LET'S JUST BE FRIENDS

The perfect, feel-good romance

KATY TURNER

Joffe Books, London
www.joffebooks.com

First published in Great Britain in 2023

This book is a work of fiction. Names, characters, businesses, organizations, places and events are either the product of the author's imagination or are used fictitiously. Any resemblance to actual persons, living or dead, events or locales is entirely coincidental.
The spelling used is British English except where fidelity to the author's rendering of accent or dialect supersedes this.

Cover art by The Brewster Project

ISBN: 978-1-80405-830-5

To Jake

CHAPTER 1

You know that feeling when the rug has been pulled out from under you? That was exactly what Holly was experiencing. Although in her case the rug had been rolled up, ready to chuck in the back of a transit van.

'A year in Scotland?' She repeated Judith's words.

'It'll positively fly by,' said Judith. 'It's a real shame that the vet who you were taking over from decided to stay in Ascot. Something to do with her husband having a last-minute change of heart, and him doing one more year in the London office. But she's another former student of mine and she swears they'll make the move to Manchester next year. And then the job will be yours, I promise.'

Holly put her fist in her mouth, trying to contain her frustration. She *had* to get out of London. Until about five minutes ago, she thought she was about to. This new role at VetCo Ascot had been the answer to her desperate prayers. When her last job had gone disastrously tits-up, Judith, her old lecturer from university and Holly's mentor, had immediately pointed her to the Ascot position. It had sounded perfect.

When Holly didn't respond, Judith carried on. 'And Eastercraig is one of the loveliest places in the British Isles. A little corner of paradise.'

Little corners of paradise were all very well, but — Holly frantically found a map on her laptop — Eastercraig was a long way from Ascot. In fact, it looked a long way from anywhere. She stared around her room, looking at the towers of boxes containing all her worldly possessions.

'I was ready to dive right in.' Holly tried not to sound desperate. 'And . . . I've had my things packed up ready to move for ages.'

She bit her lip. Forget rugs being pulled — the ground beneath her was crumbling away. Ten minutes ago, when she had answered the phone to Judith, she'd expected a few friendly pointers about the surgery. What her new colleagues were like, or dirt on the main clientele. She had not expected to be told that instead of moving into the jaw-droppingly amazing VetCo Ascot in Berkshire she was headed off to some far-flung backwater she'd never heard of in the Highlands. For an entire year.

'I've just emailed a contract over. You just need to print it and scan it back to me with your signature,' Judith was saying.

Holly winced. A contract. She hadn't actually signed a contract with VetCo, but in her defence it had sounded like a done deal. The lead vet had told her told there was a flat for the locums she could stay in, that the job would start in a month and that she came highly recommended. It had sounded like her stars had aligned, and Holly had no reason to believe the job wasn't hers. It had been offered. The contract was a mere formality, ready to be signed on her first day. Had she really misread the situation so badly?

Mind you, it wasn't the first time she had assumed she had scored a job, only to find out she hadn't. More fool Holly. Perhaps in her haste to get out of London she had jumped the gun, with the job in Ascot the shiny pinnacle of wishful thinking.

There was a pause. When Judith spoke again, she sounded warm but unwavering. 'I know it's a bit of a surprise. The position does come with a fully furnished cottage, so I can look after anything you don't want to take with you — I've got space here in an outbuilding for them. And you said you'd not worked with big animals since uni — I thought you'd appreciate the chance to do so.'

This was something else Holly wasn't ready for. 'But the job description and interview . . . I thought Ascot was a small animal role.'

'Holly, love, it's a senior vet role, and a senior vet needs to know *exactly* what's what in every situation. A solid reference or letter of recommendation stating you're a good all-rounder will do wonders when the Ascot job comes up again. Lots of ponies round there, that sort of thing. Besides, the Eastercraig position — it's a favour to an old friend of mine from my uni days. Last locum left abruptly and he needs someone in quick-sharp.'

Holly rubbed her eyes and ran through the immediate pros and cons. Pro: it wasn't as if she had any other job to go to, so she could start straight away, saving herself the worry of a few months with no income. Con: it didn't sound as if she had a say in the matter. 'I suppose it could be nice,' she managed.

'In your CV you claim to enjoy a challenge.'

Damn it! Judith had used Holly's own words against her! 'I do. Although—'

'And it said you like the great outdoors.'

'I love it. I just—'

'Then you will *love* Eastercraig. Shall I tell Hugh you'll start in a week?' asked Judith.

'I guess so,' Holly tried not to sound too downtrodden. A job was a job, after all. Beggars couldn't be choosers. And she'd still be leaving London. She needed to remember that. 'Thanks, Judith. I appreciate your help.'

'I'm sorry for the shock, but I'm glad we've sorted this all out, Holly. I can't wait to see you back down south in a year, and I'll check in with you along the way. Wonderful to talk. Goodnight.'

"Wonderful?" It was not how Holly would describe their chat. How had this happened? Not that it mattered — she'd heard herself weakly agreeing to it all, the usual confidence she possessed stymied by Judith's bombshell that the Ascot job wasn't as in the bag as she had assumed. That it was very much out of the bag.

'Goodbye,' she said, her voice a faint croak.

Judith hung up and Holly sat stock-still on her bed. Closing her eyes, she processed the news. Not Ascot, Berkshire, but Eastercraig, Scotland. Not small animals, which she had been prepared for, but work on farms, for which she *really* hadn't. Not the sought-after job at a leading practice, but one that sounded like a post from which its prior incumbent had fled.

Holly had been so sure she had everything back under control. It was only a few weeks since she'd had to leave her last job at the Francis Practice. And now she felt as if another had been snatched from her when she wasn't looking. She looked at the map again.

Eastercraig truly was the back of beyond. And then some. Although, perhaps after the humiliating fiasco with the Francis family, some distance — and there was a hell of a lot of distance — would do her good. Maybe this wasn't such a bad plan after all.

* * *

All of which was how, on an icy January day, Holly Anderson found herself standing on the front at Eastercraig taking in the view. She had her back to the MacDougal Veterinary Practice and wondered how cold the sea was. Bracing probably didn't cover it, she reflected, but she still wanted to be in it. Or on it. Once she had got over the shock of being posted so far north for such a long period of time, she had decided she was going to enjoy herself.

She'd driven up from London the day before, stopping to stay with friends in Edinburgh overnight, then started early to get to Eastercraig by mid-morning. As she'd left the Lowlands, the wide motorways had given way to narrower, serpentine roads, and occasionally her ears would pop, reminding her she was navigating higher altitudes. Onwards and upwards.

Eventually, after wending her way through winding passes, heathery moorland and dark pine forest, Holly had rolled down a long hill and arrived at the coast. And then, having parked in the only car park in Eastercraig, she'd taken a stroll along the sea front, where a wide footpath ran alongside the road.

There was the North Sea, as gentle as could be. It was almost flat, save the odd, lazy swell that rocked the fishing boats at the far end of the natural harbour. A few puffy clouds rested in an otherwise bright blue sky, the hint of a breeze hardly moving them. Holly took a deep breath, the stingingly cold salt air tasting deliciously refreshing after her years in the city.

She pulled her coat around herself tighter. Behind her was the town itself. At least, she thought it was a town, although it wasn't especially big. Maybe more of a substantial village. Either way, it was nothing like Milton Keynes, where she'd grown up. Or London, where she'd spent most of her twenties. Or leafy Ascot, where she had expected to be working.

'Bloody Ascot,' she said aloud, feeling the shock of Judith's words afresh.

However, Eastercraig appeared to be — and here Holly conceded a point to Judith — a little corner of paradise. It was incredibly pretty, romantic even, with whitewashed cottages and a couple of grand brownstone affairs. Further along the front, sweet terraced houses were painted in joyful rainbow hues. At one end of the harbour, she'd clocked a pub, and she had also spotted a general store, a pharmacy and a community café with pyramids of buns in the window. At the sight of the cakes, she felt marginally less unhappy about her abrupt dispatch to Scotland.

Officially, Monday was Holly's first day, but she'd wanted to arrive before the weekend to meet the staff and have a couple of days to navigate her new surroundings. When she had unpacked, she intended to pop on her trainers and go for a long run. And if the weather was fine, she might take her paddle board out and make her way along the coast, maybe encountering the odd seal on the way. Basically, do anything but sit still.

Turning around, Holly eyeballed the practice nervously, as if it were a snorting bull at the other side of a bullring. Judith had given her scant information about Hugh MacDougal or his staff. She'd had a curt email from Hugh about her role in Eastercraig — when to start, where the surgery was — but nothing else since. Everything was a wild unknown, and she felt her stomach do an acrobatic flip.

There was no need to be afraid, she told herself, and took a deep breath. She was a good vet. She knew her stuff. And what she didn't know, she'd pick up, wouldn't she? It hadn't been *that* long since she'd been at uni. Small animals would make up the bulk of the load, and maybe Hugh would be willing to split the work so he went to the farms and she could man the surgery. Although that letter of recommendation hinged on her having a rounded experience . . . Another shudder worked its way through her guts.

Finding a fraction of her usual confidence, but mainly unable to put things off any longer, she pulled herself up to her full height and marched across the road with her head high. The practice bell rang as she pushed the door open and a sweet-faced brunette with bright pink lipstick looked up from front desk.

'Good morning. Can I help you?' she asked, in a cheerful Highlands accent.

Holly paused and glanced around, while the young woman smiled expectantly at her. The reception looked tired. Peeling paint flaked off the walls and the sofas spewed out stuffing through multiple holes. For a second, Holly felt a ripple of panic. What if she'd imagined the entire thing? Perhaps this was an anxiety dream.

'I'm Holly Anderson. The new vet?'

It came out as a question, rather than a statement. A great, roiling wave of dread hit her this time. Perhaps she was about to wake up and start her first day working at VetCo.

She mentally shook herself. Good God! Where was her resolve? It was like she'd left it on the counter of the coffee shop at the Watford Gap services.

The young woman's face lit up, and she stood and offered a hand. 'Chloe MacKenzie-Ling, receptionist. We've been expecting you.'

It wasn't a dream after all, thank heavens. Holly breathed a sigh of relief, took Chloe's hand and shook it. 'Nice to meet you. I thought I'd pop in, say hello. And apparently you have my house keys?'

Chloe rummaged through a drawer and produced an envelope. 'Of course. It's right here on the front — Sea Spray. The pretty blue one with the bench outside. I'm *super* envious. Fabien recently did it up. Hand-painted tiles, antique brass fittings, neutral but not *too* neutral décor. Once you've settled in can I come and have a nose?'

None of this made much sense, but Holly was keen to make some friends. 'Absolutely! Come and have a cup of tea this weekend — I've got nothing in the diary.'

Chloe scribbled on a Post-it. 'I'd love to. Here, take my number.'

Holly began to wonder what might await her at the cottage when a door to the left of the desk opened and through it walked a man with tanned skin, a mane of dark curls and twinkling brown eyes. He straightened his scrubs, leaned up against the desk and crossed his arms.

'Ah — the outlander has arrived,' he said, raising an eyebrow. 'What shall we do with you? Feed you to the locals?'

Oh gosh. This she hadn't reckoned with. People taking a dislike to her. Holly began to feel tingling nerves take hold again, her toes going numb.

'Don't be such a troublemaker.' Chloe shot the man a look. 'This is Paolo Rossini, our veterinary nurse.'

Paolo chuckled and moved his hands to his pockets. 'Just messing with ye. I'm only glad there's someone new in town. I've been enduring the sideways glances and unsubtle whispers for fourteen months. Now you're here, they'll take an interest in you instead. Not least because you look like you were magicked up from some Norse saga.'

Holly barely noticed people turning to stare at her — she'd got used to it a long time ago. But it happened a lot. At 5' 11", she was taller than both of her new colleagues by a number of inches. Her flyaway blonde hair in its usual scruffy plait framed piercing blue eyes, and Paolo was right — put her in a tunic and armour and she wouldn't have looked out of place in a Viking longboat.

'I'll take that as a compliment,' she said.

'Aye,' he continued. 'It was meant as one. And besides, everyone loves the vet.'

'If that's a truism, it'll certainly make my sojourn more palatable than if they want to see me off with pitchforks,' said Holly, and Paolo grinned.

'You'll be wanting to go and unpack, but do you fancy joining us at the pub tonight?' asked Chloe.

'Really?' Holly was grateful for the invitation, and the change of subject. 'I'd love to.'

'We'll be there from eight-ish,' said Paolo. 'And don't change. It's a jumpers-and-jeans joint, in case you were wondering. Having come up from the city and everything. Don't get all blingy, because you'll stick out like a manicured sore thumb.'

Holly glanced down at her outfit, an old jersey and skinny jeans. 'I live in these. Any good?'

'Perfect,' said Chloe.

'Thanks. I'll see you both later,' she said. She made to leave, then spun back at the last minute. 'Hang on — is Hugh in?'

'He's in Ullapool today, doing his fortnightly surgery there,' said Chloe. 'I think on Monday he plans to divvy up the timetable a bit, so you can get to know the area. You'll meet him then.'

'Great! I'll look forward to it,' said Holly. 'See you both later.'

Once out of the door, she let out a huge sigh of relief. Although she was one to put on a brave face, she'd been stressing about this job. A long way from home, Eastercraig looked, sounded — even smelled — disarmingly unfamiliar. Not in a bad way, but it had been enough to make her stomach erupt with snakes of unease the second she'd stepped out of the car.

VetCo Ascot materialized in her head, with its shining entrance vestibule and doors that opened automatically. Her future — the one she had been toiling for — had been tantalizingly close. The shabby interiors of the Eastercraig practice made her feel like this was a massive step down. *Mind you*, she told herself firmly, *you shouldn't judge a book by its cover*. It wasn't only about the facilities. The people were important too, even if she hadn't met Hugh MacDougal yet.

Now she'd met Chloe and Paolo, though, the clouds of uncertainty that had been fogging up her brain had begun to evaporate. They'd been so welcoming. And a trip to the pub on the first night would be a good way to find out all she needed to know about the town. Or was it a village? That she could ask Chloe and Paolo later.

* * *

Back in the surgery, Chloe looked at Paolo.

'What do you make of her?' she asked, the moment Holly stepped out of the door.

'She's tall,' said Paolo.

'Don't wind me up. Come on.'

Paolo collapsed into one of the waiting room chairs and stretched out his legs. 'Dunno yet. We can give her a proper grilling in the Anchor later.'

If Paolo had anything else to say, he was interrupted by the practice phone. It rang twice before Chloe picked it up.

'MacDougal Veterinary Practice, Chloe speaking . . .' she said, summoning her telephone manner. She'd perfected it so it sounded breathy, but the right side of professional. Like a toned-down, Scottish Marilyn Monroe.

The gruff voice at the other end was instantly recognisable.

'Hey, Chlo! Can I double-check I've got Hugh coming next week? I didn't write it down.'

'Angus! You need to get a diary,' said Chloe, immediately switching back to her usual burr.

She glanced up from her desk to see Paolo giving her a knowing look. When she didn't answer immediately, he started gesticulating, as if to say "go on". Chloe felt her hands grow clammy as she fumbled her way around the online diary. *Cursed Paolo.* Bearing witness to her ruffled-ness in the face of a call from Angus.

'I'm looking it up.' She eyed Paolo, whose hand-waving resembled that of a conductor at the frenzied climax of a symphony. 'How are you, Angus? Coming to the pub later?'

This earned a silent thumbs up and a wink from Paolo. Chloe bit her tongue as she waited for the answer.

'Might pop in.'

'We're taking the new vet.'

'Aye.'

Chloe wasn't sure what else to say. Angus wasn't the most loquacious man in Eastercraig, not by a long shot. And with one syllable, he had stopped the conversation in its tracks. Totally bloody banjaxed it in fact. Chloe stifled a sigh and got back to business. 'Hugh's due Monday. After lunch.'

'Thanks, Chlo. Catch you later.'

'Bye, Angus,' she said, wondering if he could detect the note of longing in her voice, before hanging up.

Aware her cheeks were blazing, she clapped her hands to her face and groaned. One day she would channel her inner Holly Golightly and be a beacon of glamorous confidence. Right now, she was a Belisha beacon, and a sweaty one at that.

'Well, *that* was awful,' she said, wrinkling up her forehead.

'Is he coming to the pub?' asked Paolo.

'Unclear. My being there didn't sound like it would entice him.'

'You need to be aggressive, Chloe.'

Chloe glared at him. She was the least aggressive person she knew. Had she not known better, she would have thought herself half dormouse. Paolo might be supporting her from the sidelines, but it was hard not to be a bit defeatist when the man you wanted to have a deep and meaningful conversation with was a man of so few words.

'Thanks for being my personal cheerleader,' she managed. 'But maybe I need to move on.'

'Move on from what? You've not gone there yet?'

A painful reminder, but entirely true.

'Haven't you got animals to care for?' Chloe changed the subject.

Paolo grinned. She gave a small smile, grateful he was still fighting her corner, even if she wanted to give up.

'Off you go. Shoo. I think I can hear Tiddles calling your name,' she continued. 'It's time for his drops.'

'All right, I get it.' Paolo got up and raised two imaginary pompoms. 'Be aggressive, be, be aggressive,' he chanted.

Chloe watched as he disappeared into the back of the surgery, still dancing around. If only it were as easy as repeating a few mantras.

CHAPTER 2

One positive for Holly was that she had landed on her feet with Sea Spray. The cosy cottage was like something out of the pages of a design magazine. She would have been happy to stay in and put her feet up with the log burner on, only it would have been a bit antisocial.

After unpacking, Holly insulated herself against the chill with her long Puffa jacket and pottered along the front to the Anchor. In the dark, she could make out the outlines of the waves that she could hear slapping against the harbour wall. On the outside, the pub was a dull, unassuming building. Inside, though, it was warm and welcoming. The walls were festooned with fishing nets, buoys hung from the ceiling, and the voices were loud and the accents thick.

She was beckoned over to a small corner table by Paolo, who quickly initiated a conversation aimed at her getting to know him and Chloe.

'We were discussing the best way to introduce ourselves. Basically, we'll tell you about the other one,' he announced, pouring her a dangerously large glass of wine. 'A mixture of facts and opinions.'

'Whoa! Opinions? You'd better be planning on playing nice,' interrupted Chloe.

'Do I ever do anything else?' Paolo asked.

'You're pretending to be all innocent, but you'd better not spill any of my deepest, darkest secrets.'

Holly raised an eyebrow, keeping up with the fast pace of the conversation. 'Do you have many?'

Chloe shook her head, grinning. 'Och, no. Not really.'

Paolo held up a hand. 'We're losing focus, team. You first, Chloe. You can tell Holly anything about me you like. I have nothing to hide.'

'His best traits,' Chloe commenced, 'are he's thoughtful, and generous, and quick-witted. But on the flipside, you wouldn't want to be on the end of some of his crueller barbs.'

'Och, you're a sensitive flower,' said Paolo. 'But in the nicest sense. And like a flower, Chloe always smells good. And she loves old stuff. Especially old films, and old clothes, which she looks lovely in.'

'Ta, Rossini — you're not too shabby yourself,' Chloe replied. 'Meticulous, is our Paolo. Nattily turned out, despite the fact the uniform round here is woolly jumper and socks that ought to have been binned decades ago.'

'You're hardly in jeans,' Holly pointed out.

Holly had come in the clothes she'd worn earlier, as directed, but noticed Paolo had changed from his scrubs into something amounting to French peasant style, with a waistcoat and a necktie. Chloe wore what she had on in the surgery, a tie-waisted dress in a floral-print fabric.

'Aye. Chloe doesn't own trousers. And I don't do denim,' said Paolo. 'We have standards.'

'Hold up,' Holly protested, gesturing to her outfit, which now felt a little scruffy. 'You said this was fine.'

'It is. We didn't want you thinking you needed heels and a bandage dress,' said Paolo.

'Do I give that impression?' she asked.

'Not especially,' said Chloe. 'But every so often it happens.'

'And the whole room goes still, very still, until that person feels compelled to go elsewhere. Like back to Aberdeen,' Paolo continued helpfully.

'Right. Noted,' said Holly. 'That's a shame. I'll leave the bandage dress in the wardrobe.'

Chloe's eyes grew round. 'I thought you said earlier . . . We didn't mean to offend.'

'I had you for a moment,' Holly grinned. 'I own two dresses, and they rarely see the light of day.'

Paolo smiled, and Chloe exhaled.

* * *

Having bought the next bottle, Holly placed a tray down on the table and poured glasses for all. She had, on their advice, introduced herself to Mhairi, the publican, a woman in her forties with two sleeve tattoos and rambling roses adorning her décolletage, and at least six earrings in each ear. It paid, Paolo had said, to be on Mhairi's good side — because this was the only pub in town.

'Is Eastercraig a town, by the way?' As Holly sat down, she remembered to ask. 'It's not exactly big.'

'Oh aye,' Chloe nodded enthusiastically. 'The best things come in small packages, and Eastercraig is tiny. But a town none the less.'

So far, Holly was warming to Paolo and Chloe, whose easy back-and-forth banter led her to believe the atmosphere in the surgery was going to be cheerful. If Hugh was the same, the practice would be a pleasure to join. She found herself relaxing into the evening. It was, she noted, also to do with the fact they were now on their second bottle of white.

'Ta for this,' said Paolo, taking his glass. 'So . . . how did you find the house?'

'Perfect,' Holly replied, picturing the dreamy, light interiors at Sea Spray, which appealed to her sense of orderliness. 'The downstairs is open-plan, with a lovely new kitchen and a sofa with a sea view. Upstairs there's a big bedroom in the eaves, and a small bathroom with a shower. But the amazing bit is in my room there's a big white tub next to the window so you can lie in the bath and watch the sea.'

She really had lucked out, big time. A teeny fisherman's cottage in a long terrace, it was approximately a four-minute walk to the surgery. The one downside was there was no excuse for being late — not that she ever was. It was so glorious she had snapped some photos for her friends in London, and even sent one to her recalcitrant mother.

Paolo put a hand on his heart. 'Bloody Fabien.'

Holly glanced at him. 'This is the second time I've heard his name mentioned. What's the deal? Who is he and why would he leave such a gorgeous house?'

'He was the love of Paolo's life,' said Chloe, putting a hand on Paolo's arm.

Paolo frowned. 'He's gone, though, the wee shite. I'm trying not to take it personally, but it's hard not to.'

'So . . . you and Fabien were going out?' Holly asked.

'Me and Fabien — we were a thing. Or maybe we *had* a thing. I don't know. But it's over. It wasn't common knowledge either way though, so don't tell anyone.'

'Paolo's gay,' Chloe leaned towards Holly and whispered. 'If you'd not worked it out. And you *definitely* were a thing, Paolo, even if it was only for a few months. It was tricky because Fabien — delightful lad as he is — hadn't told his very conservative parents he was gay. Instead of biting the bullet and introducing Paolo to them, Fabe ended it and took a two-year contract working for a Swiss bank. In actual Switzerland.'

'Where he'll be mingling with hot international guys in tailor-made suits, far from the watchful eyes of the town,' said Paolo.

'I'm sorry he's gone . . . but I'm sure the right person will come along soon,' Holly tried to sound upbeat. 'How's the gay scene in Eastercraig?'

'You're looking at it,' said Paolo. 'Me. I'm it. What a cliché.'

'Paolo's cut up about it all,' said Chloe. 'He's right though. Take a look around, Holly — all the lads in here are *totally* hetero.'

As Holly scanned the pub, Paolo continued. 'I don't want to dwell on it though. What about you, Holly? Do you have someone back in London?'

'No. I don't do men,' she said.

Paolo seemed to forget his misery, and looked delighted at this. 'Wait — we can represent together. Take on Eastercraig.'

'Or women,' she added.

Chloe tilted her head to one side. 'You're not into anyone? You don't want to be matchmade?'

'Whoa. No. None of that. I'm not looking for anything at the moment.'

Both Paolo and Chloe looked downcast for what, Holly suspected, were different reasons.

'Nobody,' Holly continued. 'I've not got the time or the inclination, what with work. I want to get my career sorted before I settle down.'

It was a good enough reason to give for now. She didn't want to weigh them down with her life story. Not the gory bits, anyway.

Paolo leaned in conspiratorially. 'Apparently you can have both.'

Holly nodded. 'I know, but I've seen it happen. You fall in love. You lose focus. You end up with a broken heart. You lose more focus. And I've worked so hard to get this far I don't want to throw it away. Besides, it's hard to find someone when you look like you're from a Norse saga.'

'I meant that as a compliment!' Paolo protested, and Holly gave him a reassuring smile.

'You could have a wee fling then,' said Chloe, eyes glittering at the prospect. 'I know *everyone* here. Give me your preferences and I'll fix you up.'

'I'm not sure I want a fling either,' Holly said, shifting in her seat.

'Go on,' said Paolo. 'You're here for a year. You could have some fun with any one of these sexy fishermen. You've heard of "shore leave", haven't you?'

'*Jeez*, Paolo,' Chloe looked faux-appalled. 'Don't give the poor lass the heebie-jeebies.'

'Hey — no strings attached,' he continued. 'You could *net* one of these guys easily.'

'You seriously just said that?' Holly groaned.

'Yeah. Good, no?' said Paolo.

'Thanks for offering me a set-up,' Holly smiled. 'But I'm OK for now.'

She could not get side-tracked. She *had* to keep her mind on work. There had never been enough money when she was growing up, and she wanted to stop worrying about the fact she had zero to fall back on. And men? They just threw you off course.

You only had to look at her mum to see that. Holly loved her mother — in a rather mandatory fashion — but Jackie Anderson was a stiletto-clad, kohl-eyed maelstrom when it came to men, leaving destruction in her wake. And if Holly ended up anything like her mother during a relationship and at its subsequent end, she might be the derailer of her own destiny.

Ever since Holly could remember, Jackie had put the "over" into "lover". Doomed affairs had punctuated Holly's childhood, rendering her mother a model of irresponsibility, and as far as she could tell, relationships were a one-way ticket to disaster. Some had ended as well as they could, the exes giving a kindly wave to Holly before disappearing. Others left plenty to the imagination, with cruel retorts or ear-aching expletives exchanged. And the worst one . . . ? She fought off the thought, not wanting to dwell.

No, only once she had some financial security would she contemplate settling down. But until then she intended to steer clear of the opposite sex.

'Let me know if you change your mind,' said Chloe. 'And I'll *hook* you up.'

Holly grinned. 'Good *line*,' she said, joining in.

'See. You're punning with the best of them already. You've barely arrived, but I can tell you're going to fit in perfectly,' said Paolo, holding up a hand. 'Non-ironic high five?'

Holly obliged. Paolo was right. She had only been in Eastercraig for a matter of hours, but she had an inkling she was going to be fine. More than fine, in fact.

'Thanks.' Then, 'Heeeeey—' following Chloe's gaze — 'who's that?'

Chloe was fixated on someone who'd appeared at the door, as if she'd been hypnotized.

Paolo turned his head. 'Now, if *he* was gay, *I* wouldn't say no to a fling.'

Holly studied the incomer. He was tall and muscular, with a strong jaw, fiery hair and deep brown eyes. In a muddy wax jacket and heavy-duty boots, he walked thuddingly to the bar and Holly could feel the floor shaking as he passed.

'Hey, Chlo,' the man nodded as he went by their table.

'You'll be seeing plenty of him. Angus Dunbar from Auchintraid Farm — cattle, and a large herd at that,' Paolo continued. 'Earth to Chloe, are you OK?'

Chloe blinked. 'What?'

'Checking out Angus, is it?' he asked.

Chloe blushed and mumbled something Holly couldn't work out. But a picture was worth a thousand words, and Chloe's face was a Louvre-worthy masterpiece.

'Something going on there?' Holly asked.

'There might be, if Chloe could pluck up the courage to talk to him. As it happens, she turns into a sweaty mess whenever he appears,' said Paolo. 'Look at that upper lip. Someone give the poor girl a flannel.'

'*Hush*, Paolo,' Chloe whispered, looking dismayed. 'Can we change the subject?'

'Fine.' Paolo rolled his eyes, then turned to Holly. 'Why don't we give Hols — can I call you Hols? (Holly didn't have a chance to say "yes") — why don't we give Hols a quick rundown of the Eastercraig year. The highlights and lowlights.'

'Oooh — please,' said Holly, rubbing her hands together. 'That would be a massive help.'

'So while you're here, there'll be a ball at Glenalmond Castle. They've not announced it yet, but it's usually in late spring or early summer,' Paolo began.

'Shame you missed Burns Night,' Chloe interrupted. 'Mind you, we can always do a pretend one for you.'

'Then there's the Eastercraig Run, a half-marathon, in autumn time. It's pretty hilly, but if you're at all sporty you could join,' Paolo continued.

'Or you can join me on the sidelines,' added Chloe. 'If you're not into sports. Are you a runner?'

'I actually *love* running,' said Holly, excited by the prospect.

'Then there's the local show next month,' said Paolo, with an exuberant flourish.

Chloe looked thrilled. Holly tilted her head to one side, uncertain how this could provoke so much enthusiasm from two people her age.

'Don't look sceptical,' said Chloe. 'Last year Janet Murray hurled Doreen Douglas's carrot cake in the sea. And then they had a fight, and it turns out Janet's beautiful hair, which is the envy of Eastercraig . . .'

'Is extensions!' cried Paolo. 'I get it, Hols. I felt the same way you did last year. Bewildered. But it was hysterical. They were proper brawling. Someone was going to call the police but then Mhairi stepped in and pulled them apart.'

'If it gets that wild, I'll definitely come,' said Holly. It sounded weird, but she'd certainly go and take a look.

Paolo fixed his eyes on her. 'And what about you, Hols? We told you about us. And Eastercraig. Now buckle up, we're going to Spanish Inquisition the crap out of you.'

Holly must have pulled a face like a rabbit in the headlights, because Chloe held a hand up to Paolo. 'Easy there, Chablis-chops. Let's be nice, shall we? Ignore him, Holly. He's drunk.'

'*Emboldened*,' Paolo rolled his eyes. 'Fine. But you never get the full story if you don't ask incisive questions.'

Holly smiled. 'Where do you want me to start?'

'The beginning, natch,' he replied.

It was like an interview, not that she'd ever done one in the pub after a few drinks. She wondered if it was a pass-or-fail situation.

Chloe was first. 'What do you like doing in your spare time?'

Phew. An inoffensive start. 'Seeing friends, and being outside. I love hiking, running, cycling and I'm getting into paddle boarding — I invested in an ultra-thick wetsuit so I could do some up here.'

'Nice. My turn,' said Paolo. 'What's your favourite book?'

Another gentle enquiry. 'I like detective stories. Like Agatha Christie. And I obviously loved James Herriot as a child.'

'I'll not judge you too harshly,' said Paolo.

Chloe raised her eyes heavenwards. 'Paolo's a literary snob. Moving on: why did you leave your last job?'

Holly wavered. She'd had a huge falling out with Rob Francis, her boss, after he hired his son as partner, even though Peter was barely out of university and had never shown much interest in working alongside his father. Holly had been there for eight years and had frequently been told by Rob she was a superstar, on track to take over.

Worse, however, at a drinks party, not long after Rob had announced his intention to retire, Holly had told half her colleagues that she was going to get a promotion. Not in a braggy way, and only the ones she counted as friends . . . Holly flinched inwardly as she recalled it, fearing how it must have sounded like boasting. She'd been unable to help it though. It had been a hard slog, and she was ecstatic.

Two weeks later, though, Rob let the surgery know that Peter would be taking over his stake in the practice. The news blindsided Holly and left her deeply wounded, as Rob, with no apparent guilt, had told her it had always been his dream to pass his surgery on to his boy. Her premature pride a source of shame, coupled with the fact that Rob had betrayed her, Holly felt like she had no choice but to leave. She would rather that than go in and see smug-arse Peter every day, who swanned around as if he owned the place — which, of course, he did.

It wasn't only the surgery that Holly wanted to put behind her. She had to get out of London. She needed to reset, get out of the city, away from her peers who were all racing up the ladder, leaving her behind. Away from her colleagues who, aside from Peter, she felt now looked at her with pity. In fact, even the animals she was treating seemed to be giving her funny looks. She had needed to take her bruised confidence somewhere else.

After phoning Judith, who set her up with the phantom role in Ascot, Holly handed in her notice. Peter, who was that awful combination of arrogant and not especially good at his job, had simply nodded and wished her the best. Chucking London in felt dramatic, an un-Holly thing to do, but she couldn't bear it any longer.

'I had a difference of opinion with management,' she said diplomatically.

'Intriguing. We'll get to the bottom of that vaguery another time,' said Paolo, who must have sensed her reticence. 'What are you most frightened of?'

This *was* an interrogation, she thought. Her mind flickered through all the things she was scared of, like a rolodex of fear: relationships, not having a place of her own, farm animals (one that had only now popped back on to the list). None of which she wanted to talk about. Luckily the door opened, and an elderly man tottered in. 'Sporran's out there again,' he grumbled to nobody in particular. 'Someone go and sort the fecker out.'

Paolo and Chloe leaped up, pulling Holly with them. 'Grab your drink,' said Paolo.

Holly, bemused, was dragged through the door, barely managing to grab her coat on the way. Given it was Friday night at the pub she'd been expecting a boozed-up local bobbing up and down in the water, but instead her eyes alighted on an enormous seal.

It looked at them expectantly and Paolo raised a palm in greeting. 'Hullo, auld friend.'

The seal flopped around until it was floating on its back, sculling with its flippers. It barked twice, as if it was responding.

'Are you telling me *this* is Sporran?' Holly peered over the edge of the harbour wall.

'Indeed. Hugh tended to him once after he got caught in a net. You can recognize him by the long scar over his nose, and the fact he likes to come to beg for chips,' said Paolo.

'That won't be good for him,' said Holly.

She slowly sank to her knees, wanting to get nearer. She hadn't been this close to a seal before. There was something unearthly about his onyx-black eyes, the way they sparkled in the moonlight. He had an almost longing look about him, like a puppy wanting to be taken home. It was all Holly could do to stop herself reaching out to pat him.

Chloe knelt next to her. 'Tourists like to throw him bits of their supper, and he's grown rather large. We've been trying to discourage it with signs, but Sporran is so gorgeous people do it anyway.'

'It's the main reason why, if he makes an appearance, we dash out to keep an eye on him. He's a daft bugger, but we love him,' said Paolo. 'Most of the villagers are pretty good about it, but there's always one idiot.'

Holly nodded. She could imagine people doing it. Beside her, Chloe yawned.

'Keeping you up, are we?' Paolo asked.

'I was in early this morning,' Chloe replied. 'All that paperwork. You know what Hugh's . . .'

She tailed off, and Holly turned and glanced at her, waiting for the rest of the sentence. 'What Hugh's . . . ?'

'Nothing,' Chloe said, quickly. 'I simply like being organized. Anyway, I'd better be off.'

She got up and went to collect a bicycle that was leaning against the pub — a pink sit-up-and-beg with a basket. Holly and Paolo waved her off, Holly wondering exactly what it was about Hugh that Chloe was reluctant to tell her. A fresh round of gut-twisting nerves about Monday made its way through her, and she bit her lip.

'Walk you home?' Paolo asked Holly, gesturing along the road.

'Go on,' she said. It had been a long day and she'd feel much better about starting the job after a good night's sleep and a relaxing weekend.

They began a gentle stroll back to Sea Spray. Holly noticed glittering lights now decorated the houses on the harbour front, looking for all the world like stars that had fallen from the skies.

'Tell me what it is about Hugh that Chloe clammed up about,' she said to Paolo.

Paolo smiled. 'She's very loyal, is Chloe. She was trying not to say that Hugh can be . . . feisty.'

'Is that why the last locum left?' Holly joked.

'You could say she had a difference of opinion with management.'

Holly looked to Paolo, who gave a knowing smile. 'Fine. I asked for that.'

'How *did* a girl like you end up in a place like this anyway?' Paolo asked. 'I mean, it's lovely, but you've been sent from a practice at the other end of the spectrum. Your old place in London is all jazzy machines and computing systems. Chlo and I googled it.'

'I thought we'd established I came by longboat,' she said.

'Am I ever going to live that down?'

'Give me a week or two, and I'll get over it. You?'

Paolo looked relieved. 'I love the outdoors, and when I finished my training I worked at home in Glasgow for two years, but then got a bit bored and wanted something new. When the job at a remote practice by the sea came out, I took it. I'd not reckoned with the recent dumping and lack of other men but, that aside, it's amazing here.'

Holly watched as he looked out to sea. She followed his gaze. Shadowy anchored boats bobbed on the gentle tide, the top of the water reflecting the moon above.

He held out his arm to Holly, and she linked hers through it. 'Thank you, kind sir,' she giggled.

'An honour, my lady,' he said, and tugged her along. 'It *is* nice to have a new face in town, you know. Maybe you can provide some drama. Distract me from my failed romance?'

Holly laughed wryly. 'I told you. No flings for me.'

'Not even a tiny one? A flinglet?'

'Nice try, but a rose by any other name . . . If you're bored, though, why not come paddle boarding with me tomorrow?' Holly suggested. 'I promise you'll feel wonderful. 8.30 a.m.? Ready for sunrise?'

'If you provide the coffee, you're on,' he said. 'I'm in a flat the far end of the harbour, but I can meet you here.'

They'd arrived at Holly's cottage. Holly waved Paolo off and stood on the doorstep for a second, looking at the sea one last time.

* * *

Paolo pulled his jacket up around his neck, then strode the last few hundred yards home, tightening his scarf for good measure. He rubbed his arms, wondering if he had been mad to accept Holly's offer of paddle boarding. It was bloody January, after all.

Mind you, he needed some new distractions. Any hour not wondering what Fabien was up to was time well spent. Not that he minded his own company. But when you spent a day pottering around the shops alone, or took a long, solitary walk, you relished the thought of having someone to chat to. For months, Fabien had been that person.

Paolo had been *so* sure it was going well. OK, so Fabien hadn't wanted anyone to know about them. That hadn't been ideal. But he had held on to the thought that, one day, Fabien would see the light, and merrily shout his love for Paolo from Eastercraig's rooftops. With a massive megaphone.

That day had never come. Instead, Fabien had left the country on a one-way ticket to Geneva. It was an almighty slap in the face, and had ruined Toblerones for him for ever.

One day, however, his prince would appear. Granted, as he'd mentioned to Holly, it was unlikely he was going to appear in Eastercraig, but stranger things happened at sea. And the sea, Paolo told himself, was right outside his front door.

CHAPTER 3

Stepping inside, Holly slung her coat on a hook. The house was gorgeous, bijou. The polar opposite to the worn-out surgery down the road. Tugging her hat off, she remembered her mother again, and grabbed her phone.

As it began to ring, the tone elongated. Jackie was abroad, and hadn't thought to tell her. Of course she hadn't. Bolting off without telling anyone was one of her top skills. Holly wondered if she was on holiday, or if she had quit her most recent job — she rarely lasted more than six months in most of them.

Nobody picked up, so Holly left a message. 'Hi, Jackie! It's me. I think you may have jetted off somewhere and not told me. Anyway, hope you're having fun. Go easy on the pina coladas. Don't do anything I wouldn't do.'

She hung up. As if. Jackie's boyfriends weren't the only part of her life that was chaotic. Where Holly made sensible, well-thought-out decisions, Jackie was impulsive, spending money (when she had it) like water on things like new shoes or a blow-dry, at the expense of paying the bills. Other times she would decide to go on trips at the drop of a hat (if she hadn't spent the money on shoes or blow-dries). When Holly was younger, Jackie would leave her with neighbours, then when she was older, alone. At the age of thirteen, Holly had come home from school once to a couple of tenners and a note stating that her mum had gone to Bournemouth with Richard for a night, to treat herself to some pizza, and if she needed anything to knock on the neighbours' door. It was the first of many similar experiences. Holly often marvelled that she had grown up to be such a normal person.

She pulled off her shoes, vowing to call again the next day to make sure Jackie was OK, and a chill ran through her as her feet hit the wooden floor. She needed to warm up.

'Oh my God!' Holly cried, remembering the giant tub in the bedroom. This was the kind of evening it was made for.

Mood lifting, she bounded upstairs to run the bath, taking the steps two at a time. As it filled up, she ran back downstairs and bounced on each foot, wondering if this was the moment for a tea, wine or whisky. The latter had never been her drink, but the girl in the Eastercraig Stores had said it was from the local distillery, and it felt like a fitting drink to have in the cupboard. And Holly had thought if anyone came over, she ought to be able to offer a glass. When in Rome, and all that. She chucked a generous amount in a tumbler and dashed back up.

Having turned off the taps, Holly undressed, lit a candle and popped the whisky on a stool before climbing into the tub. It was the kind of bath people fantasized about, long enough to stretch out in and deliciously deep. She slid down into the water and leaned her head on the rim.

Yes, this was an unplanned move, one that interfered with her neat career plan. But the combination of beautiful surroundings, welcoming colleagues and a boozy night in the pub had gone a long way to alleviate some of her doubts. She pinched herself and, in her haze, decided the constellations were looking down at her, winking happily. The low lullaby sung by the sea floated through the windows, and she shut her eyes, ready to relax.

But before she had a chance to do so properly, Holly heard an odd noise. Like a key in a lock. She listened out.

There it was again. A tinny clunking. Her eyes sprung open as the front door clicked, then slammed shut. Shoes echoed on the wooden floor.

Holly froze. *What the hell?* Her skin prickled, goose-bumps forming.

The intruder downstairs echoed her thoughts exactly. 'What the hell?'

It was a man's voice. There was a man in her house!

Was this a break-in? Holly's eyes darted around the room, looking for something with which to defend herself.

The stairs creaked as the person began to climb them. Oh God! He was coming upstairs! Holly leaped out the bath and threw on her dressing gown. Putting the whisky on the floor, she grabbed the stool. Her feet still wet, she slid across the boards, tucking herself behind the door.

The footsteps stopped. Silence. Holly pressed herself up against the wall. The door creaked open. This was it.

'What in the blazes?'

The lights came on and Holly made to hit the man on the head. She let out a yell and brought the stool down hard.

'*Jesus* . . .' The man ducked out of the way as it crashed on the floor. '. . . Mary and Joseph! What the heck?'

'Get out or I'll call the police,' Holly said, as steadily as she could. She clung to the stool, raising it up in case she needed to wield it again.

'Whoa. Steady on. Calm down,' the man stood up slowly with his hands in the air. 'I was planning to crash for the night. What are *you* doing here?'

'I live here!'

It came out as a cry that occupied a curious middle ground between terror and exasperation. Which was exactly how she felt. Adrenaline pumping, Holly glared at him.

The man stepped back and considered this. 'I see. Fabien has let the place.'

'Yes!' she fumed. 'To me! And I was having a bath when you scared me half to death!'

Holly continued to hold the stool at chest height. She wasn't willing to part company with it yet. That, and it was holding her dressing gown together.

The stranger broke into a smile.

'There's nothing funny about this,' she snapped. 'You could be anyone.'

'In Eastercraig? Unlikely. I honestly didn't know there was anyone here. Fabien told me where the spare key was ages ago.'

Tentatively, Holly lowered the stool. She tightened her dressing gown and walked back across the floor to the bath. Picking up the whisky, she took a large gulp. The man didn't seem to be about to attack her, but if he tried, she could hurl the rest in his face.

'Any more where that came from?' he asked, nodding at the glass.

He had some nerve! Holly's blood began to boil.

'I beg your pardon,' she bristled. 'I said "you could be anyone", but what I meant was "who the hell are you and why are you here?" You're yet to convince me you're not the local burglar. Or murderer.'

At this the man threw back his head and let out a roar of laughter. Holly did her best to stop herself growling at him as her initial fright gave way to annoyance. He'd turned up in her house, frightened the life out of her and not yet apologized. And now he was asking her for a whisky?! He hadn't even done her the courtesy of checking she was OK. What a prick!

He stuck out his hand. 'Gregor Dunbar.'

Holly didn't take it. 'Care to elaborate?' she replied, gritting her teeth.

'I'm a bit short of a bed for the night, and Fabien didn't think to tell me the place was let. If I'd known there was somebody here, I'd never have done it. Sorry if I scared you. You can't have been here long . . . ?'

'I arrived today. I've been drafted in to work at the vet's.'

'Then you can call Hugh. Or Chloe. They'll both vouch for my good character. Look, I've nowhere else to go. Do you mind if I . . . ?'

Holly stared at him. '. . . if you *stay*?'

She let her shoulders drop, the adrenaline dissipating. There was something about him that led her to believe he was telling the truth. And that he wasn't about to bind and gag her and steal all her possessions.

'Aye. I'm a good egg. Promise.'

'I'd rather you didn't.' But as she said it, Holly felt herself wavering. It had been a long day.

'I *genuinely* have nowhere else to go right now. I'd be eternally grateful.'

'Listen,' she looked him straight in the eye. 'Gregor Dunbar you may be, but I don't know you from Adam. This is against my better judgement, but you can stay on the sofa. I'll be putting the doorstop under this door. This aerosol—' she waved a can of deodorant at him — 'is going to be next to my bed. If I so much as hear a creak on the stairs, it'll be in your eyes.'

He grinned. 'You're sure you don't want to join me for a dram?'

This guy was unreal!

'I'm fine, thanks. But knock yourself out. Literally. I'd feel safer if you did.'

'I appreciate it,' said Gregor. 'Letting me stay, I mean. And please, call me Greg. Now we're better acquainted.'

'Thanks,' said Holly, wearily. 'And goodnight.'

She moved to shut the door. Now her pulse rate had returned to normal, she examined him properly for the first time. He was big, significantly taller than her, with deep auburn hair and a hint of stubble on what was a sharp jaw.

'Hang on,' he said. 'I don't know your name. How rude of me.'

It was back to earth with a bump. 'That's what you consider rude? Not the breaking-and-entering, bed-demanding and whisky-sampling parts?'

Here he had the good sense to look shame-faced. 'I can't apologize enough.'

'Thank you,' she said, vaguely satisfied. 'I'm Holly. Holly Anderson. I've just started at the—'

'At the vet's. I remember. I'll get out of your hair now. Goodnight, Holly Anderson.'

'Goodnight, Greg Dunbar.'

Greg looked at her once again and Holly met his gaze. She intended to stare him out, let him know this was highly irregular, except all she could see was how good-looking he was.

He retreated downstairs, and Holly went into her room, closing the door firmly behind her. She didn't think he was a murderer but, in case, she jammed the wedge under the door as far as it went. And then put her deodorant next to her bed, cap off and ready to spray. Only a fool failed to plan.

Flopping on to the bed like a starfish, she wondered if she'd be able to drop off. In those moments after she'd first heard the key in the lock, she must have produced a huge amount of adrenaline. On top of that, there was the mildly unsettling fact she'd allowed herself to consider how attractive her intruder was, and that she was still ruminating on the last look they'd shared. He had dark eyes, navy like the distant seas.

She gave herself a mental slap, wriggled beneath the duvet and prayed for sleep.

CHAPTER 4

Holly woke up to her alarm beeping and remembered she'd promised to meet Paolo. Only after a minute did she realize a certain Greg Dunbar was probably passed out in the sitting room, stinking of whisky. Her whisky. She rolled her eyes, threw a jumper on top of her pyjamas and went to investigate.

As she got the bottom of the stairs, Holly hesitated. What were you meant to say in this kind of situation? It wasn't exactly written down in etiquette guides. Did you have to entertain an intruder? Or could you simply show them the way out?

Rounding the stairs, it turned out she didn't have to do either of those things. There wasn't anyone there. Holly exhaled loudly, and rubbed her face with her hands, unable to believe the night's events. Perhaps she had invented him?

She made her way to the kitchen, ready for a cup of tea, when she tripped and fell flat on her face. Rubbing her knee where she'd landed on it, she looked back and saw a large overnight bag on the floor. Holly groaned as the front door clicked open.

'What are you doing down there?' Greg wandered across and held out a hand.

Holly took it and pulled herself up. 'Tripping over your suitcase, that's what. You're still here, then.'

'Aye. How did you sleep?'

'Badly.' Surely that would have been obvious.

'Aye. It's quiet, isn't it. Sometimes makes it hard to drop off,'

She gave him a look. 'It was more the fact there was a strange man on my sofa.'

'Look, I'm sorry about last night. Really, I am. And to apologize, I've been and got breakfast. I'll make you a proper Scottish fry-up. I'm a half-decent chef.'

He lifted up a carrier bag and Holly felt her hands ball into fists. He was so presumptuous. Turning up in the house last night, scaring her out of her skin. Staying over. Leaving his bags in the way. And now he was making himself at home, heralding his own cookery skills. Frustration got the better of her.

'Are you for bloody real?' she blurted.

Greg put the food on the table and raised his hands in the air. 'I'm trying to make it up to you.'

'You do know you don't live here, right?'

His hands still hovering mid-air, he stopped for a second and looked around.

'I'll get out of your hair, shall I? I would appear to have outstayed my welcome.'

Their eyes met and Holly felt oddly guilty. Maybe throwing him out on the street wasn't entirely fair.

'I'm meant to be down on the beach in an hour to go paddle boarding,' she said crossly, glancing up at the clock on the wall.

'Coffee's already brewed,' he said, with a hint of a smile.

She followed his gaze over to the worktop, where two mugs were already set out next to a cafetière. The sound of a fry-up was tempting. 'Fine.'

'Don't thank me.'

'Don't push your luck.'

Ten minutes later, Holly had set the table and was enjoying a steaming coffee as Greg dished up a plate of scrambled eggs, mushrooms, tomatoes and black pudding.

'Here we are.' He put a plate in front of her. 'Ketchup? Brown sauce?'

Holly's mouth watered. She was going to ignore all the advice about not eating before swimming. This was a feast. She looked down, paused and gritted her teeth.

'Something the matter?' Greg took the seat opposite and offered her toast and butter before he froze. 'You're not a vegetarian, are you? I should have asked.'

Holly smiled. 'I know it might be at odds with choosing a career as a friend to animals, but I'm fully carnivore.'

Relaxing, he smiled back. 'Why the grimace then?'

'I've not had black pudding before. The thought of eating congealed blood makes my stomach churn.'

'You're missing out!' Greg said. 'And I can assure you this stuff is the real deal. It comes from a farm about ten miles away. They sell it at the shop on Fridays and Saturdays, in case you decide it's amazing.'

'Which sounds great, only I'm not sure I can do it.' Holly held back in hesitation, trying not to think about the ingredients.

'Sure you can. You tackled an intruder with aplomb. Go on . . .'

Holly examined it closely, took a deep breath as she speared a piece, then closed her eyes to take a bite, praying it didn't make her throw up. But, to her amazement, it was, as Greg had suggested, really good. Crumbly, dense and rich. Weirdly tasty.

'Like it?' he asked, watching as she ate.

'I'm pleasantly surprised. Mind you, all this food is a bad idea. If I don't get cramp, I'll sink anyway from the sheer quantity I've consumed.'

Holly thought again about going out on the sea. If she taught Paolo what he was doing first, she'd have enough time to let her enormous breakfast go down.

'You do realize it's January, right?' Greg buttered his toast. 'You're not some kind of sports masochist, are you?'

'I'm well aware of the calendar, thanks, and reckon it doesn't matter — I'll be on a board. It wouldn't be so time-sensitive though, only I persuaded the nurse at the practice to come along. He's meeting me here.' She checked her watch. 'Twenty minutes, I reckon.'

As she said it, Holly became aware that were it not for the fact she couldn't let Paolo down, she would have been perfectly happy to give the paddle boarding expedition a miss and chat a bit longer with Greg. She was obviously forgiving last night's transgressions. That, and she wanted to know why he'd spend the night on her sofa.

'I've never tried it,' he said. 'It looks great when you see it in brochures for tropical destinations. Not sure it'll be the same in the chilly North Sea.'

'Scared of the cold water?'

'A native like me? Never. I'm impressed you're going in though — you could have been a lily-livered southerner.'

'Well, next time, you'll have to come with me,' Holly said, pouring more coffee.

'Love to,' he said, giving them both a dash of milk.

Their eyes met and Holly grinned at him. This morning, his short hair was dishevelled, and he was a bit more stubbly than yesterday. Over smart jeans he wore a navy Guernsey jumper that emphasized his strong frame. There was no denying he was an attractive man, she thought, and felt a little twinge somewhere beneath her ribcage. Holly reassured herself it was fine to find someone handsome, as long as you kept them at arms' length.

Actually, now she could see him in the light of day, Holly felt like she'd seen him before. Then, annoyed with herself that in the face of his charm and good looks she'd forgiven all his presumption, she decided she needed a few answers.

'Why did you come here last night? I'm guessing you've no family around, otherwise you'd stay with them.'

His face darkened. 'My family live here all right. They've lived here for centuries. Up at Auchintraid Farm.'

Holly frowned at Greg. Greg Dunbar. He had given his surname last night, only she'd been too busy readying herself to knock him out to make the connection. That must be why he looked familiar. 'Are you related to Angus?'

'Aye. My brother. He lives up on the farm with our mother.'

'So why not stay with them?'

'I had a row with Angus yesterday. A bad one,' he said, frowning. 'I'll pop back to see Mum when I know he's out the house.'

'Oh,' Holly managed.

There was a pause in the conversation. Greg looked at her, and Holly could tell from his knitted brow he didn't want to be asked about it. Not that it was any of her business — he was, after all, a relative stranger. The silence hung in the air for a second, until to Holly's great relief, Greg spoke again.

'I'd like to hear about you. Like why you're here. And how you've got this far in life and are only now trying black pudding.'

Pulling herself upright, Holly took a sip of coffee. 'I'm on a year's placement here, getting experience with farm animals, before I go to a new practice in Berkshire. I want to move up a rung, but I've not worked with cows or anything since school — I'm a small animal vet. But if I'm going to get anywhere, I need to do it, apparently. And it's a favour for my new boss — Hugh's an old friend of hers.'

'You sound a little reluctant to be here.'

'It's not that. I thought I was going to be somewhere else. I'd worked my arse off to get a role like the one at the surgery in Ascot — it was *such* a great job.'

'It sounds like you're career-focused, then.'

'Absolutely. I want my own practice one day. Be my own boss. The works. I know it's not the done thing to confess to being super ambitious, but I am.'

Holly had to be. She didn't have much option. Her dad had never been in the picture and while her mum had worked every job that came her way, the wages never came to much. And if they did, they often got frittered away when her mum was having one of those days. Or just disappeared, like that time that Holly hated to think about.

Holly was smart, though, and she knew good grades were her ticket out of the house on the estate, with its leaky roof and tired furniture. All through school she worked hard on the basis that the first thing she wanted when she grew up was financial security. Marriage, maybe — if she ever found the time for a relationship. Children, perhaps. But a stable career that paid the bills? Non-negotiable.

'So, when did you know you wanted to be a vet?' asked Greg.

'Early,' said Holly, and told him how as soon as she was old enough, she had found a part-time job, helping out at the kennels down the road. Mrs Barron, the kind lady who'd run them and who often looked after Holly when her mum disappeared for a weekend, had said Holly was a natural and asked if she would like to do some work experience at her sister's veterinary practice — even offering to keep paying Holly's wages while she did it. Holly had gone during the holidays for a week and not looked back.

'You've been working towards it since you were a teenager?' Greg looked impressed.

'I guess so. I loved being with the animals. I was never allowed a pet growing up, too expensive — although I wished for some each year when I blew out my birthday candles. Working with them took the place of having one of my own. And — slightly less romantic — I knew it would pay a decent wage and be a job for life, if I wanted it to be.'

'I know that feeling.'

'Really?' Holly nibbled on another slice of toast.

'Sure.' He shrugged. 'I grew up on a farm, and the living can be precarious. Anyway . . . then what?'

By the time she was sixteen she was the Saturday receptionist at Hill View Veterinary Practice, always offering to help the vets and nurses with the animals. Not only did she like seeing the balance of her bank account totting up, but she realized she adored helping save clients' pets, seeing how happy they made people. Two years later she was on scholarship at Bristol to study veterinary science. At the degree ceremony she had looked into the crowd and seen her mother beaming, her face shining with tears. Feeling a tidal wave of relief that she'd done it, Holly could have wept herself.

'She must have been proud of you,' said Greg.

Holly thought of her mother. The cynic in her wondered if her Jackie had been crying because she was finally free of responsibility for looking after her only daughter and could now cavort to her heart's content. Or was that too cruel?

Anyway, here she was. Poised to take the next step. Once she'd worked in Berkshire for a few years, she might be able to buy her own practice and expand her business. She could take on her own employees. And, by that time, she'd have some of the other things her childhood had led her to desire: a house of her own, some savings and investments, and — although it would be utterly frivolous — maybe a designer handbag. In reality, it wasn't her thing — she was more of a rucksack girl. But the option to buy one would be nice.

'There you are,' said Holly. 'I realize I sound like an intense workaholic. But it's only because I want to be in control of my life.'

Greg was looking at her. 'I get where you're coming from.'

'Really? Or are you being polite?'

'No, really. Like I said, money matters. It might not be everything, but it sure helps.'

This was exactly how Holly felt. Taking a sip of coffee, she realized she was feeling a tad lightheaded under his gaze.

'So what's your story?' she asked. 'I'm guessing from what you said, and your mud-free shoes, that you don't work on the farm.'

'A tale for another time. If we talk any more, you'll miss the boat, or rather the paddle board, you mad Sassenach.'

'Sasse-what?'

'English person,' he said, and gestured up at the clock on the wall.

Holly leaped up. 'Bugger! I know it's a bit weird, but I'm going to have to leave you here.' She spun around the room like a tornado, gathering things she needed for the outing, dumping them in a pile by the front door while Greg watched.

'Can I help at all?' he offered.

'If there's any coffee left, could you decant some into my thermos please? The big one? It's in the cupboard next to the sink.'

It was forecast to be a bright day, and Holly would warm up on the water, but she reckoned her toes would fall off after the session. She hoped Paolo had a decent wetsuit. If not, she'd be hauling him to the shore with icicles hanging from his ears.

'I've got to get dressed, and then I'll be down,' she called, running upstairs.

Three minutes, one inflatable paddle board, a paddle and a packed rucksack later, Holly was ready to go. She felt like a tortoise, carrying everything on her back. If she fell over, she'd never manage to get up, and would have to lie there on the beach until someone took pity on her.

'I've got a spare carabiner on my overnight bag,' Greg said, looking at her in amusement. 'In case you want to attach the kitchen sink.'

'Oh, ha ha,' said Holly, with a grin. 'You can keep it. Although speaking of sinks, maybe you could do the washing up.'

'Hang on,' Greg protested. 'I made breakfast.'

'Hang on, I didn't call the police on you last night.' She gave him a pointed look.

He waved a hand, batting the suggestion away. 'Ach. The nearest station's miles away. They'd never have caught me. Thanks for letting me stay, by the way. I'll be gone by the time you get back.'

A quiver of disappointment ran through her, which was odd, because less than twelve hours ago she'd been threatening to hit him over the head [illegible] with the nearest object she could find. 'Sure. Catch you around,' she said, with mixed feelings. 'And maybe post that spare set of keys to me.'

'You're saying you don't want me dropping by unexpectedly in the future? I'm hurt.'

'Goodbye, Greg Dunbar.'

Holly gave a tiny wave as she left — almost flirty — feeling as if she was saying goodbye to a friend, rather than a virtual stranger. She'd go so far as to say she had enjoyed her encounter with Greg. Indeed, if anybody had spied them through the window, they'd have thought they'd known each other for years.

CHAPTER 5

Paolo was leaning against the railings in dawn's pale first light. It looked like Holly was saying goodbye to somebody, which couldn't be right, because she lived alone.

She jogged over to him, a sweater over her wetsuit and a colossal rucksack on her back, looking for all the world like a marine out on an exercise. No — she looked like some kind of Amazon. If he'd been that way inclined and a foot taller, he'd fancy her. Some people looked great in surf get-up, and she was one of them. Last night at the pub, however, he had got the feeling Holly wasn't remotely aware of her striking looks, dressed down in her jeans and jumper without a scrap of makeup. Which made him like her even more.

He bounced up and down on the spot, feeling like a bit of twit. Whereas Holly looked fantastic, his figure had not been made for neoprene. He was slim — wiry, even — with a frame that was suited to marathon running or climbing. He loved going out for a long walk, preferably when it wasn't raining, but, really, he was built for museums, libraries or antiquarian bookshops. Warm places, with radiators, preferably with top-notch flat whites on tap.

The sun was coming up, and the sea glistened under the glowing rays. On bright days, Eastercraig could sometimes pass for the Mediterranean, especially when the turquoise waters around the shallows went out, revealing a narrow strip of sandy beach bordered by rocks in which nestled hidden pools. But the quick breeze reminded him this was not Italy, Spain or Greece, and when they got in the water, he might regret his decision to go in at all.

'Why are you doing this, Paolo?' he asked himself out loud. 'It's insane.'

He knew the answer. Because without Fabien there, his weekends were quieter. Yes, he had Chloe to hang out with, but she also spent time with her family, or her friends Isla and Morag from school. And he went out with the village ramblers sometimes, but it wasn't the same as having that one person. Without that intimate connection with someone, he was a teeny, tiny bit lonely, and in the sober light of day, first thing in the morning, it always felt worse. Holly, he reflected, might be lonelier than he was, although she appeared to be reasonably self-sufficient. Thank heavens she was good craic and was happy to have company on the water.

'Looking great,' he called to Holly as she crossed the road.

She grinned at him. 'Are you ready?'

Paolo held up the life jacket he'd borrowed from Dave downstairs and gave his best 007-style eyebrow. 'Does this pass muster?'

'Oooh — now that *is* a good pun.'

He offered to help her carry everything and ended up with the paddle. They must have made an odd couple, Paolo realized, walking along the sea front so early on a Saturday. The only other people who were out were dog walkers and shoppers.

'Good sleep last night?' he asked. 'I always find the first few nights in a new place weird. I think when I moved here from the city the silence and darkness freaked me out and it took me at least a week to get used to it.'

'I couldn't sleep all right. But it wasn't the noise and light levels keeping me up. You would not *believe* what happened when I got home.'

He listened in amazement, revelling in the drama. 'I love that you almost whacked Greg Dunbar with a stool,' he hooted. 'One of the town's favourite sons almost comes a cropper up against the new vet. Can't believe you let him stay.'

'Nor can I.'

'He's charming, apparently,' he said, giving her a sideways look that Holly ignored.

'Do you know him? He didn't talk about himself much. Let me ramble on.'

They jogged down on to the slipway and between them pumped up the board.

'Aye, well, I know of him. He's from Auchintraid Farm — Angus took over after their father died. Greg left a while ago to live in Aberdeen, to follow the dollar out there. I think he's an accountant, or a lawyer. Your type, is he?'

He watched as Holly blushed. 'He's not *unattractive*. But like I said, I don't need anything right now. I need this job to work out. No distractions.'

'What about a wee flirtation here or there? As far as I know he's single and *loves* a fling. Flings, plural, I should say. A one-man sexual blitzkrieg.'

That was a polite way of putting it. Greg Dunbar had a reputation as a ladies' man. That's what Chloe had told him, anyway. And Angus. And a few other people in the pub. That Greg tended to go out with girls for a month or two, and then it would all fall apart.

Holly looked appalled. 'If you're trying to encourage me, you'll fail. I have nerves of steel.'

Much as Paolo didn't want to live vicariously, there didn't seem to be many options in Eastercraig. The town was tiny, everyone knew everyone, and if there had been a man there for him — other than Fabien — he'd have heard about it now.

'A shame,' he sighed. 'Seeing as circumstances have forced me to live my dream of finding the right person through someone else.'

Holly gave him a sympathetic look. 'What about Chloe? You could you matchmake her. Set her up with Angus.'

'Nigh on impossible. I'm trying and failing. You can quiz her about it later. Isn't she coming over for coffee?'

'This afternoon,' said Holly. 'Anyway. Let's go before the tide changes.'

Paolo stood in the shallows, dancing on his toes as tiny waves lapped at the jetty, glad he owned two rash vests. Holly picked up the board, then, without announcing her intention, she ran into the water with it and leaped on, padding for a couple of metres.

'It's bracing,' she called, sliding off into the water. 'Come on.'

Paolo took a deep breath, then roared as he ran into the water. It was, as he had predicted, freezing. He got on the board with what felt like all the grace of a hippo, then took the paddle from Holly.

'Off you go,' she said, moving through the water beside him.

'What if I fall in?' said Paolo, his teeth chattering. 'I'll die.'

'You *can* swim, can't you?'

'Of course. But it's arctic in there. I'll get hypothermia.'

'You'll warm up,' said Holly, smiling. 'Keep paddling.'

That summed up life at the moment, Paolo reflected. He manoeuvred the paddle through the resistant currents. His head was above the water, and on the outside he appeared to be doing fine. But underneath he could feel the chill. Keeping paddling was all he could manage.

'You make it sound easy,' he replied.

Half an hour later, though, Paolo had to admit he was enjoying the paddle boarding. He had been regretting the drunken decision when he'd woken up. On top of the crack-of-dawn chilliness, it was a bit too trendy. And if you'd asked him, other than tuning into the latest Attenborough documentary, the best way to enjoy nature was to put on a pair of sturdy boots, pack a flask and some snacks, maybe a book, and hike somewhere peaceful. He liked to cocoon himself in the bracken and read. Or watch the wildlife. If someone had called him a young fogey, he'd have been thrilled.

The paddle boarding was invigorating though, and he'd worked muscles he didn't know existed: his calves were on fire. And aside from that, he'd been able to see the shoreline from a different angle. For a while, Holly had paddled as he sat cross-legged on the board in front, like a floating Buddha. Paolo's heart sang a peaceful — if cold — song, and he was able to forget about everything troubling him on dry land.

As they paddled back to the shore, Holly took off her lifejacket and dropped into the water, disappearing for a second before resurfacing. Paolo leaned over the board and looked at her in disbelief. 'Have you gone berserk?'

'Nothing like a brisk dip. Join me? It's only twenty metres.'

He shook his head firmly. 'You're turning blue. And I ought to guard the paddle board.'

'From what?'

'This guy,' Paolo pointed.

Coming towards them was Sporran, who gave a jubilant bark at seeing someone in the water with him. Paolo hoped it was jubilant anyway. It would be a shame if he tried to take a chunk out of the practice's new recruit.

'Should I get back on?' Holly looked unnerved.

'I don't know if anyone's been in the water with him before. I'm sure it's fine, but perhaps pick up the pace a bit. Be assertive, and don't do anything to scare him.'

Paolo began to paddle again gently. Grey seals might bite, and while it wouldn't kill you, you'd need a whopping dose of antibiotics. He'd never heard of anyone around Eastercraig being attacked by one, but there was a first time for everything. And he didn't want it to be now. Holly was a strong swimmer, at least, and they were close to the shore.

A small crowd had gathered on the sea front — presumably wondering who was daft enough to be out on a day like this — and watched as they landed the paddle board on the slipway. As Paolo put the kit down, Holly stood up and jogged the remaining few feet out of the water. They stood next to each other, simultaneously examining Sporran, who was bobbing about in the water. He appeared to be frowning, perhaps put out he'd been left behind.

'Glad he didn't nip me,' said Holly, looking relieved. 'Friendly as he is.'

'Agreed,' said Paolo through chattering teeth. 'It's a wonder he's never done it before, considering how close people get to him when he wants feeding.'

'Sporran aside, how did you enjoy it?' Holly turned to face him. 'Converted?'

In venturing out, Paolo had surprised himself. His skin didn't feel like his own. From his head, where his hair was stiff with salt, right down to his frozen toes, his body felt different and his mind relaxed. In the best possible way.

'My goosebumps have goosebumps, but I think I could be persuaded to go out again,' he said. 'Same time next week?'

'If I'm not on call, then yes. We can make it a regular thing.'

This would do him a world of good. The less time he spent longing for Fabien, longing for anyone, the better.

CHAPTER 6

Holly stepped through the front door. Her body shook with cold, and she needed to get in the shower and warm up. She made to take off the wetsuit then paused.

'Greg?' she called.

Even though she had a reasonably modest bikini on underneath her vest, she didn't want to take anything off right away in case he was still in the house. An impromptu striptease might send the wrong message.

There was no answer, however, and scanning the room, she noticed his bag was gone. He had said he would go, but she felt oddly disappointed he wasn't there.

When Paolo had teased her about Greg, she'd denied it — of course she had, he was still virtually a stranger — but she knew her blush had betrayed her. And not only to Paolo, but to herself. Despite having barely known the guy five minutes he'd wormed his way into her head. Now she was standing in her hallway, thinking it would have been nice if he'd stayed.

That said, what Paolo had mentioned about him being a serial flirt had put Holly off a bit. No — *a lot.* Nobody wanted to be the latest victim of a ladies' man. She had always imagined her dad to be of that ilk — her mum never talked about him, refused point blank. The term itself made her want to run a mile. It was like an ear-splitting alarm, reminding her of some of Jackie's least savoury boyfriends. But, when they'd talked that morning, she had the distinct feeling there was more to Greg than that. Although it was probably tactics on his part, giving off a good impression. After years of rehearsing, Greg could blatantly play the part of "charming stranger #1" with ease.

'Keep focused,' she said to herself, peeling the wetsuit off. 'You don't want a man getting in the way.' Leaving drops of saltwater on the floor, she carried it quickly through to the back door.

Outside was a tiny yard — it didn't merit being called a garden — with an outdoor shower. She rinsed the wetsuit and hung it on a peg outside, then ran upstairs and into the bathroom.

Fabien, who she had a lot to thank for in the cottage, had seen fit to add a rainmaker shower. It would certainly come in useful. Presumably there were many days up in Eastercraig when, after being outside, you felt like you might never warm up again.

Holly turned it on, let the steam fill up the bathroom and stepped in. When she had a moment during the week, she'd get some nice shower gel and moisturiser so she could turn the place into her own personal spa. Or, more likely, a useful place to wash off the cow muck.

Not long after, dressed in a pair of thermal leggings and a baggy hoody, Holly went downstairs. She planned to spend a bit of the day studying her old uni textbooks swotting up on cows, sheep and horses, then see Chloe, and maybe go for a walk or run, but nothing until she'd had lunch. Feeling thirsty, she went to make a hot drink, when something on the counter flickered and caught her eye.

A note! Greg had put the cafetière on it, so it didn't blow away. With an unanticipated frisson of excitement, Holly picked it up and began to read.

Holly! Thank you so much for your hospitality, and the pleasure of your company. I hope you survived the paddle boarding and weren't capsized by dolphins, or the wily Sporran, or a large wave. Good luck on Monday, and hopefully see you again soon. I pop over often, and it would be nice to see you next time I'm in town. Yours, Greg

PS — I've left you a Dundee cake. I happen to know if you want to charm Mr MacDougal on Monday, you should go in armed with it.

Realizing it hadn't been there earlier, Holly spotted a tin on the counter. Inside was the most delicious-looking fruitcake, decorated with concentric circles of almonds.

Greg hadn't left a number, Holly noted. She would have liked to thank him. Perhaps, though, as he suggested, they could catch up next time he was in town. Or, as her sensible side clucked at her like a mother hen, for now she should forget about him.

She shivered, still not feeling warm yet. Could she justify turning the radiators up? It was only January after all. Smiling at the thought she'd even considered such an extravagance, she clicked the kettle on and went to throw on a second jumper and an extra pair of massive socks. Oh, to be somewhere hot!

The thought of warmer climes reminded Holly that Jackie was likely somewhere in Europe, by a beach or a pool. She should call her again — Jackie ought to be awake by now. If not, Holly could act as an alarm and drag her out of bed.

The phone rang, and Holly pictured her mother, with her peroxide blonde hair, neatly manicured talons and sparkly caftan, topping up her tan on a lounger.

After a few seconds, Jackie picked up.

'Hello, Hollybobs. How are you?' said Jackie, her usually chirpy voice edged with a rasp Holly recognized as a hangover.

'I'm well. I got to Scotland yesterday. How are you?'

'Never better, darling. Nursing a slight headache, mind. Few wines last night.'

There it was. And at what point was Jackie going to tell her she wasn't in Milton Keynes?

'Got weekend plans?' Holly nudged her mother towards a confession.

'Not much, love. Partying, sleeping, going out for lunch. I've met a wonderful guy named Marco.'

Wow! Jackie was holding out this time. 'And where is Marco from?'

'Malaga. In fact—' and here her mother gave a little giggle — 'I'm there right now! That reception job at the builders' merchants wasn't doing it for me and then I met Marco and . . . you know me!'

The revelation was followed by a bout of her mother's inimitable machine-gun laughter. Holly rolled her eyes, wondering how long it was going to last. She reminded herself she no longer lived at home, hadn't done for a long time, and she didn't have to witness the demise of this relationship. She shook her head, despairing of her mother's true-to-form behaviour. The hopeless romantic in Jackie was going strong, still looking for the perfect man — ideally one who could fund her dream life. You had to admire her optimism, really. Holly would have done if it hadn't been such an endless source of anxiety as a child.

'I should go,' Holly sighed. 'Let you get back to Marco.'

'Thanks, doll. And I know you don't always approve but he's lovely, promise. And good luck with the new job. I might get one myself out here. Marco owns some bars.'

'Speak soon, Mum. Love you.'

'Love you too, Hols. Bye.'

Holly hung up. God, her mum was such a flake.

* * *

What if, the morning after, Holly was less fun? Or less chatty? Conversation had flowed the night before, loosened by a few rounds. Now the time had come for a cup of tea, Chloe felt nervous the new vet might not be her type of person. What if she was bossy? Or imperious? Uninterested in anything she had to say? Without Paolo as backup, the shyness was trickling back.

Chloe knocked on the door, ready to present her warmest smile and a box of shortbread. You couldn't go wrong with either of those things. Besides, Holly *had* accepted the offer of an afternoon meetup.

'Come in,' said Holly, as the door opened.

Chloe thrust the box towards her. 'A wee something to welcome you.'

She looked Holly up and down. She was more casually dressed than yesterday, if it was possible. Chloe, on the other hand, was neat as a pin in her tweed pinafore and hand-knitted cardigan. Sure, you shouldn't judge people on appearances, but where she loved vintage everything, Holly looked permanently outward-bound. At least they had animals in common. She could use that as a conversational fallback, if it came to it.

'Wow! Thank you. Let's crack these open,' Holly's face lit up on seeing the tin. 'Coffee? Tea? Something else?'

Thank heavens! She liked biscuits. Chloe followed Holly into the house.

'I like your necklace, by the way,' said Holly. 'I'd love to wear jewellery, but it's rarely practical.'

'Thanks.' Chloe put a hand to her amber Bakelite necklace. 'It's from a nearby vintage shop. I can take you there if you want. It's mad, but a real treasure trove.'

'I'd love to. Now . . . what can I get you?'

'Coffee, please,' she said. Her eyes alighted on a tin on the kitchen counter. 'That's one of Fiona Dunbar's, isn't it? *Please* tell me it's one of her Dundee cakes. Or is it shortbread? Oh, bugger and balls — you'll be drowning in the stuff.'

'The former. From Greg Dunbar as an apology.'

Chloe's eyes grew round. Had Holly said that? Her residual nerves disappeared immediately. 'Greg Dunbar gave you this? How on earth . . . ?'

Her mind whirred, unable to imagine how one of Fiona Dunbar's cake tins had ended up in Holly's cottage overnight. Or how, between arriving yesterday afternoon and now, Holly had encountered Greg. She stared at her new colleague, who shifted from foot to foot in an uncomfortable fashion.

'Come on. Out with it. How did you get it?'

'He broke in, only he didn't.'

As coffee was made, Holly told her of the night's events.

'Oh my gosh. What a story!' Chloe shrieked, picking up her cup.

'Exactly. Not the welcome I was expecting.'

Chloe tilted her head. She'd known Greg for ever, and he was a good guy. Mind you, his well-earned reputation was exactly that. 'He *is* on the dangerous side. If you went in with your eyes open, maybe you'd fare OK.'

'Dangerous?'

'I know him reasonably well — our mums are friends. He's great — warm and generous. And always popping back to check on his mum and the farm. But — and it's a *big* but — he left his fiancée about a week before they were due to marry. With no good reason. I think he got a bit lost after that, and now he's a smooth-operating serial monogamist. Och — *he'd* make a fun fling, if you wanted one.'

At this, Holly threw her hands up. 'Yeesh! He's good-looking, I'll grant you, and charming. But no, I'm not up for anything like that. Honestly, between you and Paolo, you could set up a dating agency. What about you? And Angus.'

Chloe should have seen this coming. If she was going to prod Holly about Greg, then she ought to have expected Holly to reciprocate.

'Och. There's nothing there. He's just a nice guy,' she said, attempting to sound breezy.

Her tone convinced no one, including herself.

'A nice guy you'd like to be going out with?' Holly encouraged, a mischievous look flitting across her face.

Chloe let out a sigh. She might as well share it. Paolo would tell Holly at some point. Or she might, after a few drinks one Friday night.

'I've liked him since school, but he was always one of the popular guys. And I was way too shy to talk to him. Even though we're adults, it's even worse now. I'm fine when I'm "Chloe from the surgery", but the rest of the time I'm a wreck. It's like being fourteen again.'

As she said it, her stomach twisted itself into further, familiar knots, and her pulse sped up. It was a feeling she knew well, excitement with a trimming of angst. Or perhaps it was anxiety edged by excitement. It was a feeling she'd known since she was a teenager, and she'd arrived at a point where she could scarcely tell if her state of mind was positive or negative. She pulled her hands into the sleeves of her cardigan.

'He spoke to you on Friday night,' Holly said.

'To say "hello". That's common courtesy.'

'But he barely acknowledged the rest of us — only you. He's easy on the eye. I can see why you like him. Like a brooding version of Greg.'

'Aye. That's about right,' said Chloe. 'He's the opposite of his brother. Greg is smooth, gregarious and clean-shaven. Angus is quieter, moodier and hairier.'

Holly snorted. 'You make him sound like a gorilla.'

Chloe laughed. 'I mean that in a good way. He's rough round the edges, but he's thoughtful and kind at heart.'

'So, when are you going to ask him out on a date?'

Chloe had asked herself that question on many occasions and had always given herself exactly the same response. 'I wouldn't dare.'

'Why not?'

For a hundred reasons. Because she was too shy in the first place. Because he would say no. Because he wouldn't say anything at all. Because there were loads of nice girls in these parts who might catch his eye first. Because she would rather have a passively, slowly breaking heart than risk it all and have it actively broken. She could go on . . . Chloe began to play with her necklace like a rosary. Praying she might find the courage to do something about the Angus situation.

'I don't think it would work,' she said, picking a bland answer in the hope of shutting down the conversation.

'Oh, come on,' Holly scoffed. 'How can you know that?'

'Why wouldn't a fling with Greg be the best thing that ever happened to you?' she countered.

'Touché,' Holly laughed. 'It's not my thing. Maybe we should make resolutions to break out of our comfort zones. I've already started by moving a few hundred miles from mine. It's your turn.'

Chloe smiled. Eastercraig was her comfort zone. Her parents' bungalow, where she still lived, the quilt she'd made herself from old scraps of fabric on the bed she'd had for ages. Her friends from school, and the pub she went to a couple of times a week. And the warm locals she'd grown up with, who always greeted her with a smile as they walked past.

But it was also the place where she was quiet. A place where things never changed, and where no time soon did she think she'd be able to locate the requisite bravery with which to ask out Angus. She groaned inside. Living in Eastercraig was, most of the time, a blessing. Occasionally, it was a curse.

'Talking of comfort zones, how was Paolo? That man likes dry land. And tasteful interiors,' Chloe said, directing the subject matter elsewhere, and hoping Holly would take the hint.

Holly smiled. 'Like a fish out of water.'

Chloe giggled, took another biscuit and wriggled back into the sofa.

CHAPTER 7

On Monday morning, Holly woke up before her alarm, fuelled by so much adrenaline she'd be able to run a marathon and have plenty left to spare. She sprang up and examined the outfit she'd laid out for her first day.

Sometimes, when she was covered in drool, poo and worse, she dreamed of floating about in cashmere jumpers and silk blouses — anything with a dry-clean-only tag. Her time so far had taught her, however, if it didn't go in the machine, it wasn't worth the bother. She recalled being recently vomited on by a spaniel and shuddered.

She'd laid out a pair of slim black trousers, a blue shirt and a dark grey V-necked sweater. It was highly washable, but for a hint of excitement she added a pair of tiny emerald stud earrings — seeing Chloe's outfits, she wanted to add some glamour. Holly wasn't ready to get dressed, however.

Outside, it was pitch black, and undoubtedly icy underfoot. Not ideal conditions for a run, but it was the best way she knew to get her head clear. She dressed quickly, put on the headtorch her friends from London had given her as part of a Highland survival kit, and sprinted out the door.

Holly jogged along the front and towards the headland, checking her watch every so often. The surgery wasn't open, and nor was the shop. In fact, there wasn't a soul in sight — they were no doubt still snuggled up under downy duvets. She carried on past the rest of the houses, and over the gorse-covered headland towards Finnen Beach, which she was yet to see. On Saturday, Paolo had told her it was one of his favourite spots: bright but blissfully chilled out in summer, wild and haunting in the winter. If she got there for 8.30 a.m., the sun would just be coming up.

As the fingers of light reached over the headland, she saw the sandy cove was indeed ravishingly beautiful. As she ran down on to it, over gentle dunes and through tall marram, she realized how secluded it was. A small V-shaped inlet, it had sands as white as any in the Caribbean. Waves lapped at the shore, a light spray filling the air as they crested against the rocks that curved along the sides. Holly turned back to the land. There wasn't a house in sight.

"Seriously romantic", was how Paolo had described it. 'If someone was going to propose to me, it would be on Finnen Beach. Ideally it would be deserted, on a cold but cloudless day, with a bottle of champagne on a tartan picnic blanket.'

'It sounds like you've thought about it a lot.' Holly had replied, smiling.

'Maybe,' Paolo had sighed. 'When you'll see it, you'll know.'

Now she was here, she could see he had been telling the truth. Even in the cold, half-lit January morning, it was dreadfully romantic. Greg crossed her mind, and she briefly found herself thinking of sharing a glass of champagne on the beach with him. Not the proposal bit — that was taking a fantasy step too far — but if he appeared on the doorstep and said he'd set up a second brunch for them down on the sand, she wouldn't say no. In a platonic way, of course.

The thought of food reminded her she had to be at the surgery by 9.00 a.m. to meet Hugh MacDougal and start work. And before that she would need a slice of toast. After drinking in the view one more time, Holly turned on her heel and raced back towards the town.

* * *

Tentatively, Holly opened the door to the surgery. From a room off the side there came a clattering, clanging noise.

'Hello! It's Holly,' she said, popping her head around the door to find a tiny kitchenette.

Chloe looked up. 'Cuppa?'

Holly hung up her coat on a hook behind the door. 'Please.'

Chloe looked mischievous. 'Thought any more about Greg?'

Holly was about to say "no" — even though it would have been a lie — when the door swung open and Paolo appeared. Holly was glad he'd arrived when he did. He leaned against the desk and rolled his sleeves up.

'Are we all prepared for today? Lists ready?' he asked. He spotted the tin in Holly's hands. 'Straight to the top of the class, Anderson. You know what's needed to go into battle.'

'Hugh — Mr MacDougal — do I need know anything? There've been a couple of comments that suggest I might be up against something,' she said.

Chloe and Paolo shared a glance, and an awkward pause followed. Holly knew each was waiting for the other one to speak, a gnawing anxiousness appearing in her stomach.

'Come on. Forewarned is forearmed,' she persisted.

'The thing about Hugh is . . .' Chloe said, and hesitated.

Paolo inhaled deeply, then spoke fast. 'The thing about Hugh is he's been doing this for decades. He's set in his ways, and sometimes when you disagree with him, he tends to get a wee bit grumpy.'

Chloe nodded. 'And other things make him grumpy too. Like lateness, rudeness, hunger and perceived stupidity.'

'Perceived stupidity . . . ?'

'He's polite, on the whole,' said Paolo, 'to clients, and us. But he's prone to the odd blow-up. We call him "the Volcano". Usually dormant, but occasionally erupts spectacularly. He'll like you though. You're prompt, keen and look like you'd be fine pulling out a stuck calf . . . If need be, tell him you like boats.'

'That I like *boats*?'

'Aye,' Chloe agreed. 'He's been doing one up for the last year or so. Loves it. Maybe you could bond over it.'

'I've nothing against boats, but I'd be lying if I said I knew anything about them,' said Holly.

Paolo grimaced. 'Oh well. I'm sure it'll be fine. Why don't I show you the surgery?'

He put a hand on her arm, guiding her past reception. 'The consulting room, X-ray equipment, pharmacy cupboard, lab and kennels are through that door at the end. If you go round the corner and up the winding staircase there's a small staff room, and the loos. Watch your head when you're up there, it's all built into the eaves. Come through here, though, seeing as it's where you'll be spending a lot of your time.'

Holly followed him into the consulting room. It was light, with a small window, and the table set up in the middle. She paid attention as Paolo began pointing at the drawers, telling her where all the equipment was kept, making mental notes for when she needed them.

'It's in need of a refurb,' said Paolo. 'But Hugh's got a tight budget. Best not mention anything yet.'

Holly gave an "mmmm" of agreement. She wasn't going to say it on her first day, but the room looked sorrier than reception. The grey cupboard doors hung a bit askew, and the plastic was peeling off the surfaces. And while the equipment was probably fine, she had been used to state-of-the-art stuff back in London. This was all dated. And yet, considering lots of the work was going to be outdoors, perhaps a basic approach was all that was needed.

'Any questions?' Paolo asked. 'Or shall we go and see what today has in store? We begin Monday with a look at the timetable, a quick run-down of animals we've had over the weekend — although there haven't been any — and anything anybody wants to flag up.'

'I'm ready to go. Itching to get started.'

'I can give you something for that.'

'Very funny,' said Holly, grateful for Paolo's easy manner.

As they stepped back into reception, Holly straightening her shirt for the hundredth time that morning, the front door flew open, and in walked a small man with a lined face, a scrape of white hair and watery blue eyes that were emphasized by his glasses. Without acknowledging any of them he took off his coat and hung it on a stand by the door. Beneath it he had on black cords, a blue shirt and a granite V-neck jumper. Holly cringed as she realized they were wearing the same thing.

'Chloe, Paolo,' he nodded. Then he spotted Holly. 'Oh.'

Holly gave her biggest smile and stepped forward, her hand outstretched. 'Holly Anderson.'

'I know who you are,' he said, in a level but not entirely welcoming voice. 'I'm not an imbecile.'

Holly was flabbergasted. 'I didn't think you were,' she stuttered.

'Somebody does, otherwise they wouldn't have foisted you on me.'

Holly felt herself lean backwards in shock, so far that she almost hit the ground. 'Excuse me?'

'You heard me. I didn't ask for you to come here. Judith thought it was a good idea.'

'I thought you were short-staffed,' Holly turned to Chloe and Paolo, who both looked as stunned as she felt. She stood rooted to the spot, unable to move.

Hugh glared up at her. 'I was doing fine. I didn't need some young flibbertigibbet here to interfere. Now, I suggest you keep your head down and work hard. Then we'll all survive the imposition, and you can go back to Hampshire.'

Of all the things he had said, it was at this that Holly woke from her momentary catatonia. 'Berkshire,' she said. 'I'm meant to be in Berkshire.'

Hugh looked like he was about to snipe back when the door opened, and in stumbled a woman who appeared to be wrestling an enormous ginger cat. Claws out, it squirmed in her arms, and she crashed into the desk trying to hold on to it.

'Quick, Hugh!' she squealed, sinking to the floor, still clinging on to the furious animal. 'You need to take him.' The cat continued to fight against her, and the poor woman looked like she was trying to keep hold of jelly.

'Why isn't he in a bloody cage, Jeannie?' roared Hugh.

This suggestion elicited a yowl from the cat, and he finally managed to break free. Holly stepped back as he made a dash for the kitchen. She winced at the sound of china smashing on the floor.

'Terence!' the woman leaped to her feet.

'I'll go,' said Chloe, lines forming on her brow.

'No. I will,' said Hugh.

Hugh rolled up his sleeves and marched towards the kitchen. Holly stepped to the side and peered over Chloe's shoulder. Behind them, Paolo put a hand on Jeannie's arm.

'Come on, Terence,' Hugh clicked his tongue.

Terence resolutely refused to come any closer, instead knocking a second cup off the work surface. He took a few steps, giving an almost taunting glance towards them as he did so. Hugh lunged for him, and there was another scream — Holly wasn't sure if it was Hugh or Terence — before Terence leaped over Hugh's shoulder and bolted back into the waiting room.

Hugh spun around, revealing rows of scratches running the length of his arm and a face that was a nasty shade of puce. He went to chase the cat, but as Holly and Chloe parted to let him through, he slipped on the spilled tea on the floor and crashed over in a blur of arms and legs.

'Someone get that bloody cat,' he yelled.

Holly turned and crouched down, and a pair of ears poked out from behind the reception desk. Slowly the cat peered round at her, and Holly gave him what she hoped was a sympathetic look. After all, she too knew exactly how it felt to be on the end of a blast of rage from Hugh MacDougal. The cat came forward and — rather inexplicably — wound itself round her ankle. She scooped him up and held him firmly.

'Now, what are we going to do with you?' she asked softly, standing up.

'I'm sorry,' said the woman, rushing forwards. 'I'm Jeannie Douglas, and this is Terence. He was in a fight with another cat last week and got a bite on his front leg — the left one. And I looked after it at home, but I think it's infected. I only carried him because he hates coming in so much.'

Holly took a breath. She was going to treat this cat and sort out the carnage, before calling Judith and telling her Hugh had some serious issues. That instead of needing a new member of staff, he required urgent anger management sessions.

'Hugh,' she summoned a calm voice. 'You see to your scratches. Paolo, you come with us to the consulting room and we'll see what's up.'

Not daring to wait for a reply, she walked to the consulting room, before gently settling the cat on the table.

'Now, Terence,' she examined the leg. 'What mischief have you done yourself, hey?'

An abscess had formed where the tom cat had been bitten. Terence gave a tired mew, exhausted by his failed break for freedom. This should be simple. All she needed was for Paolo to remind her where everything was.

'Paolo, I need to lance the abscess, flush with saline and then give a shot of antibiotics. Mrs Douglas, once I've sorted this, you can take Terence home, but keep an eye on the wound,' she said, starting to explain to Jeannie what she needed to do once they were home.

Shortly after, a relieved Jeannie Douglas and a happier Terence were waved off and Holly found Hugh sitting on a chair in reception, talking to a lady with a beagle. He got up, his jaw clenched. Surely he wasn't going to shout at her again?

'Holly, a word, please,' he gestured towards the door to the consulting room.

Holly glanced at Chloe, who shrugged apologetically, and Paolo, who made a "no idea" face. Hugh wasn't about to fire her, was he?

Hugh held the door open to the consulting room. Holly entered, and felt her guts flip as he shut the door, remembering the last conversation she'd had with an employer — the one where she had ended up resigning. She wasn't in the position to do that again quite so soon, and with that realization the bravery she'd found in the consulting room a moment ago deserted her. For a hideous second she thought she might burst into tears.

Hugh looked at her over the top of his glasses. 'Ms Anderson, I need someone who knows what they're doing. I didn't need that old busybody Judith to post me some green twenty-something who wouldn't know a cow if it bit her on the nose. I'm a vet, not a babysitter.'

At this, Holly forgot the desire to cry. If she didn't need the job to work out, she might have told him what for. But she did, so that probably wasn't a great idea. Nor should she correct him on her age, although it was nice to be mistaken for a twenty-something. Wait — scratch that thought — *none* of this was OK.

She took a deep breath, summoning a calm voice. 'Hugh, Mr MacDougal . . . I was as surprised as you were to find myself working for you. I'm really sorry that this feels like an imposition. I'm certain we can make this work, though, and see the year out.'

'A whole bloody year,' Hugh huffed. 'Christ!'

'I'm a really hard worker, and a fast learner, and . . . I'm a good vet.'

'That remains to be seen, as far as I can tell. Now, I'm going to make another cup of tea and watch you deal with that beagle. Make sure you know what you're doing.'

Holly followed him at a distance. She had never worked with anyone like this and didn't know if she could. Not for a whole year.

* * *

At midday, Chloe took her lunch outside to eat on a bench overlooking the sea, and two minutes later Paolo joined her. It was their Monday ritual, regardless of the season. Chloe would zip to the café at 11.50 a.m., collect their crab sandwiches and cakes, and they'd eat together, assuming the weather allowed. She rarely picked one up for Hugh — he liked to get his own — but, thoughtful to the end, she'd grabbed one for Holly and left it on the side in the kitchen in foil with a pink Post-It on top.

She looked up for a second and closed her eyes, letting the sun warm her face. Today had been beautiful so far, although having lived in Eastercraig all her life, Chloe knew it could change in seconds. Best to make the most of it while you could.

Sitting upright, she gazed over the water. A few boats slid slowly along the horizon, far out at sea. Closer to hand, the tiny harbour hummed with gentle activity. The tide was out, revealing the sliver of beach and network of rockpools where in summer small children with buckets would wade excitedly. Fishermen called to one other from their boats, locals popped in and out of the shops and the odd car chugged along the road behind them. She smiled to herself while overhead circling gulls shrieked, reminding her to eat her lunch before they did. Only two weeks ago, she had witnessed one steal a four-finger KitKat right out of her friend Morag's hands.

'Come on then,' said Chloe. 'Spill. How's she doing? It wasn't the most auspicious start to the day.'

She was dying to know what had been happening back in the consulting room. Normally, she was in control of the flow of gossip, sharing with Paolo the titbits she'd picked up behind reception. But not this time. And it was killing her, especially considering Hugh had thrown a wobbly within seconds of his arrival.

After spending Friday night and Saturday afternoon with her, Chloe had decided she genuinely liked Holly. She hadn't liked Bronwen, the locum who'd preceded her. Bronwen had been ultra-efficient, and the surgery had run smoothly, but she'd been a bit snooty, and rejected any invitations to join her and Paolo at the pub on Friday nights. To top it off, she'd also told Chloe, within days of arriving, she wasn't "a girl's girl", and preferred hanging out with lads. To Chloe, that was the same as holding out a stick of kryptonite, and she'd quickly dropped any ideas of making life-long friends with her. Holly, on the other hand, had real potential, even if she was only staying a year.

'Not much,' said Paolo. 'She was a pro with Gogo's hips. Didn't quail under pressure. Or Hugh's intense glare.'

'And how does Hugh like her, do you think?'

'To be honest, I think he's a bit intimidated by the fact she's about a head taller than him. She might fare OK — after the initial hiccup she flew through the list easily enough, even with Hugh breathing down her neck. She's confident — with small animals at least.'

'I wouldn't describe Gogo as small. That Great Dane is bigger than a Shetland pony.'

Paolo laughed. 'They're off to Auchintraid this afternoon.'

'I know. Aren't you going too?'

Chloe shot him a sideways glance and Paolo gave her a knowing look. 'Wondering if she might try and steal Angus and want me to keep an eye? Don't worry, I don't think he's her type.'

'I wonder if Greg might be though.'

'Don't deflect. If you don't go for it with Angus, he'll get taken by somebody else, cantankerous bastard that he is.'

'He's not cantankerous. He's tempestuous.'

'Same thing,' said Paolo, taking a sip of tea.

An image of Angus Dunbar, in a pair of mud-spattered coveralls, sprung into Chloe's mind. He was so tall and broad, and she often fantasized he'd scoop her up into his arms, as if she were as light as a feather. Although perhaps not while he was covered in muck. She'd have to re-jig the fantasy so her clothes didn't get wrecked.

She gave Paolo a nudge in the ribs. There was no point hiding anything from him. 'Bring me back some of the gossip?'

'Aye. All right. Anything for you, MacKenzie-Ling.'

Holly came out of the surgery, bundled up in her coat, with a cup of tea and her sandwich.

'This looks delicious — I love crab. Thank you *so* much,' she called, lifting the sandwich up. 'Hugh went home for lunch so reckon I can sit out here for ten minutes. Room for a tall one?'

'You're funny,' said Paolo. 'So yes.'

Chloe gave a small smile, immensely relieved Holly liked seafood. She budged Paolo along and Holly came round and sat down next to her.

'Getting on with Hugh?' Paolo asked.

Holly looked at him with the face of someone upon whom an uncomfortable truth has recently dawned. 'My mentor said that my predecessor left "abruptly". Is that because Hugh is, how can I put it . . . very angry a lot of the time?'

'They might have had some . . . arguments,' Chloe said, reluctant to give anything away.

'About what?'

Chloe shot Paolo a pleading look. He was a far more comfortable gossip than she was.

'Everything,' Paolo said, picking up the conversation with evident relish. 'The computers, the clients, the payments. And then she suggested he might consider finding someone to tackle his management style, smooth it a little. Not in those words, though. They were permanently at each other's throats. It was best she left because one of them would be dead by now if she hadn't.'

Holly looked alarmed. 'Oh Christ!'

Paolo apologized. 'Sorry. I was painting a picture and it got a bit dark. Be patient with him, persevere.'

Chloe remembered taking Munchkin, her hamster, in to see Hugh when she was a child. For a shorter man, he had loomed large, even then. But he had been kind too. While there was no denying Hugh had become snappier over the last couple of years, Chloe wanted to defend him.

'He's a pussycat really,' said Chloe, eliciting a snort from Paolo. 'He is! He's missing Dorothy, his wife. She died a few years ago. He's lonely, is all, and it comes out in spikiness. Paolo's right. It'll just take some time for everything to settle.'

There was a lull in the conversation while they all ate their lunch. After a bit, Holly sighed. 'You've lived here all your life, right, Chloe? Do you ever get tired of this view?'

Chloe looked in front of her, at the mesmerizing undulations of the dark waters, and the occasional white wave tip that appeared and disappeared in the blink of an eye.

'No,' she said. 'Never. I sometimes lose track of time when I watch the ocean.'

'Hey Chlo — can you give Holly any tips about Auchintraid?' asked Paolo. 'You know plenty about the farm. And the farmer.'

Chloe shot him a look and flushed a deep crimson. She didn't like the implication she was an obsessed woman. Even though she was exactly that.

Chloe considered Angus once more. The younger of the Dunbar brothers by three years, where Greg was every inch the smart businessman, making his way in the city, Angus was a farmer through and through. The man surely slept in his wax jacket. He'd taken the farm over when their father had died ten years ago, and his weather-beaten face often bore a look of concern as he juggled the hard tasks of the farm. But Chloe knew that when he took his mind off the all-consuming duties of Auchintraid, he had a smile as wide as could be, and a laugh that shook the surrounding hills. And his arms were as strong as any man's, and . . .

'Errrr — Chloe?' Paolo poked her.

Oops! She'd disappeared into her own wee fantasy land while thinking about him, the one where she had no fears about expressing her deepest feelings for him.

'It's no good,' she said, glumly. 'He'll never know me as anything other than Chloe, the mousy girl from the year below, who occasionally answers the telephone when someone's required to stick their hand up a hairy coo's arse.'

'*You* think that,' said Paolo. 'Nobody else does. They know you as Chloe, the eternally thoughtful, kind and generous girl next door. And who is utterly gorgeous and doesn't know it.'

Chloe wished she was that girl. After two slices of Dundee cake she had eaten that morning, she felt rather like a land-based cousin of Sporran.

She let out an enormous sigh. 'Really?'

Paolo's lip twitched. 'I'm rarely so laudatory about anyone, so I'd take it if I were you.'

'Seconded,' said Holly. 'I've been here less than a week, and you've invited me to the pub, got me a sandwich — let me give you some money, by the way — and I heard the way you calmed Mrs James earlier when her rabbit went under anaesthesia. That's exactly how you come across.'

'Thanks, guys,' she said, smiling.

The flattery was enough to push out the doubt for the time being.

CHAPTER 8

Holly held tightly to the Land Rover's grab handles as they sped out of Eastercraig. She glanced back at Paolo and noticed he'd done the same. It was the sensible thing to do, considering the hair-raising pace at which Hugh took the corners.

'Beware of Fiona,' Hugh yelled over the rattling engine. 'Don't let her get talking as she'll never stop. Angus is a good lad, though. Hard-working.'

'I saw him in the pub on Friday night,' she replied.

Paolo leaned over from the back seat. 'He lives and breathes farm. Nice enough when he's not frowning.'

'Weight of the world on his shoulders, that lad,' said Hugh, shaking his head. 'Needs to find himself a girl. Can't live with his mother for ever.'

Holly craned her neck around again and Paolo gave her a wink. Poor Chloe, so shy she didn't want to ask him out. From what it sounded like, though, Angus was either too crabby or so busy he'd not get round to it, even if he did fancy her.

They flew over the headland and joined the main road, which they followed for a couple of miles. Holly gazed out the window at the soft hues of the heather, glad it was enough to distract her from her mounting queasiness. On the other side of them stood a large pine forest. The proud trees looked ancient, like they'd always been part of the landscape. For a second she let go to peer round at a rocky outcrop, then regretted it as Hugh swung off the road round a hairpin turn and tore over another bump in the road, nearly causing her to slide into the footwell despite wearing her seatbelt.

'Never met a pothole you didn't like, did you, Hugh?' said Paolo, laughing.

'Pipe down, cheeky,' said Hugh. 'There. That's it, down the end of the track.'

'Wow,' Holly breathed out, forgetting her mounting need to hurl.

Auchintraid Farm was *gorgeous*. Where Eastercraig was jolly, with its bright buildings and friendly locals, this was the exact opposite. It was wild and windswept. A long, dark stone farmhouse sat in the farmyard, a mongrelly collection of barns and sheds on either side, with the sea right beyond. Holly imagined that on a stormy night, the place would be battered by the winds and rain — there were no trees to protect it. Or if the fog rolled in it would feel isolated, or haunting. *Wuthering* — that was the word. If Angus wasn't moody by nature, living and working in a place like this could surely make you so. She hopped down from the car and stood looking over the fields.

Paolo came to stand beside her. 'On a day like today, I can't think of any farm that's more wonderful.'

Holly nodded. Despite the isolation, he was right. She was glad the weather was good, because today the sea shone under the winter sun, and birds rose and fell around the cliffs. As she breathed in the salty air, which mingled with the smell of the farmyard, she had a fleeting but strong suspicion any farms she was going to work on in Berkshire were going to feel pedestrian by comparison.

She followed Paolo round the back of the car and they lifted out their bags, and zipped themselves into matching green jackets and over-trousers, tugging on wellies over extra socks. Hugh had mentioned he would be taking a back seat while Holly did the work, adding to the nausea she had been feeling on the way over.

'Paolo,' she said in a low voice. 'I'm a little worried about this cow business.'

'Which bit? Has it been a while?' he asked, wiggling a foot into a boot.

'You could say that . . . I've not seen any since uni. And I got kicked in the head by one. I was fine, but I decided I preferred the slightly more predictable workings of the surgery. I'm out of practice and reasonably anxious.'

'Bad luck,' Paolo shot her a sympathetic look. 'But there are plenty of us here. You can ask Hugh for help, remember.'

'What, and let him think I'm incompetent?'

'Good point. OK. Don't sweat it, I'm sure you'll be fine.'

Holly was about to insist otherwise when a woman in wellies came out of the house, greeting them with a wave. She was tall — as tall as Holly — with masses of flyaway red hair.

'Hugh, Paolo,' she said, with a smile that took up half of her face. 'And you must be Holly Anderson. Angus is over in the fields somewhere. Let me give him a call.'

To Holly's surprise, she pulled out a massive walkie-talkie.

'Not much signal out here,' Paolo explained, as Fiona called Angus in.

Moments later, a quad came hurtling down the lane, and off hopped a burly man in coveralls. In the light of day, rather than the gloom of the pub, the similarity between Angus and Greg was obvious.

He didn't smile as he shook her hand. 'Angus Dunbar,' he said, then nodded at Hugh and Paolo.

'I'll go and get tea. And some flapjacks?' Fiona clapped her hands together. 'Come in and tell me all about yourself, Holly.'

Angus's eyebrows knitted together and Holly wondered if he grew frownier as Fiona grew chattier. He shook his head, exasperated. 'Not right now, Mum.'

'That sounds great, Fiona, but I'm not sure we have time,' added Paolo, diplomatically.

'I'd love to at some point, Mrs Dunbar,' Holly said, politely. 'But it's my first day on the job and I'd love to see the herd. Maybe afterwards?'

She didn't dare mention she'd already made great inroads with one of her Dundee cakes that morning, and prayed Hugh and Paolo exercised some tact too.

'Well, I'll get the flapjacks out ready.' She beamed. 'When you're all done, pop down to the house.'

Holly watched as she pottered inside, and momentarily wished she could go and have a natter rather than tackle the cows. She reckoned the interior was full of squashy chairs, and blankets and cats. And cake paraphernalia. Instead, though, as her colleagues went to unload the car, she looked to Angus.

'Are we going back over there?' she asked.

'Fold,' Angus grunted.

'I'm sorry? Fold what?'

'You called it a herd. Highlands are a *fold*.'

'Oh. Accept my apologies — to you and the fold. I hope they're not offended.'

She grinned, but Angus didn't look amused. It was definitely time to get going.

Angus gave a slight tilt of his head over towards the hills. 'That way.'

Hugh looked up from where he was throwing the bags on to the quad. 'Off you go, Holly. Paolo and I will take the spare from the shed. Keys in the kitchen, Angus?'

'Aye,' said Angus. 'We'll be over in the far field.'

Holly watched until Hugh disappeared into the porch. 'I've not been on one of these for a while. So if you wouldn't mind taking it easy . . . It was a bumpy drive over.'

Angus raised an eyebrow. 'Hugh drove?'

'He has a reputation?'

He smiled, and his face was transformed. 'Aye. You're pale green. Have a sip of water and you'll feel better.'

For the last few minutes, Holly had begun to wonder what a sweet person like Chloe saw in a man like this — he'd looked surly, and unapproachable, and you'd never describe his conversational style as chatty. But as he handed her a bottle, she realized that — as Chloe had insisted — under the grumpy exterior there *might* be a gentle side to him.

'It tastes a bit special,' he said, as she took a sip. 'Comes from a spring further up the hills. Beautifully soft, no?'

She held the bottle up to the light. 'A spring?' She took another mouthful. 'It's wonderful. You could bottle it and go into business.'

'Och. There's only one business round here and that's the coos.' He gestured to the quad bike. 'Hop on.'

Holly wasn't sure she was ready for four wheels again yet, but at least she wasn't with Hugh, who suddenly zoomed past them at breakneck speed. Holly was grateful it was Paolo and not her who was clinging on for dear life. Hopefully he wouldn't fly off the back.

* * *

Up in the top field, Holly looked around her. Highland cattle were dotted all over the grass. Only there was something different about these ones.

'Aren't Highland cattle usually brown?' she asked. 'I've not seen these black ones before.'

Angus nodded. 'Lots are. But they come in all manner o' colours. And they're *very* friendly.' He held out a hand, and the nearest one padded over to greet them. 'This is Maud.'

'They're gorgeous,' said Holly, slowly putting her palm forward, which Maud licked. 'Hello, Maud.'

'And if you're wanting to fit in, you can call them hairy coos,' Angus added. 'If you remember that, and to say "fold", we'll make a local of you yet.'

Another smile crept on to his face, and Holly dared to believe he was warming up a bit. Hugh and Paolo were already up at the top of the field, and together she and Angus walked up to join them.

'These are my hobby,' said Angus. 'They spend most of the year over at the Glenalmond Estate, roaming over the moors there.'

'And the main bulk of the farm is a beef herd?'

'Aye. And yes, they're a herd, not a fold. You're actually here to do some toenail clipping — Hugh may've explained — but I wanted to introduce you to this lot. They're what everyone thinks of when they think of Scotland. Plus, I didn't want you getting shat on as soon as you'd arrived.'

'What?' said Holly.

Angus shrugged. 'Occupational hazard when you're trimming their hooves. We'll hop back on the quad in a mo and go back to the barn. I'll help you to get them all in the cattle crush.'

* * *

Back at the farm, Holly pulled Hugh to one side. 'Can I have a word?'

This wasn't ideal, considering Hugh had told her that morning he didn't need her help. But she could hardly go off and begin the job when she wasn't sure if she was about to balls it up. She elected not to tell him about her fear of cows, just the bit where she hadn't been within ten feet of one since she was in her early twenties.

'Fire away, if you must,' he huffed.

'I've not worked with big animals for a while. To be honest, I'd decided not to go down that career path, and I'm not sure I remember the finer points.'

'For God's sake . . .' Hugh frowned. 'What finer points are there? Head end, rear end, middle bits. And besides, you're here for toenail clipping. It's not rocket science.'

Holly was dubious. Not rocket science, perhaps, but it was a branch of veterinary science she had not had any contact with since university. Literal contact, seeing as one had attempted to plant its hoof in her skull. The idea of being behind a massive cow was making her feel wobblier than a blancmange.

Hugh let out a harrumph. 'Pop your gear on. I'll talk you through the first one, but you'll be doing the rest.'

* * *

As Holly had cut the hooves of the herd with the pliers-like trimmers, one or two had, as Angus had said, pooed on her. It stunk, splatters reaching up her knees. At least her face had been spared. And she hadn't been kicked either. Yet.

The poo wasn't the worst bit though. It had been over a decade since she had done work with farm animals and she wasn't used to such an energetic job. Before long, her arms were beginning to visibly shake. Every muscle was burning, but she couldn't stop. Hugh and Paolo had watched, or passed her equipment, Hugh giving "mmmmms" of approval (she hoped), and Paolo flinging the occasional thumbs up. Angus, when he wasn't helping move the cattle, stood with his arms folded, nodding. She prayed he was happy with her work.

At the end of the afternoon, having said goodbye to the Dunbars, Holly flung her bag in the back of the car. Paolo came round to join her.

'How do you think I did?' she whispered, so Hugh didn't hear.

'Looked fandabidozi to me,' he replied.

'I think my arms are about to fall off!'

'Don't tell Hugh you're tired,' he warned.

Holly looked at him. 'Really?'

'Nah — it's probs fine. But don't make yourself out to sound like a wuss.'

Blimey, she thought, crashing down into the passenger seat. This was a serious change of scenery.

CHAPTER 9

Utterly shattered, Holly sat in the pub with Chloe and Paolo, trying not to fall asleep. The end of the week had come around fast. Holly had worked in Eastercraig most mornings. On Thursday she'd been along the coast, where she'd held a small animal surgery in a village hall there. And in the afternoons, she'd gone on visits with Hugh to see more farms.

Each evening, she had been mentally and physically exhausted by the farm work, and on the verge of frustrated tears from the pressure of having to show the pernickety Hugh that she was a competent vet. He had spent most examinations peering over her shoulder, watching her every move. During one awkward consultation she was examining a mouse when it escaped her grasp, and even though she had caught it before it went off the table, Hugh's canyon-depth frown lines suggested he thought she was a complete moron. It was shattering, and after falling asleep in the bath on Thursday night, Holly realized she was going to have to revert to showers if she didn't want to accidentally drown herself.

Hugh was a nightmare. It came as a reassurance when Chloe told her that Hugh probably had a PhD in belligerence, and Paolo had nodded in agreement. 'Honestly,' Paolo had said that morning, 'if Hugh didn't yell at you at least once a day I'd begin to be concerned.'

Her career hung on Hugh writing her letter of recommendation though, and unless he mellowed out she was going to struggle to last the year. In a text where she had told Judith how tricky he was to work with, Judith had told her to "hang in there". But Holly couldn't make any promises.

'Want another?' Chloe asked, finishing a white wine.

'Thanks, but I can't,' Holly stifled a yawn. 'I'm on call tomorrow afternoon and I don't think I've ever felt this drained in my life.'

She took a deep breath and felt a second yawn coming. In front of her was a plate of Cullen skink — a deliciously warming haddock soup — made earlier from the catch of the day. It was wonderful, but if she wasn't careful she'd end up face down in it, snoring. She'd barely touched her pint.

'If you're not up for an all-night party, why don't you have a hot chocolate?' suggested Paolo.

'Go on then,' Holly smiled. 'Man — when did this happen to me? Friday night at the pub and I'm having soup and a hot drink.'

'Gotcha,' said Chloe, getting up.

The door of the pub swung open, bringing in a blast of cold air. Glancing up, Holly watched as Angus Dunbar strode in. He nodded to them both as he slung his coat up before carrying on to the bar. Holly looked at Paolo, and as their eyes met, she knew they were both thinking the same thing: Chloe.

'Will she even say hello to him?' Holly leaned in and lowered her voice.

'Yeah,' Paolo whispered. 'But she'll say something polite in her sweet, sing-song way, then dash back here.'

Holly instantly felt a desire to give Chloe a hug. And a pep talk. She scanned the room, her eyes alighting on a table of men. They weren't bad-looking, she thought. Not the best, but passable. They had been there the other week, and she'd seen them around and about in Eastercraig. 'What about those lads? Would she go for any of them? For practice, perhaps?'

'Och, Callum and Rob Grey, and Sandy Alexander? Local fisherman. I wouldn't touch them with a bargepole.'

Holly's brain veered off on a tangent. 'Wait — isn't Sandy short for Alexander?'

Paolo grinned. 'So good they named him twice. Only he's not in the slightest. He had a conviction for theft a few years ago.'

'Not Chloe's type, then.'

'Exactly. In terms of relationships, the only thing you'd want from any of them is a clean bill of health.' Paolo pretended to gag.

Holly giggled. Looking over towards the bar, she could see Chloe talking to Angus. She silently rooted for her from the sidelines.

Paolo followed her gaze. 'She'll blush in about five seconds and shy away. All coy.'

That jinxed it. As soon as Paolo had said it, Chloe turned a deep shade of beetroot, scooped up the drinks tray and scuttled back over. She sat down and puffed her cheeks out.

'How was Angus?' Paolo asked.

'Fine.' Chloe's voice was high-pitched. She paused and looked for a second like she was going to cry. 'I have no idea what to say to him.'

Chloe looked so lost Holly wanted to wrap her up in a blanket and give her a hot water bottle.

'You chatter away to us every day at work,' she pointed out. 'And everyone else who comes in. It's not like you lack people skills.'

'Whenever I see him my heart rate increases, and I get butterflies,' said Chloe earnestly. 'As he gets closer, my mouth dries up, my tongue feels too big, then it gets knotted up, and I can barely manage to emit a squeak.'

She took a huge breath and looked from Holly to Paolo.

'Doesn't help that he's the least conversational man this side of Scotland,' Holly said sympathetically.

‘We need to build up your confidence,’ Paolo added, sounding mischievous. Holly frowned. They had just discussed this idea, and dismissed it. ‘Not one of this lot?’ she asked, incredulously.

‘Oh no,’ said Chloe. ‘We’ve talked about this before, Paolo. No way.’

‘I’m not talking about this rag-tag bunch of crabs-ridden degenerates. We need more opportunities for you to talk to him. Until talking to him becomes totally normal and you don’t start sweating at the mention of his name. I’m thinking the Eastercraig Show. You bake some cakes and chat ever so nicely to him, perhaps get your flirt on a little.’

‘What?!’ Chloe stared at Paolo as if he were mad.

‘All I’m suggesting is some light chatter. So you feel more at ease with him.’

Holly felt the same way Chloe looked. It didn’t sound wholly convincing. ‘Won’t it be hectic, and full of people Chloe knows?’

Paolo ignored her concerns. ‘He’ll definitely be there. You can casually bump into him, again and again. Offer him something you’ve made for the cake stall. The way to that man’s heart is through his stomach.’

Paolo stretched back and crossed his arms with an air of satisfaction. Holly looked to Chloe, whose brow was wrinkled in contemplation.

‘I guess I’m OK at baking,’ she said slowly.

Paolo rolled his eyes. ‘You’re more than OK. You’re amazing. And then you put on your phone voice, and don’t pretend you don’t know what I’m talking about.’ Paolo put on a not-bad impression ‘“Oh, hi, Angus. Would you like to sample my wares?” Oi!’

Paolo un-sprawled hastily as Chloe went to kick him in the shin.

‘No need for the sleaze, Rossini. What do you think, Holly?’ Chloe looked to Holly. ‘You’re more sensible than this guy.’

It wasn't an overly bad idea, Paolo's dubious innuendo-led scripting aside. And Holly could see Chloe needed a gentle nudge — if not a shove — to get going.

'It's as good a place to start as any,' she said.

'That's three weeks to work out how to get Angus to come and look at your buns,' said Paolo, causing even Chloe to giggle.

'Do I have any say in this?' Chloe asked with the air of the defeated.

'No!' Holly and Paolo replied in unison.

* * *

Cycling home, Chloe contemplated the Eastercraig Show. She'd been every year since she was little. Then, it had been burgers, petting the farm animals and hanging out with friends, and as a teenager, eyeing up the boys. Now it was . . . well. It was basically the same. Eyeing up Angus and simultaneously trying to work out how to approach him and avoid him, wanting to engineer a situation that was completely natural — a contradiction in terms if ever there was one.

Isla and Morag, her schoolfriends, had decided her crush on Angus was so long-standing it was a personality trait, rather than something to be acted upon. There had been a couple of boyfriends here and there, never anything serious, but after those had fizzled out, her heart always came back to him. Then, last summer, everything had changed.

When Angus had broken up with his girlfriend Dani in the July, it had dawned on Chloe that neither of them were getting younger. At some point they'd both settle down. And that bit of Chloe that had always carried a torch for Angus had started to whisper to her that if he didn't settle down with her, he would do so with someone else.

If only she could gain some confidence. But for as long as she could remember, it hadn't been in her nature. She hadn't been programmed that way. Maybe it hadn't helped her mum had been unwell when she was a teenager — when everyone else had been chatting to the boys with the gusto of the carefree, Chloe had been worrying about things at home. Perhaps that had left her feeling fragile, cautious. Then again, she was inclined to think she simply wasn't one of life's go-getters. Not everybody was, were they?

Paolo was right, however. She needed to take steps to find her inner warrior.

CHAPTER 10

After a paddle boarding session and the subsequent hot shower it necessitated, Holly pulled on some jeans and a thick jumper, ready for the Eastercraig Show. When not taking flak from Hugh, Holly's conversations at work had revolved around buoying Chloe up, readying her to talk to Angus. On the last couple of Friday nights in the pub, Chloe had virtually ducked under the table every time he had appeared.

'What are the odds?' Holly had asked Paolo as they'd walked up the slipway that morning. 'Do you think that somewhere inside Chloe there's a foxy temptress, a seduction pro?'

'No,' Paolo replied emphatically. 'Really, no.'

'Then what are you expecting from today? Have we just been prepping her for failure? Because if so, we ought to have some wise words on hand for when it doesn't come off, some kind of strategy to keep her spirits up.'

'That's what the pub's for.'

Holly had shot Paolo a look.

'What!' He grinned. 'Either we keep giving her nudges in the right direction, or we just stomp on her dreams. You might be happy to avoid men, but Chloe isn't, despite the fact she literally hides from Angus. Over the year I've been here she's bolted from every opportunity, some of which would have been prime. They were both really drunk at Burns Night and Chloe was going to do something then until she saw him talking to some blonde from Ullapool and changed her mind. She needs a push.'

'Paolo . . .'

'Just a wee one,' he insisted. 'Not a break-your-teeth-on-the-pavement whack.'

As she pulled her trainers on, Holly thought about Paolo's matchmaking scheme. Today Chloe was going to suggest Angus go with her to the cake stand and offer him a pecan blondie — which she had baked. On the face of it, it was nothing too terrible.

The thought, however, made Holly a little uncomfortable. But that was on her. It wasn't that she was anxious for Chloe — well, she was, in case it didn't work — she was anxious for herself. That she might become a victim of something similar.

A victim. It said it all, didn't it, that the first word to spring to mind when it came to relationships was so negative. Undoubtedly it was because that was how she saw her mother. Permanently broken-hearted, crying on the kitchen floor after one too many glasses of wine, before careening into the next guy a few weeks later. She had to get going, before she dwelled on it anymore.

Slamming the door behind her, Holly stepped outside, grateful for her parka. In London she would have swapped it for something lighter by now, but even though it was nearly March it was still shockingly bitter. Eastercraig necessitated extra layers. A storm was due tonight — it would be nice if it would hold back until after the show had finished.

Why on earth would anyone hold a show today? Holly watched as the whistling wind whipped up frothy waves, the spray hitting her in the face as she headed along the front. Chloe had told her it was because they didn't want to compete with the bigger summer fairs, and besides, it was something to do during the shorter, colder days. When Holly had pointed out that meant it was the wrong season for local produce, Chloe shrugged. 'Who needs giant marrows when you can have cake?' she had asked, to which Paolo had added: 'Says Eastercraig's very own Marie Antoinette!'

Sure enough, the heavy drizzle, cold air and a lack of outsized vegetables hadn't held back the town's residents. Crowds milled around the street, ducking in and out of the village hall and the school, which had both been opened up for the day to house food stalls and bric-a-brac. Back towards the car park, the old livestock market erupted with noise, and Holly popped her head in to see pens holding sheep, Shetland ponies, miniature goats and llamas. A few of Angus's Highland cattle were tethered outside, and she could see him introducing them to small children.

Holly smiled. It was quaint. Far more authentic than the "country fair" she had once gone to in Richmond.

* * *

Paolo loved people-watching, and the Eastercraig Show was perfect for it. He'd waved hello to the Sandersons who had a croft out of the village, Joe the harbourmaster, Graeme Innes who was in his book group and a handful of other people. Cheery Hamish from Glenalmond had come and shaken his hand, and Paolo had introduced him to Holly. The pair of them were now stood outside the café, waiting for Chloe.

'Chlo!' Paolo spied her in the crowd and beckoned her over. He brought her and Holly into a huddle. 'Let's talk tactics.'

'Slow down.' Holly shot him a warning look. 'It's only ten. We've got lots of time. And I've already spotted Angus. He's over with some of the Highlands.'

Chloe straightened up. 'Yeah. Let's take this easy, shall we?'

Paolo sighed and took a step back. It was hard rallying these two, both of them were so resistant. One of them was vehemently anti-relationship, and the other was desperate for one but just couldn't get going.

Not that it mattered. Resistance was futile, and Paolo was going to take that saying and run with it.

'No worries,' he said. 'Let's spend half an hour doing the rounds, and then go from there. Can't wait too long, Chloe, or all your blondies will have been sold. And then you'll not be able to ask Angus to come and try one.'

'I'll find you in the school hall,' Holly said. 'I'm just going to check on the animals. Hugh mentioned he knew most of the farmers here but not all. Just need to run my eyes over them to make sure they're all well. And then I'll grab a tea. Would either of you like one?'

'You're keen to get away.' Paolo gave her a wink. 'Are you really planning a beverage trip, or is it because you're hoping to catch a glimpse of the other Dunbar?'

Holly's eyes widened. Paolo continued to stare her out, and Holly, looking a little less polished than usual, started to go pink. It was at this that Paolo realized that he had hit the jackpot.

'Nothing of the sort,' Holly managed, pursing her lips. 'Let me do a round of the pens, and I'll see you in a bit.'

With that she walked off. Paolo, his chest swelling with excitement, turned to Chloe. 'Well, we might have unearthed something. Somewhere, buried deep within Holly Anderson, are some feelings. I'm like a love archaeologist. Getting ready to dig.'

Chloe stared at him for a moment, and then her face softened. 'Paolo, at some point you're going to have to focus on yourself.'

Paolo shook his head. 'Perhaps. But not right now. Let's go and people-watch.'

He took Chloe's elbow and steered her through the crowds. Focus on himself? He didn't want to do that. Because every time he did it reminded him of how Fabien had barely explained his leaving, ending their relationship as if it had been a fling. Like it had meant nothing to him. Like Paolo had meant nothing to him. God, he had to move on.

* * *

Holly looked around her. She couldn't see Greg Dunbar anywhere. Although why was she even looking for him in the first place? Because, she told herself, over the last few weeks she had been thinking about him more than she would like to admit. More than she would like to admit to herself, and *definitely* more than she would like to admit to Chloe or Paolo. *Especially* Paolo, who was on a potentially doomed mission to set Chloe up, and if that failed she knew he would swoop in on her.

'Come on, Anderson,' she muttered to herself.

She was stronger than this. Strong enough to repress the slight heat she felt radiating through her body whenever he'd crossed her mind. And strong enough to remind herself that he was a one-track-minded Casanova reminiscent of some of Jackie's greatest hits. That thought was, she noted pleasingly, enough to wipe him from the front of her cerebral cortex, and she set off towards the pens.

When, after locating Hugh and reassuring him that all the animals were well, she found Chloe and Paolo, they were lurking by the cake stands in the school hall. Chloe was shifting her weight from one side to another, biting her lip.

'What's the matter?' Holly asked.

'Nothing.' Paolo put a hand on Chloe's shoulder. 'We just spotted Angus on the move so headed into position. Did you spot Greg?'

'Nope,' she said, curtly. 'Are you ready, Chloe? Or is that a silly question?'

Chloe looked as if she were about to face a task on which the future of humanity depended. 'He's about ten metres away. I don't know if I can—'

'Deep breath,' said Holly, giving Chloe's arm a squeeze.

'Oh gosh. I can't.' Chloe wriggled out from where she was standing next to the cake table and disappeared into the crowds.

'Are you kidding me?' Paolo asked, as Angus walked past them, nodding in greeting. Paolo handed over some coins to the lady behind the stall and took a piece of the blondie.

'Can't believe she bailed. This stuff is the absolute bomb. I've had one slice already. Want a bite?'

Holly shook her head as Chloe reappeared next to her. It looked like all the blood had drained from her face.

'I wasn't ready after all,' Chloe said apologetically.

Holly watched as Paolo pushed his eyebrows as close together as he could. 'I'm *apoplectic*, Chlo. You wouldn't know because I'm eating cake so I don't scream, but that was a real missed opportunity.'

Chloe frowned back at him. 'I couldn't. I could feel my temperature rising — not in a good way — and had to cool down. Maybe it's a sugar low?'

Paolo, with a roll of his eyes, held out the cake and Chloe leaned in a took a bite.

'There's no urgency, is there?' Holly asked. 'Other than the fact he might get snapped up because he's pretty good-looking.'

'Does he remind you of Greg?' Paolo looked impish.

'He's right behind you,' whispered Chloe, spraying them all with crumbs. 'Oh God. Sorry.'

Holly looked behind Paolo. Greg caught her eye and smiled, and Holly felt herself take a tiny breath. She hoped it was imperceptible to the naked eye. If not, Paolo and Chloe wouldn't let her hear the last of it.

Holly raised her hand. 'Hi, Greg. You're here.'

She felt Paolo give her the side eye at such a lame comment, and was grateful when Chloe leaped in.

'Greg! How are things in Aberdeen?' Chloe asked. 'What news?'

Greg leaned over and gave Chloe a peck. 'All well, thanks. Long time, no see. And hi, Paolo. And Holly, great to see you again.'

He leaned over and gave Holly a kiss too, and she felt her cheek burn where his lips had touched her skin.

'We heard you spent the night at Holly's,' said Paolo.

Holly fought down a blush, the heat spreading through her chest. She exhaled slowly, trying to halt its progress, aware now that Paolo and Chloe were looking at the ground because they were corpsing.

'How are you?' Holly looked to Greg.

'I'm well,' Greg replied, choosing to ignore Paolo's comment. 'I've been looking for Mum, actually. I spotted Angus a moment ago too — hard to miss that towering frame. Do you think it's possible for him to still be growing at this late stage?'

Chloe giggled. 'He's a head taller than everyone else in here. With that and the hair he doesn't blend in.'

Greg looked at Holly and put a hand on her shoulder. 'And how have you been? Paddle boarding the high seas? Settling in at work? How are things with Hugh?'

Holly was about to tell him, when a high voice interrupted.

'Greg! Darling.' Fiona wrapped her arms around her son. 'And hello, you three. Thick as thieves are this lot from the surgery. How's your mum, Chloe? I haven't seen her since she came over for coffee a fortnight ago, and she was tired then.'

Chloe had barely replied when Fiona pulled Greg away, trilling that she needed to talk to him. Greg looked over his shoulder and gave a wave, one that — Holly could have sworn — was directed at her, rather than her colleagues.

'Wow!' Chloe turned to her, eyes round. 'He likes you.'

'What? No! No, he doesn't. He barely knows me.'

'He asked you *questions*. Ones that show he paid attention last time you met. When he crashed at yours,' Paolo said, grinning.

'On which note, thanks a lot for the suggestive spending-the-night comment.'

'I noticed you blushing,' said Paolo.

'Understandable. It was totally OTT.' Although as she said it, a tingle ran up Holly's spine.

'Well. We both think he's into you. Holding your gaze while talking, that hand on your shoulder. Man, he can be really charming,' said Paolo.

Of course he was, Holly thought. How else did he get into the pants of legions of women? Charm made her wary.

'Hey — look over there,' said Chloe, taking another bite of blondie.

'Was that a decoy? Because I saw that, you tiny thief.' Paolo held the cake closer to his chest.

Chloe pointed. 'By the door. All the Dunbars. Maybe they're making up after whatever that row was that Greg mentioned to Holly.'

'Doesn't look like they're making up, Chlo,' said Paolo. 'Maybe they'll be this year's Doreen and Janet. And Angus will hurl Greg into the sea. God, I love a bit of drama.'

Holly turned to look. Angus was red in the face, his eyes full of fury. He was jabbing a finger at Greg's chest, stepping closer and closer. Greg held his ground, but he too was becoming more animated. It didn't look like a happy fraternal catch-up to her. It was too hard to hear what Greg was saying, but over the clatter and chatter she picked up Fiona's voice saying: 'Not here, you two. Can we carry this on at home?'

At that, Angus walked out the door, his mother and brother close behind.

'I'm not sure that was the end of hostilities,' said Paolo. 'Angry Angus looked like he was on the warpath. Shall we follow them?'

Holly, aware that the set-up with Angus was over for the day, shepherded everyone over to the door. 'I think that's enough for now. Shall we go and see the llamas and then come back when someone's judging the cake competition?'

Llamas would make everything better.

CHAPTER 11

'I don't want to impose, but do you mind if I come in?' Greg asked.

That evening, after the show, Holly was surprised to get a knock at the door. She opened it to see Greg on the step, bag in hand. His hair was looking more windswept than when she'd seen him that morning. Mud spattered his smart jeans and once-clean boots. It suited him.

Did she mind? On balance, Holly decided she was happy about the imposition. It would be nice to have company. Especially Greg's company. But she chided herself for letting that thought even enter her mind.

'Of course not.' She took a step back. 'Everything OK?'

Greg came inside and put his bag down and rubbed his face with his hands. 'If I give you a good enough reason, would you be able to put me up for the night?'

Holly's heart stopped. 'Tonight?'

'I wouldn't ask, but the B&B is closed between January and March, Mhairi has no space at the Anchor, and a guy I'd otherwise crash with has a new bairn.'

'And you can't stay at the picturesque, sprawling farm with your family because you've still not made up with Angus yet?'

He made a face. 'Exactly. I thought a few weeks or so would give him the time he needed to cool off, but apparently not. We gave it a shot today but we're still at loggerheads. I'd have called if I had your number.'

Holly gave him a long, hard stare. It was maddeningly presumptuous. Surely he knew other people. And even if not, he could have managed to get in touch somehow — it *was* the twenty-first century.

Her heart began to beat louder and faster than she'd like it to as she considered the request. It was acting at odds with her head, which was telling her to calm down and be sensible. He was a player, and this turning-up-on-the-doorstep schtick was all a ruse. Not normally one to let her emotions run roughshod over her brain in these matters, she was surprised to then hear herself saying: 'OK, then.'

'Thanks, Holly. I appreciate it.'

He followed her further into the house. While he owed her an explanation, maybe now wasn't the time to ask for it. That aside, putting him up was the right thing to do, she reasoned. She was simply helping out a friend, if someone you'd barely met twice could be termed as such.

'I mean it,' Greg continued, sounding grateful. 'I really do appreciate it. You're a top banana. Funny how last time you were going to bludgeon me, and now you're offering me bed and breakfast — or at least tea and cake?'

He said the last bit with a twinkle in his eye.

Holly laughed. 'I can put the kettle on, but I'm all out of snacks.'

'Fear not! Greg the bringer of cakes is here.'

She watched as he pulled out a tin from his bag. Having eaten her way through another two of Fiona's offerings in the previous weeks, she worried her body was about fifty per cent dried fruit. If she started drinking sherry, she would turn into a Christmas cake by December.

'It's shortbread from the show, some of Mum's.' He reached into the bag again and presented her with a bottle of whisky. 'And this as an extra mark of my gratitude. We can put the world to rights later. This is an older one, smokier, posher barrels. For your collection.'

'Thank you! But I haven't finished the last yet,' she said. 'And I'm on call after 5 p.m., so I can't partake in even the tiniest of drams.'

'That's a shame,' he said, sounding like someone who'd had his grand plans chucked out the window.

Holly sensed his disappointment. Weirdly, she felt the same way. 'But next time you're here, hopefully we can sample it. And for now we can have some of that shortbread.'

She went over to the cupboard and placed a couple of mugs on a tray as the kettle clicked. Flinging teabags in the pot, she filled it up, and carried the lot over to the coffee table. Greg, as if it were his house and not hers, collected some plates and set out the shortbread.

'What have you been up to since I saw you?' he asked. 'We were interrupted earlier.'

'Exploring the beautiful Highlands and trying to keep my head down at work.'

'MacDougal a challenge? He does have a reputation. Just try to stay out of the firing line.'

'Impossible. I'm the prime target,' Holly joked lamely.

Greg gave a sympathetic look. 'Mum said you'd been to the farm.'

Holly took a piece of the shortbread — neatly cut into a petticoat tail triangle — wondering how Fiona found time to bake so much as well as do all her farm work. Sitting back, she began to tell him all about what she had been up to in Eastercraig, and when she finished he told her she ought to go to the Spring Fling at Glenalmond Castle.

'It's one of the biggest nights of the year round here. You'd better get the tickets quickly, before they sell out,' he said.

'Two steps ahead of you,' she replied, a smile flitting across her face. 'My colleagues and I have booked ours.'

'So you're spoken for?'

Holly gulped, the question seeming harder than it should to answer. 'I mean, kind of, but not entirely. It's . . .'

Their eyes met, and right then, Holly found herself imagining what it would be like dancing with Greg. The thought of his arm around her waist, holding her close to him was . . .

Her pocket began to vibrate, and she pulled out her phone and answered the call.

'You all right?' Greg asked, as she hung up.

'No. I have to run. Someone's dog is having puppies and one's stuck. Spare key's now in a drawer under the microwave if you need to get in or out. I'd say to make yourself at home,' she gave him a wry smile, 'but you already have.'

Two hours later, Holly arrived back at the house, leaning momentarily against the door to steady herself.

The dog breeder, Geri Logan, who was expecting a litter of cocker spaniel puppies, had realized early on there was a problem: a water bag had been passed but nothing had emerged after that. An old hand, she had phoned the surgery immediately.

Holly had told her to come in, readying herself to perform a C-section. Adrenaline surged. She had done this before plenty of times, but this was a different surgery, and Hugh's equipment left plenty to the imagination. And after realizing her new boss was not only keeping a close watch, but was also a potential psychopath, she had to get it right. Ideally without calling him out of bed to help. She couldn't blot her copybook. But it would be fine. Of course it would.

'No complications with the pregnancy otherwise?' Holly asked Geri, ushering her into the surgery.

'All fine and dandy,' said Geri. 'Nothing to give any cause for concern.'

Holly gave Geri a smile. She paused for a second and took a breath.

'You all right, lass?' asked Geri.

'Fine,' said Holly. 'Gathering my faculties.'

And remembering where all the instruments were kept.

Gently, she lifted the spaniel up to the table, ready to operate.

Turning around to wash her hands, Holly heard a gasp. She spun back to face to Geri, fearing something dreadful had happened, only to see the dog yelp, as a small, wet ball of fur slid out. Quickly, Holly put in in front of its mother, who started to lick it. When she saw it breathe, Holly remembered to do so herself. She exhaled quietly.

'Often happens,' she reassured Geri, as they peered at the dogs.

'Aye,' said Geri. 'About five years ago I had the same thing, only for the dog to give birth in the back of the car on the way here. Boot was a right mess, I'll tell ye.'

Holly waited until the last of the puppies was out, and once satisfied they were all healthy, said goodbye to Geri, telling her to get in touch if need be. Then, having cleaned up and completed some paperwork, she had locked the surgery and made her way back to Sea Spray, pleased to have done a good job, and relieved that Hugh shouldn't be able to find fault with her.

Realizing now that she'd been standing outside for no reason, Holly pulled her head up from where she had been resting it on the door. The icy drizzle that had begun earlier that day was giving way to heavy drops of rain and Holly paused to look out to sea. The waves were choppier than they had been, and she remembered the forecast had predicted a storm over the weekend. If the spaniel was her only call, she'd be happy.

As she stepped through the door, the first thing that struck her was the wonderful smell of cooking. She remembered her uninvited guest, then wondered how on earth could she have forgotten him.

In an armchair, Greg was reading the paper, legs crossed on the footstool. 'You're back,' he said, getting up. 'How was it?'

'You *have* made yourself at home.' She laughed. 'And it went well, thanks. Seven healthy puppies are all snuggled up next to their mum. Which I count as a success. I'll tell you all about it in a second. I need to wash my hands and splash some water on my face.'

'Great. And I've made supper, because — let's be honest — it was the least I could do. Beef ragu and pasta,' said Greg, making his way to the kitchen. 'I'll dish up.'

Holly pelted up the stairs. The adrenaline surge she was experiencing now was on a par with the one she'd had over at the surgery.

In her room, she checked herself in the mirror. Should she put on makeup? The rational part of her brain stepped in — she was being absurd. Still, a hint of mascara wouldn't go amiss.

After putting on the lightest brushing of it, she came back downstairs. The lights were dimmed, and Greg had put a steaming casserole dish on the table. There was wine, but she was touched to see he'd also bought a bottle of sparkling water. Sliding into a chair, it was only when he took the lid off that Holly realized she was utterly starving.

'This looks fantastic. Thank you,' she said, her mouth watering. 'I'm ravenous.'

'I'm glad,' he said. 'I'm a man who likes a recipe, and forgot we're two, not four, so there's plenty. Leftovers will freeze if you need to, though.'

'I'm sure I can manage,' she said, as he piled up tagliatelle on her plate. 'It's going to be a job not to shovel it in like an animal.'

'Talking of animals, what happened?'

Holly relayed the drama, and as she finished, she slumped back in her chair, defeated by Greg's portion sizes.

'You must think I'm a pig,' she said. 'I've eaten half the ragu.'

'Nope. I think you know your stuff. This is one of my mum's top hits. She used to cook it whenever I came home from uni.'

Holly raised an eyebrow. 'Did you cook it because you've been cast out from the farm and needed something to remind you of home?'

He looked a little sheepish. 'Maybe. But I also thought you might appreciate some hearty fare. Comfort food. What did you used to have when you were little?'

Holly made a face. 'I . . . umm . . .'

'Come on. You have to have a favourite. Mac and cheese? Sausages and mash? Sunday roast?'

'It's not that I don't have a favourite, but my mum didn't cook much. She was always out at work, so I tended to make my own stuff. I reckon I was a latchkey kid from the age of about ten.'

'Oh,' said Greg. 'Sorry.'

'Don't apologize. Plenty of kids are. I just rarely came home to a great big meal. If I did, I was the one cooking it.'

When Jackie did cook, Holly thought, she did a pretty abysmal job. She tried, but it was always out of a packet. Consequently, Holly never knew if she loved whippy strawberry mousse puddings or loathed them. Her poor mother. When she wasn't preoccupied with one of her feckless boyfriends, she was working all hours at the office, or the salon, or one of her other short-lived roles. No wonder three-course meals were low down the list.

'Do you see much of your mum?' Greg asked.

Holly shook her head. 'Not often considering how close Milton Keynes and London are. In fact, I've discovered she's recently shacked up with some guy named Marco and is currently living it up in Malaga.'

'She sounds wild.'

'That's one way of describing her,' Holly rolled her eyes. 'Anyway. Thank you for the dinner. It was amazing. And sorry again I ate so much. Not sure there's anything left for the freezer after all.'

'Well, I hope you have room for pudding.'

Holly raised her eyebrows, and put her hands on her stomach. 'Can we have a hiatus? I think I need to collapse on the sofa.'

'You don't have space for brownie and ice cream?' Greg protested. 'I was going to try to make a hot sauce for it.'

'Oh, go on then,' said Holly, wishing she'd worn leggings and not jeans. She could have done with a stretchy waistband.

Holly watched a little while later as Greg tidied up the plates from pudding. The brownie had been the icing on the cake. No — it *was* the cake. And cake with ice cream was always welcome. And that meant Greg was welcome . . . Her reasoning skills sounded impaired, she noted, with a flicker of panic.

Greg had just gone to open the fridge when his phone rang. He answered, and Holly got up and carried on clearing the table, seeing a frown form on his forehead while he listened to the voice at the other end of the line.

'Will he be OK?' Greg sounded worried. 'Do you want me to meet you there?'

There was a pause. He caught Holly's eye and pointed wildly towards the front door.

'I'll go up to the farm and help. I'll ring you when it's done,' he continued, then hung up. He looked at Holly. 'Get ready. You've got a call coming.'

Before she could comprehend what was happening, her mobile began to buzz. She picked up to hear Fiona's voice on the end of the line.

'Hugh? Holly?' Fiona sounded breathless. 'Who am I through to?'

'It's Holly. Is everything OK?'

'It was getting windier, so Angus went to check on the Highlands. One got scared by something, knocked Angus down, and somehow he got kicked in the face. He was out in the top field, and he turned up back at the door, covered in blood and disoriented. I've taken him to A&E.'

Holly shuddered at her memory of getting got by a cow. Poor Angus. Fiona was now talking nineteen to the dozen, and Holly had to close her eyes to concentrate. 'What do you need me to do?'

'Can you go up and find the cattle and check they're OK? There should be seventeen of them. I'm worried that in his haze, Angus didn't close the gate. It's blowing a hooley out there now. Could you try and get them into the old barn?'

Her eyes widened. This could be bad news. If the fold got out it could cause no end of damage, to itself, or to anyone else. Even if one wandered up on to the road on a night like this it could cause a fatal accident.

'I'm on my way, Mrs Dunbar. And I'll call you the moment I've got it all sorted.'

'Thank you, Holly,' she said fretfully. 'The main herd ought to be fine, but can you look in on them as well? We left in a rush. Greg, my other son, says he'll go too. He'll wait for you in the yard.'

Holly rang off and turned to Greg. 'She doesn't know you're here, then?'

Greg gave her a look. Rolling her eyes, she threw on her jacket again, slipped into her trainers and grabbed her wellies before running out to the car.

CHAPTER 12

Heavy drops of rain hammered on the windscreen, the wipers on the old estate barely able to keep up. Unused to the road, Holly drove cautiously. She didn't want to take a bend too fast in this weather or hit a puddle. Or a cow, come to think of it. Hairy coos blended into the scenery more easily than your average Friesian, especially in the dark. The car growled as it struggled up a hill, and she wished she had something heavy-duty like Hugh's Land Rover.

'When are you going to tell me what happened between you and Angus?' she asked, glancing at Greg. 'I don't like the fact your mum doesn't know you're staying at mine.'

Greg looked straight ahead and didn't reply immediately. 'It's complicated. Maybe a farm emergency isn't the time to talk about it.'

'Fine. But when this is done, you owe me an explanation. You're staying on my sofa for a second time, and I had to lie to your mother, who — by the way — is a really nice woman, and someone I don't want to upset. Nor would I want to get on the wrong side of your brother.'

Greg gave a hollow laugh. 'He's moody all the time, it wouldn't matter.'

'Maybe if you two talked about the situation, the air would be clearer,' Holly suggested. 'Honestly! Why can't men discuss their feelings?'

'We're both perfectly comfortable expressing our feelings. Only our feelings fall at opposite ends of the spectrum. Watch out!'

Holly slammed on the brakes, her stomach giving such a lurch she had to pat her jumper to check it was still inside her body. On the road in front of them stood a great, shaggy cow.

Climbing out of the car, Holly's breath made huge damp clouds in the air. Far from being one of the relaxed, cud-chewing beasts she had encountered the other week, the cow's eyes were wide in terror. It was unlikely to hurt them, she reasoned, but if they scared it any more it might gallop off into the dense trees on the other side of the road. She felt a shudder of nerves and looked at Greg.

'What do you think we do?' she whispered. 'I ought to put the hazards on but the poor girl's terrified. But if anything comes over the hill it might hit it, or us.'

Not only were they getting drenched, but it was freezing, and Holly could already feel her fingers itching with the cold. Time was of the essence.

'I'll go behind her,' said Greg. 'Try to shoo her along. It's not far back to the turning. Give me some space, then carry on slowly behind us with the hazards.'

'You sure you know what you're doing?'

'I grew up with this lot, remember?'

Holly got back inside the car, wiping her hair from her forehead, and watched Greg approach the cow cautiously. He walked around the side, waited for it to acknowledge him, and calmly laid his hands on it. And then, as far as she could tell through the driving rain, he began to talk to it. After a few seconds, it started to move. Holly exhaled and dropped her shoulders as the pair began to walk up the hill, slowly at first and then faster. She turned the ignition back on and trundled along after them.

Once they'd taken the turning, Greg shooed the cow down the track to the farm. It took off at a trot, and Greg walked behind it, Holly following. When she got to the yard she slammed on the brakes and jumped out.

'Are you OK?' she called. Holly grabbed her spare waterproof from the back seat and ran over to Greg. 'Put this on.'

Soaked to the skin — his jacket was wholly unsuited to the weather — his teeth gritted, he turned to her, a look of palpable relief in his eyes.

'Crisis one averted,' he said, pulling the coat on. 'I can see the rest of the fold down in the yard. Let's get them inside.'

'I have to say, I'm relieved you're here,' Holly said as they walked over together. 'I've felt a bit uneasy around these creatures. I'm still not one hundred per cent used to them.'

As Greg herded the cattle back into the barn, sliding round on the mud, Holly stood at the door, counting them in. Aside from being sodden, they looked fine.

'Wait!' She put a hand on Greg's arm. 'Did you hear that? Lowing.'

He shook his head. 'It's the wind. It sweeps straight in from the sea.'

Holly stood stock-still. 'No. Listen. There it is again. Out beyond the farmhouse.'

'Hold on. I'll grab some torches.'

He ran in, then reappeared with two large torches, and together they followed the track between the barn to where it ran down to the fields that lay beside the sea. She was grateful he'd thought of them as she shone the beams around her feet to avoid falling. The ground beneath them was a mudflow, and Holly wondered if she started sliding, whether she might go all the way to the cliffs and into the sea.

Then she halted, grabbed Greg's jacket. Their torch beams picked out two nervous eyes staring through the darkness. Holly took another step, gradually picking out its shape. Smaller than the others, she reckoned it was only a year or so old.

'I'll get this one,' she said, sounding braver than she felt. There were no two ways about it though, she was going to be in Eastercraig for a year and *had* to get to grips with all manner of large animals. Had to be able to face up to a hefty ruminant without wanting to run for the hills. Her guts contracted.

'Are you sure?' Greg asked. 'He's young but he's still a hefty fella.'

'I'm nearly as tall as you.' Holly was spurred on by indignance. 'And I'm the vet, after all.'

Her heart in her mouth, she took a step towards the bullock. It eyed her with suspicion. Holding its gaze, she inched closer until she was near enough to place her palms on him.

'There, there,' she said, in a low, reassuring voice. 'Time to come back to the barn.'

The bullock appeared to nod, and then let out a huge huff, almost grateful to be told what to do. He must have been alarmed by the whole ordeal, Holly thought, giving his shaggy hair a gentle stroke.

Pleased with herself, she was about to urge him on when spiked forks of lightning illuminated the sky, and a clap of thunder sounded. The bullock leaped with surprise, and went to bolt. Holly, her reactions fast, tensed and stood her ground, blocking it.

But he was determined, and went round her. As he brushed past, Holly slipped on the mud, and watched in dismay as the bullock broke into a run. Thankfully Greg managed to catch up with the animal, calmed him again with soothing whispers and nudged the would-be escapee in the right direction before shutting him in the barn.

Rolling her shoulders, Holly got up from the floor. She was going to ache in the morning.

'Are you OK?' Greg called. 'Are you hurt? That was close.'

Holly walked towards him. 'Only wounded pride.'

Greg held the barn door open again. Holly walked in, pulled her drenched hair back from her face and puffed her checks out. Her jeans were now brown with mud, and the water had soaked all the way through to her skin. Never had she felt less attractive in her life. Not that it mattered, she reminded herself. She wasn't here on a date. She glanced at Greg. He also looked as if he'd been dragged through a hedge, and a loch, backwards. And yet he still managed to look sexy. She gritted her teeth, frustrated by the devil on her shoulder who was trying to distract her.

'You take the far side, and I'll scan this one. Then we'll switch to double-check they're all OK,' she said, getting back to the task in hand. 'Then I'll go and see the beef herd too.'

'You know what you're looking for?'

'Is it the ones lying on their backs with their legs in the air?'

'I see you're getting the hang of this.'

She looked down, trying to make sure he didn't see her grinning.

CHAPTER 13

Confident all the cattle were well, Holly allowed herself to go and wash her hands. Sitting down on a straw bale next to the animals, which were now snoring peacefully, she checked her watch. It was nearly 11 p.m., and Fiona and Angus would be back soon. Stifling a yawn and realizing she was about to fall asleep, she looked to the door to see Greg returning from an expedition to the farmhouse. In one hand he held a thermos flask of tea and in the other a bundle of clothes.

'Sorry. Took me a while,' he said. 'Had a root around through my old chest of drawers to find something dry. Want a couple of jumpers? And you're so tall you might fit my joggers too. Don't worry — we can both turn around.'

Holly felt her cheeks burn as she took the bundle of clothes. She faced away, and checked over her shoulder to make sure he'd kept his side of the bargain. Reassured, she peeled the jeans from her legs and pulled on the joggers, then switched her jumper for the moth-eaten Aran knits he'd passed her. Warmth and comfort trumped vanity: she was too tired to be bothered that she was a decent fit for his clothes.

Dryer, she turned to face him, but he still had his back to her. He'd got on some ancient jeans, a flannel shirt and a shabby jumper, and she felt he looked more at home in those than the city clothes he usually wore. More at home, and weirdly more attractive. She felt faintly flustered, and tried to ignore it. 'Thanks,' she said. 'That's much better. I imagine I looked like Nessie, but frankly I'm too tired to care.'

'Don't be hard on yourself,' he said, he glanced at her over his shoulder. 'Maybe a selkie.'

'A what?'

He turned and as he pulled his sweater down, she got a glimpse of smooth, toned skin. *So* toned. Her insides did a tiny cartwheel.

'A seal-woman,' he said. 'A mythological shape-shifter from the sea. Captures the unwary.'

She caught his eye. 'I bet you say that to all the girls.'

'No. Just you.'

The atmosphere was instantly charged, and Holly knew it was nothing do with the storm in the air. All of a sudden she felt lightheaded. Not like herself. She needed to change the subject and not get caught up in all of this.

'Does this all bring back happy childhood memories? Mucking out on the farm?'

Greg went and sat down on a bale, poured a cup of tea and held it out for Holly. She went and sat next to him, making sure there was a good ruler's length between them.

'A bit, yeah.' Greg poured himself a cup and took a sip. 'But while people look at this place and think how wonderful it is, there's a lot of worry that comes with it.'

'That there's always stuff needs doing?'

'Aye. However much stuff you do, you're never on top of it. And it's not like you make any money. It's a stressful life . . .'

Here Greg tailed off, and looked at the cattle, who were dozing beneath the dim light of the bulbs that hung from the ceiling.

'I guess so,' said Holly. 'So you were never the tiniest bit tempted to stay? Auchintraid looks idyllic.'

'Looks can be deceiving. Remember the first time we met, and I told you how precarious the whole farm thing can be? When I was a teenager, I remember coming downstairs once, only to find my dad staring at a pile of unpaid bills on the table, his eyes bloodshot. It was two in the morning, and he'd been there for hours, wondering which ought to get paid first. He told me not to tell Mum because she'd only worry. I think from that moment on I decided my future lay somewhere else. Hence ending up in the less idyllic but rather more stable world of tax law.'

He grimaced slightly and turned so his knees were pointing towards her. Holly mirrored his actions, shifting ever so slightly closer to him. 'I know how you feel, remember? I always wanted a steady career,' she said.

He caught her eye. 'Does that mean you're disappointed to find yourself up here when you ought to be earning a real packet down in Ascot?'

She thought of the fact that she still felt out of place, that Hugh made her life miserable and that she hadn't lost her healthy distrust of cows. But the beautiful scenery and the fresh air was blissful, and she had already made new friends. Somehow, she also had more spare time, more space to breathe here up in Scotland. In London, she had been living life in the fast lane, working every hour possible and squeezing a social life or the odd run into the gaps. Here work often finished at 6 p.m. on the dot — on-call emergencies aside — and Holly was getting used to the gentler pace her life was moving at. But . . . Hugh popped into her mind again, all angry face and spluttered annoyance.

Holly was about to reply when the barn door flew open to reveal Angus, his face a smashed palette of purples and greens. Fiona appeared behind him, hovering in the doorway as Angus marched towards them.

'Thanks for coming, Holly,' he said. 'I'll talk to you in a moment.'

'Are you OK?' Greg stepped towards his brother, concern etched on his face. 'You took quite a hit there.'

'Get out.' Angus halted in front of Greg, crossing his arms. 'How dare you even step foot on this farm after this afternoon.'

Greg spoke calmly. 'I have every right to be here. And when Mum called to tell me there was an emergency I came as quickly as I could. So did Holly.'

'Funny, there seems to be only one car in the yard.'

A pit opened up in Holly's stomach, and she realized there was no way she could deny that they'd come here together. Worse still, she could tell from Angus's tone that he wasn't pleased about it.

'I know where she lives,' Greg said. 'And when I got the call I ran over to her cottage. It's a good job we were both here. The Highlands were out and it was a two-man job.'

Angus looked at Holly. 'Is this true?'

Holly drew herself up to her full height. 'We encountered one of them on the road over and the rest out in the yard. I was glad to have an extra pair of hands.'

She hadn't lied, merely withheld the incriminating details. And the ends justified the means, didn't they? She'd rather avoid Angus's wrath.

Fiona gave a cough. 'Let's all go into the house, shall we? I can make us some tea.'

'He's not coming in the house,' Angus snapped.

Greg looked him straight in the eye, then paced right past him, stopping on his way out to give his mother a kiss. 'I'll wait in the car,' he said, looking to Holly before disappearing through the door.

Holly looked from one Dunbar to another, then reminding herself this was nothing to do with her, she took a deep breath. 'I'll give you a quick run-down, shall I?' she said, firmly, as she heard the door of the car slam shut.

Ten minutes later, Holly climbed into the driver's seat. Greg was looking at the barn, watching the shadows of his mother and brother as they moved around inside. Even though she was more curious than ever as to why the two of them had fallen out, she knew better than to ask now.

'Let's head home,' she said. 'We might even catch a few winks before sunrise.'

Greg turned to her. 'Sorry you had to see that.'

She dismissed his apology with a wave of her hand. 'I'm sure whatever it is, you'll both get over it. You'll reconcile and this feud will become a distant memory.'

Holly turned on the engine and flicked the wipers on to their top speed, which was enough to keep the windscreen clear.

'Don't bet on it,' he said, sighing heavily. 'Great job with the cattle, by the way. You're settling into this big animal business with aplomb.'

'I'm glad someone thinks so. I couldn't have done it without you, though. Thank heavens you were there. And you knew where there was a stash of dry clothes.'

Her mind leaped suddenly back to the sight of his bare stomach. *Stop it,* she said to herself. *You're being ridiculous.* She put her foot down.

CHAPTER 14

On Monday in the surgery, Chloe hung on to Holly's every word. She could practically see the drama as Holly recounted it. She had already heard about it through her mother, who was a friend of Fiona's, but nothing Mei had said was especially salacious and Fiona had clearly held back on the juicier details.

'I can't help. Greg still wouldn't say what's going on between him and Angus,' said Holly, finishing her side of the story. 'And he left on Sunday before I'd woken up, leaving me another note, telling me he didn't want to cause trouble for me by staying at the house again.'

'My mum doesn't know either,' said Chloe. 'All Fiona said was the boys had an almighty bust up and you were there to see it. I think she's embarrassed.'

'I had a drink with Graeme Innes on Sunday,' Paolo interjected, emerging from where he had been making tea in the kitchen. 'And he said Angus has a massive bruise on his face and a broken nose. Was it fisticuffs? Should we await a duel?'

'No, and not least because it's the twenty-first century,' said Holly. 'He was kicked by a cow.'

'This is how rumours start, Paolo,' Chloe said.

She thought about Angus, wondering if he was all right. And if his nose was going to have a permanent bend where it had been broken. Maybe he needed some TLC. Maybe she could provide it.

Hugh broke through her reverie, flying through the door as if blown in by the high winds. Chloe glanced outside. The gales that had begun on the weekend showed no sign of abating. The waves weren't breaking over the road yet, but if it got any worse they would.

'I hear you didn't kill anything on Saturday night, Holly,' Hugh shouted as he disappeared into the kitchen.

Chloe gave Holly a thumbs up, even though it was hardly a compliment. After Hugh's unpredictable eruptions over the past month, even the seemingly resilient Holly might appreciate some support. As Hugh reappeared, Chloe passed him the list and watched him scan it.

'Bloody hell,' he growled. 'This again?'

He turned to Chloe, who bit her lip. 'Mr Rayner called. And he thinks there's something wrong with Perky.'

Hugh's nostrils flared. 'I'll sort out the table for the first consultation. Holly, Paolo, I'll see you in a minute.'

With that, he disappeared into the consulting room.

'I'm guessing now isn't the time to ask him about a new socket in the consulting room,' said Holly, dismay in her voice. 'It wasn't working last Friday. I had to ask the owners to hold the plug in so the lamp worked.'

'It is *never* the time to ask Frugal MacDougal to spend money on anything,' said Chloe. 'I once asked for a new computer, and he told me it would be throwing good money after bad, and I should be grateful I didn't still have a typewriter. And the locum before Bronwen asked for an expensive brand of painkillers and he bellowed expletives at her. He thought he was being put on the spot, or the locum was secretly an agent of big pharma. Or whatever the animal equivalent is . . .'

'Big farmer?' Paolo suggested, giving jazz hands to his own joke.

'What's he so grumpy about this time?' Holly ran her eyes down the list.

'What isn't he grumpy about?' Chloe peered over her shoulder. 'Mr Rayner keeps a parrot — Perky — that is on the verge of taxidermy. But whenever it's off its food, it comes in. Then there's a hamster with an abscess. He finds them fiddly — he'll delegate that to you.'

'Who's Lady Moira Glennis?' said Holly. 'Bringing in a wolfhound — imaginatively named Wolfie.'

Paolo let out a wistful sigh. 'Hamish's mum. She lives at Glenalmond.'

'What's got into you?' Chloe asked.

'I can't wait for the ball. That place is like a fairy tale — a big castle with turrets, with a river at the end of the garden. And you reach it through a large pine forest.'

'Sounds like *Macbeth*,' said Holly.

'It is,' Chloe said. 'Without the murders and all that.'

Paolo looked misty-eyed. 'When I went once before, Hamish had got some venison back from the butchers and gave me and Hugh a couple of steaks . . .'

As Paolo fell into a rhapsodic description of Glenalmond's game, Chloe's mind wandered to Angus. Perhaps later, on a coffee break, she could glean a few more nuggets about what had happened at the farm. Mainly the Angus-related bits.

* * *

'Hello, Hugh,' said Moira Glennis, wrestling a colossal, hairy dog through the door of the consulting room. 'And welcome, Holly. How are you settling into the surgery?'

'Well,' said Holly. She didn't dare look to Hugh in case he contradicted her. 'And this must be Wolfie. Hello, chap.'

'He's being such a pickle. Didn't want to come today at all. I think he's scared of Hugh.' Moira gave Hugh a wink. 'And before you ask, I *know* they're Irish, and I ought to have deerhounds if I was being patriotic, but there were none available nearby when we were last looking for a dog. Then we found Wolfie and it was love at first sight.'

The dog gave a deep bark and sat down by the door. From under a scruffy fringe, he gave Holly a knowing look.

'It's all right,' Holly said to him. 'You come along here. You're too big for the table so let's do this down here.'

She knelt down. Wolfie got up slowly and padded towards her, apparently resigned to his fate.

'You said you think he's breathing quickly?' Holly asked Moira.

Moira nodded, lines forming on her forehead. 'Could he have a virus? The poor wee darling. Will he be OK?'

'He's hardly wee . . .' Hugh muttered.

Holly ran through her usual questions and clinical examination, and finally took her stethoscope and had a listen to Wolfie's chest. After his reluctance to come into the room, he was now behaving perfectly, letting her do everything she needed to. She gave his ears a quick scratch before stepping back.

'The chest is a bit muffled, and he has a temperature . . .' Holly began. 'Which indicates an infection, and so I'll give him some medicine for that. I'd also like to do a chest X-ray too, in case. We've had the next person cancel so we could do it now.'

Holly and Hugh took Wolfie through to the other room, manoeuvred him into position and put him under anaesthetic. Moira agreed to come and pick him up later.

That afternoon, when Wolfie was awake, Holly invited Moira in from where she had been waiting in the hall.

'I'm afraid what we're seeing is pneumonia, Mrs Glennis. We can start him on treatment today. And we'll need to book him in for some follow-ups.'

A tear ran down Moira's cheek, and she ran a hand along Wolfie's back. 'My poor love. Lovely old boy.'

'It's OK, Moira,' Holly said reassuringly. 'Like I say, we can treat it. Most animals will make a full recovery.'

As Holly stepped back, Wolfie looked up at her quizzically. She barely realized what was happening before the dog threw his paws to her shoulders, knocking her to the floor, before attempting to plant slobbery kisses all over her face.

'Oh good grief! Are you OK?' Moira cried, pulling Wolfie off her. 'You can normally stay upright, if you recognize when he's about to hug you.'

Holly sat up. 'I'm fine. A bit taken aback perhaps.'

'I think he likes you. Don't you, you soppy thing, poor old chap.' Moira wiped her face. 'Right. Run me through what we're going to do.'

Holly gave Wolfie an affectionate pat on the head, and started to explain the course of action.

* * *

As they were closing up, Chloe was starting to regret pestering Holly for the finer points on Angus and Greg.

'I don't want to gossip, and I swear I don't know anything about the argument, but what I will say I think is Angus is a *major* hothead. Compared to Angus, Hugh could be described as placid,' Holly was saying, as she wrote up the last of her notes.

Paolo nodded exasperatedly. 'It's what I've been trying to tell her!'

Chloe felt like she should stand up for him. Yes, he had a reputation. But he didn't deserve it. 'He's got a lot on his plate,' she said quietly.

'Like what?' said Paolo.

Chloe looked out to sea. It did sound like Angus had been on the brink of madness on the weekend. He'd raged at Greg in front of Holly. Whatever it was must have been pretty serious.

But she *knew* he had a soft side. It was just very, very deeply buried. Chloe thought back to the time when, as a teenager, she'd watched Angus pick up a wounded seagull Rob Grey had felled by throwing stones. He'd carried it over to the surgery and left it with Hugh. She'd been sat on the front with Isla and Morag, who had been busy reading *Mizz*, and had marvelled at how he cared more for rescuing the creature than preserving any reputation for being cool. What had happened to that gentle soul?

'How was Hugh today?' she asked Holly. If there was someone who was having a harder time than she was, it was Holly.

'So-so. He only huffed twice. I've been keeping a tally on a notebook tucked in my pocket,' Holly said. 'Did he actually want another member of staff for assistance? Or was I hired as a human punchbag?'

'Don't say that,' said Paolo. 'You're doing great. He's just notoriously hard work.'

'He *hates* me,' said Holly. Neither Chloe nor Paolo responded to that. 'Thanks for the reassurance, guys.'

Behind them, the door swung open, revealing a glaring Hugh. 'Holly. Can you come and check on this cat we've got in tonight?'

Chloe patted Holly's arm. 'Deep breath.'

As Holly followed Hugh into the back, Chloe turned to Paolo with a worried look. 'Reckon she'll last?'

Paolo gave a non-committal shrug.

CHAPTER 15

Holly sat in the Anchor, feeling her glass of red slowly warm her up. She needed it after Hugh had asked her to stay late to go through some paperwork. Tempted to tell him it was Friday night and that none of it was urgent, she bit her tongue as she sat down behind the reception desk. She had finished it though, eventually sending a message that Hugh had not deigned to reply to.

She took another sip of her drink. All she needed now was a pie, and the end of the week would at least finish pleasantly. A naughty voice pointed out that if Greg turned up, her week would be complete, but she tried to ignore it. The man was a player, and she didn't have time to be played.

Opposite her, Paolo was trying to coach Chloe on how to approach Angus: she was planning on taking him some tiffin on the weekend. All it needed was for Chloe to be able to speak to him. Holly tuned back into their conversation, pushing all thoughts of Greg, and those square inches of his abdominals, aside.

'Repeat after me,' Paolo was saying. 'Angus. I've made you some tiffin. How are you?'

Chloe wrinkled her nose. 'That is lame. You can do better than that. *I* can do better than that. I doubt lines like that are how you ended up with Fabien.'

Holly laughed. 'You need some farm puns. Can we do something with horns? Or hay?'

She allowed herself to think about what she might say to Greg next time he came. *If* he came. That thought stopped her in her tracks. What if he didn't return? Maybe he'd retreat to Aberdeen for a while, and not come knocking on her door. It would be nice if he turned up tonight, though, with a bottle of wine, and his hair mussed up from the winds outside. She gave an internal sigh, then realized from the looks on her friends' faces she'd done it out loud. The pair of them rounded on her, sharing impish looks.

'Thinking of Greg, by any chance?' asked Paolo.

Holly kept her lips tightly shut.

'Your silence speaks volumes. Maybe you should test your lines on him first,' said Chloe. 'Seeing as you clearly fancy him.'

'I don't fancy him,' Holly protested. Paolo's gleeful expression suggested she was unconvincing. 'I don't. We get along fine, and besides, I've not got time for it.'

Paolo took a sip of wine. 'Sure. You keep telling yourself that. But if Greg appeared right now and offered to whisk you off for a cosy dinner somewhere, you'd say yes, wouldn't you?'

It was an exercise in holding her nerve. Gritting her teeth, she attempted a chilled expression. It made her face ache.

'I give her ten seconds,' Chloe looked at her watch. 'Come on, Holly, confess. You'll feel much better. And you'll be able to unclench your jaw.'

The cajoling was too much. Holly gasped and took in a huge breath, as if she'd been underwater too long and had finally resurfaced. 'Fine. You both win. I can't push him out of my mind. He's interesting, clever, funny, and last time we saw each other I could practically see the sparks.'

'And he's super ripped from trail running,' said Paolo.

'Aaaaaand that. But he doesn't sound like he has much respect for the many women he dates. And I don't have time. And I don't want anything like that. And, finally, I barely know him,' she said, with the air of someone successfully concluding an argument. Holly decided not to muddy things by telling them the part where she had exchanged a few texts with him that week. There was nothing too incriminating in them, not even kisses at the end — it was chat about work, and box-set plans — but Chloe and Paolo would go to town regardless.

'In fairness, I don't think he ever has more than one girl on the go at once,' said Chloe.

'Still not a glowing advert for commitment,' said Paolo. 'And by now we know Holly wants that.'

'But only when I've . . .' Holly started.

'Sorted out the rest of your life,' said Paolo. 'So you keep saying.'

'There's more to life than a job, you know,' said Chloe kindly.

'I know.' Holly gave a small shrug. 'And one day I'd love to find a balance, but when you've got nothing to fall back on, you need to make sure your career is stable.'

'But a fling?' asked Paolo.

'I said it before, and I'll say it again. I don't do flings.'

'I don't want to sound like a prick, but the world doesn't end when a fling does,' said Paolo. 'You seem like you've got your head screwed on about everything else.'

'Is there something more to it?' asked Chloe. 'I know it's nosy but I can't hold it in any longer. Curiosity killed the cat, and I don't want it to get me too.'

Holly swallowed, her throat growing dry. Maybe now was the time to get it into the open. It was bound to happen at some point. She took a steadying sip of her drink.

'My dad left before I was born — I guess *I* was the product of a fling, but I don't know — Jackie never liked to talk about it. Ergo, me and flings were on bad terms from the outset.'

She told them that from her father, a man she'd never met, to Tony the Stoner from the pub, to seemingly-nice-Fred who decided to stay with his wife, her mother had failed to demonstrate there were any good men out there. None who would stick around. And that when they didn't, her mum usually lost the plot.

'Some men want to stay around,' said Paolo. 'Sorry — that was insensitive. I just mean that some relationships do work out.'

'Exactly,' said Holly. 'They go on for more than a few weeks, but that's when they get more dangerous. You think you might be on to something. You might commit to someone, give them your heart and soul, only for them to destroy you.'

Chloe's eyes widened. 'Did someone do that to your mum?'

'Yup. The worst man Jackie ever found,' Holly took such a deep breath she felt lightheaded, 'was Gavin Grey, who was around when I was eleven or twelve. He was charming and while there was something a little off about him, Mum liked him, so I was on board. And things were better with him around, to begin with. Mum always remembered to pick me up from school, cooked nice meals. We even went to the seaside for the weekend once, which was amazing. They managed about six months before things went wrong, which was a record.'

She shook her head. 'Mum had opened a post office account. She had decided to start saving, which was incredible, and had stowed away nearly £500. I knew it was there in the little book, and I liked to count it and dream of holidays, trips to theme parks, school uniform that didn't come from the second-hand table. But then . . .'

Holly tried to neutralize the anger that was rising up her throat, making her eyes begin to burn.

Paolo put a hand on hers. 'You can stop if you want, Hols.'

'No. It's OK. Gavin found the book. He told Mum he would invest the money in a scheme he knew of. And thus far, he had given Mum no reason to believe he wouldn't. Later, Mum told me there had even been bits of paper, with authentic-looking logos on them, that she had signed. Over the next months, she kept giving him money to invest, even working overtime for that bit more, and taking out a loan from some dodgy guy down the road. Gavin kept saying "every penny helps".'

Holly had cried enough tears over it at the time. Now, as she came to the worst bit, she could feel herself vibrating with a pent-up hatred for Gavin. Hate was a strong word but Holly felt nothing less than that for him, and however much she tried to let it go, a part of the hate remained. It lurked in a corner of her mind like a gremlin, waiting to undermine the calm, focused persona she clung to.

'He was part of a gambling ring, and he was a crap gambler. Mum's earnings were covering his debts. When she asked for some money back to pay a bill, the whole lot had disappeared, something that Gavin did too, although not before they'd had an almighty row and the police got called by a neighbour. He scarpered before they arrived.'

Out they came, all the feelings she liked to keep inside. Chloe and Paolo seemed astounded their otherwise calm and collected colleague held in so much pent-up emotion.

'We never saw him again. Mum was floored. She had dated some toads, but this guy was something else. There was no money, and after the thug she'd borrowed money from called his loan in, no TV or sofas either. She was devasted by the whole thing, drinking lots, going out, not coming back until daybreak. Good thing I knew how to wash my own clothes, and thank God for free school dinners.'

Paolo and Chloe looked appalled, and Holly felt bad for lumbering them with all her baggage. She didn't like anyone to see her less put-together self. Everyone had a side like it, but she felt hers was worse than most.

'I'm fine,' Holly added, lightly as she could. 'Totally rounded as an adult. For the most part. And after a year Mum recovered too, and went off fishing for more toads.'

'Wow,' Paolo whispered.

'I can see why you put your career first,' Chloe added. 'Sorry we've been pushing you on the Greg thing.'

'No worries,' said Holly. 'It's no massive secret, but it's not the kind of thing you tell people when you've only known them for a week. Aaaaaand — for the record — I *know* not all men are love vampires, waiting to drain the life out of me.

People fall in and out of love all the time, and survive it. But it's not a niggling doubt for me — it's a big voice yelling in my ear to look after myself and stick to my priorities. And I know that money doesn't buy you happiness, but it certainly greases the wheels. Life for me and Mum would have been infinitely easier with some extra cash. Once I've sorted that, I'll look for someone, even though right now I must admit Greg is giving me all the feelings.'

'Where's your mum now?' asked Paolo. 'You don't mention her much.'

'Malaga — don't ask. As you might have twigged, she's a total rollercoaster of a woman. We see each other when we manage, but we don't have one of those relationships where we chat every day. Or week. Or month sometimes.'

And Holly didn't mind that. She liked to keep a healthy distance between herself and her mother. Not have to listen to her mother's woes and provide solutions. It wasn't as if her mother had always been there for her. She was too busy being "wildly bohemian" as she had once described herself when Holly was in her late teens. Holly had countered that with "immature mess".

So ever since she had been young, Holly was determined to be the opposite of her mother. To remain cool and detached, like an iceberg. Unsinkable. Although — she realized — icebergs tended to have a lot going on under the surface. Right now, that was certainly true with regards to Greg. Whatever . . . she would find her perfect match when the time was right.

And talking of which . . . She turned to Chloe, who was at that moment eyeing the door to the pub.

* * *

'The herdsman cometh,' Paolo whispered in Chloe's ear.

Chloe barely heard him. All she could see was the horrific state Angus was in. It was as though someone had tossed a caber and he'd had the misfortune to look directly up as it landed on his face.

'Chloe,' Holly nudged her. 'Didn't your mother ever tell you it's rude to stare?'

Her eyes remained glued to Angus. 'You said he only had *some* bruises. His entire face is a bruise.'

Finally aware she was looking at him as if she were a slack-jawed yokel, she closed her mouth and turned back to her friends.

'It'll heal,' said Holly, putting a hand on her arm. 'Honestly. He had scans. His nose may be a bit broken, but it can be reset if need be. Surgeons can work wonders.'

Paolo made a coughing noise, making Chloe and Holly look up simultaneously.

'Oh!' cried Holly. 'Hi, Angus!'

Chloe took a sharp intake of breath. In the time Holly had been reassuring her, Angus had silently crossed the floor and was standing beside their table.

'I see that aside from the man himself, Hugh's crew is all present and correct,' he said.

Chloe watched as he tried to smile but ended up wincing from the effort. A desire to wrap her arms around him threatened to overwhelm her.

Nobody spoke, so Angus carried on. 'Holly, I owe you a pint — you were a rockstar the other week.'

'I reckon you owe me one too,' said Paolo, casually. 'For helping Holly with the admin for it.'

Angus chuckled. 'Go on. And Chloe, I'll get you one too because you're a top lass.'

Chloe felt herself flush crimson. She avoided the ecstatic gazes of her colleagues, which were so unsubtle she didn't need to see them to know they were there, and looked Angus straight in the eye. This was it. Now or never.

'Thanks,' she said. 'A gin and tonic for me, please. And while I'm sure your mother is trying to smother you with cakes, I've made you some tiffin. Can I drop it off tomorrow?'

'Are you saying I need sweetening up?' Angus said, smiling, raising an eyebrow into his green forehead.

'I'm not sure even I've got enough sugar for that, darling.'

The words just slipped out!

For a second, she was mortified, but then Angus winked at her before heading to the bar. She'd got away with it! Smiling, feeling a wicked excitement bubbling inside her, as if she'd stolen the crown jewels from the Tower of London and escaped scot-free, she turned back to her friends, both of whom looked suitably impressed.

'Cheeky cow! I didn't know you had it in you,' said Paolo, raising his glass.

'Nor did I! Nobody's more surprised than me.'

It came out as a squeal, as if the control she'd held as she'd spoken to Angus had gone, and all that remained was one final peep. She held up her glass.

'Cheers,' said Holly. 'Now, let's plan what you're going to wear.'

'What?' Chloe felt the wind knocked out of her sails. 'I was going to wear a dress and cardi.'

'In fairness, she's going to a farm. It's not the time for sultry eyeliner and unbuttoned tops. And I don't reckon that's Angus's style anyway,' said Paolo. 'He's one for a homely outfit, although if you were wearing a silk camisole underneath I reckon he'd be pretty happy.'

'I don't own a silk cami,' said Chloe, sounding panicky. 'Besides, he's not going to be ripping my clothes off — I'm taking him a traybake.'

'You never know,' said Holly. 'Might be all it takes . . .'

Chloe noticed Angus returning from the bar, and shushed her friends, anxious not to be exposed. Expressions like naughty schoolchildren, they obliged.

'Would you like to join us?' Paolo asked, gesturing to an empty stool.

'Aye, for a moment,' said Angus. 'Ferdie Taggart's coming shortly, and we'll be propping up the bar.'

'You'll be propping him up by last orders,' said Chloe. 'That man can't handle his drink.'

As Angus sat down, Chloe thought for a moment of Ferdie Taggart, who worked over at an energy company towards Inverness and lived out of the village. Poor Ferdie, built like a string bean, could barely down three pints before his legs lost the will to keep him vertical.

'Then I'll have to rely on you lot for some quality conversation,' Angus said. 'How's this week been at the practice?'

Technically, it was a question he was asking to the group, but Chloe could feel his eyes on her. She became aware of the wool of her jumper scratching her neck, making her hot, and she tugged at it as she searched for words. Panic began to rise up in her, making her feel spaced out.

Chloe felt a kick under the table. It wasn't clear if it was Holly or Paolo, but it was enough to stop her drowning in blushes, to lower the heat that was making her body prickle. She took a sip of her gin and tonic.

'Tell Angus about the parrot,' Paolo said to Chloe.

'His language was foul. No! It was fowl! God, Paolo has got us all punning constantly,' she said. Angus smiled at the lame joke though and — emboldened by it — she carried on. 'Bluer than Hugh's, if you can believe it.'

And at that, she relaxed into the conversation, recounting the tale, thriving on the encouraging nods from her colleagues, but mainly those from Angus.

CHAPTER 16

Paolo watched Chloe unwind, gaining confidence as she talked. He glanced at Holly, who gave him a gleeful look. If Chloe could last until Ferdie made an appearance, she'd have made great strides.

Then, from over by the bar, a shriek rose above the warm hum of chatter. At first, Paolo thought it was a laugh but, craning his neck around, he saw it came from a place of pain. Hamish Glennis stood looking awkward, drawing his chin into his neck, seemingly dismayed. But he wasn't the source of the shriek.

That had come from the girl standing opposite him. Daisy Morello, his glossy sylph of a girlfriend, stood with tears rolling down her cheeks, her hands running through her curly brown hair. Along with the entire pub, Paolo found himself goggling at the tableau, wondering what could have happened. As far as he knew, Hamish wasn't one for brawling: on the occasions he'd met him, he'd been very private, the epitome of reserved.

Paolo had met him a few times at the castle with Hugh, when they'd been up seeing to the animals there. Moira and David Glennis's only son, he worked on the estate as a ghillie. As a way of making Glenalmond pay its way, the family opened it to visitors who came to fish and shoot game, and Hamish acted as their guide.

It sounded grand, but Paolo knew the Glennises were anything but. In fact, despite the colossal house, they were down to earth. Instead of marrying within the aristocracy, David Glennis had fallen in love with a waitress at a café in Edinburgh and within six weeks had married her. While Hamish had been surrounded by material comfort, Moira had never let him assume he could rest on his laurels and rely on his title for the rest of his life. Instead, he had to earn a living, and as far as Paolo could tell, he did it well. Word had it Hamish was knowledgeable, enthusiastic and highly dedicated, ensuring guests would be keen to return.

'What do you think that's all about?' asked Holly.

'I can't tell,' said Paolo. 'I can see Hamish and he'd not hurt a fly.'

'And the girl who's auditioning for a role in a horror film is . . . ?'

'Daisy Morello, the girlfriend. Fun, but prone to drama. She's from Glasgow, and is never knowingly underdressed. Remember when I told you what the dress code for the pub was when you first got here? Well, either Hamish was too polite to tell her, or he was ignored. I think she's a wannabe influencer and her daddy is funding it all.'

He studied Daisy's outfit. Not unusually, she was dressed up to the nines. On top of a pair of black skinny jeans she wore a sequinned top, and teetered on studded heels. There was no evidence of a coat, and Paolo felt chilly looking at her.

A hush fell over the pub as Daisy howled like a banshee. 'My shoooooooooes,' she wailed. 'They're ruined.'

By now, everyone in the room was glued to the argument unfolding before them. Even Mhairi, normally not swayed by dramas in her bailiwick, had put down the glasses she was holding. Hamish looked like a scared animal, ready to flinch at the slightest movement. Daisy snatched her clutch bag from the bar and stormed out of the pub, slamming the door behind her. A stunned silence reigned.

'Nothing to see here, you nosy bunch!' Mhairi eventually clapped her hands, and the noise levels in the room returned to their previous volume.

Hamish shuffled over to the door, presumably ready to plead forgiveness for whatever had happened to the shoes. Angus grabbed him and pulled him over. 'What happened there, mate?' he asked gruffly.

Hamish looked agonized. 'I don't know. It wasn't about the shoes, I don't think. Although they were exorbitantly expensive. She and I . . .'

Paolo watched as he tailed off. Hamish didn't often bring her to the pub — presumably they spent most of their spare time in Glasgow. But — Paolo knew from being a native — Hamish would have looked distinctly out of place in the kind of bars Daisy dressed for. It wasn't that he wasn't turned out well — in fact, he cleaned up nicely when he wasn't in khaki overalls and a waterproof. When you mentioned the term "ghillie", it conjured up the image of a portly tweed-wearing man of middle age, with a hoary beard and nostril hair. But Hamish was clean-shaven, with a round, friendly face and ruddy skin. He simply didn't exude glamour, whereas Daisy oozed it from every pore.

Hamish failed to find the words to finish the sentence, then rolled his eyes and gave up, defeated. 'I ought to go,' he murmured apologetically. 'Bye, all. Catch up soon.'

Hamish pulled his coat from the stand, and threw it hastily over his shoulders before following Daisy into the dark night. At the same time, Ferdie appeared in the doorway, and Angus bade them goodbye before they got up and went to the bar.

Holly stood up. 'I ought to go — I want to get some paddle boarding in first thing tomorrow while the tide's in.'

'Me too,' said Chloe. 'I'm taking Mum to Inverness to look for gowns for the ball. I wonder if Daisy will be going. They're an odd couple, aren't they?'

They *were* an odd couple. Warm, kind Hamish, and pouty, angular Daisy. Paolo thought on it for a second.

Would he rather be in a relationship with the wrong person, or alone? It was a tough call and, as he considered it, he felt a shadowy unease creeping over his skin. It wasn't like he had a choice anyway.

'I'll join you, Hols,' he said, quickly. 'See you bright and early on the front.'

CHAPTER 17

'I'm going to stay,' said Chloe to Paolo and Holly. 'Maybe go and see what's happening at the bar.'

'Oooooh,' said Paolo. 'I'll be texting for all the gossip in the morning. If you want to come and join us in the sea, let me know.'

'You two are hardcore,' she said, shaking her head. 'I might take a rain check. But I'll message if anything important happens.'

Chloe waved goodbye to her friends and then looked over to the bar. She had done well earlier, and was riding along on that swell of success. Angus had fully shed his outer layer of irascibility, and was now roaring with laughter at something Ferdie had said. She could well believe it — Ferdie was quite the comedian until he'd had one too many. Then her confidence wobbled. Angus was having a nice time. Would he be annoyed if a girl came and interrupted a manly drinking session? She looked at her feet, hesitating.

'Chlo!' Suddenly Angus bellowed across the room. 'Over here.'

Joy! He had asked *her* over. She practically skipped towards him. Heart thudding, she put the dregs of her gin and tonic on the bar, and Angus pulled a stool in between him and Ferdie, who was tucking into a plate of chips and talking to Mhairi.

'Where are your colleagues?' Angus said.

His voice had a deliciously low growliness to it. She could listen to him talk all day.

'Done for the evening. They're going paddle boarding tomorrow at first light.'

'You're not joining them?'

'I'm not tempted to get frostbite.'

Angus laughed, and Chloe smiled from having made him do so, and decided she wasn't completely socially awkward.

'And what do you make of the new vet. Got the measure of her yet?' he asked.

Chloe hesitated. Did Angus have a thing for Holly? It wouldn't surprise her — Holly was stunning, even when she was in her filthiest outdoor gear. And confident too. Compared to her, Chloe blended into the background. But Chloe liked Holly and, being the unceasingly honest person she was, she couldn't do anything else but sing her praises and hope Angus was only asking out of politeness.

'She's great. She's fitted in at the surgery well — I mean, we come here together on Fridays out of choice. Hugh's tolerating her too. Well, tolerating is probably too strong. He hasn't fired her, at least. And she hasn't quit. Bronwen only managed a month after all.'

'And how is MacDougal? Mood swings still very much present?'

Chloe paused, forgetting her worries about Holly. Hugh's mood swings weren't only just "present", as Angus had put it. They were a daily occurrence. He'd not shouted at any clients, but she could see him getting frustrated by silly things, like a bottle label facing the wrong way, or his tea being too hot. Only that morning he'd yelled at her for chatting to Mrs Hargreaves for too long. As for Holly, she kept getting it in the neck for no apparent reason.

'You know, they've been bad of late. The last few months he can barely set foot in the surgery without smoke coming out of his ears. I wonder if he's threatened by Holly.'

'He probably fancies her.'

Oh God, her fears were founded. She gathered herself, finding the courage to investigate. 'I think most men do, don't they? She commands attention.'

'Och — she's not my type,' said Angus. 'Mind you, I'm not sure who is. Someone who could be a farmer's wife. And I wouldn't wish being a farmer's wife on someone. Brutal work, long hours and endless money worries.'

'I'm sure there are plenty of girls who wouldn't mind,' said Chloe, quietly.

She didn't look him in the eye. It had taken all her remaining guts to even suggest he'd be an attractive prospect. At least, that's what she'd intended. That he'd know she meant him, rather than any old farmer.

'Even you? With your comfortable upbringing and neat skirts? You'd be willing to shack up with an old curmudgeon like me?'

'You're a young curmudgeon,' Chloe finally looked at him.

She spied a hint of a smile under the bruises, and lit up inside but couldn't find the words to continue the conversation.

'Well, it isn't for everyone,' Angus said finally. 'It wasn't for Dani. Sometimes I think it isn't for me. It wasn't for Greg, after all.'

'Would you ever give it all up?'

'Never. But I don't think it's helped, me and Greg have fallen out.'

'What happened?' Chloe knew it was none of her business, but she had to ask.

He looked furious. 'I don't want to go into detail, but let's say Greg is a treacherous, selfish bastard who has forgotten where he came from.'

Chloe felt her heart sink. A minute ago, conversation had been going in the right direction, and now it had taken a distinct wrong turn. From what Holly had said, it was a nerve that didn't want striking. What could Greg have done that had upset him so much?

'I'm sure you'll make it up,' she said hopefully.

He snorted. 'Not until he comes to his bloody senses.'

Chloe's mouth formed a small "o" as she realized there was nothing she could say that would make it any better. She searched for a way to change the subject. Angus didn't need to dwell on the feud. A drunken Ferdie came to the rescue.

'Chloe! I didn't see you there!' he said, cheerfully. 'Would you like a chip?'

And with that, Ferdie slid off his stool.

'Might be time for me to go home,' said Chloe.

She'd put in enough groundwork for one night. And maybe her foot in it, at the same time.

CHAPTER 18

Paolo took a sip of coffee. 'The Glenalmond Ball is rapidly approaching. Me and Holly can go as a pair, and you and Angus. We'll call it a foursome if that's less intimidating. Chloe — you've been all shy again after that burst of energy — you can get up close and personal with him. All that dancing.'

Holly cringed inside. She had two left feet, and when she danced people tended to give her a wide berth. 'I'm useless.'

When they'd booked the tickets back in February, it had seemed like a good idea. But May was coming around fast and the night was nearly upon them.

'I've thought of that,' Paolo continued. 'I thought we could head to the Country Dancing Society for some practice.'

Chloe looked unconvinced. 'Over towards Inverness? My grandparents used to dance there, and not when they were youngsters. It's the waiting room for heaven.'

'It'll be fun,' said Paolo, ignoring her comment and getting animated. 'Think of the leaping! Me and Fabien went a few times and had a lovely night nattering to all the folk there. They're all so happy to see anyone under fifty they descend like vultures, so it's the ideal place to brush up on your reeling. You'll be fully prepared to dance with Angus all night long. And you with Greg, Holly?'

Paolo sprawled back and crossed his arms with an air of satisfaction. Holly looked over to Chloe, whose brow wrinkled in contemplation.

'I doubt Greg'll come, as I imagine he's still avoiding Angus. But I'm totally up for some practice,' said Holly, deciding to get over her fear of dancing for Chloe's sake. 'I really can't dance for toffee though.'

'And I'm totally out of practice. We can look like idiots together,' said Paolo.

Holly leaned out and held up a fist which Paolo bumped.

Chloe raised an eyebrow. 'I'm guessing I don't have a say in this either.'

* * *

The following week, Paolo drove home along the dark, winding road from Inverness, and realized he'd not seen another car since they'd left the glorified log cabin that was home to the Country Dancing Society. Holly dozed in the back — she was on call again the next day — but Chloe was talking nineteen to the dozen.

'I loved Mr Henderson,' she said. 'The one with the massive beard.'

Paolo laughed. 'He was great! And he had some good stories about when he'd met his wife there in the sixties. And he was forgiving about Holly standing on his toes so often.'

'Aye. But she was better by the end of the night.'

'You've been hiding your light under a bushel, by the way.'

It had turned out while Holly had been a dictionary-definition novice, Chloe could dance like a demon. She had not only known the steps to everything, but she had perfect posture too. Paolo had heard a couple of the older attendees commenting on how neatly she had pointed her toes.

'What light? What bushel?' Chloe asked.

'You were up there reeling with the best of them. Have you been doing the steps in your bedroom all week? Watching videos on TikTok?'

'I used to dance all the time,' she said. 'Not only at school, but there was a club each Thursday in the village hall. It closed down a few years ago, which was sad. Miss Goldie moved away.'

'Well, you were excellent. No wonder that old chap Duncan wanted you for more than one dance. He was having the time of his life.'

'*I* was having the time of my life,' she said. 'When I was dancing I disappeared for a moment.'

'We did the right thing, then? Dragging you an hour into the middle of nowhere to dance a jig with some doddery strangers?'

'Aye. I had a wonderful evening,' Chloe replied in a dreamy, far-away voice. 'Did you?'

Paolo smiled to himself. The night had not got off to an auspicious start. As he had been getting ready, he'd gone online and seen a picture of Fabien with a friend. Only, the friend was more than a friend. If the location of lips on Fabien's cheek hadn't been enough to confirm it, then the text below was: *Raclette with the boyf — requires cheesy picture.* Paolo had left the house in a blur of emotion, feeling the heartache afresh. Heartache, and a giant kick in the gut.

But, lo and behold, as he stood at the bar, watching Chloe whirling and Holly stumbling, he'd become aware of a man standing next to him. Having said the place was full of people over the age of seventy, he was surprised to see this man was his age. And gorgeous, with blond hair, and green eyes.

Paolo had flashed him a smile. 'I thought I was the youngest one here.'

The man had laughed and stuck out his hand. 'Ritchie. Nice to meet you.'

'Paolo. You come here often? I've been before but not seen you.'

'It's only my second time. I came with a friend the other week. It was wonderful. And I love talking to this lot.' He gestured to the dancers. 'So many interesting stories. Don't get me wrong, I love a bar or club, but this is great fun. Love your shoes, by the way.'

Paolo looked down at his brogues, polished to perfection. 'Thanks. Yours are pretty jazzy too.'

'Fraser and Sons. Expensive, but worth it. Like me!'

Paolo let out a laugh. The guy had chutzpah, not to mention a dress sense, and he liked it. 'Funny. So, Ritchie. What do you do and where do you come from?'

'Well, Cilla . . .' Ritchie began.

Before he'd had a chance to say more, a diminutive lady with permed grey hair tottered over. 'Would you care for a dance, Ritchie?'

'It would be an honour, Maureen,' Ritchie replied.

He winked at Paolo, then offered the lady his hand, accompanying her to the centre of the room. Paolo watched as they disappeared into the crowd, ready to start the next dance. He waited at the bar, hoping to catch a glimpse of Ritchie as he danced. He felt oddly tingly, like he'd had one too many coffees.

At the end of the night, as Chloe and Holly jostled him to the front door, he spied Ritchie chatting to another elderly lady. Quickly extricating himself from the coat queue, he snuck over and tapped Ritchie on the shoulder.

'Maybe see you again some time,' he said, his blood moving through his veins faster than normal.

'Aye,' said Ritchie. 'I'd like that.'

Paolo was ready to move on. Normally he wouldn't have been this bold, but seeing Fabien cosying up to Pierre had given him the brutal shove he needed. Hell, even the quickest of rebounds had the potential to become long-termers. And Ritchie seemed like a good chap — he was happy to dance with all the old ladies for a start. Always a good sign.

'Can I give you my number?' he asked. 'Make it happen, rather than rely on chance?'

'Pass me your phone,' said Ritchie.

Paolo handed it over, and watched with bated breath as Ritchie tapped his number in, then pressed save.

'All done,' he said, handing it back. 'Hopefully see you sooner rather than later.'

'Hopefully indeed. Night.'

He went to rejoin the girls, brimming with excitement.

Now, as he turned the last of the bends into Eastercraig, he wondered how long he should leave it before contacting Ritchie. Tonight would be too desperate. And he would only lie awake waiting for a reply. Tomorrow was a new day. A new dawn, a new day and a new man.

* * *

They arrived home after midnight. Chloe waved Paolo and a sleepy Holly goodbye, and then snuck up the gravel drive to the white, pebble-dashed bungalow where she lived with her parents.

As carefully as she could, so as not to make a sound, she turned the key in the lock. After hanging her coat up and tugging off her heels, rubbing her sore but happy toes, she stole across the hallway towards her attic room.

'Chlo?' came her mother's voice.

Chloe cursed inwardly and tiptoed back to her parents' room. She pushed open the door, went in and kneeled next to the bed. Her father was snoring loudly, and she hoped it was that which had woken her mother, rather than her coming in.

Her mother, Mei, lay on her side, and Chloe could see her eyes glinting in the dark.

'What have you been up to?' Mei whispered.

Mei held out a hand, and Chloe reached for it giving it a squeeze, then lay her head down on the pillow next to her mother. She smelled of lavender face cream. 'I was at the Country Dancing Society near Inverness,' she whispered. 'With my colleagues from the surgery. Remember?'

Mei breathed in. 'Of course. I love that place. Your father and I went there a few times. Remember all your steps?'

Chloe nodded. As soon as the music had started she recalled PE lessons and classes in the village hall where she'd danced the Dashing White Sergeant, skipping up and down the school hall while a teacher tapped out a beat. The names themselves were like a favourite blanket, and she felt she could wrap herself up in them — the Gay Gordons, the Flying Scotsman, the Eightsome Reel. Chloe had always loved the feeling of being fleet of foot, and how even the coolest of children were thrilled when the class all reached the end of a number standing in the right place.

More than that, the classes had been an escape for her when her mum had been sick. When Chloe was fifteen, Mei had had a stroke. It had taken months of rehabilitation to get her up and about again. Now that nightmare was distant, but at the time Chloe had ended up stressed and anxious. Once a week, however, in the village hall, under the tutelage of the formidable Miss Goldie, she could forget. Concentrating on everything from the larger formations to the tiniest tilt of her head forced her to push everything else out of her mind. She could leave that fog of worry at the door. Come to think about it, she had done that tonight.

'I did a few reels with an old man who used to dance with his wife before she died.'

'Oh wonderful, darling. Tell me which ones.'

Chloe listed the dances, and her mother smiled as she listened.

'And tell me, were there any younger men there? Anyone to take your fancy?'

'Och, Mum. Leave off!' she shrieked, forgetting to be quiet.

For a moment her father, Jack, stopped snoring. Chloe caught her mother's eye, and they shared a look, breathing sighs of relief when the snorts started again.

'Paolo, Holly and I significantly lowered the average age. I think you'd be the next youngest,' she whispered.

‘Count me in,’ Mei whispered gleefully. She gave Chloe a teasing look. ‘Would you like me to dig out your old outfits for you next time?’

Chloe leaned over and kissed her mum on the forehead. ‘Thanks, but no thanks. Night, Mum.’

‘Goodnight, darling.’

As she climbed into her own bed, she wondered if Angus still remembered the dances from school. And if he would be up for the ball. She crossed her toes in the hope he would agree to go.

* * *

Holly stepped inside, glad of the warmth. The five steps from the car to her front door had been enough to set her teeth chattering.

She was never going to make it as a professional dancer — she had fallen over twice tripping over her own feet while trying to work out where to stand — but she had been able to dance out some of the stress that had been making her shoulders ache for the last week.

Eastercraig was like a postcard, and most people had been nothing but kind. True, a few people had eyed her as if she might be coming to steal their pets, rather than treat them, but it was a close-knit community. They’d warm up. Hugh, on the other hand, might not. Another week of constant huffing and nit-picking had made her feel tiny, and she was 5’ 11”, so that was saying something. Every time he had given criticism, which was often (and as far as Holly could tell, usually unnecessary), he failed to use the “praise sandwich” approach, preferring borderline derision. Sometimes he barely managed to say “good morning”.

She had to keep reminding herself that she *was* a good vet. Judith thought so, even if Hugh didn’t. If she was going to stay sane, she was just going to have to grin and bear it.

Her phone buzzed. Greg. The sight of his name filled her with a warm glow. Their weekly texts were something she increasingly looked forward to.

How've things been? Any good tales from the surgery?

She went upstairs, threw on her PJs and composed a reply. A platonic reply, she reminded herself, forcing herself not to smile as she typed. This was polite conversation. Nothing more.

Besides, this was a good way of keeping her mind off her worries about Hugh.

CHAPTER 19

'Do you know what it is, Holly?' asked Hugh, his eyes boring into her.

While the days were longer and slightly warmer, despite the fact it was May, Holly could still feel her fingers burning with the cold. Across from her, Mandy Lewis stood biting her lip, stroking one of her five alpacas, as Holly examined the painful lesions on the mouths of the others, her rubber gloves offering her no protection from the chill. Across from her, Hugh stood with his arms crossed, waiting for her to make her diagnosis.

Mandy, who Hugh had described as an "ageing hippy with about as much grasp of husbandry as of space travel", was on the verge of tears, and every so often took a shuddering breath. Hugh had told Holly on the way over that Mandy had bought the alpacas on a whim after seeing some being reared on the TV and wanted to do something similar. Judging by the way he delivered the story, Hugh didn't approve.

Mandy seemed nice enough though, and after seeing the smallholding, Holly was happy they were well cared for.

Holly looked at Mandy. 'It's orf, or sore mouth. A pox virus. Highly contagious.'

'The rest of the animals on the farm are well?' Hugh asked.

Mandy looked worried. 'The sheep are fine, I think. The alpacas were grazing over with some of Lindsey Harris's lot at her farm for a few days, while I was away last week — maybe they got it there? The goats are well, and the donkeys.'

Holly cast her eye around the farm once more, the grazing areas separated by wire fencing.

'Lindsey Harris?' Hugh asked, fixing his eyes on Mandy.

'Yes. My sister came and looked after most of them, but Lindsey offered to have the alpacas because she thinks they're cute.'

Hugh rolled his eyes and looked to Holly. 'Bloody Lindsey. I heard from someone in the pub she'd had an outbreak with her sheep.'

Mandy's eyes widened.

Holly looked at Mandy. 'Tell me, have your sheep been in the same field as the alpacas since they've been home?'

Mandy let out a whimper, and her hands flew to her mouth. 'Not since they got back — a couple have just had lambs. But they're all so fond of one another they tend to nuzzle through the fence.'

She flung her arms around the neck of the nearest alpaca, and Holly patted another on the head gingerly, glad of her rubber glove. 'Maybe don't cuddle them too closely, Mandy. You can catch it from them, and it's not pleasant.'

Holly walked with Hugh over to the sheep field, only to find the small flock also showed the same spotty rashes around their mouths which were afflicting the alpacas.

'That's it then,' said Holly. 'The alpacas caught this at Lindsey's and Lindsey either doesn't know, or doesn't care.'

'Lindsey's a sloppy individual,' Hugh said in a low voice. 'I'm surprised Mandy left the animals with her, but she must have had her reasons. But at least we're at the bottom of it. Let's go and school her about looking after the lambs. She'll be needing to watch out because they have lower immunity and it might be more serious.'

* * *

All the way home, Holly barely felt her usual carsickness, she was so elated. She and Hugh had practically been getting along. Hugh hadn't criticized her work. The huff tally had been low that week, and she was getting to grips with this big animal stuff. In her most recent email exchange with Judith, she had been able to say, quite honestly, that she was finally settling in.

Hugh's bonhomie (if it could be called that) didn't last though. After she'd pulled a deep splinter out from a dog's paw that afternoon and charged the owner for it, he was yelling at her that she was trying to wring money out of people for trifles, his face florid from the effort of raising his voice so much. 'These are *friends* as well as clients. I won't have you reaching into people's pockets for things like that.'

Holly gawped. 'This is a business, Hugh, not a charity.'

'And it's my business, and I'll run it how I see fit. The sooner you learn that the better.'

'Calm down, poppet,' said Paolo, who'd appeared from down the hall and was now stood at the doorway holding a ginger cat.

Hugh spluttered, perhaps wondering what missive he could throw at Paolo, but nothing came. Holly had come to notice Paolo had a calming influence on Hugh, and was grateful he'd turned up before things got worse.

Whatever, Holly told herself. She wasn't going to let it overshadow her weekend. She wasn't on call, and Saturday was the night of the ball. Only yesterday — in a passing good mood — Hugh had said he was happy not to drink, and she could let her hair down. Holly strongly suspected Paolo and Chloe had encouraged him to switch on-call shifts with her.

The prickly atmosphere dissipating, Holly felt as if she could cross the room without being shouted at again for no reason. She lifted the cat from Paolo's arms, and spoke to it.

'It's all right,' she said, as it purred. 'We'll check you over and make sure you're ready to go home.'

The beetroot hue that had temporarily afflicted Hugh's face disappeared. 'Next time, just think about what you're charging for. You won't make any friends round here if you hold people to ransom. You have to be reasonable.'

For a second, Holly felt a lump in her throat. She willed it away, telling herself Hugh wouldn't know reason if it hit him in the face. And that if she was to last in this job and get the CV points, she needed to save face. 'Why don't you finish for the day, Hugh? There's nothing else major, and you're on call tomorrow anyway. We can ring if we need you.'

Hugh took a deep breath, and Holly held hers. Being magnanimous was a good technique for getting over difficult situations. That, and she would rather not spend another moment around him today.

Hugh gave a small cough. 'That's kind of you. Sorry. I'm tired and hungry.'

Holly smiled at being proven correct. 'Apology accepted. We'll see you at the Spring Fling.'

Unprecedented volte-face complete, Hugh lifted a hand above his head and began to dance a jig. 'I hope you youngsters are ready.'

'We've been practising, remember,' said Paolo. He joined Hugh in skipping on the spot and started to sing the tune to 'Scotland the Brave'. Hugh began to mime a pair of bagpipes.

Holly let out a snort, trying not to stare at her suddenly carefree boss, before the cat let out a miaow, reminding her she had work to do.

'There's a time and a place,' she called over the cacophony. 'And that's tomorrow night.'

Hugh stopped. 'Aye. I'll preserve my energy. I'll come and pick you all up from Sea Spray.'

As he left, Chloe appeared at the door. 'Is everything all right in here? I heard the yelling. Are you OK, Holly?'

'I'll survive. Hugh had one of his moments. But we've made up — kind of, and he's going home to relax before the weekend's festivities.' Holly gave a tired smile. 'Also, in a min can you call Mrs Roberts and tell her Ginger's ready to be picked up?'

'Sure thing,' said Chloe. 'And are you all ready for tomorrow? Have you got something to wear? You can't roll up in your hufflebuffs.'

'My what?'

'I don't know what you're talking about either,' said Paolo.

'Your comfy clothes. Jeans, jumpers, woolly socks. Have you got anything else to wear?'

'I've got a party dress, if that's what you mean,' said Holly. 'Black and sparkly, above the knee. And some heels.'

Chloe looked aghast, and Holly wondered how she could have possibly said the wrong thing.

'What? No! This is your chance to go *big*.' Chloe stretched her arms out wide. 'It's a ball, not a bar. You need something floor-length, something you can move in, and that moves with you. A *gown*. And flats, or you'll regret it after twenty minutes of reeling.'

Holly felt a twinge of regret. It would have been nice to wear heels. She loved to, even if it made her the tallest woman in the room. But Chloe had a point. And it would also make dancing with Paolo tricky: the two of them had connived — if you could connive kindly — to partner up on most songs to ensure Chloe danced with Angus as much as possible. She did have some ballet pumps she could use. A long dress though . . .

'Where can I find a dress at the last minute?' she said. 'And also, won't I look absurd? Like a Viking in taffeta.'

'This is Eastercraig, not the nineties,' said Paolo. 'We can find you something perfect. And maybe then we can find you the perfect man at the ball. There'll be plenty of handsome princes. Well, handsome lairds. And farmers.'

Holly and Paolo looked at Chloe, who went a shade of crimson deeper than that of the pencil skirt she was wearing.

Perhaps there would be someone at the ball for Holly to dance with, other than Paolo. Maybe someone tall, dark and handsome. She felt a pang as she thought of Greg, knowing it was unlikely he'd turn up. Considering the falling-out he'd had with Angus, she imagined he'd be holed up with work in Aberdeen. He'd surely have forgotten all about her. Or — if he was being true to rumoured form — found someone else.

'Changing the subject!' Chloe cried, and Holly zoned back into the conversation. 'Paolo, are you ready for your date with Ritchie tonight? Come on, what are you wearing? Where are you going this time?'

* * *

Later, Holly lay in the bath, taking in the inky twilight. Even in spring, this far north the days were so much shorter, and before she'd left the surgery the sun had already disappeared, the first of the stars appearing to sparkle in the sky. She had opened the window so as to hear the hushing waves of the sea, and the knock of the boats bouncing off one another as they sat in the harbour. She sunk back into the tub, enjoying the chill air on her face while the rest of her was submerged in the hot water.

Could you even see the Milky Way in Berkshire? she wondered. You certainly wouldn't hear the sea, let alone be able to skip across the road for an icy swim in it. She had sent a text to Judith only that afternoon letting her know that even though the secondment to Scotland had been a drastic change of plans, she was enjoying herself.

While nearly every moment with Hugh made her question her ability to last the coming months, the slow tempo of life in Eastercraig wasn't so bad, now she was growing used to it. She ought to make the most of it, seeing as the fast pace of the new surgery would keep her so occupied it was unlikely she'd be able to spare a moment for such delights as luxuriating in bubbles while staring up at heavenly bodies.

Talking of bodies, try as she might, she had been unable to shunt Greg from her mind. He was so annoying. Appearing and disappearing without a by-your-leave, then lingering in her thoughts and refusing to be shut out. She had to keep reminding herself that she found his attitude towards relationships inexcusable. She ignored the fact that the texts they exchanged always brightened up gloomy days.

So Holly found herself checking her phone, even though she'd not sent him any message to reply to, and she was still hoping he might knock on the front door again, even though it had been over two months since he had last done so The taut slice of skin she had glimpsed up at the farm crept into her mind once more.

She berated herself again for wasting time thinking about him and then, noticing the wrinkles on her fingertips, got out of the bath, put on a dressing gown and padded downstairs. Finding some leftover soup in the fridge, she put it on the hob and went to check her texts.

She froze.

There was a message. Greg.

Long time, no see, Anderson. Still going to the ball tomorrow? Got one of the last tickets. I hope you'll save me a dance. G

It was as if some higher power was laughing at her. Throwing her hard-kept resolutions in her face.

Holly read it a second time, and she bit her tongue as she composed a reply. Even though she'd spent the best part of her bath thinking about him — appraising his best features then using his faults to write him off — she sent a flirty one. One which demanded a response.

I thought you weren't coming. Afraid I'm already promised to Paolo. But sure I can find room on my busy dance card, especially for a partner who is taller than me. Have you got your kilt ready?

Holly waited a second, eyeing the dots that indicated he was typing. They disappeared, and Holly found she was holding her breath in anticipation. Then Greg's name flashed up on the screen, and she answered immediately.

'Thought it would be easier to call,' said Greg's deep voice down the phone. 'And it would be nice to hear your Sassenach tones.'

Holly's veins began to thrum. 'Here I am. Loud and clear, I hope. You changed your mind then?'

'Och — was getting a touch of FOMO. Here's the thing. I need to plan a quick heist to get my kilt from the farm.'

'How are you going to manage that?'

'Mum'll text me while Angus is out with the coos. I'll dash in and grab it, and then I'm off to help Hamish set up.'

Holly groaned. 'You know your falling out is getting absurd,' she said.

'I'm aware of that. But we'll get over it. One day. How are you?'

'I'm OK. I've been enjoying a calm evening in preparation for tomorrow.'

'Great. I have a feeling it's going to be amazing! I've heard rumours of fireworks.'

'Me too. I can't wait!' said Holly. 'It sounds like it's going to be magical.'

'How will I spot you?'

'Don't be daft. I'll be hard to miss. With heels I'll be the one a foot taller than everyone else.'

'You're hard to miss even without heels. Anyway, I'll let you go. Like I said, I thought it would be nice to hear your voice. Goodnight.'

'Night,' she said, wondering if he could tell she was smiling.

Holly hung up, and curled up on the sofa with her soup. A moment later, a message came through.

Really looking forward to seeing you x

Her stomach lurched. It was *not* a necessary message. He was flirting with her, wasn't he? A teeny, tiny bit. Should she send a kiss back? Maybe she ought to compose a message first — one of those wouldn't go amiss.

Looking forward to seeing you too x

OK, so it wasn't especially original, but there was no need to throw caution to the wind entirely.

* * *

Paolo drummed his fingers on the dark wooden table. He had been waiting at Ocean Bar for twenty minutes, sat like a plum. The waiter had brought him not one, but two, saucers of nuts — which meant the staff would be running bets on him by now.

He checked his watch again, and then looked up at the clock. Ritchie had stood him up. It had seemed too good to be true. The first two dates had been great, and three was meant to be the magic number. Or something. Paolo scanned the room, trying to find an eye to catch. Waiters were like buses — you waited for ages and then three always turned up at once, bearing their tiny bowls of sympathy pistachios, when all you wanted was to get the bill and disappear.

He had been certain there had been a spark with Ritchie. They'd been roaring with laughter the other week. Ritchie had obviously thought differently. He felt his face slip that bit further. Any more, and it might fall off completely.

Paolo heaved a sigh. Perhaps he should just swear off men for a while. Make like Holly. Focus on other things.

CHAPTER 20

'It's amazing,' said Holly, staring at herself in the mirror.

That morning, she, Chloe and Paolo had spent an hour in Carousel Vintage Emporium, a weird and wonderful shop fifteen minutes from Eastercraig. It looked like a hoarder's dream, with piles of clothes and little in the way of coat hangers. Chloe, who had already bought her dress, had scaled each mound and rooted out all manner of wild items. The shopkeeper, Mrs Butowski, kept thrusting them through the gap in the curtained corner that passed for a changing room with a speed Holly couldn't keep up with.

'More, darlink,' said Mrs Butowski, in her heavily accented English, passing her a long, swishy red dress. 'If they don't fit, we alter. Try this. Maybe is too big but Chloe can put a stitch in.'

Holly had never tried on so many clothes in her life. There had been some taffeta — which Paolo had forbidden — but eventually they'd rooted out a slinky silk dress, which reminded Holly of Keira Knightley's green number in *Atonement*, only this one was a midnight blue. As a bonus, it was long enough for her, and fitted perfectly.

Hugh would soon turn up at her cottage to drive them all to the ball but Holly couldn't help but turn in front of the mirror, examining every angle. It wasn't often she dressed up, but tonight she felt sparkly, rather than someone for whom muddy trousers were a second skin, and momentarily pictured herself with Greg.

'We all scrub up very nicely indeed,' she said, turning to Chloe and Paolo.

'Don't we,' said Paolo.

'And we've got enough time for some fizz,' said Chloe, tilting her head towards the stairs.

The three of them made their way to Holly's kitchen, and Holly poured out three glasses. Sure, she missed the hustle and bustle of the city, and going out with her friends. Not as much as she thought she would, though. Despite her work woes, something about Eastercraig was worming its way into her subconscious, whispering to her, the quietest siren song. Just like Greg. She took a slug of her drink.

'Hugh's here,' said Paolo, as a horn sounded. 'Ready to fasten your seatbelts?'

'As ready as I'll ever be,' said Holly, as Chloe dragged her through the door.

* * *

Twenty bumpy minutes later, the car pulled up outside Glenalmond. Chloe paused for a moment, and slid out into the chill, clear evening, pulling her coat around her. Her fifties-style ballgown had thin straps and her shoulders were freezing. She focused on the pines, trying to shake the queasiness she was feeling after the ride.

'Castle's that way,' said Paolo, putting a hand on her arm.

'I know,' said Chloe. 'I want to stop feeling sick first. My first view of Glenalmond all decked out shouldn't be marred by my puking prosecco all over the gravel.'

She took another deep breath, in through the nose and out through the mouth. Chloe had only been in Hugh's car a couple of times, and not recently enough to remember how hideous his driving was.

'Angus has arrived,' Holly whispered in her ear. 'And my, has that man been concealing some good looks under that beard. Here — have a sip of H_2O. I've taken to bringing a bottle when Hugh's driving.'

Chloe took the bottle from Holly, wishing it was whisky, not water. Taking one last breath, she turned around, and her heart soared.

There, with Fiona on his arm, stood Angus. He looked fantastic. Like a matinee idol. His unruly hair had been tamed, brushed away from his face, and he had shaved, revealing his strong jawline. It was a transformation. True, he was more built than Cary Grant or Clark Gable, but tonight he looked ready to hand her a martini and stare deep into her eyes.

'Och, now I'm having an attack of the nerves,' she said. Their insistent jangling was worse than the car sickness.

Hugh had already crossed the gravel to see the Dunbars, but Chloe remained rooted to the spot. An attack of light-headedness had set in, and now her limbs felt like they were becoming detached from her body. Taking her coat back off, she let the cold air run over her skin, bringing her back to where she was, and she pushed her toes into the soles of her shoes, grounding herself.

'Are you OK?' Holly sounded concerned.

Chloe turned to face her. 'I've been looking forward to this ever since we got tickets — we've been practising our dancing, and I've been trying to be confident. And before we left the house, I was on cloud nine, feeling all glamorous in my dress. But what if there's too much pressure? What if it doesn't all go according to plan? What if I don't pluck up the courage to see if Angus would like to go on a date?'

'What if you spontaneously combust from overthinking it all?' said Paolo.

'I hadn't even thought about that!' Chloe squeaked in dismay.

Paolo put an arm around her shoulder. 'Life rarely goes according to plan. You know that, I know that, and I reckon even our resident control freak Anderson knows it. If you don't feel like snagging your man tonight, don't worry. It's all groundwork.'

'Which here, helpfully, is all in the footwork. Something you excel at,' Holly added.

'You're right,' said Chloe, trying to reassure herself. 'I need to enjoy the evening for what it is. Let's go and greet them. They'll be wondering what we're blethering about.'

Summoning up all the inner strength she had, which still wasn't as much as she'd hoped for, she took the hands of her colleagues and pulled them over towards the car. If she wasn't feeling ready, she could try to put on a convincing enough show.

'Hi, Fiona,' she called, as they approached. 'Hey, Angus.'

There was a flurry of handshakes, hugs and pecks on cheeks, and the group made towards the castle. Tonight, it looked straight out of a fairy tale, which Chloe decided to take as a good omen.

She fell in beside Angus. 'You're looking smart in your kilt.'

"Smart" was right, wasn't it? A way of saying someone was looking attractive, without being too obvious. Or was it too much? To her relief, Angus smiled.

'And you're looking lovely. Ready for the Gay Gordons?'

Chloe nodded. 'Of course.'

Angus stopped, and patted his leg. 'Ach — my sgian-dubh's in the car still. Will you wait for me?'

Yes, thought Chloe. *You don't need to ask*. He ran back to the car to fetch the knife that would slip into his sock, and Chloe was glad he'd not told her to go on with the others. Then, concerned she was reading too much into things, she took a deep breath as he returned.

He crouched down to arrange the knife, and while he wasn't looking straight at her, she felt she could ask.

'Would you be my first dance?' The words rushed out of her mouth. 'Only, I thought your mum and Hugh would pair up, and I think Holly and Paolo might too . . .'

She could hear her voice tailing off, doubt slipping back into her mind.

'I'd love to. I was about to ask you the same thing. Although I'm a bit rusty.'

And breathe. She did a tiny inner jig. 'You're in luck — Holly, Paolo and I have been training in order to get the edge.'

'Do I need to be concerned you'll show me up?'

She grinned. 'I wouldn't dream of it.'

A sharp gust whipped around the gravel, and Chloe grabbed the skirt of her dress. Her neat hair, which she'd spent a goodly length of time straightening, blew around her face, sticking to her lipstick.

'Drat,' she said. 'Hang on, I need to straighten up.'

Angus leaned in close. 'You look perfect. Come on, before it happens again.'

He held out an arm. Linking hers through it, feeling like a princess, her heart going at an unnatural pace, they approached the door together.

CHAPTER 21

Arriving at the great porch, Holly stared up at the castle and grabbed Paolo's arm. 'This place is incredible,' she whispered.

'I know. And that's the ballroom.' Paolo pointed at a long, low room off to one side. 'I've not been in before, but I reckon it'll be all antlers and crossed swords.'

Holly paused for a second, taking it all in again. 'I'm ridiculously excited. Aren't you?'

'Beyond. I was chatting to someone in the surgery this week who said they've blown the budget on lighting.'

Holly could well believe it. The grounds on the way in had suggested as much. They'd come through the woods, clenching their teeth as Hugh thundered in and out of pot-holes. But once they'd left the forbidding conifers behind, they'd arrived on a large drive surrounded by topiary pyr-amids, all of which had been strung with twinkling lights. Enchanted, Holly had been mesmerized by them, not even noticing the castle.

But as Paolo had pulled her towards it, following Hugh and Fiona, she'd found herself in thrall of Glenalmond itself. The colossal grey building, tall with round turrets at the top, had surely been drawn from the pages of a book. On a vast scale, her cottage could have fitted comfortably in the main porch, and the large windows either side were over six feet high. Like Narnia, it had its own lamp post, which only added to the magic.

Floating through the crisp air came the sound of bagpipes, the piper standing on the steps, serenading partygoers through the door. Holly upped her pace, dragging Paolo along with her, desperate to see what the castle looked like inside. They joined a line waiting to get in, the air buzzing with the anticipation of revelry.

'It's like I've gone from the sublime to the sublime-er,' she said as they got into the entrance hall. It was vast, and she wondered how long it must have taken to build. Or to fill it, for the walls themselves were a monument to history, suits of armour vying with tapestries, crossed swords and taxidermy for attention. Holly could see how Wolfie would fit here. A huge house called for a dog of similar proportions.

'I wish I lived in a place like this,' sighed Paolo.

'I bet Daisy does too. Maybe that's why she's with him.'

'Hell, I'd go out with pretty much anyone if it meant I could come and live here. I'd be especially persuadable if there was champagne every time I stepped foot through the front door and bagpipes to herald my arrival.'

'Same. I'd totally marry someone for a castle like this. I might even give up my job if they asked me to.'

Paolo passed her a glass from a tray being held by a waiter, and clinked his own against it. Holly took a sip, letting the bubbles effervesce.

'And there was me thinking you were a woman of principle,' said a voice behind them.

Holly jumped and spun around. Then she began to feel that excited lightness that had occasionally come to her over recent weeks.

'Greg,' she said, trying to sound casual.

'You look fantastic,' he said. 'And Holly, you don't scrub up too badly either.'

Holly smiled, as Paolo raised his eyebrow. Greg leaned forward and gave Paolo a handshake, then gave Holly a kiss on the cheek. As he did so, he whispered in her ear. 'You look beautiful.'

Heat flooded Holly's body, and she felt herself go red. Aware Paolo was staring at her, twitching with mirth at the exchange he'd witnessed, she decided to talk about something else. 'Have you seen your mother? She was in front of us until a second ago?'

'No, and in fact I ought to find her. Try and see how she is before Angus realizes I'm here and starts making a scene,' he said. 'Paolo, if I may, I'd love a dance with your date for the evening. I'm flying solo tonight.'

'You ought to ask her,' Paolo replied. 'She's an independent woman, as you heard a moment ago.'

With a flicker of smile on an otherwise serious face, Greg said: 'Holly Anderson, would you do me the honour of a dance tonight?'

Even though Paolo was pretending to examine the button on his cuff, and nobody else was paying them one iota of attention, it was as if she were under the spotlight, with all eyes on her. It had to be the champagne.

'Of course,' she said, as calmly as she could.

He gave a nod, and wandered down the corridor to the ballroom. Holly poured the contents of her glass down her throat, making the backs of her eyeballs burn.

'Dear lord, you're as bad as Chloe,' said Paolo, tugging her out of the centre of the hall.

'No, I'm not,' Holly protested. 'Here, pass me another of those.'

She tilted her head at the man with the tray of drinks, and no sooner had Paolo passed one to her than she'd downed half the glass. 'Be honest. Did I look like a complete idiot?'

'It was delightful to watch. You looked utterly adorable. There's a real sheen on you, though.'

'It's only because a question that usually starts off with "would you do me the honour of . . ." ends up with the man on one knee. Ugh — I feel all sticky.'

'Isn't success ninety-nine per cent perspiration?'

'Pipe down. I don't want sweat marks on my silk dress. Anyway, I bet his compliments are like confetti — flung into the wind without much care.'

Paolo pointed a finger at her. 'You're in trouble. You're wondering how you can reconcile your nun's vows with the fact you've got the major hots for him.'

'If I do, it's because I never see him, so he's hardly a real option,' countered Holly. 'When you're a nun, like me, it's OK to fancy a guy you're in no danger of bumping into on the front in Eastercraig.'

It was meant to sound conclusive, but Holly realized she had merely confirmed everything Paolo had said. She gave Paolo a shrug, with an expression that suggested the quandary was frying her brain.

'Come on, let's find the main event,' Paolo said, giving her a sympathetic look. 'Get your mind off that man, if that's possible. And I need to get mine off Ritchie. God — my relationships are ending before they even begin.'

'Ghosting is another reason I don't want flings,' said Holly. 'It's cruel and cowardly. You need to forget him, Paolo. Stop dwelling on him. He was a time-waster.'

Holly followed Paolo into the ballroom, then stopped, paralysed by wonderment. She'd been to smart parties before — university celebrations, the odd corporate dinner with colleagues. But nothing compared to this.

A cat's cradle of golden bulbs had been strung from the ceiling, illuminating the crossed swords that were dotted along the whitewashed walls. At one end of the floor was a collection of round tables, and the other a stage. In the middle was an empty space for dancing, on which couples and groups were chattering to one another. A ceilidh band was warming up on stage, and there was a palpable excitement in the room.

'Do you think this lot know all the steps?' Holly asked Paolo.

'A lot of them, aye. But that's what the caller's for. You're not getting cold feet are you?'

'Me? I rarely get cold feet — you've seen me on a Saturday morning. I'm practically impervious to fear.'

Holly stopped as the caller banged a drum and the chattering died away. Without being asked, the crowd redistributed itself, until everyone in the room was standing around the edge of the dance floor. Through the silence came a sharp clicking of heels, and Holly looked over the floor to see Laird and Lady Glenalmond come to stand before everyone.

The drummer began her beat, and one by one the instruments joined in. Then, with even and confident footwork, they began to dance. Someone clapped in time with the music, keeping up with the enthusiastic fiddle and guitar, the jollity of the accordion and the haunting pipes that whistled the top notes. It was contagious, and before she knew it, Holly was clapping with the rest of the room.

Moira and David Glennis were well practised. Cheerful Moira spun with all the grace of a ballerina, her skirt flying out like a whirling dervish's. David, who until that moment had looked like a placid man, lit up on the dance floor, matching his wife's steps. Soon, they were beckoning people to join them, and before Holly knew it the hall was full of twirling couples, the raucous music of the band rising above the thunder of shoes on the floorboards.

Holly, dragged on by Paolo, found herself dancing with the abandon of a small child, feeling utterly un-self-conscious. She'd worried she'd feel nervous on the floor, towering above people as she did, particularly as she was a relative newcomer to a ceilidh. But it was such an utterly intoxicating sensation, reeling and clapping and being swung in circles like you were on a fairground waltzer, she forgot her fears immediately. She didn't care she couldn't keep up with the steps, or remember who she was meant to be dancing with.

Finally, the tune came to an end and, breathlessly, Holly retreated to a table. It felt as much of a workout as any jogging or paddle boarding session. She grinned at Paolo, who looked as if he felt the same.

'That was so much fun! Like the dance society gone large!' she said, feeling dizzy. 'Although I think my shoes are going to be an issue before long.'

'That's why Chloe recommended flats to change into.'

Paolo pointed over to the other side of the dance floor. Chloe, partnered with Angus, appeared unflustered by the first dance. She had had the sense to wear a neat pair of ballet pumps. Holly gave herself a mental facepalm for deciding against hers.

The caller announced the next song, and the drum started again, its hypnotic beat tempting couples back. Holly watched as Angus led Chloe on to the floor. Her hair had frizzed up, and under the lights it looked like a halo. Angus, a man transformed for the night, waited for the instruction, and then they were off.

'They're amazing!' said Holly. 'He's so nimble on his feet. And Chloe's obviously a pro.'

'You could say they're made for each other,' Paolo replied.

'Do you think it could ever work? He's so stormy, and she's so sweet. What if something happened, and he crushed her feelings.'

'But what if he didn't? Maybe she's exactly what he needs, and vice versa.'

Holly watched. Opposites did attract, after all. And seeing them on the floor tonight, they made a handsome couple. How they'd make the leap from friends to more still eluded her though. Chloe might be confident on a night like this, but most days she'd not say boo to a goose. Or even a gosling.

When the dance ended, she watched the groups depart the floor. Chloe and Angus, chatting with Fiona and Hugh, disappeared out of the door. Presumably they needed to catch their breath, but Holly crossed her fingers Chloe and Angus would find time to talk alone. Ideally in a dark corner, away from prying eyes.

After some more dancing, if what Holly had been doing could be called that, she and Paolo went to sit down once more. But she'd barely slumped back in her chair when she received a tap on her shoulder.

'Are you free for the next dance?'

Greg. She looked around for the right words, even though she knew she only needed to say "yes".

Paolo saved her. He got up and stepped to one side. 'I think I'll potter off to explore the castle.'

'I noticed my brother slipping out, so I thought now was the perfect time to ask you,' Greg said, as Paolo disappeared through the crowds.

He reached out a hand, and Holly took it. 'Doesn't Angus know you're here?'

'I might have kept it a secret,' Greg replied, looking a bit sheepish. 'I know it's cowardly, but I didn't want to miss a party like this.'

'Or cause a scene?' Holly raised an eyebrow.

'Or cause a scene. So if you see him, let me know. Hold on — you're looking sceptical.'

Holly wasn't convinced. Having seen Angus in all his raging glory, she felt it was risky. She had a vision of him charging across the dance floor to fight with Greg, sending guests flying in a tartan tsunami.

'I think you ought to be able to talk things over. You know, two grown men and all that.'

'Maybe. But no time to talk now. Take a deep breath, we're about to start.'

And with a twinkle in his eye, knowing the steps before they were called, Greg began to lead them into the melee.

'I can't remember how to do this one,' Holly said, as he whirled her in great sweeping movements across the floor.

Before he had a chance to reply, Holly found herself facing him, as part of two opposing lines. A couple cantered up and down and disappeared, and before she knew it, she was holding arms with him again, being spun around.

'Enjoying yourself?' Greg asked.

'Yes. I think. I'm not sure. I have two left feet.'

They parted again, Holly desperately trying to make sure she was standing in the right place. When she was reunited with Greg once more, she felt unsteady under his gaze. Hell — she felt unsteady full stop. He put out an arm and spun her in a circle and, now distinctly off-balance, she felt her plait beginning to fly loose, and let out a laugh. As he pulled her back towards him, her heart was racing.

Their eyes met, and Greg grinned. 'You're getting it.' He tucked some strands of hair behind her ear.

'I'm never going to win any medals, but yes,' she admitted, a wide smile on her face.

'We could get a drink in a bit. But I think you should try a few more dances. You're not the type to give in, are you?'

'No! Let's keep going,' said Holly, spurred on.

She wasn't the type to give in, was she. Was she? She could feel her resolve shifting inside her like tremors before an earthquake, precipitating a large-scale disaster. For now, dancing felt like it might keep it at bay.

CHAPTER 22

Paolo stared at the walls. There was a lot of grey stone and simple whitewash. He'd seen the outside of the castle before, and parts of the estate while working with Hugh. But inside was something else. He'd imagined dark wood panelling, burgundy carpets, a stale air of gloom. Not so. While there were suits of armour, grand tapestries and life-sized paintings of long-dead Glennises, it was lighter than he'd expected. Almost modern.

When Holly had formed a couple with Greg, he'd gone for a stroll. Not wanting to interrupt Chloe, who was getting on well with Angus by the bar, he'd slipped off into the belly of the castle.

So far, he'd found a dining room, its table significantly larger than his whole flat, and a comfy sitting room in which a few of the older residents of Eastercraig were having an evening nap. The enormous kitchen, which looked like it was where the Glennis family usually spent their time, had been a hive of activity, catering staff moving about at twice the pace of normal people.

Coming to the end of a corridor, his bearings gone, Paolo pushed tall, heavy double doors to reveal the most amazing library. Aside from a colossal window, books covered the walls, with a ladder on a rail to get to the ones on the highest shelves. In the centre, two squashy sofas faced each other, with heavy tartan blankets draped over the back.

This was it. He had found his spiritual home.

The ancient leather-bound volumes were calling to him, so he walked over to one of the walls, and ran his fingers over the spines. They were beautiful. He pulled one out, opened it and breathed in the delicious scent of musty paper. At this point, if someone had told him he had died and gone to heaven, he would have believed them.

The door opened, and Paolo spun around to see Hamish. 'I'm so sorry. I'm sure I'm not supposed to touch any of these,' he said awkwardly.

He clutched the volume to his chest. Then, afraid he looked like a thief, he replaced it quickly — but carefully — in its rightful place.

'Oh, you're welcome. Browse away,' said Hamish distractedly.

Paolo watched Hamish cross the room and collapse on to one of the sofas, then reach over to a small side table and pour himself a whisky from a crystal decanter. 'Want one?'

'Me?' said Paolo. 'Sure.'

He sat on the sofa opposite Hamish. For a night of absurd glitter and gaiety, he appeared downcast.

Paolo took the glass. 'Is something the matter, Hamish? You seem a bit low.'

Hamish groaned. 'I guess I had a wee argument with Daisy again. I didn't want to hang out with her glossy friends and do shots. They're all a bit . . .' he stopped and waved his hands. 'Shrieky, and shiny. So I've come here to recharge.'

'You didn't fancy the dancing?'

'Och — I'm abysmal. My feet get all tangled up. I'd rather be in a smoking room, chewing the fat.' He glanced at Paolo. '*You* looked like you'd been having lessons.'

Paolo paused, and took another sip of whisky. 'We have. Well, Chloe, Holly and I have been going to a group. We didn't want to look like oafs lumbering around on the dance floor.'

'Well, you looked super. You all did. Although Holly's a little tall for you. Mind you, I didn't think she was your type.'

Paolo let out a laugh. 'Not really. She's a woman for starters.'

'I thought so,' Hamish chuckled. 'But it would have been impolite to ask.'

They shared a look of amusement, and Paolo's instincts suddenly sprung to life — barely only slightly, but there — appearing as a brief thrumming in his chest that had gone as soon as he'd felt it. Was Hamish gay?

He'd not noticed it before. But why would he? Daisy might have been jamming the signals. He'd never been wrong though. In fact, he prided himself on his instincts — as much as he prided himself on his knowledge of Victorian literature, which was a lot.

Weird. It was entirely possible Hamish was gay, wasn't it? Or bi? Maybe Hamish himself didn't know. Or didn't want to know. Paolo's mind spun, but there was no denying the peculiar feeling he'd had.

The door opened, and Holly appeared. 'Hello, you two! We were finding somewhere to sit down.'

Paolo set his suspicions to one side.

Hamish jumped up. 'Come and join us for a tipple?'

'That's kind of you, Hamish,' said Holly.

'Ham! My man.' Greg appeared behind Holly. 'So this is where you've been hiding.' He bounded over to the sofa, giving Hamish a huge hug, then addressed the group. 'Our Hamish's natural habitat is outside but, when the weather is too bad even for him, he likes to retreat to the library to read classic adventure books. Much like he did when he was a wee lad.'

Which ones?' asked Paolo. '*Swallows and Amazons*? *Treasure Island*?'

Hamish poured a drink. '*Harry Potter*.'

'That's *not* a classic,' said Paolo, in mock outrage.

'What are you talking about? It's one of the most famous works of the late twentieth century . . .' He tailed off, as he realized everyone was looking at him. 'Sorry. Let me get you two a glass each.'

'This is a beautiful room,' said Holly, who had sat down next to Paolo. 'Some of these books look centuries old.'

Paolo leaned in. 'It's like *Atonement*, isn't it. And with you in that dress it's doubly like it. If we weren't here, you'd be being seduced right now.'

Holly turned and whispered into his ear. 'Don't be obscene. There's nothing going on with Greg.'

'You're fibbing. The air between you is crackling with passion,' Paolo muttered. 'The guy can't keep his eyes off you.'

'Stop winding me up!'

He shrugged. 'I'm just stating the obvious.'

Across from them Hamish and Greg were chatting. Greg glanced up from whatever they were saying and gave Holly a smile. Paolo reached over to the decanter and topped them both up, ready to carry on ribbing Holly.

Just then, there was a cough, making all four of them jump. There in the doorway, looking unimpressed, stood Angus. Chloe hovered behind him, biting her lip in concern.

'What were you thinking, coming here?' he barked, glaring at Greg.

Paolo looked from one to the other with a sinking feeling. This couldn't be good.

* * *

Holly was unable to take her eyes off the pair as Greg got up and walked calmly over to Angus. It was like watching a meeting of fire and water. Water usually won, right? Her legs tensed, and she shifted to the edge of the sofa.

'You should have stayed away,' Angus growled.

'I'm just as entitled to be here as you,' said Greg, his face betraying no emotion. 'I'm happy to stay away from the farm until you see sense, but anywhere else I can go as I please. I want to see my friends, not to mention Mum.'

'As if you care about her.'

Greg's eyes narrowed, his nostrils flared. 'How dare you,' he said, his voice dropping to a dangerous whisper.

Holly hadn't seen Greg angry before, and it put her on edge. Up to this point he'd been kind, thoughtful, polite — even when she'd been threatening to knock him out with a stool. Nothing but a perfect gentleman. That said, she could see what Angus was saying was provocative.

'How dare *I*?' Angus looked around the room, his eyes glinting. 'If the other people here knew what you were doing, do you think they'd feel the same way about you?'

Holly's heart pounded as doubt crept into her mind. He might have been a serial flirt, but she was sure underneath that Greg was at least a decent guy. She could handle a crush on a ladies' man. But if Greg was a fraudster, gangster or trained hitman, she'd need to rethink.

'I'm trying to help! Can't you see that? Tell them, if you like. You're the one who's acting like an idiot,' said Greg.

What on earth was going on?

Hamish stood up. 'Come on, guys. It's a ball. Why not put your differences aside for the night. Talk business over a brew tomorrow.'

'With all due respect, Hamish, keep out of it,' Angus snapped.

Hamish looked shocked. In the doorway, Chloe's hand flew to her mouth. Holly looked at Greg. He briefly caught her eye, then took a deep breath.

'Angus is angry because I had a meeting with a developer. The farm is struggling and we need to stabilize the accounts,' he said.

Holly looked around the room. Chloe, Paolo and Hamish looked stunned, as if the very idea were criminal. Angus looked so angry his fury could have been bottled and used as an explosive.

'And there's the problem,' he said angrily. 'When our father died, he wanted the farm to stay in our family. Not only did you fanny off to university and Aberdeen, but then you returned with ideas to sell our inheritance. Some of us gave up our chances to study and see the world to care for the place.'

'He never wanted this,' Greg couldn't restrain his annoyance any longer. 'He never would have wanted Auchintraid to be a burden. Or for you to give up on your own ambitions to keep the farm running. You've turned suffering into an art form, Angus, pretending it's loyalty.'

'And you've betrayed your roots. I used to think you were the most amazing guy in the world. My big brother, who I would do anything for. Now you're nothing to me.'

The entire room was transfixed, as if this was a tragedy unfurling on a stage. None of them had dared shift an inch since Hamish had been shouted at. Instead they all watched with horror as the secrets the brothers had been holding in flooded out.

'I think Hamish is right. This ought to wait until the morning,' Greg said.

'Of course you do, you traitor.'

'For heaven's sake,' said Greg, sounding tired.

He made to leave the library, but before he could manage, Angus flew at him and barrelled him over the sofa. Holly leaped to the side, her heart in her mouth, pulling Paolo with her.

'Angus! Stop!' Chloe ran over to the middle of the room. 'What do we do?' she cried at Holly. 'You're tall — pull them apart!'

But Holly didn't know what to do. Angus and Greg were now wrestling, as if they were schoolboys having a playground tiff. Only they were much bigger, and much stronger. So far, neither of them had punched the other, but if someone didn't step in, it mightn't be long. If she did what Chloe said, however, she'd end up with a fat lip.

'Should I find Fiona?' Hamish asked, looking around at them all.

'Christ, no,' said Chloe. 'She wouldn't want to see this.'

The pair were now pulling each other to their feet, locked in a violent dance, like two stags butting heads.

'Stop it, both of you,' she shouted, in as commanding a tone as she could manage.

Angus, holding Greg's shirt, heard her. He turned, and registered the onlookers as if he was seeing them for the first time. Greg, who up until that point had been gripping his brother's shoulders, trying to hold him back, let go. He brushed his hair from his face, and with his arm knocked one of Angus's hands off.

Greg shook his head. 'Sorry, Hamish, everyone. That was uncalled for.' He looked at his brother. 'Let's talk about this tomorrow.'

Angus glared at his brother. 'Fine.'

Holly's shoulders dropped. It was over and, better still, nobody had been hurt, herself and the other bystanders included. She waited for Angus to let go of Greg's collar, the last evidence any ruckus had taken place. Then they could all return to the dance.

But at the last moment, Angus gave Greg a push to get past him. Only it wasn't a gentle shove, but — as far as Holly could see — a knock intended to topple Greg and send him to the floor. If he'd been verbal, Angus would be having the last word.

Unprepared, Greg staggered back and fell on to the side table. There was a tremendous crash as the tray bearing the decanter and glasses smashed into thousands of glittering shards. A collective gasp went up. Angus halted and turned on his way out the door, consternation crossing his face before disappearing from the room.

Holly went and knelt down next to Greg who rolled over and sat up, rubbing his head. Blood trickled down his cheek from a gash in his temple.

'Are you OK?' she asked, examining the wound.

'Pride in tatters, relationship damage with sibling potentially irreparable, but otherwise fine,' he said. 'Hamish, I am *so* sorry. Was this an antique? Can I replace it?'

'I think it's from John Lewis,' said Hamish. 'So not to worry. Say, do you need to go to hospital?'

'I'm fine,' said Greg. 'Chloe, can you go and make sure Angus is OK? Keep an eye on him? Hamish, let me know where a dustpan and brush is? I'll clean this up, then maybe I ought to head home.'

'Please, I'll do it,' said Hamish. 'You go and get some rest. And text me in the morning to let me know you're OK.'

'I'll help,' offered Paolo.

The room emptied, leaving Holly alone with Greg.

'Do you feel at all dizzy?' she asked, still concerned.

'Aye, though I've had a number of drinks and a fight with my brother. It's hard to tell what the root cause is. I think I need to get in a cab.'

'To Aberdeen? It's miles away. Stay at mine.'

Holly thought there was a high chance he might have concussion. If he stayed at hers, she could keep an eye on him. That *was* the main reason, she told herself.

'Are you sure? I feel like I've caused enough trouble this evening.'

'I'm sure. And I can stitch you up too.'

'Wouldn't Hugh think you were squandering vital resources?'

'I have my own emergency kit. Don't tell me I don't know how to live.'

She leaned in to look at the cut. It wasn't deep, but a few Steri-Strips wouldn't hurt.

'If you're sure — that'd be great,' Greg got to his feet. 'You get the coats, and I'll get the cab.'

CHAPTER 23

'Are you sure your eyes aren't about to roll back into your head?'

The taxi lurched along the stony drive back to the main road, back through the acres of dark conifers. At least the driver was less erratic than Hugh, Holly thought.

'I'm fine,' Greg insisted. 'I'm sorry your evening was cut short.'

There was genuine regret in his voice. Holly, even though she'd been enjoying herself, felt better knowing she was going home with him. *Because of the head wound*, she reminded herself.

'I don't mind. I'm not used to heels, and I was getting a blister. I'm not sure I could have danced for much longer.'

'You're lying, but I appreciate your dishonestly. Now, I'm going to close my eyes for a second,' said Greg. 'The left side of my head feels a tad tender.'

By the time they got home, Greg had dozed off. At least, she hoped he had. If not, she had a problem on her hands. She gave him a shake, her body flooding with relief when he opened his eyes.

After paying the taxi driver and opening the front door, Holly directed Greg to the sofa. 'Don't worry. This is going to be much easier than normal because you're not covered in fur.'

'Not my face, perhaps. But under this shirt my chest's hairier than a hairy coo.'

'Stop it,' Holly protested, feeling herself blushing at the thought. 'I need to have steady hands for this, so please don't make me laugh.'

She collected her kit from the cupboard under the stairs and sat down next to him. Greg stayed stock-still as Holly leaned over to examine the cut that ran all the way from the top of his cheekbone to above his eyebrow. Needing brighter light, she pulled the lamp on the side table closer.

Moving nearer with a sterile wipe to clean the wound, Holly felt the cool attitude she usually possessed during a procedure evaporating. She could feel his breath on her collarbone, and she looked down for a second, remembering she was still in her ballgown.

Holly bit her lip, determined to stay professional. Greg didn't wince as she gave the cut another clean for good measure.

'Much pain? Are you OK?' she asked.

'Never better. Say, am I going to get a scar?'

'Hard to know. It's not a deep wound, and I've not spotted any glass in it. With any luck you might escape scot-free, as they say. But don't quote me on it — like I say, humans are not my forte.'

Taking the Steri-Strips from the pack, Holly kneeled up on the sofa and gently applied each one. For all her willing it to stop, her heart was hammering, and she wondered if Greg was able to hear its quickening thud in her chest. Or maybe he could see it. Although that would mean he was looking at her chest. She brought her focus back to the task in hand, then pulled away to examine her work.

It was a neat job. 'Not too bad, if I do say so myself.'

Holly went in for one last look. As she did so, Greg turned his head. It was practically touching hers. Their lips were dangerously close.

'Holly,' Greg said, his voice low.

Holly's pulse quickened, her emotions racing off like a runaway train that was about to jump the tracks. She was frozen to the spot, willing herself to move, but she couldn't. This was madness. This was complete and utter madness. She couldn't do it.

Looking anywhere but at him, Holly forced herself to sit back on the coffee table, and zipped up her medical bag. 'Would you like some water? I might have some with a slice of toast.' She couldn't let anything happen.

Greg cleared his throat. 'I'd love some of both, if you're offering. I can't apologize enough for wrecking your night.'

Holly sensed a hint of disappointment in his voice. And she reckoned it wasn't only about the fight. It was time to change the subject. She paused, then took a deep breath, forcing them both to think about something else. 'Are you genuinely selling the farm off to developers? All that beautiful land.' She stood up and headed to the kitchen, and hunted out the remains of a loaf.

'Do you I think I'd do that?' he asked, and Holly could feel his eyes on her.

Heart still merrily pounding away, she avoided his gaze. 'I don't know. You've dodged the question of what happened with your brother every time I've asked. Why do that if it's not something big?'

'And you've not heard rumours around the village? It's not been local gossip? They'd all loathe the idea too.'

'Angus hasn't said anything, as far as I know. He might hate your guts enough to give them a good punching, but not so much as to shame you in front of everyone who lives here.'

Greg frowned. 'You think I should be ashamed? I'm not the one who's taken his eye off the ball and let the farm run into trouble. I wouldn't be thinking about selling if I didn't have to.'

There was the confession. Holly could only stare at him. 'So Angus is right . . . ?'

'Not necessarily. And not to some massive builder who wants to build a new village. Or a golf course. Or a superstore. Angus has blown it way out of proportion. And there's more to it, isn't there? He said it tonight. Angry I deserted him. Look. Could I have a bite of toast, and maybe a whisky? And then I'll tell you all about it.'

'Sure. Hold on.'

Holly clanked around collecting the wherewithal for a drink, and set it out on a tray with the toast. She felt she was finally getting to the bottom of Greg and Angus's feud.

'Remember I told you about that time I found my old dad down in the kitchen, breaking into a million pieces over the accounts?'

Holly sat down — in the armchair so she wasn't too close him — and handed Greg a plate. 'Yes, and it dissuaded you from taking over the farm.'

'Well, it wasn't the only time it happened. I became a light sleeper, and every so often I would hear him shuffling around. I'd sneak downstairs and look through the door, and see the stress in his face — his dull eyes, his clenched jaw. After he died, I told Mum and Angus I would sort out the finances. Well, they were in a tangle, I can tell you. When I totted it up, the debts were huge. I told Angus, we agreed not to mention it to Mum. Angus, meanwhile, said he would do anything he could to make the farm more profitable, and I believed him when he said he had tried.'

'And I'm guessing he didn't manage.'

'I got busy and started taking on more work. Angus said he was on top of it, and as far as I knew that was the truth. Anyway, end of last year, Mum called me up saying she had found a shocker of an unpaid bill. Angus had told her not to worry, but there was so much to do on the farm Mum didn't think he'd been able to give it enough attention.'

Holly looked at him. 'And she called you to have a look?'

'Exactly. I went to stay for a week, and while Angus was out, I trawled though the mountains of papers he'd bunged in folders. If he was on top of it all, it looked like a haphazard way of managing it. After a couple of days I worked out the farm was no better off than it had been when Dad was alive.'

'What happened when you told Angus?'

'He said it was fine. That farms are often in debt. But I hated the thought it hadn't improved. You know, I think the financial strain was one of the things that killed Dad. He had a heart attack, eventually, out in the fields.'

'I'm so sorry,' said Holly. 'That must have been tough.'

She thought of her own childhood and wondered how her mother had managed not to let her own meagre bank balance worry her more.

'Aye. Harder on Angus, perhaps. He had been such a cheerful soul, and then along with the farm he inherited the moodiness Dad had been famous for. Anyway — I knew unless I fixed the finances, or improved them at least, he might end the same way.'

'Who are you selling the farm to?' asked Holly.

'Jeez! Not you, too!' said Greg. He put his head in his hands. 'I've not agreed to anything. I had a preliminary talk with some developers. You can put ten decent houses on an acre of land, and I told Angus that he could give up two or so acres and then keep the farm safe for the next generation. The instant I brought it up he had a fit and told me that if I sold it there would be nothing left for the next generation. Then he claimed I think about nothing but money. The guy doesn't realize that he's screwing that place up.'

Holly could hear the frustration growing in Greg's voice as he spoke.

'I didn't mean to pry,' she said.

'Och — I know,' said Greg. 'I didn't mean to snap. But it's a real sore spot.'

He reached up and placed his fingers on his stitches again, his eye creasing as he did so.

'Along with that one?' said Holly. 'Can I get you something for the pain?'

'A large cash injection ought to do it,' said Greg, with a wry smile.

'I was thinking paracetamol.'

'Go on,' he said. 'And another glass of water, if I may, please.'

A minute later, Holly set both on the coffee table and looked to Greg, only to realize he was fast asleep. The moment had passed, and she had emerged from her temporary insanity unscathed. Their lips had been *so* close, but — Holly told herself — she had plenty of chaos in her life already without having to add an extra layer of the stuff.

CHAPTER 24

Chloe got out of the car and watched as Angus went round to help Fiona out of the passenger seat. He beckoned her with a nod of his head, so she followed them to the house.

The kitchen was warm, the Aga blasting out heat, and Angus clattered through the cupboards, producing cups and saucers, finally banging a tin of cake down on the table. He went to put the kettle on and Fiona, exhausted after a night's dancing, collapsed on the shabby sofa that ran along one wall of the kitchen and pulled off her shoes. Silence reigned.

The scene left Chloe feeling dreadfully confused. Here was Angus the protector, helping his mother indoors, making tea and setting out sustenance after a night of dancing. But that night she'd also witnessed Angus the destroyer — of tables, at least, thankfully nothing more.

The latter Angus was the one making her doubt her feelings for him. Why did he have to be so fiery? Where his sweet side had gone remained to be seen, but Chloe wondered if Angus had had it removed from his body and flung into the North Sea.

'I'll be back in a minute. Need to change out of all this,' he gestured to his kilt.

'Did you enjoy yourself tonight, Chloe?' Fiona asked softly, as Angus handed her a cup of tea and left.

'I did,' she began slowly.

As she leaned against the counter, she could feel Fiona's eyes on her, and wondered if she was going to ask about the fight. She took a breath, readying some kind words, but Fiona spared her a maternal interrogation.

Fiona sighed. 'I'm appalled you had to witness that. It showed the worst of both of them. I certainly didn't bring them up to behave that way.'

'I know you didn't. And so does everyone else at the party.'

'Do they? Or will they be dissecting my life between dances? Discussing the fact Greg deserted us for the city, and Angus felt lumped with this place?'

'Nobody will be gossiping,' Chloe was keen to reassure Fiona. 'It must be frustrating they've fallen out because, at the end of the day, they're both trying to look after you and the farm.'

Fiona sighed. 'One of life's little ironies, I suppose. And the one person who would have known what to do isn't with us any longer. None of this would be happening in the first place.'

Chloe watched as a tear rolled down Fiona's cheek. She leaped up and snatched a tissue from a box on the work surface, and passed it over.

'Thank you, darling,' said Fiona, taking it and wiping her face. 'Ah look, here's our Angus. I think I'm going to retire. Leave you two to chat.'

Angus stood in the doorway, looking more at ease in a pair of flannel pyjama bottoms and a raggedy jumper. Fiona stood up and gave him a kiss on the cheek, before nudging him to one side and disappearing upstairs.

Angus came and sat down at the small table. Chloe took the chair opposite him.

'Shall I be mother?' he asked.

Chloe nodded and he topped up her tea.

'Talking of mothers, your mum is devastated. Look, Angus, it's none of my business . . .'

'No. It isn't,' he said, a note of caution in his voice. 'But I'm sorry about earlier. I'm not that guy. Not the guy who beats anyone up, and especially not his own brother. Except I am.'

Chloe knew she was pushing it, but after seeing Fiona cry, it was only right to tell Angus what she thought. After all, she'd known him a long time — perhaps he'd respect her opinion. She had a brief flashback to Angus snapping at Hamish, and held on to the table, in case she was blown away by the force of Angus's reaction.

'You need to work something out. You and Greg. Did you not see your mum was crying? It's breaking her heart.'

Angus gave a small shrug. 'What's going to break my mother's heart is seeing this farm disappear. Today Greg's talking an acre or two. But what about tomorrow?'

'I think tomorrow he'll be rubbing his head, wondering how it went so wrong with you. I don't think he wants to destroy the farm.'

'Sure he does. He's a massive sellout. The guy hasn't done an honest day's work since he left for college. Sits on his arse in his air-conditioned office, forgetting any connection he has to this place.'

'You don't really believe that, do you?'

'Aye. Today he's talking about selling off a field. But that's only the start — it always is. Planning will get given, and more developers will come nosing, asking if we're keen to sell more. Auchintraid's been in the family for decades, providing for us and the people of this town. These ancient tracks, these walls, these trees, they are my life. Before that it was our father's pride and joy.'

'Maybe his sons were your father's pride and joy, and if he were here he would rather you weren't throwing punches at one another.'

'I never meant to hurt him.'

The confession was a chink in his armour, a chance for her to probe. To get closer to him, and find out what lay beneath the layers of anger. Maybe a tiny, exploratory prod wouldn't hurt, but on a different tack to begin with.

'Did you want to go to college?' she asked tentatively. She picked up her teacup and almost hid behind it, then lowered it. As if china could ever make an effective shield.

'Me? Uni? Nah. Would have been a waste o' time.'

'Not even agricultural college? That might have been for you. And you could have cut loose.'

Chloe paused as a frown gathered on his forehead, and then the lines relaxed.

'I didn't have time to cut loose,' Angus said, his shoulders dropping. 'Dad died, and someone had to take over. We could have hired someone, but it's *my* legacy. I didn't have time to wait. Maybe it would've been great to go yomping around campus and partying . . .'

'Maybe a tiny bit of you resents Greg for getting that chance. That he got to revel in his youth a little longer. Misspend it.'

Angus met her eyes, and she felt her heart skip a beat. 'Aye. Perhaps.'

There was a pause, and Chloe took another sip of tea. And then another. It was like she couldn't drink it fast enough.

'What about you?' Angus eventually asked. 'You've not exactly gone off to explore the world.'

Chloe smiled. 'I guess not. But I've always been happy here, and after Mum's stroke I've felt the need to stay close. No — I've wanted to stay close. I mean, she got better, but she's never been quite one hundred per cent. Although really I've never wanted to live anywhere else. Sure, I like a holiday, but there's no place like home.'

As she said it, it was as though a cloud covering Angus's head had been lifted. He let out a sigh. 'Aye. I might complain, but there's nowhere else I'd rather be.'

Slowly, Chloe thought, he was shedding the frustrations of the night. Unwinding, piece by piece.

'Slice of toast?' he asked, getting up.

'Do you have marmite?'

'Do *I* have marmite? What a question!'

Chloe laughed. 'Hugh thinks it's an abomination and won't have it in the surgery. He says it's a stain on the good name of spreads. Puts it in a category with fish paste and Nutella.'

'He can keep his fish paste, but he's wrong about the Nutella. The nerve of the man.'

'I'm inclined to agree with you there. Nutella and banana sandwiches are my nirvana.'

Angus turned around. 'OK, Chlo. Your top three things on toast. Go!'

'Marmite, blackberry jam, plain butter. You?'

'Marmite, peanut butter or raspberry jam — home-made. Next: top three dances tonight.'

'Gay Gordons, Strip the Willow, Dashing White Sergeant. I'm old-fashioned, me. Top three cows?'

'There is only one type of coo. And that's a hairy one. Everything else pales in comparison,' Angus said, a note of triumph in his voice.

Toast flew out of the toaster, making Chloe jump. Angus, clearly aware of the machine's cannon-like tendencies, caught a slice in each hand.

'Pass them here, I'll butter them,' she said, reaching over.

His fingers touched hers as he handed the toast over, and Chloe felt a tingly warmth spread through her hands. She put them on the plate, and reached for the butter dish and a knife, and a moment later pushed the plate of buttered toast between them, watching him surreptitiously as Angus gave each piece a scraping of marmite.

His hair, which at the start of the evening had been brushed back from his face, had returned to its normal state: dishevelled, rebelling against all attempts with wax and gel. In fact, now he was out of his kilt and back in a jumper, he looked entirely his usual unkempt self. Chloe preferred it that way. Under the table, his foot grazed hers, and she felt her heart do a flip as he left it resting there. Desperate to distract herself, she reached for some toast and took a huge mouthful. Angus did the same, and for a minute there was silence as they ate.

'I'm sorry if I ruined your evening,' Angus said.

'You didn't,' Chloe placed her toast back on the plate. 'It was lovely. I got some dancing in, sipped some champagne and got to wear my fave dress.'

And got to come back to the farm, she also thought. Spend the evening talking to the man whose image intruded on her thoughts at least ten times an hour.

'You were a dancing pro,' he said. 'But I do mean it — the apology, that is. You deserve better than being back on a lonely farm with me, before the bell has even chimed midnight.'

She shrugged. 'I'm like Cinderella.'

'Aye. Only Cinders had a handsome prince.'

She was aware he was looking at her, and Chloe wished she could say that *he* was her prince. That sitting in the kitchen, their feet touching under the table was — to her — perfect.

'I'm still having a lovely time,' she said, not quite meeting his eye.

'Listen. I've no' got champagne, but would you like a drink by the fire? We can watch a film or something — you love all those old ones, don't you? We've got a few here.'

At this, she finally looked at him again, trying to stop herself from grinning like a loon. 'Sure. I'd like that.'

CHAPTER 25

Wearing his shirt, a pair of black boxers (Holly had studiously looked elsewhere) and a frown, Greg appeared in Holly's bedroom doorway on the Sunday morning, bearing a tray.

He placed it on the bedside table then pointed a finger to the cut on his face. 'I've had a look at this. No wonder you're a high-flyer — if this is what you can accomplish after all that champagne, I can see why sober you're a force to be reckoned with. You're a veritable life-saver and literal face-saver. Legend.'

Warmed by his compliment, Holly had smiled, but — modest as ever, and desperate not to get carried away with the "legend" bit — replied: 'It's grown-up sticky tape. It's not as if I held a needle over a candle and darned it with silk thread.' She laughed. 'But thank you — it's nice to hear someone say it.'

'Hugh still giving you grief?'

'Every single day. No worries though. I reckon I can grit my teeth hard enough to cope.'

A paused followed, before Greg took a deep breath. 'I wrecked your night. I feel like a complete idiot.'

'It's not the end of the world. I could have managed a few more dances. But I'd rather it ended there than in casualty.' All of which was true, and she didn't want to add to his guilt — Greg's remorse was clear.

'Look. Is there anything I can do to make it up to you? Dundee cakes only go so far.'

'If you tell me some of that's for me,' Holly motioned to the tray, 'you'll be making a good start.'

Greg nodded. 'Aye. *All* for you. I got the Sunday papers too, if you fancy a read.'

'Are you not having anything?'

'Had a fight. Slept on your couch. Thought it might be a bit much to assume I can have breakfast here too. I'll clear off in a minute.'

'It's never stopped you before.'

Greg smiled. 'I know. You've been good to me. I'll pass this time, though.'

'But you've gone to such an effort. I can't eat all of this.'

Holly gestured to the tray, hoping she might persuade him. It was groaning with toast, scrambled eggs, a glass of orange juice, the cafetière and the newspaper.

'Go on then. A wee bite,' he said, and poured himself a coffee. 'Thanks.'

Holly took the plate of eggs and began to eat. Greg reached for a slice of toast and covered it with marmalade.

'You are *such* a prat,' Holly said, unable to keep it in any longer.

'I know.'

'I mean, I don't mind. I had fun the rest of the evening. But Hamish, Paolo, Chloe? And your mum? And that mess in the library! Both of you leaving looking like you'd gone ten rounds in the ring! You're grown men!' She felt her exasperation bubbling up.

'It'll keep Eastercraig chatting for weeks,' he said, trying to lighten the tone.

It didn't, and Holly felt even more frustrated, thinking of her own, unsatisfactory family set-up and how she longed for bonds that weren't often stretched to breaking point. 'Listen. Auchintraid is running into trouble. You two need to fix your relationship. If all you do is butt heads it's not going to happen. You were tight-knit before this — don't squander that. The rift will get deeper, and the farm will end up in further debt.'

'I'm trying,' said Greg. 'It's Angus that's the problem. If he won't even be in a room with me without trying to punch me, how are we going to have a sensible discussion?'

'Call in a moderator.'

'Are you joking?'

'No. I'm not. You need someone to umpire you. Who can keep the peace. And possibly who can pull you apart when one of you flies across the table in a rage.'

'Putting yourself forward?'

'Don't be absurd,' Holly rolled her eyes. 'Clearly, your mum is the best person for the job.'

'Dad would have been the best person for the job.'

'Maybe, but you have a mother who functions like a normal human being, which is more than I have. Do this for her. Let her help.'

Holly paused, wondering if she had gone too far. It was none of her business. But then, it also was, because it meant every so often Greg Dunbar appeared in her life, a distraction she could do without. Her mind flitted back to the almost-kiss from last night, and she pursed her lips, trying not to overthink it.

'You're right,' Greg said eventually. 'I'll talk to her. Meanwhile, what are your plans for the day?'

'I was intending to sleep off my hangover, but that forecast storm isn't in full swing yet, so I might go on a run round the cliffs.'

'Sounds nice. Fancy company? I've got my gear at the B&B. Give me ten and I'll be ready.'

Holly froze. Hadn't he said he was going back to Aberdeen last night? Maybe he hadn't. When she'd told him not to go all that way in the cab, he'd not corrected her, not mentioned the B&B. Perhaps he had wanted to stay at hers . . .

Was he being drawn to her in the same way she was being pulled towards him? And had he not fallen asleep, might something have happened? Neither of them had acknowledged how close they had been last night. Noisy thoughts began to race around her head, and she did her utmost to shut them out. *He probably forgot, in the wake of the punch*, she thought. She didn't need to be inventing scenarios in which Greg devised increasingly creative reasons to stay over because he fancied her.

She gave him a put-upon look. 'I thought you were meant to be getting out of my hair. Besides, are you sure you should run after a head injury?'

Greg grinned. 'You've proven you're calm in a crisis. You can step in if need be.'

'I'm a vet, remember. Not an ambulance service.'

An hour later, however, Holly ran along the coast path in Greg's wake. She'd agreed to go but she was regretting it: Greg was a formidable runner. Considering the shape he was in, she had suspected he liked to stay fit, but she was struggling to keep up. She found herself breathing through a stitch that had set in on the third mile, and blamed the scrambled eggs.

'How far are we going?' she said, catching up with Greg.

He had slowed down and was jogging on the spot. 'Too fast for you?'

'No,' she lied. 'I was just asking. I'm fine.'

'You look uncomfortable.'

'Tiny stitch. Nothing another mile won't sort out.'

She put on a burst of speed and ran up the next hill. Keen to leave Greg behind, she powered ahead, taking in deep breaths of the tangy sea air. Before she got to the top, she realized she was feeling lightheaded. Maybe she was dehydrated. Hearing Greg behind her, she turned to check how far back he was. Maddeningly, he was right there, and had barely broken a sweat.

Her competitive streak kicked in, and she made one final push for the top. When she got there, she stood and looked down at Greg, ready to crow. Instead, as he got close, little white stars speckled the scene in front of her.

'Holly? Are you OK?' Through her tunnel vision, he looked genuinely worried.

'Fine. Not taken in enough air,' she said.

'Here,' he put an arm around her. 'We'll pause for a second.'

Holly felt herself leaning into him, putting her head on his shoulder and closing her eyes. As she did so, she could have sworn he was holding her more tightly, his thumb grazing her waist. He felt strong, and she felt an undeniable pull between them. She opened her eyes and her mind began to wander as she looked over Finnen Beach.

'The sea is so clear,' she said. 'You could be down there drinking rum, thinking you were in the Caribbean.'

'Or some cider. That's always a good one for Finnen. Maybe we should go and have a picnic there sometime. I'll take you rockpooling.'

She tried to concentrate on her nun's vows, as Paolo had called them, to little avail. Maybe she needed to think about some of her mother's boyfriends instead. That normally worked. But oh, it sounded so tempting, and she could see herself there with him.

'Sounds . . . Famous Five-y,' she giggled and glanced up at him.

He grinned, looking down at her. 'So will you be entering the Eastercraig Run?'

The spell was broken. She was back to real life. A life, she reminded herself, in which Greg was a serial monogamist at best, and a dangerous heartbreaker at worst. Holly needed to keep him at arm's length. And right now, his arm was *far* too close.

She unpeeled herself from him.

'I'd forgotten about that. When is it again?' she said, determined to look like she hadn't been wrapped up in a momentary fantasy.

'It's usually the first week of September.'

'Are you running it?'

'Why? Think you can beat me?'

'I can try,' she said, even though it would be nigh on impossible to keep pace with him for thirteen miles. 'You're doing it?'

'Seeing as I'm trying to maintain a low profile in town, it's best I don't. Besides, I don't want to show you up.'

'As if,' said Holly, and she nudged him in the shoulder.

'I could train you, if you like. Set you challenges.'

'Ha-bloody-ha. You're the last person I would take lessons from, you smug git,' said Holly, causing Greg to laugh. A raindrop landed on her nose. 'Come on. Let's go home before it pours. Here a single drop seems to be the prelude to a storm.'

They jogged back to Eastercraig. Greg didn't stop to come in before returning to the B&B. Instead, he gave her a peck on the cheek and said he owed her one.

'More than one, I'd say,' said Holly.

'Fine. I owe you two. Maybe even three. Thanks again. I'll see you soon, I hope.'

And with that, he gave a wave.

Holly stood and watched him jog along the harbour to the B&B. She was troubled by how she felt. He was everything she had spent her entire life trying to avoid. And she couldn't wait to see him again.

CHAPTER 26

'I need to inform you there's been a development,' said Paolo seriously. 'Have we got five minutes before the next patient?'

It had been a hectic Monday morning, and there had been little time to discuss the events of the ball. Holly nodded. Something in Paolo's tone made her pause, as if he were going to tell them news that was either utterly wonderful or truly awful. Paolo drew himself up to full height and assumed the air of a prime minister about to announce a national holiday.

But before he could say anything, Chloe shrieked, 'You're finally online dating!'

A smile twitched at the corners of Paolo's mouth. 'More exciting.'

Holly waited. The energy he was radiating made her forget about Greg, and the fact she was utterly dripping wet. She had gone to the shop in a downpour, and had been marvelling at how, even in May, the rain in Eastercraig got you from the side, as well as from above.

'I think . . .' said Paolo slowly. 'I think Hamish is gay.'

'What?' Holly thought of Daisy at the ball, in a slinky sequinned dress.

'Bear with me. Let me tell you what happened after you all left,' said Paolo.

* * *

Paolo looked at the damage on the library floor. It looked for all the world as though a cat burglar had been caught in the act and dropped a sack of diamonds. After a moment, Hamish materialized at his side with a dustpan and brush and together they peered over the sofa at the shattered glass that lay strewn across the carpet.

'Was it really John Lewis?' asked Paolo.

Hamish turned to face him, grimacing. 'Nope. Georgian. It's been said Robbie Burns himself poured a wee dram from that very one.'

Feeling the blood drain from his face, Paolo stared at Hamish. 'Christ! Was it insured?'

'Ach, I'm just messing with ye,' Hamish let out a hoot, leaving Paolo's cheeks to rapidly turn pink. 'Dad got them in Aberdeen in the eighties. House of Fraser.'

'Are you heading back to the carousing after this?'

'Carousing?'

'Carousing: having a wild time. You know this is *your* party?'

'I know what carousing is. But I'm not the party type,' Hamish stared out the window into the darkness.

Hamish swept up then collapsed in an armchair by the fire. Paolo took the seat opposite.

'What type are you then?'

'I'm a beta-male, no — zeta-male, no . . . I'm zeta-snail, but happily so. Outdoorsy, with a preference for a slower pace of life. I'd rather have one or two amazing whiskies than neck a load of rubbish. And I enjoy the quiet of the country, the stillness. Daisy thinks it's a bit bleak out here, prefers the city. All things considered, I don't think we're best suited.'

'No offence, but why are you going out then?' Paolo wouldn't have asked normally but Hamish was being open with him.

'She pursued me. It was nice to feel wanted, even if I didn't think she and I were a good fit. And at first I quite liked it — she's smart, witty, a total knockout, and . . . she's super outgoing, and I felt I needed someone like that. Someone to draw me out. But actually, I think we're too different.'

'Have you ever met anyone you felt was a better fit?'

Hamish considered the question for a second. 'In fact, no. It's always started off well, but eventually cracks have appeared. What about you?'

'To be honest, Eastercraig doesn't have many options. I'm starting to get worried.'

'I can appreciate that,' Hamish said. 'It's a small community.'

'Small indeed. Most of the time, I wouldn't change living in Eastercraig for the world. It's beautiful. But man-wise, this place is sorely lacking.'

'Fabien not coming back then?'

Paolo blinked, then he stared at Hamish. 'How do you . . . ?'

'I knew. A few of us did. But I wouldn't have thought of you as a natural pair.'

Paolo laughed. 'I know. I'm not shiny and in your face.'

'Exactly,' said Hamish. 'Flash Fab . . . Sorry it didn't work out.'

Paolo, emboldened by the openness of the conversation, asked what half of Eastercraig would have done, given the chance. 'If you don't think Daisy's the one, why not end it?'

'Och. I don't know.'

'Come on. You don't *have* to be with the wrong person.'

'Maybe not. But I've never had that thunderbolt moment. I guess I've given up on that idea now I'm mid-thirties and am just hoping to find a companion to muddle along with. Love complicates everything.'

'But it can be wonderful,' said Paolo, unleashing his inner romantic. 'The flush of first love, all the uncertainty, the agony, the ecstasy.'

'And you've had that? Did you get it with Fabien?' Hamish looked at him, 'And has it always been men for you? Or did you ever feel that way with a woman?'

At the uncontrolled barrage of questions, Paolo looked at Hamish, and tilted his head to one side.

* * *

Holly stared at Paolo, taking in the revelation.

'I'd had my suspicions, but at that point it was literally like someone had flown into the room, hung a lightbulb over my head and said "ding",' said Paolo excitedly.

'Get off it,' said Chloe.

'I'm pretty certain he is,' said Paolo. He folded his arms and leaned back on the reception desk.

'While the internet signal in Eastercraig makes me think it's the 1950s here, it's actually not,' said Holly. 'Wouldn't he be out? He's in his thirties, right?'

'Holly's right. I know he can be quiet, but he's never shown even an inkling,' Chloe continued. 'I've never seen him with a guy *or* heard him mention one.'

'It's a small town. You could be forgiven for keeping things to yourself here. Anyway, we carried on talking about it. About all the loves of our lives — his all sounded a bit rubbish, because he's gay, obvs. Or bi. Or something. And then we ended up talking about books. He's invited me back to come and look at the library again.'

'As if Hamish is gay,' Chloe snorted. 'Wishful thinking on your part, Paolo?'

'What? You think that because I can't find a date I'm now just fashioning gay men out of straight ones? I've sworn off dating, as you well know. Besides, he's not my type.'

Holly watched the conversation ping-ponging to and fro. She didn't know Hamish well enough to offer an opinion. But it didn't matter — it was entertaining enough watching Paolo and Chloe argue about it. It was a bit of fun in an otherwise driech — Chloe had taught her the word, meaning wet and dreary — day.

The front door swung open, and Hugh appeared on the doormat, his mac billowing up like a parachute. Holly pushed the door shut behind him, fighting the force of the gales that seemed determined to stop her.

'Why are you all bloody standing here? Haven't you got anything better to do?' he barked, wiping the rain off his face.

Chloe took his coat from him. 'Mrs Cromarty is going to be late because of the inclement weather, and Tony Pennington cancelled the guinea pig neutering. He doesn't want to drive in all this stoating rain.'

Hugh harrumphed and made his way to the surgery door. 'Bunch o' ninnies, the lot of them. You three need to find something useful to do. Holly, why don't you delegate some jobs? If you want that bloody recommendation letter you need to show some nous.'

Holly could think of a few things needing doing, but she hardly wanted to boss her friends around. Then again, as Hugh's eyes bored into her like red-hot lasers, she thought it best to come up with a couple of meaningful tasks.

'Paolo, can you please check the drugs, and Chloe, please chase the stationery order. I'll go after the outstanding invoices,' she said.

'Good,' Hugh nodded, and disappeared down the corridor, but not before he could bellow: 'And somebody fetch me a bloody tea.'

'Blimey. He's extra snippy today,' Holly lowered her voice, not wanting to get caught out. 'And we barely scratched the surface of the weekend's goings-on.'

'I'd say he's increasingly worse,' said Paolo. 'Bouncing up and down like a rubber ball. I'm off to the drugs closet, and while we're talking of closets, I *would* put money on Hamish being gay.'

He disappeared, and Chloe handed over a long printout of outstanding invoices. Picking up the spare phone, Holly sat down and prepared to start dialling. It was never her favourite job, chasing debts. She remembered the pit-of-the-stomach feeling of wondering if there was enough in her current account to pay for things as a student.

She scanned it. There were a few big bills [illegible] she ought to prioritize those. Honestly, Hugh's accounting was utterly dire. As she got down the page, her eye was caught by the name "Dunbar".

Holly pictured herself walking along the coast path with Greg, running through the grass to Finnen Beach, where they'd chase each other into the shallows. Then they would sit down on a picnic blanket, sharing a rug over their shoulders to keep warm, and fall upon a hamper of delights. Only they wouldn't eat it because they'd be too busy staring at each other. And then they would fall upon each other, and . . .

Holly chided herself, knowing if she was going to run a practice, cash flow was high up the admin list, and fantasy romantic liaisons didn't feature at all. She dragged her gaze from where she been staring out at the waves, and back to the paper in front of her.

Not long into the task, her phone buzzed. A message from Judith.

> *How are you, Holly? Catch up soon? Maybe we ought to schedule a halfway conversation with Hugh in June for an interim report. Call if need be. J*

Ha! An interim report? If Hugh gave her anything less than short shrift on that she would be blown away. She had to worm her way out of this. Honestly, between the weather and Hugh and Judith's suggestion of a check-up, today was not working out for her.

> *We're really busy. All going well. Is a halfway conversation really necessary? Think everything fine. Holly*

She held her breath.

> *Glad to hear that. Maybe I'll just have a quick chat with Hugh at some point. Ring him and see what he thinks. J*

Holly wasn't sure if that was better or worse.

CHAPTER 27

Holly thought she was getting the hang of things, Hugh included, although she imagined she would later kick herself for thinking that was the case. One lunchtime, on a sunny June day, when Hugh was out on a call and Holly was just tidying up, the bell on the front desk rang. She wasn't expecting anyone but, as Chloe and Paolo were out, she made her way to reception. There in the waiting room stood Gordon Laurence, a giant of a man with windswept grey hair and a weathered face, a floppy-looking collie under his arm.

Holly paused. Gordon kept sheep on a farm outside the town and — according to Chloe — rivalled Hugh for bad-temperedness. He and Hugh were good friends, and Holly wondered if they had an in-joke running as to who could make the most aggressive-looking face when greeted.

'How can I help you, Mr Laurence?' she asked.

'Tess fell in a rabbit hole while we were out in the fields. She's limping, and whimpers if I touch her leg,' said Gordon through thin lips, his habitual frown in evidence. 'Is Hugh in?'

'He's on a call,' said Holly. 'I can see to Tess.'

'I'd rather have Hugh,' Gordon muttered. 'Hugh knows what he's doing.'

Trying to disguise her annoyance, Holly held out her arms. 'If she's in pain, it's best we see her as soon as possible.'

With a look of resignation, Gordon passed Tess over. Holly carried the dog through to the consulting room, put her on the table and started examining her, giving her soft coat a gentle stroke.

The door to the consulting room swung open, and Hugh looked from Gordon to Tess, and then to Holly. 'Everything OK?'

'Poor Tess here's broken her leg. I'm going to sort her out now, admit her for general anaesthetic so we can X-ray and cast it. Mr Laurence, we'll keep her in overnight, give her painkillers, but she ought to be fine to be picked up in the morning.'

'Thank you, Ms Anderson,' said Gordon. He smiled at Holly, in a gurning way that Holly took to mean it was an unusual effort for him.

'Holly, I'll call Paolo back in and you can begin,' said Hugh. 'Gordon, you're welcome to stay but we can take it from here.'

Through the door, she heard Gordon saying: 'Don't know what you've been talking about, Hugh. The lass seems perfectly competent.'

'She has her moments.'

Well, that was practically a compliment.

* * *

But, as Holly had feared, Hugh's approval — as ever — was a fad. One Friday night after a heavy week, Hugh erupted in spectacular style and, like Vesuvius, he was flattening everything in his path.

'Don't you think I've got enough on my bally plate?' he said, thumping his cup on the reception desk so hard tea sloshed out.

Holly watched Chloe mop the mess up with tissues then carefully remove herself from the waiting room into the kitchenette. Holly envied the safe haven.

She took a breath, wanting to give a considered response. What she'd done was perfectly reasonable: she'd heard about a sheep farmer a little further away who wanted to move to a new surgery, and had made an approach. In Holly's eyes, it made business sense, as it ensured another potential income stream for Hugh.

'Like I said, it's more revenue for you. I don't see how that's an issue!'

'But once you're gone, who'll handle it? It's extra accounting.'

'You'll be getting a new locum, won't you?'

'For God's sake, woman! Sometimes you make me rue the day I agreed to hire you.'

'I'm trying to help!' Holly said, as levelly as she could.

At this, Hugh growled then huffed off down the corridor. Holly collapsed in Chloe's chair, but almost as soon as the door had clicked shut, it opened again. Holly braced herself for another tirade — like most volcanoes, with Hugh's tempers there were usually leftovers to be spewed out. Thankfully, it was only Paolo.

He put his hands on his hips. 'Can you not get to the end of a week without sending the poor man into spasms of rage?'

'I suggested a way to make money. Won't make that mistake again,' Holly replied gloomily. 'I'll have jeopardized my reference there . . .'

'Pub in ten?'

Paolo already had his parka on. It was tempting, but the latest bout with Hugh had made her feel tired, and in want of a warm bath and an early night.

'I might go home. I'm shattered.'

'Boo. Not even a swift one?'

'No, but I'll be up for a paddle tomorrow, if you want to join?'

'Count me in, if I'm not utterly hanging. And remember, Hugh has his ways. He might come round to it over the weekend. Wait and see.'

Chloe peered out of the kitchenette. 'Sure you can't be tempted to the pub? Might take the edge off a bit.'

Holly rubbed her temples. 'Neither of you have this effect on him.'

'We've learned how to handle him,' said Chloe. 'Although he is noticeably grottier with you. Much worse than with Bronwen, the last locum who was here.'

'Did she quit or did he fire her?' asked Holly. She envisaged Hugh chasing her off down the main street, wielding a scalpel.

'Hugh yelled her to death . . . kidding. Bronwen went back to work in Edinburgh,' said Paolo. 'I think she'd landed here with grand ideas about living in a hobbit house off the grid and soon realized she missed the comforts of the city . . . And she couldn't hack MacDougal.'

Holly managed to laugh, in a strangled way. 'Well, he's not getting rid of me that easily. Whatever it is he doesn't like about me, he's going to have to lump it,' said Holly, expressing her resolve with a determined tone, even though inside she felt like the cracks were deepening. She had only made it halfway through the year.

'Are you *sure* you don't want to come to the pub?' Paolo raised an eyebrow. 'Couple of tequila slammers will see you right as rain.'

'Thanks again,' said Holly. 'But I'm going to double-check the rest of the book before an early night. How can Hugh be annoyed at me after that?'

'If you change your mind, you'll know where to find us,' said Chloe, pulling her coat on.

Paolo opened the door to the sound of hushing waves, letting in the mild sea air. Holly waved them goodbye quickly, before getting some tea from the kitchenette.

Sitting down in front of the computer, she took the folders out from under the desk and started going through the books. It might have been repetitive and simple work, but for someone who had a sharp eye for their finances, it was immensely satisfying. If Holly could get all the stuff on to spreadsheets, it would make life so much easier for whoever took over from her. Perhaps, if she caught him on a good day, Hugh might be persuaded to invest in some accounting software. Or a new calculator at the very least. She smiled at her own joke.

And, speak of the devil, at that moment, Hugh appeared over her shoulder. He clicked his tongue as he examined the screen. Holly braced herself.

'Judith said you were diligent,' he said. Then he took a deep breath. 'My wife used to do all this stuff. She had an excellent head for numbers.'

Holly looked at him and instead of seeing an angry man, saw a widower, adrift without his soulmate.

'I don't mind it,' she said gently. 'I like having everything in order.'

'And I do too, only I'm not very good at it. Dorothy could pick them up, and out of chaos came order. God, I miss that woman.'

'What happened to her?' Holly asked.

Hugh's face softened, and he leaned against the back wall. Holly spun her chair round to face him. 'Cancer, it was. Three years ago.'

'I'm sorry, Hugh. It was just the two of you, right?' Holly asked. Paolo and Chloe had told her all about it, not long after she had arrived, but she had never asked Hugh himself. The moment had hardly presented itself.

'Indeed. We never had children. It didn't happen for us. A shame, but we were happy together. And we have our lovely niece, Skye. She's my sister's daughter. Lives in Edinburgh now but used to come up here every summer. She used to get packed up here as a teenager to keep her out of trouble.' Hugh chuckled.

Holly took a momentary step back from her opinions about Hugh. It was the first time he had ventured to tell her anything about his private life, and for a second he was human, rather than an alien beamed down from Planet Fury.

'Any plans for the weekend, Hugh? Working on the *Dorothy-Jo*?'

Hugh smiled at the thought of his boat. 'Aye. She's looking wonderful. Maybe apply a coat of paint if there's a gap in the weather. You?'

Holly thought Hugh could apply a coat of paint to the walls in reception, but knew better than to wind him up again.

'Might go for a run. Try to relax.'

'Sounds like a good idea. Just make sure you get this all sorted.'

Of course, Hugh couldn't leave on a positive note.

* * *

Back in the cottage, Holly pulled the practice laptop out of her bag, vowing to do one last hour before a box-set binge. As she opened up the spreadsheets, her phone rang.

Dear lord! It was Greg! Not simply texting, but calling. *Keep it together, Anderson*, Holly said to herself. *It's just a man. A handsome man who might be trying to lure you into his bed, who makes you melt as soon as you see him. You have to resist.*

'Holly! How are you?'

Trying not to sound too excited, Holly pushed the laptop away and curled her legs up beneath her. 'Fine. Doing some work.'

'Not in the pub with Chloe and Paolo? It's a Friday night, isn't it?'

'I didn't fancy it.'

'Well, I for one am glad. It means you answered your phone.'

'Hang on.' Suspicion crept into Holly's mind. 'Are you about to ask if you can sleep on the sofa?'

'Why would you think that?'

'It's the basis for our friendship, isn't it? You're not on the doorstep, are you?'

A thrill ran up her spine at the thought of him saying he was outside with a bottle of wine, ready to come and crash at the far end of the couch. She had recently taken to shaving her legs on a Friday morning in case he showed up unexpectedly.

'I like to think there's a bit more to it than that.'

'Hmm, sometimes I'm not so sure.'

'You have a point,' he said. 'And the reason I'm calling is to suggest something to make up for it. I don't want to be the man who breaks into your house, or requires your steady-handed needlework, and then buggers off in the morning.'

'Thanks for acknowledging it, at least.'

Greg laughed. 'Would you like to go to a supper club next weekend? There's one at the Old Lookout, which is about forty-five minutes along the coast. I rang earlier and they had two tickets left.'

Any last frustrations at Greg's unpredictable comings and goings disappeared without a trace.

'I'd love to,' she said, and pinched her leg to make sure she hadn't fallen asleep and was dreaming the invitation up.

'Phew. I'd hoped you'd say yes, because I've already taken the liberty of buying the tickets.'

'What time, and what kind of place is it? As far as I can tell, the dress code up here is either jeans and jumper, or black tie.'

'Smart casual, but make sure you've got a jacket and your wellies in case the track's muddy. It starts at 7.30 p.m. with drinks, so I'll get you at 6.45 p.m., and drive us home afterwards.'

Holly's pulse raced. This was an actual date, in all but name. Now she found herself glad he wasn't on her doorstep, so he didn't see how ridiculously widely she was grinning.

'Looking forward to it,' she said. 'See you then.'

'Night,' said Greg. 'Sleep well.'

'You too. Night.'

With a yawn, Holly stretched her arms into the air, and did a quick double air punch for good measure. Wait — had she done that? She looked up to where her fists were raised above her head. Yes. It would appear she had. *It's just a crush*, she told herself quickly, lowering them. *Nothing you can't handle.*

* * *

Paolo had gone to the bar, leaving Chloe alone with her thoughts. To be honest, she had nothing to offer to the conversation that night. She'd not seen Angus since the day after the ball, and it had been weighing heavy on her mind.

After a night spent watching *Casablanca*, talking for hours and falling asleep on the sofa, Chloe had been given a lift home by Angus and subsequently spent the day after the ball floating around on a cloud of happiness. So, they hadn't kissed, but she had felt closer to him. Closer than ever. He had told her he would see her soon, and Chloe had been beyond overjoyed.

Since then, though? Nothing, bar a couple of texts to see how she was. Hardly special. And she hadn't seen him in person once. That wasn't completely out of the ordinary, because he was often busy on the farm, but she usually saw him once a week or so. If he had been into town, he had been invisible. Or perhaps *she* was invisible. Like a ghost. Hang on — had she been ghosted? If it could happen to an urbane fox like Paolo, it could certainly happen to her.

'Cheer up, Chlo. It might never happen,' called Rory MacShane, a fisherman who'd tramped in.

So accurate was Rory's unwitting insight, Chloe didn't even bother to smile. Paolo elbowed his way back through the crowds and pushed a glass of wine towards her.

She grabbed the drink and took two huge gulps, awaiting sweet intoxication. 'It's been so long. He's hardly been in touch.'

'He's probably busy. The guy works all hours — you know how much he's got to do.'

'Oh, pipe down,' said Chloe. She felt her face crumple.

'Hey,' Paolo leaned in. 'Come on. You've not seen him, that's all. No need to cry.'

Chloe looked down, her cheeks getting all hot. Her fringe was sticking to her forehead.

'Paolo. It's not going to happen. Fetch me some crisps, now! All of them.'

Before Chloe knew what was going on, Paolo was leaning over and wiping her face with a tissue. Then he was straightening out her hair. 'Not if you sit here crying about it.' Then suddenly, 'Hey, Angus!' he called. Then, lowering his voice, he whispered: 'Now smile. He'll never say yes if you're a grump.'

'Say yes to what?' she hissed. Just in time, she looked up and saw Angus standing there. Swallowing a gasp, she managed to say: 'Oh! Hi there. How've you been?'

Angus pulled off his jacket before crashing down on a spare stool. 'I'm good. Coos are good, so I'm good. If you'd ever asked me at school if my mood could be swayed by a herd of cattle, I'd have laughed. But look at me now. How are you both?'

'Fine. Discussing the upcoming run,' said Paolo, getting up. 'About to get another round in, too. What'll you have?'

Angus surveyed the table in front of him. There were two full glasses on the table. As if it were normal behaviour, Chloe picked hers up and drank the contents in three large mouthfuls.

'Same again for me,' she said, and raised an eyebrow at Paolo.

It was so obvious. If he hadn't realized already, Angus would know it was a ruse.

'Chloe thought you'd be up for it,' said Paolo. 'Back in a sec.'

He disappeared towards the bar. Chloe looked to Angus, nerves making her feel like a giant jelly, praying she'd be able to string a sentence together without a wobble.

'The half-marathon?' Angus asked. 'You thought *I'd* want to do it?'

Bloody Paolo! There was nothing for it. 'Maybe. Holly and Paolo are running and I might join them. What do you think? Keen?'

'I'm less track. More field.' He grinned.

'Very funny. But would you like to? I'm game if you are.'

She was game. Oh-so game. Especially if he was.

* * *

From over by the bar, Paolo watched Chloe for signs of success. Or panic. It was hard to tell in the low lights how flustered she was.

'Paolo!' A hand clapped him on the back. 'What are you having?'

He turned to see Hamish next to him.

'Hamish!' he said, as they shook hands. 'It's my round. Say, you're in a good mood.'

Hamish rocked back and forwards on his toes. 'I've broken up with Daisy. I feel light as a feather. Mine's a whisky, please.'

Paolo put in the order and looked Hamish up and down. 'I can see that! You're not exactly moping.'

He was springier than usual, bouncing about on the balls of his feet like a spaniel with a stick.

Hamish looked shame-faced for a second. 'Ought I be in mourning?'

'Dunno. How upset was Daisy?'

'I'd say she was annoyed more than anything. If I didn't know better, it was because I'd pipped her to the post. She said, "You know I'm a great catch," and I said, "So's a twenty-inch trout, but you still have to throw them back."'

Paolo guffawed. 'I'm guessing she didn't like that.'

'She said, "If you love fish so much, why don't you marry one, you tweed-encased twot?" and stormed off.'

They began to chuckle as Mhairi plonked a round of drinks in front of them. Unable to stop, Hamish began to weep with laughter. Paolo felt his shoulders start to shake — it was contagious.

'That'll be £12.80,' Mhairi said. 'What's so funny?'

'Hamish broke up with Daisy,' Paolo wiped a tear from his eye.

He paid as Mhairi stared at them. They leaned against the bar a second, allowing the last of the hysterics to leave their systems.

'Want to come and join us at our table?' Paolo asked, finally getting over his giggles.

'Don't mind if I do,' Hamish replied. 'I'm seeing Ferdie, and he's not due for a bit, but I was so happy I came early for a celebratory tot.'

'And then out on the town?'

'Are you kidding? I am going to enjoy a well-earned break from the opposite sex.'

There it was! There was a subtext in what Hamish was saying, wasn't there? It was *so* obvious.

CHAPTER 28

Holly wriggled into a yellow cotton halterneck dress. It was summery, but pretty glamorous, especially compared with the leggings or jeans Greg usually saw her in. Underneath, though, she had on a pair of large, intentionally boring pants. It wasn't as if Greg would be venturing there tonight. She didn't want him to, after all . . . did she? The voice inside Holly's head sounded doubtful and she searched for some conviction.

A knock sounded, and Holly ran downstairs. She ran across the floor and skidded to a halt, shifting from side to side in order to achieve the perfect "relaxed" pose before opening the door.

Greg stood there without a coat, the evening was mild. 'You look gorgeous,' he said, and gave her a kiss on the cheek.

Any remaining resolve deserted her instantly. Turning around to hide how flustered she was, Holly grabbed her denim jacket off the coat hook, pulled it around herself then headed outside.

'Do you want me to shut the door?' Greg called.

Holly looked back. She had left it wide open. The man was causing her to lose her grip on reality.

Greg drove them up the hill out of the town and on to the main road. The evenings were light now, and the sky tonight was dotted with pink candy-floss clouds. Holly wound down her window to watch as the sun gave the gorse an ethereal lustre. On the edge of one of the fields, she spotted some of Gordon Laurence's beehives, and remembered she needed to bring some money for the honesty box next time she came running. During a recent visit to the surgery with Tess, he had told her about his hives and that he ought to have a decent stock of honey soon.

'So what's this place all about?' she asked. 'I tried to find it online, but their website is like a front.'

Greg glanced at her and grinned. 'It's highly secretive.'

'Come on. Give me some clues.'

'I've not got many to give. I know it's all locally sourced, so it'll be top-notch. The couple who run it do it as a sideline. She's an architect, and he works in oil — he's a client of ours, and mentioned it a few months ago.'

'And the place? The Old Lookout? I found pictures of that.'

The photographs were of a small white building next to a pebbled beach, alone but for some seagulls, wheeling through the sky. It was surrounded by grass, which gave way to dunes. Holly could almost feel the grains of sand between her toes as she imagined walking down to dip her feet in the water's edge, then meandering through the shallows with Greg, her hand in his. Oooh — she *had* to stop the incipient fantasies.

'Ah yes. It's a bothy, albeit a privately owned one.'

'A bothy?'

'They're like rest cabins for walkers or campers. Sometimes it's a bit cold to camp, and the bothy is a shelter. Anyone can use them. Kirsty and Rod got permission from the owners to do a couple of nights here.'

'So it's like a campsite?' Holly tried to get her head around it all.

'Not exactly. There's no running water or electricity. And they're often pretty isolated. It's a great way to spend a holiday. Angus and I went on trips together when we were younger. We'd eat beans all weekend, and hike up hills.'

'Hang on, go back. There's no hot water or heating?'

Greg laughed. 'They've got portable generators, and a loo now. It'll be positively luxurious. A far cry from the ancient camping stove we used to take.'

'Did Angus want to go to uni?' Holly asked, aware she'd abruptly changed the topic of conversation. 'And did he feel like he missed out because your dad died?'

They had clearly been so close, and it made it even harder to understand their feud. She felt her pulse quicken as she awaited a reply, but there was silence. As it persisted, Holly wondered if and when Greg would shut her down.

'I think so,' he replied at last. 'But he loved the farm more than I did, being out in the wild, and I guess when Dad died there was nothing for it but to get straight to it.'

'It must have been hard on him.'

'Aye. He had always been Dad's wee shadow, trailing around the farm after him. It must have been hard, not having Dad around to ask for advice.'

'Did he ever talk about it to you?'

'Nah — not really. We soldiered on for Mum's sake. But I could sense the weight on his shoulders. And that he missed having Dad there.'

Holly brushed a strand of hair out of her face. 'You should talk to him about *that* first. Then the development.'

Greg kept his eyes on the road. 'If he'd let me.'

'Could he take some time out now? He's still young. You could get a stockman in to look after the herd day to day.'

'I don't know if he would. Anyway, I couldn't persuade him to go. He'd worry in his absence I'd give the go-ahead to a giant retail park or something.'

The land sale. As someone who wasn't going to live in Eastercraig for ever it hardly affected her, but she could see why Angus was bothered by the idea. Aside from that, it was such a beautiful spot, isolated and untamed. It would be a shame to build on it. Holly wasn't going to say that to Greg, though. He wouldn't appreciate her input if it sounded like she was siding with Angus.

'Hey — you never talk about *your* dad. Or your mum, really. What are they like?' Greg asked.

Holly bit her lip. He *had* told her about Angus and their dad and the land sale.

'Dad left before I was born. To be honest, I think he left the day after I was conceived, if you catch my drift,' Holly said. Telling him felt OK, and she continued. 'And because Mum went off the rails a bit when it came to men, I never got a decent replacement father figure either,' she said.

He turned his head quickly. 'Och, that sounds hard. Your mum had a few boyfriends, then?'

'Many, many boyfriends. Each one more of a feckless moron than the last,' Holly said.

She detailed some of her mother's worse moments, starting with Dan Glossop, who she renamed "the bogeyman" because of his habit of picking his nose at the table, and ending with the time her mother had got drunk after breaking up with Scooby Benton, and set her apron on fire while tearfully trying to make chips. Thankfully, Holly had got in from school at that moment, and had managed to help put it out before any harm was done. And Gavin. She told him about that too. Holly told the stories in a jokey tone — which she always did because it helped her not get upset by it all — but Greg looked horrified.

'Not what a child needs, is it,' he said.

'Not really. I mean, she tried to be a good parent. Well, sometimes. She just always got distracted by the weasels she went out with.'

'That sounds tough, Holly.'

Holly looked at Greg. Given the number of boyfriends her mum had had, Holly had developed pretty reliable instincts about men, and what they wanted. It occurred to her that, for all Paolo and Chloe's words of warning about Greg, her gut had never told her to run from him. She didn't get the bad vibes with him that she used to feel whenever her mother turned up with her newest boyfriend.

Before either of them could say more, they rolled off the road and headed towards the neat little building, its windows aglow with the reflection of the sun's golden light.

'Is this it?' Holly asked. 'It certainly feels like we're a long way from anywhere.'

Greg reversed into a space. 'It is. And please, can we not talk about the feud for the rest of the night? It's nice to tell someone about it, but this evening is about having a good time.'

Holly laughed. 'Sure. But only if we don't talk about my mother's boyfriends. Let's keep it upbeat.'

'Deal,' said Greg. 'Hey — this looks great!'

Up close, the bothy was not much larger than a double garage. Strung between the door and a couple of spindly trees in front were lines of fairy lights, ready for nightfall. A brazier sat beneath them, around which were arranged log benches draped with heavy sheepskins and blankets, for when the temperature dropped.

Greg offered her an arm — the track through the grass was uneven — and she took it, not wanting to slip.

Before they had a chance to knock, the door opened. 'Greetings,' said a slim man with neat hair and horn-rimmed glasses. 'Ah! Greg Dunbar. Good to see you. And you must be Holly. I'm Rod.'

He pulled them in, and without Holly noticing it getting there, she discovered she had a tumbler in her hand. 'A Twilight Bramble,' said a petite woman with a short afro, who had materialized next to Rod. 'I'm Kirsty. Here, let me take your coats.'

As Kirsty spirited them away, Holly looked at the room. It was tiny inside. At one end there was a square table with benches. At the other, Kirsty and Rod had set up a tiny bar and kitchen area, leaving a small space for milling about in the middle. Greenery had been brought in to decorate above the widows, and garlands of dried flowers were draped around the walls. Strands of bulbs were suspended from the ceiling, bathing the room in a bewitching glow.

'Look up.' Greg nudged her. 'If you came to stay here, that's where you'd sleep.'

At either end of the building, in the roof space, were two mezzanine levels, each big enough to hold two people.

'How do you get up there? Even someone your height would need a ladder.'

'There's probably one somewhere. Or you use sheer determination,' said Greg. 'These are great, aren't they? Shame I'm driving. I'll just have to exert a little self-control.'

He tapped his glass, and Holly nodded. The combination of whisky, berries and sugar was delicious and dangerous, slipping down easily. One more and she'd be drunk.

By the time it came to supper, Holly felt wobbly. Worse than that, she felt loose-tongued. The second bramble had indeed been her undoing. And who cared? She was here to have fun. Rod corralled the group to the table. Holly was glad to see they'd not mixed the guests up, and that she was on a corner, with Greg round the next side of the table.

Conversations bubbled alongside the din from the kitchen corner. The other side of her was one half of an older couple. He introduced himself as Sven Sinclair, one of Kirsty's architect colleagues. 'My mother is Swedish, and my dad's from Dundee,' he explained, peering over his arty, yellow-framed glasses. 'I always get asked, so out of habit I now tell people first.'

'What kind of buildings do you design?' asked Holly, intrigued.

'All kinds. On the whole, I take commissions for people who want architect-designed homes, but I'm trying to move the business towards sustainable opportunities for our clients. I'm particularly interested in building housing into the existing environment, so it melts into the landscape.'

A light pinged on in Holly's head. 'You need to talk to Greg. You know, for general interest purposes.'

'Your boyfriend?' Sven looked to Greg, who was talking to the woman next to him.

Holly blushed. 'We're friends.'

'Really?'

'Really,' said Holly, as firmly as she could manage.

'But you make such an impression as a couple.'

Did Sven have no shame? Perhaps he had an open, Scandi approach to relationships. Holly squirmed like a worm as she searched for a way to dodge the question. Thankfully, she was saved from having to tell him anything else by the arrival of the starters. In front of her was placed a bowl of steaming mussels in a light, buttery sauce.

Greg leaned over to speak in her ear. 'Apparently they harvested these from out in the bay this morning.'

Holly turned to face him. He was tantalizingly close. 'Amazing.'

She popped one in her mouth, but before she knew it, butter was dribbling down her chin. Fumbling for her napkin, Holly nearly gasped as Greg picked his up and wiped her chin. Feeling Sven's gaze on her, she glanced over her shoulder, where she caught him giving her a raised eyebrow. And if raised eyebrows could talk, this one would be saying "who are you kidding?"

Her cheeks burning, Holly turned back to Greg. Thankfully, the candlelight ensured he couldn't tell.

'Thank you,' she said primly. 'They're pretty tricky to eat politely.'

He looked unfazed. 'But worth it, aren't they? You'll not get them so fresh unless you pick them yourself.'

'Now I'd like to try that. I could take the paddle board out to collect some.'

Greg looked at her. 'That's not a bad idea. We could go out and forage for them round the headland. Or past the farm. You know they're an aphrodisiac?'

We?

She gulped, searching for something to say. 'What is it about ugly seafood and aphrodisiacs? Oysters too. They all look like vaginas!'

Dear Lord! That was the worst thing she had ever said. Desperately, Holly tried to halt the fluster that was overtaking her.

'How's your starter? Let me top your drink up,' said Rod, coming to her rescue.

Holly jumped, not having realized he was behind them. 'Yes please! We were saying these were delicious. And an aphrodisiac, too. Apparently.'

Kirsty appeared next to her husband. 'We've inadvertently planned a rather sexy menu,' she said, a twinkle in her eye. 'Fresh loch-caught salmon next, which is also said to raise temperatures.'

After topping up everyone's drinks, Rod and Kirsty moved around the table and fell into conversation with Sven and his wife. The noise levels in the room were rising. Greg leaned over, his temple grazing hers as he went to talk in her ear.

'Are you having a good evening?' he asked.

Holly could feel his breath on her neck, and it gave her goosebumps. 'I'm having a wonderful time.'

'Despite the fact your food looks like a . . . ?'

Holly reddened. 'Can we not revisit that?' she whispered. 'Do you think Rod heard?'

'Don't worry about it. Even if he did, he wouldn't think anything of it.'

There was a pause, and Holly let out a juddering sigh. 'This is so nice, isn't it?'

'What?'

Holly stalled for a second, remembering not to give voice to her more intimate thoughts. She sat up. 'Oh, you know. The food, the scenery, this beautiful bothy. I can't believe you used to get to come here when you were little.'

'Aye. There are a few others near here too. Did you ever go camping when you were young?'

She cleared her throat. 'Having told you about my mother, does it sound like I ever went camping? Or, for that matter, on holiday?'

Greg pulled back and looked immediately sorry. 'I didn't mean to make you feel bad.'

Holly grinned. 'It's nae bother,' she said, in a dire accent, and giggled. 'But no. Never. And I never did when I was older, either. When I've gone away with friends we tended to stay in actual houses, or hotels.'

He looked relieved not to have offended her. 'That's crazy. You're in your thirties and haven't spent a night under canvas?'

'This isn't canvas, I'd like to point out. It's definitely brick. I might have had a few drinks, but I can still tell the difference.'

'OK. Maybe your first attempt at camping could be a bothy. A bit less terrifying. The weather's warming up, too.'

Holly looked him straight in the eye, feeling reasonably bold. Greg had, after all, suggested they go off to forage mussels. 'Are you offering to take me?'

It came out sounding more suggestive than she had intended. She was feeling slightly reckless.

He leaned closer. 'Would you like me to?'

'I think I would,' said Holly, her body practically humming with the urge to kiss him. 'Yes.'

Kirsty put plates down in front of them, putting the brakes on Holly's speeding emotions. Greg smiled, and they started to chat about other, safer, things. The surgery, Greg's office, the Eastercraig Run, their parents and everything in between. But as they talked, they inched closer and closer, their heads almost touching.

Greg's company was making her feel the opposite to her normal, grounded self. Holly had the sensation she was floating. That she was lighter than air. As if she were in some kind of wonderful dream. It was increasingly hard to listen to her sensible side, she thought, as she took another sip of her drink. Hell — who *needed* a sensible side!

After a delicious salmon with summer slaw, a foraged berry crumble with local cream, and a lot of wine, the time came to go home. Holly was distinctly tipsy. Worse than that, she felt brazen, like she ought to abandon her usual inhibitions.

* * *

When they arrived home, Greg came and opened the car door, offering his hand. Feeling better than she had when they'd left, no doubt thanks to having the window down for most of the journey and blasting her face with cool air, Holly got out.

Above her, the sky twinkled with a million stars. The sea, which for the last week had been a roaring, towering mass, had finally come to rest. Gentle, lapping waves glistened beneath the silvery moon.

In the doorway, Holly stopped, her body awash with tingles of anticipation. It was now or never. If she was going to do something, this was the time. She was desperate to be near him, was ready to embrace this uncontrollable want.

'Are you coming in?' she asked, meeting Greg's eye. 'I mean, you tend to stay here anyway. I think the sofa bears a Greg-shaped imprint.'

Greg gave a smile. But it wasn't one which filled Holly with confidence. There was a definite air of it being a "let-you-down-gently" expression. The floor turned to quicksand, and Holly was overcome by a sinking feeling.

'I'd love to,' he said. 'Only Hamish offered me a bed at the house, so I don't have to impose upon you.'

'You wouldn't be imposing. I'd like you to stay.'

It came out sounding too keen. Holly instantly regretted it.

Either Greg hadn't noticed how over-eager she'd been — although it was unlikely— or he was doing a good job of sparing her feelings. 'I've had a lovely night,' he said. He leaned down and gave her a kiss on the cheek. 'Goodnight, Holly.'

He didn't turn immediately, and hesitated for a second, his next sentence stuck in his throat. Then he appeared to think better of it, gave a small cough and walked back to the car.

'Goodnight,' Holly said quietly.

She stepped inside and closed the door behind her.

Tugging off her heels, she went and collapsed on the sofa, yanking on a pair of fluffy socks that were lying on a cushion. They had been getting on brilliantly, and somewhere, between the bothy and Eastercraig he had changed his mind. Stupid, bloody Greg! It was so enervating she could have kicked herself. Holly raised her foot in the air, wondering if she was bendy enough to manage.

Then, before she found out if such contortion was possible, there was a knock at the door.

Quickly, Holly skated over to it, sliding to a halt as she undid the locks. There on the step, boots in hand, stood Greg.

He held them out. 'I believe these are yours.'

Holly took them from him. This was fate, wasn't it. He'd come back. The scene had strong romantic overtones — even if Greg held a pair of filthy wellies rather than a glass slipper.

Hardly registering what she was doing, Holly dropped the boots, wrapped her arm round his neck and kissed him. Greg's lips pressed against hers, and he stepped forwards, putting his hand round her waist and pulling her to him. For a second they were bound together, Holly's body melting into his, heat surging through every inch of her being. She ran her fingers through the back of his hair, and — even though it was barely possible — he tugged her even closer.

Then he stopped.

Greg stepped back. 'I can't, Holly. I'm sorry.'

Oh God! She'd misinterpreted it. She cast about for an excuse. 'No, I'm sorry. I shouldn't have done that. It was the brambles,' she said, desperate to come out with at least a sliver of dignity intact.

'I had a lovely evening. I really did,' said Greg, not meeting her eyes.

But he was in a rush to go, Holly could sense that. 'I've made myself a tea,' she lied quickly. 'Better get to it before it goes cold. And you ought to get to Hamish's. It's getting late.'

'Of course,' he replied, stepping outside, before turning around again. 'I'll see you soon.'

But Holly had a horrible feeling she wouldn't. Tears forming, she closed the door behind her, wanting to sink to the floor. She had taken a risk, let her heart run roughshod over her head. And it had been a mistake.

Sucker-punched and wanting some comfort, Holly nipped round to the surgery to see a fluffy lionhead rabbit called Mordecai who was staying the night after an operation. Hugh would have checked on him, but right now she needed a cuddle, and Mordecai was the closest thing she had. Not wanting to switch on all the lights, she crept in through the back door.

The rabbit was fine. She opened the cage and reached him out, giving him a hug that was far more for her benefit as it was for his.

'I'm not happy,' came a voice.

Holly eyed the rabbit, having an *Alice in Wonderland* moment. Surely he hadn't just spoken to her?

In the silence, the voice continued. It wasn't the rabbit, obviously, and she hadn't fallen down a rabbit hole. It was coming through the wall. 'It's Hugh,' Holly whispered to the rabbit. 'And he's not happy. There's a surprise.'

Holly popped Mordecai back and crept through the corridor so as not to startle him. Oh — who was she kidding? She was being Anderson PI, gathering information, and had no intention of announcing her presence. She crouched by the door, pressing her ear to the keyhole.

'Judith, I cannot put it any more simply. She may have been wonderful at interview but she has a way to come . . . No, we don't always see eye to eye . . . I'm a very long way from writing a reference. Honestly, Jude. It's one dud after another . . . No. I want to keep her here for now, make sure she improves before you inflict her on anyone else.'

Holly swallowed a gasp, tried to pull herself up to standing. Biting on her knuckles, feeling as though she might scream at any moment, she snuck out the back door, carefully locking up behind her. Had today entered a competition to be one of the worst days of her life? As well as the Greg nightmare, it turned out that Hugh, who she thought she was just about winning over, still couldn't stand her. To top it off, he was in league with Judith — someone she had always thought had her back — and worse than that, he didn't think that she deserved a reference.

Back at Sea Spray, Holly reached for her laptop, and composed an email.

Dear Judith,
I hope this finds you well. I want to check in with you because I was wondering if six months in Eastercraig might be enough? Is there an option to be seconded to another surgery elsewhere? Just to broaden my experience?
Many thanks and best wishes,
Holly

Her finger hovered over the keyboard for a second. Why was she wavering? She had to get out of this place. It wasn't a little corner of paradise after all. It was paradise lost, a hitherto unknown circle of hell.

She hit send.

CHAPTER 29

Holly removed the tortoise from the shoebox and held it up to her eye.

'And you say Bubbles has some kind of hernia?' she looked at Helena MacLeod, who was in the room with her toddler son, Harry.

'Yes. Honestly. It was just coming out of her shell,' Helena fretted.

Holly, baffled, turned Bubbles around in her hands. 'Can you point to where the hernia is?'

'There,' Helena whispered, and pointed her finger to the back end of the tortoise.

'Hang on a second.' Holly handed the tortoise back to Helena, and went to grab her phone.

She typed into the search bar wondering what kind of person had these words in their search history, then showed the images to Helena.

'That's it!' Helena cried.

'So it's not a hernia. It's Bubbles's penis,' said Holly. 'She is a *he*. Nothing to worry about at all.'

'Huh,' said Helena. 'I would never have guessed.'

'It can be quite tricky to tell. Especially when they're younger.'

As Holly waved them out of the consulting room, she paused. Normally something like this would have raised a smile or caused her to stifle a laugh. Not today. As of an hour ago, her sense-of-humour failure over Eastercraig was complete.

Judith, efficient as ever, had emailed her back early that Monday morning.

Dear Holly,
Thank you for your email. I've given your request some thought over the last few days, but I think you ought to remain in Eastercraig a little longer. I am sure you're doing brilliantly, but Hugh thinks you could still do with more big animal experience.
Best wishes,
Judith

Holly couldn't help but feel let down. Having had a deficient mother figure in the form of Jackie, she had been overjoyed at being taken on by Judith at university as a kind of mentee. Judith was a smart, successful woman with her head screwed on. Exactly the kind of woman Holly aspired to be. Judith had encouraged her, guided her and helped find her jobs. Only that included this job. It meant Judith wasn't fighting her corner at all. She was in cahoots with Hugh. One of the people she looked up to most had let her down with a painful thud.

Still in bed, Holly had let out a tiny whimper of disappointment as she read the message on her phone, then pulled the duvet over her head.

* * *

'Spirits have never felt so low in this place,' commented Hugh, as he arrived in the surgery mid-morning. 'What's the bloody matter with you lot? You're all moping around like sad sacks.'

'I speak on behalf of us all when I say: we're fine,' said Holly, poking her head out from the kitchen.

'Your tone suggests otherwise,' Hugh huffed.

Chloe looked up from the desk. 'Can I make you a coffee, Hugh? You've got time.'

'Sure. I'll go and set up the table.'

As he left, Holly heaved a sigh. She could hardly bear to look Hugh in the eye.

'Tell us why you're so off this morning, then,' Chloe said to Holly. 'I've got a min.'

'Fine,' said Holly. 'I made a move on Greg, basically tried to shove my tongue down his throat, and he rejected me. I tore my moral code asunder and threw myself on a man known to be a womanizer, who then didn't womanize me! I'm so embarrassed. I got it completely wrong. I thought I'd felt something between us, I really did, and that he did too. Perhaps after so many years of shunning dates I've got zero ability to read the signals.'

She put her coffee on the reception desk and rubbed her eyes. She hadn't slept well the last couple of nights, unable to stop playing the scene out over and over again. Greg had left her a voicemail on Sunday night but, too stressed to listen, Holly had deleted it. Out of phone, out of mind.

'And worse than that,' she continued, 'I asked Judith for a transfer. This morning she said "no" and said I ought to ride my time out here.'

'You what?' Paolo nearly dropped his mug.

'I'll fill you in at lunch,' said Holly.

'We need to sort this out. Or at least distract ourselves,' said Paolo.

'Mandy Lewis does gong baths with the alpacas,' suggested Chloe. 'We could have a group cleansing ritual, and a cuddle.'

'What the . . . ? *No*. I need to channel this anger. Put it to good use,' said Holly.

Paolo picked up a leaflet from the reception desk and waved it in the air. 'The Eastercraig Run. It'll be a challenge — well, not for you, Hols, but you can try for a PB. And Chlo, you've already told Angus you're running it. Let's train like Olympians. Exercise is great for your mental health, after all.'

Holly looked up to the ceiling. 'I run all the time. I was thinking more like doing a kickboxing class. Really letting it out and getting our minds in good shape for whatever crap Cupid slings at me next.'

Chloe tilted her head reluctantly. 'I'm not really the athletic type.'

Paolo gave a growl of frustration. 'This is not fighting talk. Come on.'

The door swung open, and in came a woman with a snake tank. Holly rolled up her sleeves, ushered the lady through, then followed her. As she did, she thought about the race. It would be fun. But would it be enough to take her mind off everything else?

CHAPTER 30

Chloe sat down on a rock, clutching her side. She had a painful stitch. At least, she hoped it was a stitch, and that she wasn't having a heart attack. Running alongside Holly and Paolo was impossible. The former's strides were about twice as long as hers, and Holly had thrown herself into training to distract herself from her doom-lunge at Greg. Paolo was lean and nimble despite his claims to hate any form of cardio, and he had confessed to having been on the school athletics team as a teenager.

'Come on, MacKenzie-Ling,' Paolo had doubled back and was at her side, bouncing on the spot.

'I can't . . . I can barely get . . . enough air in my lungs . . . to stay upright.'

Holly appeared over the crest of a small hillock. 'Stop gassing, you two. If we're going to do this, we need to train hard.'

'I hate you, Holly Anders—' Chloe ran out of breath halfway through the sentence. 'What was I . . . thinking when I . . . said I'd do this?'

Holly jogged back towards them, barely sweating. Chloe, on the other hand, felt as though she had been swimming. Her sweat-wicking leggings were almost at capacity.

'Apologies for the pun, but let me jog your memory,' said Holly. 'You said you'd been ribbing Angus, in a flirty way, telling him you could beat his sorry arse any day. So, we have until the start of September to get you there.'

'Foolish. So foolish,' said Paolo, shaking his head. 'The man's over six foot.'

'It was *you*, Paolo!' Chloe would have shouted if she wasn't panting for breath like an obese Labrador. 'It's your fault. And now I'm here. And it's nearly race day and I'll never manage.'

'I gave you a gentle push,' said Paolo. 'Remember, we are removing you from your comfort zones and turning you into an all-conquering powerhouse who feels like she can do anything, and thus ask Angus out.'

'Either way, Angus is about fifty per cent Dundee cake,' protested Chloe. 'He's fit, but not in a running-y way. He can heft a cow, but I don't reckon he'd win a speed trial.'

Chloe had ended up telling Angus that *she* could run the course, easy-peasy. It had been a drunken brag. And, like most drunken brags, it wasn't wholly true . . . In all honesty, she was as capable of running that distance as she was capable of walking on water.

'Neither will you if on your first run of the year you spend most of it sat on a rock,' said Paolo.

'You're mean,' said Chloe. But she took his hand as he held it out.

'We'll go slowly,' said Holly.

Chloe gave her a withering look, one that she hoped expressed the sentiment *you don't know the meaning of the word*. But she realized she had to get up if she wasn't to finish last of all — which would be embarrassing considering plenty of the competitors were twice her age. *I can do this*, she said to herself.

'Let's go,' she said, stretching out her legs.

They carried on along the coast path. It was exposed up there, and Chloe wondered if the fact they were running into the wind counted for anything. They were at least moving slower than before, and she managed to keep up. They were going for eight miles, in the hope that by the day of the race, Chloe could run just shy of the thirteen miles she needed. It was going to be tough — but she had said she would do it.

Finally, her face shining so much it could guide ships, they got back to the hill that descended into Eastercraig. It had never looked so welcoming. Chloe paused to look at the familiar houses, nestled into the crescent of the bay.

'Sprint to the front door?' said Holly, bouncing on the spot.

'I'll see you both there. Mine's a gigantic glass of water,' said Chloe.

She watched as Holly and Paolo, both with energy to spare, raced down the hill and towards Holly's house. She put her hands on her chest, and took a deep breath, feeling her lungs fill up to the top. Glancing at the sea, Chloe watched the waves undulating, rolling in pale blue, then being sucked back into the depths. At the edge of the horizon, the water looked almost black.

As she stared, Chloe became aware of the edges of her vision disappearing. She turned her gaze back to the white houses, but couldn't focus on those either. They'd become oddly pixelated. There was a buzzing in her ears, as if swarms of bees were inside her head.

This wasn't good at all. Everything went dark.

* * *

'Chlo? Chloe?'

A man was calling her name. It sounded as if she were underwater. Chloe opened one eye and saw a blur of colour that she recognized as Angus.

'I think I fainted,' her voice came out in a hoarse whisper.

'I'd imagine so,' said Angus. 'I came out of the shop to see you flop backwards into the grasses. I've never run so fast.'

'Oh God,' she said, trying to prop herself up.

'You'll be OK. Lie flat, and I'll hold your legs up for a moment.'

'What? No!'

This was not what she needed. This scenario was not conducive to Angus realizing she was the girl of his dreams. Cantering up and down a candlelit hall was romantic. Snuggling on the sofa watching black-and-white films was romantic. Lying on the coast path with your legs in the air, covered in skin-tight Lycra and sweat, unable to stand unaided, was absolutely not.

'I need to get back to Holly's,' she said. 'My keys. Dry clothes . . .'

'Slowly, slowly,' Angus held out his hand. 'Let's see if you can stand.'

Chloe took it, only to find her legs were incapable of bearing her weight. Dizzy again, she let go and sat back on the ground.

'Steady now,' said Angus. 'Head down until the dizziness goes.'

Leaning forward, she felt the blood working its way back up her body. 'That's the last time I go running with those two.'

'Paolo and Holly?'

'They're training me for the half,' said Chloe. Then, embarrassed, she said: 'At the pub I said I could beat you. And I don't think I can.'

'I admired your gumption. But I admit I wondered if you were bluffing. I certainly was.'

'You got me,' said Chloe, in a small voice. 'But after all that dancing, I made the resolution to keep getting out of my comfort zone.'

And a large part of that was going to be finding the balls to ask you out, she said to herself.

Chloe carried on. 'I know the running says otherwise, but I'd say I'm managing pretty well. Only right now it's returning to my comfort zone that's the problem — and by that I mean Eastercraig. My legs are still jelly — how on earth am I going to make it down the hill?'

Angus laughed. 'Like this?'

She screamed as he hoisted her up on to his shoulder in a fireman's lift. Chloe, the world more topsy-turvy than it had been five minutes ago, felt her heart in her mouth.

'It's a good resolution.' Angus started walking. 'Getting out of your usual routine. Maybe I need to do the same.'

'All you'd need to do is get off the farm for a day,' she teased. 'That'd qualify.'

Angus let out a humph, and she heard a change in his voice. 'As if. My life is not my own. It belongs to the coos. I'm practically bloody married to them.'

There was a pause. Without being able to look him in the eye, it was easier to ask the question that was always on her mind.

'Oh Angus! Really? Don't you think you'll ever settle down?'

'I wouldn't want to burden anyone else with the life I lead. Farming's hard. Auchintraid's isolated. It's easier by myself.'

'It's not *that* isolated. You've got family and friends. And, on a practical level, a car. A landline. Wi-Fi. A community right here. You're not some loner living off the grid, miles from civilization.'

But he didn't reply, and they descended the rest of the hill in silence. Chloe wondered if he was reflecting on what she'd said. Maybe realizing someone believed in him.

At Holly's door, he set her down gently, the world flipping over one last time. He gripped her, keeping her upright, pulling her in to his side. For a second, she felt his heart beating, and let herself be drawn closer.

'Thanks for the lift,' she said.

Angus looked at her, then knocked at the door. 'It was my pleasure,' he said, a twinkle in his eye. 'Now. If I let go of you, will you fall to the floor?'

'Perhaps you ought to hold me a while longer.'

The words came out without her thinking them through, and she hadn't meant them to sound so suggestive. But they did, and Chloe held her breath, waiting for a reply.

Angus tugged her closer, tucking her in under his chin. 'You daft thing.'

When Holly answered the door, a second later, her eyebrows flew up. 'We were wondering where you'd got to! Coming in for a brew, Angus?'

'Thanks, but I can't,' he said. 'I need to get back to the farm. Jobs piling up.'

Chloe looked up at him. She thought she'd detected an ounce of hesitation in his reply. And while it may have been because the jobs *were* piling up, she hoped it was because he'd far rather be with her.

She reached up and gave him a kiss on the cheek. 'Thanks for saving me,' she said.

'Any time. Call me tonight. Let me know you're OK,' he replied quietly, before nodding goodbye to the others. 'See you all later.'

Holly grabbed Chloe and wrenched her inside, almost pulling her arm clean out of its socket. 'What on earth happened?'

Chloe couldn't stop a wide grin forming. 'Give me a cup of tea, and I'll tell you all about it.'

* * *

Later, Paolo popped into the shop. At the counter, Hamish was buying stacks of smoked salmon and quickly stashing it into a bag.

'Is there a fine-foods apocalypse on the horizon? Should I stock up?'

'Shhh!' Hamish said. 'Keep it down.'

Lola Carlson, the girl behind the counter, gave a conspiratorial nod.

'What's the big secret?' Paolo whispered.

Hamish beckoned him into the aisles.

'A huge party is coming up for the weekend. We claim on the website we serve food from the estate, but we used all the trout at the ball.'

'But this is salmon.'

'I don't think they'll care. But they requested smoked fish as part of their Saturday menu. So I called up and Lola said they had tons. And she's going to keep schtum.'

'Well. I'll not tell anybody either,' said Paolo.

Hamish looked hugely relieved. Then another look crossed his face. 'Say, did I see Chloe over Angus's shoulder earlier? Is there something between them?'

'Oh, Chloe passed out while jogging and Angus came to the rescue.'

'Och! The race? Are you entering?'

'I already have,' said Paolo. He made a few exaggerated lunges, reaching for some pasta as he did so. 'I'm a seasoned pro.'

'The route comes through the grounds. Fancy a training session followed by a coffee in the library? You said you wanted to have a nose. Sorry it's been a while. I've been overrun by guests.'

Hell yeah! Of course he did. A jog through the magical castle woods, with a caffeinated chaser in one of his favourite rooms in the world? No brainer.

'I'd forgotten all about that,' Paolo said casually. 'I'd love to. I know you work weekends, but I've got a Wednesday afternoon off soon?'

Hamish beamed. 'Fab. And I'll join you. I'm out of practice — well, I can barely go half a mile — but it'll be fun. I'll text you.'

CHAPTER 31

A few weeks later, on an overcast Wednesday afternoon, the surgery was closed for a deep clean. While Paolo was off running with Hamish, Chloe was sitting in the window seat of the café enjoying a bun with Holly, discussing the upcoming race. Specifically — and it was one of Chloe's biggest worries — what to wear. Holly was telling her some more Lycra wouldn't go amiss.

'I don't want to have all the gear but no idea,' Chloe cringed.

She remembered a trip to Aviemore with school and winced at the memory of falling over time and time again, all the while kitted out in the neon salopettes her mother had insisted on getting her.

'See it as an investment,' Holly said, gently. 'You'll use it again, and it'll make you feel like a pro. You need the right mindset.'

'I have the mindset. Not the figure.' Chloe bit into her iced Danish. 'Give me a pencil skirt and I will zip myself into it. But the Lycra expands to reveal your every lump and bump.'

'You've got a great figure, Chloe,' Holly insisted. 'Honestly. And it doesn't have to be skin-tight. You could wear a looser top and shorts over a base layer. It'll help you run faster. You can't leave these things up to chance.'

'I'll think about it,' said Chloe, putting it to the back of her mind.

'Oooh — look. There's Wolfie,' said Holly, pointing out the window.

They stared out to see Wolfie leaping off the jetty into the water, something that he did about three times as Moira yelled at him to come to heel.

'He's so naughty,' Chloe said laughing. 'I think he reckons he's a fish.'

Holly nodded. 'Of all the animals I've seen here, I think he's my favourite. So much hair, and he's such a character. And he responded so well to that treatment. Look at all that energy! Although I'm not sure jumping in the sea is great for him. Hey — there's Angus.'

Chloe, rapt, stared through the window. She took in each inch of his broad frame, watched his hair get blown by the breeze. Angus paused to talk to Moira, and then looked up and spotted Chloe and Holly in the window. He waved.

'Give him your most glorious smile,' said Holly. 'Quick.'

Chloe licked her lips and beamed at him. She giggled and turned back to Holly. 'How was that for not leaving things up to chance?'

'Top notch!'

Chloe looked back at Angus, who was giving her a slightly lopsided grin in return. He gave another wave and began to walk back to the car park. Her heart thudded in her chest, ready to break out, and she placed a hand on her jumper to steady herself.

'It was easier than thinking about Lycra,' she said to Holly, by way of explanation. 'Have you heard from Greg recently by the way? You've stopped talking about him.'

Holly stared into her coffee cup. 'He's tried to call me a couple more times, but I either missed them or didn't pick up. And he sent me a message saying he'd knocked on the door the other day — thankfully I was over in Ullapool.'

'What if he's seen the error of his ways? Wants to apologize for being such an eejit?'

'Chlo, I am *so* embarrassed by the whole thing. I threw myself at a man and he rejected me. Not only has my self-esteem taken a massive thwack, but — even worse — I did the thing I said I'd never do: I let a man be forefront in my mind.'

'You can't help that you like him. And he *was* giving you all the signals.'

'I want to forget about the whole thing,' Holly said, and turned to stare out of the window.

'And how's that going for you?'

'Not especially well. Thank heavens he doesn't live here. I don't know how you've dealt with all your feelings for Angus *and* had to bump into him all the time.'

Chloe gave Holly a knowing look. 'Well, I've never thrown myself at him. He hasn't had the chance to say no. Anyway, if Greg calls again, I think you should pick up.'

'No way.'

'Come on, Holly, you are worthy of love.'

Holly rolled her eyes. 'I never said I wasn't worthy of it. Only that I didn't want it right now. I'm going to put it on the back burner and get back to it after a few years in Ascot. And that means no Greg.'

Chloe sighed. 'The course of true love never did run smooth.'

Unless, she thought to herself, she could snag Angus on race day.

* * *

Holly took a bite from her bun and watched Wolfie shake the water from his fur before barking at Sporran, who had emerged from the water.

Greg filled her mind in an expansive way, crowding everything else out. She thought again about how she had opened up to the possibility of them happening, only for it to blow up in her face. So much for self-preservation.

'Anybody in there?' Chloe interrupted her thoughts.

'I am,' Holly played with her fingernails. 'Somewhere, underneath the suffocating double act of horrible bosses and horrible romantic incidents.'

'It's not that bad.'

'Hugh hates me, and now so does Greg. I'll miss you and Paolo, and Eastercraig, but Ascot can't come soon enough,' Holly said dejectedly. 'Hey, what's that?'

Over Chloe's shoulder, Holly spied a commotion outside the Anchor.

Chloe turned her head. 'It's Mhairi, with Goose.'

Mhairi was running up the road, carrying her black Labrador in her arms. She was yelling, but Holly couldn't make out what she was saying. She slid out of her chair.

'We'll pay you in a bit, Anjali,' she called to the café's owner and pulled Chloe out of her seat.

Mhairi met them halfway along the road, cradling the dog like a baby.

'What is it?' Holly ran towards her.

'I think he's had a heart attack,' said Mhairi, tears gathering in her eyes. 'I've just called in, and Hugh says he's en route.'

'The surgery's being cleaned, but I'm sure we can use the consulting room,' said Chloe.

They went round the back of the surgery, and Holly let them in. 'Talk me through what happened.'

Mhairi followed her and Chloe inside and put Goose on the table. 'We were out walking, and there was a Shetland pony in one of the fields. Goose went over to say hello and the pony kicked. I didn't see if contact was made but Goose collapsed on the floor. When he came to he was dazed. I reckon his life had just flashed before his eyes.'

As Mhairi stifled a sob, Holly looked at Goose, who appeared to be completely fine. He panted as Holly put a hand on his head.

She gave him a scratch behind the ears. 'And is Goose healthy otherwise? I've not seen him in here this year.'

'Very healthy. He's only two. But now this! What if he has an underlying condition?'

Holly had her suspicions, but ran through her checks. A few minutes later, she gave a smile. 'There's nothing wrong with his heart, not from listening to it. Or anything else. He appears to have fainted.'

'He passed out?'

Holly nodded. 'It happens. He had a bit of a shock, but nothing that some cuddles won't fix.'

Hugh appeared at the door. 'Mhairi? Where's the dog?'

'It's all OK, Hugh,' Mhairi positively glowed, picking up the dog and carrying him to the door. 'Thank you, Holly. Send me the bill.'

'No charge today, Mhairi. We're not officially open this afternoon.'

'You're a star, Holly,' said Mhairi. 'Have a round on me this Friday.'

Holly grinned, and Hugh rolled his eyes.

* * *

'It's because we're way higher than sea level,' said Paolo.

He jogged on the spot and watched as Hamish leaned forwards against a tree, gasping for air.

'Don't be ridiculous. It's because my cardio ability is nil,' Hamish managed between puffs. 'Give me a glen and I'll roam all day at my own pace. This, on the other hand . . . Do you think there's any truth in Aesop's Fables?'

'If you're suggesting the fittest of us are all going to take a nap on the course, you're only fooling yourself.'

Paolo smiled. Hamish began to stretch his calves. They'd run deep into the woodland that surrounded Glenalmond. It was a grey summer's day, and there was a light mist between the trees, the damp air heavy with the scent of the pines. It was also eerily quiet, and if there was any noise, the combination of the weather and woodland would have muffled it.

In fact, it was a tiny bit creepy, now Paolo thought about it. Out here on the estate, they were a trek from anywhere, and they'd not seen another soul. Though he'd become accustomed to the Highlands, Paolo had been a city dweller for the best part of his life. He was used to noise, light and other people. On the odd occasion, the isolated places surrounding Eastercraig stopped being places of natural beauty and became scary. *Blair Witch* scary.

'Do you ever get angsty, tramping through the grounds?' he asked, tentacles of unease wrapping their way round his chest now.

Hamish grinned, the first time he'd done so since they'd left the house a half-hour ago. 'Woods spooking you?'

'Pshhhhh. Not at all,' Paolo bluffed. 'Look at me — I'm right at home here.'

Hamish laughed, not buying it. 'I get it. It's a dark forest. And let's face it. Nothing good happens in forests. Look at *Hansel and Gretel*, or *Little Red Riding Hood*.'

'Och, I'm not scared. I simply need to get back into my groove.' Paolo's tone was convincing nobody. Least of all himself.

Hamish had caught his breath by now. 'Don't panic,' he said, easy as you like. 'We'll not be much longer in here.'

'I'm fine,' Paolo insisted.

He wasn't though, was he. Between the dark firs, the thickening mist and the silence, he was getting claustrophobic. Or was it agoraphobic, seeing as he was outside? Either way, his hair was standing on end, and it had nothing to do with the fact he'd been standing still in the shade for three minutes. Paolo turned around, only for Hamish to grab both of his shoulders and say 'BOO' loudly in his ear.

It was the last straw. Paolo shrieked, spun round to admonish him, but tripped on a twig and fell backwards. Reaching out, he grabbed the first thing available to him: Hamish. With a dull thud, they landed on the ground, side by side.

Hamish rolled over on to his back, chuckling. 'The mud all over my arse was totally worth it for that.'

Paolo, lying on his back, stared up at the towering firs above. 'That wasn't fair and you know it.'

Hamish rolled over. 'Sorry. It was childish. But . . .'

As Hamish trailed off, Paolo realized how close their faces were. Was that what had stopped Hamish from finishing his sentence? That feeling of being so near to someone, being able to feel their breath on your cheek?

'Paolo,' Hamish said quietly.

Paolo got the strange feeling something was about to happen.

'Hamish?' It came out as a whisper.

'I can't do this,' Hamish said. And with that, he got up and ran.

Paolo, who had been so distracted by his own anticipation, took a second to register. Hamish, having complained about the run since they'd left the house, was now sprinting faster than Paolo could have imagined possible. He'd be on track for an Eastercraig gold if he kept going at that pace.

Hastily getting up, Paolo began to run after him. He had to catch up, find out what had just happened. If he didn't, he'd endure hours of confusion. Or end up lost in a forest for days.

He found Hamish at the edge of the wood. Through the last few trees, Glenalmond loomed. Hamish stood staring at the house, his hands on his hips, and Paolo could see he was out of breath again.

'Hamish?' Paolo took a step closer, a twig snapping under his feet. 'What's going on?'

Hamish turned, his face the picture of agony. 'Daisy wants to get back together. And I'm not sure she's the right girl for me. Or the right person, if you catch my drift.'

'I've caught your drift.' Paolo came and stood next to Hamish and focused on the encroaching mist. 'You know you can turn her down, don't you?'

'I think so. But then . . . in the forest. What happened.'

Paolo turned to look at him. 'What did happen?'

'We had a moment, didn't we?'

Paolo felt his eyebrows fly up. He was lost for words, and before he could confirm Hamish's suspicions — because, yes, it had felt alarmingly like a moment — Hamish had continued.

'I think it's the whole Daisy thing. Heightened emotions and all that, confusion . . .'

'Confusion about what?' Paolo could feel the anticipation racing around his body. This was going to be the confession he'd waited for. Hamish didn't answer immediately, so Paolo offered a prompt. 'Do you mean . . . your sexuality?'

Hamish goggled. 'What? No. That's never been in question.'

'But we just had a moment. You said so yourself.'

Realization seemed to dawn on Hamish. 'Ohhhhh, I guess you don't know. Of course. Sorry. I'm bi. No uncertainty there,' he said, lightly. Then his expression clouded over. 'What I actually meant was that I'm confused about what to do with Daisy. We had a rough couple of months, but perhaps there's something to salvage . . .'

Hamish looked pensive. His head must have been in a spin. But he wasn't the only one. Paolo could barely keep up — he was stuck on the first revelation.

'Hold up. Can we go back? How did I not know you're bi?'

Hamish shrugged. 'Och, I never felt it needed an announcement. I realized at uni, and when I was there I told a couple of mates, but I didn't want to come back home and make some massive thing of it, you know? And because I've only had girlfriends since I've been back working at Glenalmond, it hasn't come up. I've not been living a lie or anything. It's just the right guy hasn't been here.'

'But the wrong girl has?'

'That's not fair. I've really liked all the girls I've gone out with, at the beginning at least. And Daisy was right — at first. And then she wasn't for a bit. We were arguing lots over petty things, but she said she's had time to think and wants to get back with me. I've no idea what I should do.'

'Maybe take some time. Don't rush into it. Go somewhere quiet and have a think.'

Hamish's brow was one big frown. 'I do most of my best thinking out stalking. I like to talk to the animals. That probably sounds a bit strange.'

'You're talking to a veterinary nurse. I spend half my life doing that.' Paolo was pleased to see a flicker of a smile cross Hamish's face.

'I won't do anything rash, promise. Shall we have that coffee? Look at some ancient tomes?' Hamish asked.

Hint taken. 'I'd like nothing better. Let's go in. We can talk another time, if you like.'

But while on the outside Paolo was playing it cool, inside his heart was racing. This was not how he had expected the day to go.

CHAPTER 32

Holly stretched her legs for the hundredth time, then bobbed up and down on the balls of her feet. Once she had started running she would warm up properly, but it might take a while. Early mornings in September were chilly on the coast of Scotland.

Layered up, she'd arrived at the start line and recognized most of her fellow runners from Eastercraig. Locating her colleagues, Paolo said he'd go at his own speed, and Chloe had gamely insisted she'd complete the event but was holding on to the adage "it's the taking part that counts". Holly had nodded, her competitive side propelling her closer to the front.

She started off quickly, borne along the quayside by the crowd. Before long, though, the pack thinned out, and as the course ascended the coast path, she found herself with some space. In front of her a red-vested runner was keeping a good pace, and she decided to try to follow them.

As she cleared the coast path and headed inland, Holly heard a voice calling her name.

'Holly! Hey, Holly, wait up!'

She turned to see Greg gaining on her. Holly felt an unwelcome prickle of excitement at seeing him, which she successfully converted to annoyance. No way was she going to "wait up". The sting of rejection lingered, and she wasn't sure she wanted to look him in the face.

You are not going to distract me again, Greg Dunbar, Holly said to herself. Not romantically, nor athletically. She upped her pace.

It had been a while since the night at the bothy, but the humiliation still, on occasion, caught her out. It wasn't *all*-pervasive, but Holly would be cleaning her teeth, and there he was, rejecting her kiss. And earlier that week when she was putting a cat on a diet. Or every time she saw a couple together, enjoying each other's company, moments from their next successful snog. And now here he was in the flesh. Usually a run cleared her mind, but apparently that wasn't going to be the case today.

Small orange flags signposted the way ahead and, as the route took a turn on to a long track, Holly went into a sprint.

The course twisted and turned, bumpy underfoot, and before too long, she'd come to the woods. Swinging her neck around, she realized she couldn't see Greg. Good. Feeling blood pounding in her ears, she eased off, slowing down as she began to run on a path by a babbling stream. The burst of speed had made her feel woozy.

Just as Holly was beginning to feel ready to go again though, she heard Greg's voice. It was faint, muffled by the trees, but he was shouting her name. She glanced over her shoulder, and at the same time skidded across some moss, losing her footing and falling over.

'Damn,' Holly said aloud, getting up.

Panting, she reached out for a tree to steady herself.

'Are you OK?' Greg had caught up.

Holly felt her cheeks reddening and she frowned at him. 'Can't a girl take part in a race without being hounded? Anyway, I thought you said you weren't running.'

'I wasn't, but I changed my mind, hoping to run into you. I've been trying to get hold of you for weeks but, short of coming by your workplace like some creepy stalker, I've failed. So here I am. I want to talk about what happened.'

'*Now*? In the middle of a wood, during a cross-country?'

'No. Talking later. For now I thought it might be nice to run together.'

'Why would you think that?' Holly asked, hoping he could hear the warning tones in her voice.

'Everything is better with company, isn't it?'

Greg had caught his breath already, and looked as if he'd barely broken a sweat. Infuriated, she began to run, without giving him a response. He didn't deserve one.

'Holly. Hear me out,' he said, catching up once more.

Finding extra reserves of strength, Holly ran towards the next flag, out of the forest and into the grounds of Glenalmond. The Glennis family, staunch supporters of anything charitable, had set up a table in the grounds with refreshments. Behind it, roaring words of encouragement to anyone who passed, were David and Moira in matching fleeces. David held up a cup and Holly ran towards him.

'No Wolfie today?' she said hopping on the spot as she downed a glass of water.

'Good lord, no,' said David, looking alarmed. 'He was bred for hunting. Daft bugger would get overexcited and fell somebody.'

'And then bring them back between his jaws for supper.' Moira rolled her eyes at the thought. 'Jelly baby?'

Moira held out a pudding bowl of sweets, and Holly took a couple. Then, hearing gravel crunching behind her, she turned and saw Greg again. 'Thank you,' she said hurriedly, taking a couple more for good measure. 'See you soon.'

As Holly tore off along the drive, she was faintly aware of David engaging Greg in conversation, and felt a grim satisfaction he'd be delayed. Happy she could reach the end of the course in peace, she had a rush of energy and, approaching the final stages of the run feeling lighter, she sped towards the road.

Before long, she caught a glimpse of the sea. The sight of it let her forget Greg for a moment. In the sun, it looked like someone had thrown handfuls of silver glitter over it and Holly slowed, mesmerized by the shimmering ripples. A clutch of seagulls bobbing on the surface were disturbed by something in the deep and exploded into the sky in a chattering storm of wings. Squinting, she realized it was Sporran.

Holly smiled, realizing the course had wended its way through the best bits of Eastercraig. The wild, gorse-covered headlands, the wood and the river, bookended by the sight of the ocean, had been beautiful. Never in London had she been on a run in which her surroundings were so bewitching.

After crossing the finish line and jogging home, she'd just got her key in the front door when she felt a presence behind her. It didn't take a genius to work out who it was. Holly let out a small sigh, not even bothering to turn. 'Greg. Please go away.'

'Can we talk?'

Holly craned her neck over her shoulder. He looked so desperate to get whatever it was off his chest — and she'd hazard a guess it was an apology for being such an arse — Holly found a small part of herself relenting. All the same, she wasn't sure what to say.

Turning the key, she pushed the door. 'Why? There's not a lot to it. I had a few drinks, thought the mood suggested a kiss, and I was wrong. I got carried away.'

'No. Listen. Can I come in?'

'So *now* you want to? Not after a lovely evening out together, but after we've run a race and are both dripping with sweat?'

'I get my timing isn't great.'

'You don't say? And are you about to throw in the Angus thing as a reason you can't go back to the farm, and need to crash here too?'

'No. I'm staying at the B&B.'

'Oh.'

Truth be told, Holly didn't know what to think. Layer upon layer of confusion had built up. He'd rejected her. Then he'd basically ambushed her during the race, and the lack of warning meant she'd not had time to think how she'd approach a conversation with him. And now he was here, in her house, asking to talk. To top it off, she was feeling dehydrated. And in need of a shower. And a pee. And clean clothes. And a snack. It was hard to know where to start.

'So. Can I come in?' he persisted. 'It won't take me long.'

'OK, OK,' Holly raised her eyes to the sky, and wondered if she was about to make a big mistake. 'But let me get sorted first. Put the kettle on, will you?'

* * *

Chloe had taken a place at the back of the pack. There was no point going anywhere else, though it did cross her mind if she fainted again there wouldn't be anyone to scrape her off the gorse. But she was determined to finish it, even if she limped back into the harbour a week after the race officially began.

As the first group zoomed off, she saw Holly, layered up and looking professional as ever — Chloe wondered if Holly ever looked anything less — flying up the hillside overtaking a group of people wearing running club jerseys. And, as she tried to limber up without toppling over, she spotted Paolo too, off at a confident pace.

She sighed so deeply she nearly gave herself a stitch, then took a deep breath as the people in front of her started to move. For a moment, Chloe stood there and watched them, wondering if this was sheer idiocy. Would there even be anyone at the finish line in three hours?

'Chlo! Are you going to stand there like a melon?'

'What?' she spun around to see Angus right behind her.

'Are you going to go? I know you're worried about finishing, but you'll not do that if you stand here all day.'

He had a point. All the same, her nerves were worsening. 'It's such a long way,' she said.

Chloe began to feel hot, and a sensation like being pricked by thousands of pins spread across her skin.

'Tell you what, I'll come the first mile with you. And then I'll pop along to Glenalmond. If you've not emerged from the woods in . . .' he checked his watch, 'ninety minutes, I'll come in and find you. And if you've already gone, Moira and David can let me know.'

'You'd do that?'

Angus put an arm around her. 'Aye. For you, anything.'

Chloe wished he meant that. That he'd realize he was a total catch. That he would sweep her off her feet, literally. Although not over his shoulder again — that wasn't her best angle. His display of sensitivity only made her more certain that under the gruff, defensive interior, was a kind man who could make any girl happy. Of course, ideally, that girl would be her.

'Thanks, Angus.' She smiled. 'I'd appreciate it.'

As the last of the crowd in front spilled out over the start line, Chloe felt a last-minute shiver of nerves. Angus looked at her and gestured for her to go. Taking one last deep, stabilizing breath, she began to jog.

'Lovely day for it,' said Angus, breezily.

Chloe snuck a sideways glance. He looked totally unsuited for running. His frame suggested he'd be mainly suited to caber tossing, or hurling, or — as she imagined he did often — hefting the cattle around. Nor was he dressed for it, in his bulky waxed jacket and hiking boots. She giggled as she ran.

'Something funny?' he asked.

'Aren't you uncomfortable?'

'A little hot, maybe,' he said, pulling off his beanie and shoving it in a pocket. 'I'd look absurd in Lycra though. You, on the other hand, look great. Especially the headpiece.'

Chloe was in shades of pink and maroon, looking for all the world like she'd been dipped in strawberry jam, a comparison that would be complete when her face went red with exertion. Not that she cared. She would be too busy concentrating on reaching the finish line.

'Holly got me the furry headband,' said Chloe, the compliment putting a spring in her step. 'One for her and Paolo too.'

'Well, let's hope no birds of prey mistake you for their next meal.' He grinned.

'Oh gosh! Do you think that might happen?' She stopped in her tracks, appalled at the possibility.

Angus let out a roar of laughter. 'I doubt it . . . Now, you've made it a mile, this is where I leave you. I'll go and wait at the house for you. Remember. Be positive — it'll help.'

Chloe gave a small wave and jogged on along the coast path. With the cool wind brushing her face, she was no longer feeling the prickly panic that had threatened to engulf her. Of course, it was nothing to do with the breeze, and everything to do with Angus's presence and calm words. Positivity, as Angus had said, was going to see her through — if it didn't, she didn't know what would.

After what felt like for ever — a period of time in which she'd stumbled on slippery moss and fought off lichen-speckled branches — Chloe emerged from the trees that surrounded Glenalmond. The positivity, while it had worked a treat, was soon ousted by a more encouraging thought: that of Angus waiting for her with a cold drink, willing her to run towards him. Every so often, she'd been struck by a flash of fear, wondering if he might give up.

But he hadn't. He was there, his huge frame looming over David and Moira Glennis. It was a good thing he was handsome, because if he wasn't he'd look like Lurch from the Addams Family.

'Come on, girl,' he boomed at such volume his words echoed off the building.

For a split second Chloe felt this was how he might have addressed one of his cows. Mind you, he was utterly devoted to them. Uncertain how to process this, she made her way towards them and took a sip of water, and a jelly baby.

She bobbed up and down, aware of a blister forming on the arch of her left foot.

'Looking good, MacKenzie-Ling.' He came round to stand in front of her. 'Still vertical.'

'Yup,' Chloe breathed, unable to manage more than one syllable.

'I'm going to head to the finish line now,' he said. 'You're going to do the last bit. It'll feel hard towards the end, but at least the last mile is downhill. And I'll let your parents know you're on your way.' He gave her a clap on the arm that nearly knocked her flat.

'Sure,' she said, feeling anything but.

'Are you sure you're OK? Have another jelly baby.'

'Thanks.'

He handed her one and stepped closer. 'Pink, cos it matches your outfit.'

Chloe smiled, more grateful than he could know, and with a wave to Moira and David Glennis, started the jog down the seemingly endless drive. She could do it, couldn't she?

CHAPTER 33

While Greg clattered around in the kitchen, Holly took a quick, ice-cold shower. Freezing water eased her aching legs: running from Greg had meant she'd gone even faster than her usual pace, and her muscles had clearly been taken aback. She threw on a pair of leggings, a gorgeous green woollen jumper she'd bought over on the west coast, and some warm socks. After a quick check in the mirror, satisfied she looked marginally less race-worn than she had before, she returned downstairs.

'That was quick,' said Greg.

He was sitting on the sofa, and Holly took one of the chairs opposite him. As he poured her a cup of tea, her eyes alighted on a tube of digestives.

'Thanks for this,' she said, taking a sip and picking up a biscuit. 'And these.'

'How are you? Work going well?'

Holly was inwardly annoyed at the small talk. She wanted to get straight to the point. Politeness cost nothing though, she supposed. 'All fine. And you?'

Greg smiled. 'OK. I'm off to Edinburgh for a few months with work. And I've got a new lady in my life. A dog.'

Holly's heart, which had stopped beating for a second, kicked back into action. 'Really?'

'Yeah. A Gordon Setter, Sadie. She's excellent company. Staying with a mate this weekend because it seemed a faff to bring her here. I'm not here to talk about her, though. I came today because I wanted to apologize. I took you out, and we were having fun, and things were happening and I shut you down.'

He stopped to consider what to say next, and Holly found her pulse beginning to quicken. She leaned forward and took another biscuit.

'Leaving me feeling pretty stupid,' she said. 'Anyway. In your own time.'

'You've maybe heard by now that in the past I've had a few girlfriends, the odd fling.'

'More than the odd one.'

'We were having such a great time, but then I realized you weren't fling material.'

Holly flopped back in her chair, insulted and intrigued. 'Thanks. I think.'

'Not like that. I mean, we get on so well. I wouldn't want to ruin it by making it awkward.'

'Because this conversation is *totally* un-mortifying.'

Greg took a breath. 'It's just, you're not my usual type.'

She snorted. 'This is getting better and better.'

'Type of . . . Ach! Let me get it all out. You're not some girl I met in a bar, or at a party. You're smart and funny and can beat me in a race. And I like hanging out with you. To be honest — to my disappointment — I didn't think you were interested in me. Not in that way. You'd pulled away from me after the ball.'

'Dear lord,' said Holly, closing her eyes. 'I can honestly say I want this to end.'

'I'm not trying to make you feel bad. The opposite. I want to clear the air. So: there was something between us. But on the way home — aside from the fact you were a little drunk and I wasn't — I remembered what you said about all your mother's boyfriends, and decided that that maybe I needed to take things more slowly. I didn't want you to think . . . I didn't want you to feel—'

'Ditched, like one of many other girls?'

'That's not fair,' said Greg.

'If your relationship history went on your CV, I wouldn't hire you. I'm sorry — but it's true.'

Perhaps that had a been a bit harsh. Holly had meant it to be a joke. Well, kind of. But she was putting on her best suit of armour, fashioned from snippy remarks, determined not to get hurt again.

Greg looked floored. 'You think I'm that person?'

Holly felt a knot of regret and cast around for words to make it better. 'Everyone says you're that person. *You've* just said you're that person.' It was hardly an improvement. She waited for him to reply.

'Look, I haven't dated anyone this year.'

Holly frowned, not having expected that confession. She looked out of the window towards the sea, wanting to order her thoughts coherently. Everything he was saying was thoughtful, considered, making his behaviour forgivable. But it was futile, pretending that anything could be salvaged from this.

'Greg,' she said, opening her eyes. 'I'm going to be straight with you. I was only ever here for a year, and it's already September. And then I go to Berkshire to start my dream job. When I first arrived, I'd made a pact with myself that I was going to focus on work, and not let anything else distract me. I mean, I made that pact *before* I arrived. It's how I've lived my whole life — mainly due to, yes, you guessed it, my mum. I'm not looking for love. Or flings. Or whatever it is you're offering. Or not offering. Not right now.'

'So if I said given my chance again, I would have taken that kiss, would that change your mind?'

Greg looked at her expectantly. But she knew in her head it was going to be a no. Despite the emotions she'd been having, the ones where his presence made her feel effervescent, she had to be true to herself.

'To be honest, I'm not sure. I want to avoid romantic entanglements. Especially with practised lotharios.'

Shocked by the force with which the barbs kept flying from her mouth, she jammed yet another biscuit in it.

Greg looked hurt. 'Is that what you think? That I'm some kind of lady-killer who doesn't care about other people's emotions? I never said I didn't want to find the right person.'

'It also doesn't sound like you were trying hard,' said Holly, although she felt bad about saying it. It was a low move, trying to quieten any misery over your own choices by taking swipes at someone else's.

'I do. I've forgotten how to get past all the . . .' He waved his hands around his head for a second. 'I've not felt ready to . . .'

As he gathered his words, Holly started to feel shattered. She leaned back in the chair and ran her hands through her still damp hair, her fingers getting caught in the tangles. She was leaving for Ascot at the end of the year. And Greg was off to Edinburgh. There was no point in any of this. She cut him off.

'I don't think I'm the girl who's going to get you out of this slump, Greg. But I'm sure someone will.'

'But you felt something, right? It wasn't just me.'

Holly bit her lip. 'If I did, it was a momentary lapse of judgement on my part. Any feelings I might have had have disappeared. Just like that. Poof.'

'I know from experience that doesn't happen . . .'

They caught each other's eye, Holly feeling every cell in her body leap with anticipation. And then she found sense. 'It can.'

Greg looked at the floor for a second. 'Maybe I ought to go.'

'Probably best,' said Holly. 'Glad I could offer an ear, but I'm done in. I think I need to go and have lie down.'

And some time alone to settle her aching head.

He nodded and got up, walking to the door. 'I'll see you about, I hope,' he said, and Holly sensed a note of hope in his voice. 'Perhaps we can go for a drink — platonic, of course. Or a run, when you've recovered from this one. Or that picnic. Look — I'd rather have you in my life as a friend, than not at all. If you'll have me.'

'Sure,' she said, and gave him a peck on the cheek.

He opened the door, and stepped out. 'Bye, Holly.'

'Bye, Greg.'

As Holly closed the door behind him, she felt instantly wretched. It would be foolish to go after him, wouldn't it. Wouldn't it?

CHAPTER 34

Eventually Chloe reached the last part of the main road, ready to drop down into Eastercraig. She had no idea how she had got there — perhaps her body had gone into survival mode without her realizing. Then, as she'd thought she'd made it, everything began to burn.

She half ran, half tripped up the road, and finally the finish line came into view. There, waving wildly, was Angus. Despite her lack of energy, Chloe felt her hand shoot up. She had done it! She could do anything!

Gathering pace, because of the incline rather than any reserves she might have, Chloe barrelled down the hill. She'd imagined reaching the end, the crowd parting — although this was now off the cards as the crowd was *de*parting — and the rapturous applause. But it didn't matter, because Angus was there. Off to the side she noticed Paolo, who gave her a fist pump, then pointed at Angus and mouthed "go get him, girl", before disappearing off towards his flat.

'You look like you could do with one of these,' said her dad's voice, tapping her mum's stick.

Chloe spun around to see her parents. She'd been so caught up thinking of Angus she hadn't seen them. 'Have you been here the whole time? Aren't you freezing?'

'We've been in the pub, darling,' said her mum. 'Angus came to let us know you'd be a while, didn't you, love. Honestly, Angus, you're such a good lad, so thoughtful. And you looked so dashing at the ball. You're light on your feet for a man your size. It's a mystery why you've not found yourself a lass to settle down with.'

Angus went pink, and Chloe felt a large part of herself die of embarrassment. She couldn't bring herself to meet Angus's eyes. Instead, she looked at her father, who gave her a small wink.

Finally, when Mei's gushing praise came to a stop, Angus murmured a "thanks", and in return received a pat on the arm.

'Mum, I'm getting cold. Shall we all go home?' Chloe asked quickly.

'Och, no. We've had a call from Debbie Brewer asking us if we want to pop over for coffee. Can you walk back?'

Chloe had just run thirteen miles and wasn't sure she could. But it was important for Mei to be out and about when she felt like it. 'I'll try, Mum.'

'Thanks, pet. I'd hate to cancel on Debbie. Maybe Angus could run you back? Could you dear?' she turned to Angus.

'Oh, Mum!' Chloe said, cringing.

Angus nodded. 'Of course, Mei.'

Chloe, numb with dismay over her mother's interference, turned to Angus. 'Thank you. That's kind.'

'There's Debbie,' her father said, waving at a woman over by the shop. 'Come on, Mei. We'll see you later, Chlo. Bye, Angus.'

When her parents were out of earshot, Chloe turned to apologize. Angus wasn't the type to revel in a shower of compliments, and Mei's outpouring would have caused even the vainest of men to blush.

To her surprise, Angus let out a chuckle. 'Dashing?! Your mum thinks I'm dashing?'

At least he'd seen the funny side. 'Apparently so.'

'And "light on my feet for a man my size". I should put that on my dating profile.'

'You have a dating profile?'

'Nah. But I think I should get one just to include that gem.'

He guffawed again, and Chloe's heart — which had taken a momentary back seat when she'd thought he might be looking for love online — began to beat again.

'Well,' she said, his laugh helping her find some confidence. 'You did look *very* dashing. And you *were* light on your feet.'

'As were you. And you looked dashing too. Well, beautiful — I'm not sure girls can be dashing. Och — look at your cheeks. They're beginning to look chapped. Let's get you home.'

If he'd realized he'd made her blush, he did a good job of sparing her further embarrassment. They walked towards the car, and Angus held out an arm.

'How does it feel to have done something you never thought you'd manage?' he asked, opening the door.

If only he knew of the irony in his words. Chloe climbed up into the car. 'I'm feeling pretty proud of myself. Although I couldn't have done it without you. I appreciate it, your seeing me off, meeting me at the house.'

'It's nae bother,' he replied. 'Always happy to help out.'

The car trundled along the front, and Chloe shivered. She was still riding high on having completed the race. This was it. This was her moment to ask him for a drink, just the two of them. She took a breath.

Then, as they were approaching the pub, Chloe spotted Daisy Morello, waving wildly. Daisy was, as always, looking glamourous, with heeled trainers, skinny jeans and a shiny parka. Next to her stood a petite, but no-less-polished woman, wearing pink lipstick. Angus pulled up and wound down his window.

'Angus, darling,' Daisy said, in her soft, breathy way. 'This is my cousin, Elle. You know, I told you way back, at the ball.'

'Daisy told me you were handsome. And she was right,' Elle pouted, her big blue eyes sparkling.

'Hi, Daisy. Hi, Elle.' Angus nodded at them, with a hint of a smile. 'You know Chloe, one of Eastercraig's residents.'

'Yes, of course,' said Daisy, and acknowledged Chloe, as if only seeing her in the car for the first time. 'Anyway. Elle's up here until Tuesday, and I thought you'd like to join us and Hamish at the pub tonight.'

Angus looked as puzzled as Chloe felt. 'I thought you'd broken up,' Chloe said. Paolo had been keeping her and Holly abreast of the situation. Honestly, it was hard to keep up. She had only just got her head around the fact Paolo had told Hamish was bi, before swearing them to secrecy because it wasn't really his news to share. 'You're back together?'

A faint look of annoyance crossed Daisy's face, which was then replaced by one of smug satisfaction. 'Chloe, you'll be too tired to join us after all this running, but it was nice to see you. Catch you later, Angus.'

All this time, she'd thought she'd been making progress with him, only for him to be asked out by someone else. Seeing Daisy, with all her shiny confidence, and her equally gleaming cousin, was enough to make her feel helpless again. Helpless, and about two foot tall.

Angus nodded at Daisy, then drove up the hill back to Chloe's house.

'Daisy's back on the scene?' Chloe said flatly.

'Apparently so. I imagine Hamish will be needing some backup.'

It couldn't have been off-putting that backup would involve entertaining Elle. Chloe had always thought he'd like someone down-to-earth, comfortable in wellies and able to bake a cake, but maybe she'd been wrong, even if Elle did look like a praying mantis in a cashmere coat.

Where Daisy's cousin had the real edge, though, was sheer brazenness. Which, as Chloe well knew — she realized with a sinking feeling — she couldn't even begin to muster.

This girl was so disarmingly confident she'd tell Angus she liked him, draw him out of his shell and out of the gloom in which he existed on the farm. They'd be engaged within a month.

'I imagine he will,' said Chloe, and sighed.

They drove the rest of the way in silence. Chloe couldn't find any words. If the race hadn't tired her enough, she felt shattered Angus was going out in the evening on a double date.

'You OK? You've gone quiet.' Angus turned into Chloe's drive.

'It's been a long day. And it's not even lunchtime,' said Chloe.

'Are you going to be OK? Want me to see you in?'

'I'll be fine,' Chloe replied firmly.

Legs wobbling, Chloe hopped down from the cab. She would be fine, after a nice hot bath and a jacket potato. And several days of general wallowing.

'Fine doesn't sound like you,' said Angus. 'I thought you'd be more exuberant than this.'

'I am exuberant,' said Chloe, with all the bounce of a wilted lettuce leaf. 'Watch.'

To prove it — or rather, put Angus off the scent — she hopped from side to side.

'Full of beans,' Angus grinned. 'See you later in the week? I can give you the news on Hamish. Heaven knows what's going on there.'

'Yeah, give me a call,' Chloe replied. 'Thanks for the lift.'

Chloe shut the cab door and waved as Angus sped off down the road. Then she let herself in, ready to collapse on the sofa and retreat back into herself.

* * *

Later, as she cleared up evidence of the biscuit-binge crime scene in the sitting room, Holly reflected on the position she was in. She'd literally fled from Greg that morning. She might have been able to outrun him, but he was still at the forefront of her mind. Slumping into the sofa, dressed in her most comfortable leggings, she closed her eyes.

She wanted stability, didn't she? It wasn't a question, never had been. It was a statement of fact. That was her goal. A stable family, a stable home, all supported by her own stable job. Holly had spent her entire life aiming for this, and she was nearly there. At least, the job and the home parts. She might have enough for a deposit on a flat soon, especially with all the extra money she'd saved while being up in Eastercraig.

Greg was the epitome of everything she'd worked against. He had no potential to be anything more than a fling, not least as she was leaving. And as for Chloe saying he was "lost" . . . Holly didn't think she was the one to find him. Most likely she'd end up being the most recent notch on his bedpost.

Yet, even though he was the wrong man on *every* level, in the wrong place, at the wrong time, Holly still felt drawn to him. She was still going over their every conversation. Dissecting with great care each touch, each shared look, each moment.

'Holly Anderson,' she said to herself. 'You are losing the plot. Stay on track. This is not part of the life you want. You need to forget this pretender and keep going.'

Her mind a jumble, and hating being in such a state, Holly got up, pulled on a jacket and headed over to the practice. She could pick up some files, check the animals. Anything would be a welcome distraction.

CHAPTER 35

It turned out going to the surgery hadn't been a good idea after all. Holly was standing by Joe MacAllan, the harbour-master, trying to diagnose his cat, Dora, an old tabby. She might have stood a strong chance of doing so, only she could barely understand a word Joe was saying.

Joe, an old client of the surgery, kept exchanging concerned glances with Hugh, who was sitting on a stool by the counter. Hugh had come in as a favour to Joe, who was worried about Dora, but on discovering Holly working at the desk, he had told her to take the appointment. He must really dislike her not to have stepped in by now.

'She's been . . .' said Joe, for the fourth time.

Holly could only make out about one in every three words Joe said. His was the thickest accent she had encountered since coming to Eastercraig.

'I'm so sorry, Joe. Could I ask you to repeat that one more time?' Holly shrank backwards as she said it.

'I said . . .' Joe bellowed.

Holly felt like she might faint with embarrassment. She looked to Hugh, who glared back at her.

Joe looked at her. 'I said she's been losing weight. She's off her food, and this last week has been behaving oddly, hiding in corners and running away.' He enunciated every word in a fake English accent.

Holly bit her lip at Joe's final words. It was never a good sign when animals started to withdraw. It often signalled that whatever the underlying condition was, it had advanced to the point where the end was near, and Dora looked very unwell.

She put aside the mortification she was feeling. 'I want to run some tests, Joe. We'll get the results for you next week.'

Shortly after, having seen Joe and Dora back to reception, she pulled Hugh back. 'I'm not sure that cat's going to live much longer.'

'Joe got that cat when his wife died.' Hugh muttered.

Holly bristled at what was a wholly unhelpful comment. Was Hugh implying she wasn't going to do her utmost? She didn't reply and went to make a calming cup of tea before writing up her notes. As she put the milk back in the fridge, she pulled out her phone and composed a message to Chloe and Paolo.

> *Have you both finished? Sorry I wasn't there to see either of you over the line, but something came up. Come for a drink on the porch asap? x*

CHAPTER 36

'Elle? The one who looked like she wouldn't know a farm if she was walking through one?' Paolo gawped in disbelief.

Holly stared out at the ocean. It ought to calm her. High tide had brought the water to the wall, and she, Paolo and Chloe were sat with their legs dangling though the railings. Holly stretched out a bare toe and dipped it in the cool water, swirling it absentmindedly as she tried to silence the voices in her head, which were arguing about what she'd said to Greg, whether she had been right to push him away.

Chloe looked dejected. 'I waited for ages. I know it was never official but I felt there was chemistry. Like when you put the metal in the water and it fizzes uncontrollably.'

'Lithium,' said Holly.

'What?' said Chloe. 'Oh. Is that the metal?'

Holly nodded and gave Chloe's arm a squeeze. 'Don't overthink. It might be nothing. Same with Hamish and Daisy. It might all end in tears.'

Paolo shrugged, a look of melancholy passing over his face.

'Don't tell me you fancy him?' said Chloe. 'We've been over this.'

He shook his head. 'No, nothing like that. But Daisy is all wrong for him. He's wasted so much time on her already. How's the prosecco going down, Hols? Feeling better?'

'Nope. I feel flat. Like I've been run over by a steam-roller.' Holly took a swig from the bottle she was holding and then offered it to Chloe.

'We need to find new men. No, actually — all men are horrible wastes of space. Let's not find any. I don't want one. Not one who would go out with someone like Elle,' Chloe said. 'Do you still feel anything for Greg?'

Holly wrinkled her brow in contemplation. It was no good denying it. 'I do. But you're right. He's off to Edinburgh for a few months so it's definitely time to forget him. I need to think of stuff that negates all the reasons I like him.'

'Me too,' Chloe agreed emphatically. 'I've got some ready to let fly right now, in fact. Angus agreed to go out with Elle; is otherwise married to his cows; smells of manure, sometimes; moody, regularly. Oh, this is *so* cathartic. You try.'

Holly took a theatrical breath. 'Greg: shoes are too shiny; doesn't *live* here or in Ascot; buggering off to Edinburgh, which is even further than Aberdeen; famed as a liability with the opposite sex . . . Did he think I'd see him as having a softer side if he got a pet?'

'Holly,' Paolo gave her a nudge.

But she was getting into it. 'Honestly, as if buying a dog absolves you of being a dick.'

'Holly!' Chloe grabbed her arm and pulled it sharply.

'Ow, Chlo.' Holly turned round then froze. 'Oh. Greg.'

He was standing right behind them, hurt painted over every inch of his face. Holly felt chills run through her, as if she were neck deep in ice.

'I was just passing on my way to the pub,' he said.

'Greg . . .' said Holly.

It was too late, though. For a second Greg held her gaze as he walked backwards, shaking his head. Then he turned and went.

'Oh God,' whispered Holly. 'What have I done?'

* * *

Later that evening, after Chloe and Paolo had left, another two bottles of prosecco down between them, Holly went outside once more. She sat on the bench outside Sea Spray to watch the sunset, the remains of a glass of whisky beside her. She picked it up and gave it a sniff, breathing in the peatiness.

Really, she ought to have been in bed, but the golden September light was so enticing. Holly wrapped her blanket around her as the sun sank down, the sky looking like a watercolourist had picked up pinks and oranges and washed them across the heavens in broad sweeps.

It should have been a peaceful end to a crazy day, only she was fixating on the Greg disaster, clips of which insisted on whirring around her brain, like a horror film. Her insults had been slung like a succession of verbal grenades, each one worse than the last. She hadn't really meant any of them, which made the devastation even worse.

She picked up her phone and called. No answer. Immediately she tried again. Nothing. To be fair, it would have been more surprising if he had picked up.

She sent a text:

Can we talk. Please?

The reply was swift:

I think you said it all earlier.

Please, Greg? It wasn't what it seemed.

It seemed pretty obvious. Those were some choice words.

This wasn't going well. Holly took another swig from the tumbler.

It was a misunderstanding. I am truly sorry.

It's late. I've got work tomorrow. I'll see you around.

Temped to hurl the phone into the sea, Holly stopped, aware of something wet on her cheek. It was a tear! She cursed out loud. At some point, over the course of the year, she had turned into Jackie. It was way past her bedtime, she was the wrong side of tipsy and crying over a man. She shuddered at the thought. At least she didn't have rivers of mascara coursing down her face.

'Well,' she said to a passing seagull. 'If there's anyone who can sympathize with my plight, it's her. Lord knows how many disastrous relationships she's had.'

The seagull squawked back at her and, taking it as a cue, Holly picked up the phone and dialled. It rang a few times, then Jackie picked up, and for the first time in a while, Holly took comfort in the chirpy voice.

'Holly Dolly, it's ever so late. Are you OK?'

'Jackie, I know we don't talk about the serious things all that much, but do you have a moment to chat?'

'I know, darling,' her mum chuckled. 'And yes, I'm all ears.'

Holly sighed. 'I'll get to the point. I met a guy, fell for him and then I ballsed it up. And I feel rubbish.'

'Oh, pet. I know how you feel, you poor darling. Men are pigs.'

Perhaps her mum wasn't the right person for this conversation. Jackie had been through so many boyfriends there wasn't much scope for nuance. Once they were out of your life, all men were lumped in the same dismal pile.

She went to Greg's defence. 'But he's not a pig. He's great.'

Jackie let out an "ooooooo" like a pantomime dame. 'A good one, eh? So it's worth fixing? You've never talked about having a man before . . .'

Mainly because there had never been one. There was a pause, and the line crackled. In the silence between them, cogs whirred and something clicked. Holly hadn't called her mother to get advice about Greg. Or for a maternal ear into which to pour her woe. Of course she hadn't. She had called her because Jackie was the reason Holly was so scared of falling in love.

Holly decided to try a different angle. 'Can we not talk about him for a bit . . . Listen, Jackie, have you ever been in love? Actual, all-consuming love? I know you had lots of boyfriends, but I'm talking about the real thing.'

There was a creaking sound, followed by footsteps, and a door shutting. Her mother lowered her voice.

'Moving to the sitting room — don't want Marco hearing this, nice as he is. I liked a lot of them. Especially the ones who seemed like they'd stick around. But they always got bored, so then I'd go for a flashier one, you know, who might whisk me off my feet and off to a nice hotel for a night. But in between trying to look after you, hold down a job and pay the bills, things wobbled, without fail. And you know what, Holly, I wouldn't say I truly loved any of them. I desperately wanted to, but I didn't.'

'You've never really been in love?' It surprised Holly that a woman who had dedicated so much time and effort to finding a partner had confessed that.

'Lust, perhaps. But not love.'

'Wow.' Holly didn't know what to say. She felt her entire body slump. 'I'm sorry.'

'Wait, darling. I wasn't quite finished,' Jackie said, sounding both serious and sad. 'There was only ever one man I truly loved. It was your dad, but it ended before I found out I was pregnant. After that, I panicked. Hurled myself at every man going in the hope of getting it right. But none of them were any good.'

'You loved my dad?' Holly whispered. This was a revelation. Jackie never talked about Holly's father.

'I did, doll. It doesn't matter now, though. Can't change it — it's all ancient history. But sometimes I think about what might have been if it worked. But that's that. Nothing more to it.' Jackie let out a shuddering sigh, and Holly sensed she was unwilling to talk further about it. 'Look, darling, if you've found someone who you like, and who feels the same way, go for it! If you don't, you'll always be left wondering what might have been. And end up like me — a total mess.'

Her greatest fear writ large. The one thing that held her back more than anything else in the world. The comparison made Holly breathless.

'Christ,' whispered Holly. 'Do you think that'll happen?'

A cackle ran down the line. 'Nah. *Highly* unlikely. You might be my daughter, but we couldn't be more different. I'm a gambler, Hols. Taken many a bet on a man being the right one, and — afraid to say — usually lost. But you're a smart girl, you don't do risk. I bet you've thought this through.'

Relief that Jackie saw them as different people flooded her body. And Jackie was right. Holly *had* thought it through. She had let her head tell her over and over that it was foolish, yet still the thought of Greg persisted.

'He doesn't want to know. We had an . . .' Her throat constricted slightly and Holly tailed off, hit by the futility of it all. Her skin felt numb and she rubbed her temples, trying to restart the circulation.

'Apologize,' Jackie said simply.

'He won't hear me out.'

'Then try again.' Jackie sounded determined. 'You've *never* been a quitter, Holly. Not like me. You're a sticker. You've always worked hard and got what you want. If you want this, keep fighting. Go on. And sometimes, doll, and I know this isn't in your nature perhaps, you have to let your heart lead the way.'

'But what if it works, *then* it goes wrong. What if I don't recover?'

'People recover from all sorts of things, Holly. I've recovered from dozens of bad relationships. Sure, I have my downs, but I also have my ups. Nobody's perfect. Look, it's better to regret doing something that regret not doing it, right?'

Hard to argue with that one. 'I guess so.'

Her mother was coming off as an actual rounded person. Well, not completely round, but not the wholly disjointed individual that Holly had always written her off as either. She had always thought her mother was oblivious to her flaws, but perhaps Jackie was completely aware of them. At ease with them. Maybe Holly should be the same with hers.

There was a pause, and Holly wondered what Jackie was about to say. 'Look, darling. Now we're having a serious conversation, I know I've not always been the best mum. I want to make up for the times I was ropey . . .'

It wasn't the time to open that can of worms, seeing as there was already one to deal with. With a touch of guilt that she didn't usually feel with Jackie, Holly gently pushed away the olive branch her mother was offering. 'Can we talk about it another time?'

Her mum laughed. 'All right, darling. I'll let you know when I'm back in Blighty. Maybe come visit you.'

'I'd like that,' said Holly.

'And let me know how it goes with this chap, eh? Chat soon.'

They said their goodbyes and rang off. Holly pushed her back up against the bench. All this time she had been railing against love, unwilling to take the leap. Too scared of it and what it might do. But perhaps instead she needed to fight for it. Face her fears, put her preconceptions to one side and, for once, let her heart rule her head.

CHAPTER 37

Holly got up from the bench, walked the hundred yards down the front and stopped outside a pretty white building with blue windows. This was it. She was going to right her wrongs. She pulled out her phone and composed another text, her fingers trembling as she hit send.

Are you in the B&B? I need to talk to you.

It's late, Holly.

I'm outside. I want to apologise. Before you go to Edinburgh and I never see you again.

There was no reply. Holly wondered if it was too much to have another whisky when she got back.

A few moments later, the front door clicked open, and Greg, in a pair of old joggers and a jumper, slightly bleary-eyed, stepped on to the pavement.

'Holly, I get it. You don't approve of my behaviour. And I can understand why. But it's late, and I need to drive back to Aberdeen first thing,' he whispered.

'I am really sorry. I was angry. And Chloe and I were playing a stupid game where we were trying to stop ourselves thinking about you and Angus.'

Greg pulled the door to behind him, put a hand on her back and started to guide her back along the front.

'What's happening?' she asked.

He shushed her. 'You were talking *incredibly* loudly. Come on, let's get back to yours, and I'll tell you the whole story. And then maybe *that* will absolve me of being a dick.'

Holly bit the inside of her cheek, desperate to keep the awkwardness at bay as her words from earlier continued to echo in her ears.

They reached Sea Spray, and Holly walked in. It was a good thing it was a quiet town. She'd left the front door wide open.

Greg sat down on the sofa. 'You know when you told me you had some feelings, and they disappeared?' Greg began. 'I know feelings don't disappear. When my fiancé Ally left me the night before our wedding, I had every right to hate her, but I couldn't. I loved her, and I would have taken her back in an instant.'

Wait. *What*? Holly blinked. 'I thought you left her.'

Greg shook his head. 'No. She left me. And I said I'd take the blame for it.'

'But everyone said *you'd* got cold feet. But it was her all along?!'

'She said she hadn't felt the same way for a long time. That she didn't know how to end it and thought marriage might solve it. Only it made it much worse.'

He looked at the floor and Holly felt an ache for him. Suddenly he was a far cry from the "practised lothario" she'd branded him. 'What happened?'

Holly sat down at the other end of the sofa and turned to face him, pulling her knees beneath her.

Greg hesitated. 'I don't like to talk about it. But here goes . . . You know when you meet the right person? I'd always thought the fireworks thing was a myth, but when

I met Ally at a party it was as if an entire box of the things had gone off at once. She was incredible, and when she said yes to going on a date, I was floored. And after a few more dates we became exclusive, and after six months we moved in together. Then, after another year, I asked her to marry me. It was quick, but when you're in love, you know. And I *knew*.

'The wedding date was set, but it was as if doing that set off a panic button inside her. We began to argue about insignificant things. She'd snap when I asked her questions. Not want to be in the house. I put it down to nerves. Everyone gets stressed before the big day, right? There're tons going on. Then the night before, she told me she couldn't go through with it. Nothing else. She didn't love me enough.'

He stopped and shut his eyes, and Holly wondered how real the pain must feel even all these years afterwards.

'I'm so sorry,' she said, after a moment.

Greg opened his eyes. 'I'd been so blindly in love I hadn't realized she didn't feel exactly the same way.'

'Why didn't she tell you sooner?'

'She felt there had never been the right moment.'

'And why does everyone think you left her, and not the other way round?'

Greg ran his hands through his hair. 'She didn't want her parents to know it was her. They had put *so* much money into it. She couldn't bear the shame, and thought they would be furious. Because I loved her so much, I said I would take the blame. It would mean only one broken relationship, rather than two. I've never told anyone else, not even my best man — Angus.'

Holly's insides froze. He had let the whole town think he had deserted his fiancée because even in the throes of heartache he could still find it in himself to be the bigger person.

She shifted to the edge of her seat. 'And then what?'

'I haven't seen her since. And after it happened, I decided there was no point looking for love — not after it had got the better of me. I'd been so wrong about it I told myself I wouldn't ever make that mistake again.'

And with that comment she was back in the room. 'Hence a string of broken hearts across the Highlands . . .'

Greg frowned. 'I always make my intentions clear.'

'Crikey. What a delight you are!'

Greg gave a half-smile. 'I suppose you could see it that way. I do want to settle down one day, but at the same time I've not wanted to get too close.'

'I get that,' said Holly, which of course she did. More than anything.

So that was Greg. He'd been so hurt by what Ally had done he hadn't wanted to commit to anyone in case it happened again. Herself included.

'What about you? When will the time be right for Holly Anderson?'

Now? With Greg? No — they had already decided earlier that it was going to be friendship. On that she had to hold fast. 'I spoke to my mum earlier. Jackie opened up to me, and it made me feel like perhaps relationships might not be all bad. Up until this point it's all been self-preservation, but maybe I'm ready to let go a little.'

She looked to Greg, who held out his hand. She took it and gave it a squeeze.

'Why do you always call her that?' he asked.

'Call her what?'

'Jackie? Not Mum.'

'Oh. When I was eleven I decided she was such a crap parent she wasn't worthy of the title, so I took to using her given name. She thought it was funny, which proved my point.'

She let out a sigh and stared at her feet, recalling her mother's words. Imagine how hideous it could have been if Jackie had said "We're not so different, you and I". But she hadn't. Reassuringly, she confirmed that they were from different planets. Which *hopefully* meant letting herself fall in love wouldn't result in Holly finding herself, in her fifties, in a Costa del Sol dive, wearing a macramé bikini and cut-offs, three espresso martinis down by teatime.

The urge to be honest won out. 'Anyway. Talking to her made me realize . . .' Holly paused as she riffled through her thoughts, wondering how to phrase it. There wasn't much to lose. Apart from control. Although — she reminded herself — she had made her peace with that. 'I should let you know I really like you too. You were right about the feelings not disappearing. But . . . I go at the end of the year.'

'I know. You said so earlier.'

'Yes. So while I've said what I've said, that's all. But I'd very much like to be friends, you know, if you'll have me.'

The words caught in her throat as she said them, even though there was not an ounce doubt this was the right thing to do. A new life awaited her — even if it didn't thrill her as it should — and it would be the wrong time to start a relationship with someone at the other end of the country.

'Do you want a hug?' came Greg's voice.

She looked up. 'Reckon so. Do you?'

'I would,' he said.

'Hang on,' he said. He shifted down the sofa and put an arm round her. 'I'm sorry things haven't worked out between us. But if I've gained you as a friend, then maybe that's something.'

Holly smiled. 'Agreed. I think you might be the best thing that never happened to me.'

There was a pause, one in which Holly's mind filled with reprieves, all of which ended in Greg pulling her in for a kiss. Her body still yearned for his, and he was right there, their closeness tormenting her. She screwed up her face for allowing the thoughts to catch her out so easily.

'Let's talk about something else,' she said, bringing the conversation to a close.

And they did, talking into the small hours about everything and nothing, all the while Holly thinking how unfair it was this was never going to work.

CHAPTER 38

When you wanted more, agreeing to be friends with someone was hard. At least Greg was in Edinburgh, and Holly didn't have to worry about seeing him. All the same, the possibility of rekindling anything gone, Holly found herself trying to fill every spare moment with activity. She ran more, paddle boarded more, and one November weekend where she was at a total loose end she persuaded Paolo and Chloe, along with Chloe's friends Isla and Morag, to come and paint the surgery. It had taken the five of them two full days, but plenty of people popped their heads round the door to tell them how clean and fresh it looked.

The weekend they had painted, Hugh had gone to see his sister and brother-in-law in Edinburgh, and upon his arrival back, on a mizzly Monday, he blustered in.

'There's something different,' Hugh said, squinting around the room. 'I can't put my finger on it.'

He went through to the kitchen, and Holly, Chloe and Paolo waited behind the desk.

'Should we tell him?' Chloe whispered.

'Nah. Let him sweat it out. It's not rocket science,' said Paolo.

Hugh reversed out of the kitchen. 'Smells funny too.'

'Like . . . fresh paint?' asked Holly.

Hugh scowled. 'Ach. That's it. The walls are a different colour.'

'And Fiona stitched up the sofa cushions,' Chloe pointed to them. 'Isn't it all jolly?'

'The one behind you is yellow,' Hugh was fixating. 'You've jaundiced the place. I feel like I'm swimming in custard.'

'Everyone loves custard,' said Holly, as brightly as she could. No good deed went unpunished, a phrase with infinite applications when it came to Hugh.

'Not me,' said Hugh firmly.

They had put in hours of work. Paolo was unsurprised, and Chloe looked crestfallen. Holly threw her hands up in the air. 'I'm sorry it's not to your liking. But I think it's a big improvement.'

Hugh muttered something under his breath, huffed and made his way through the door to the consulting room.

'It's not even custard,' said Chloe, in a small voice. 'It's Dutch Orange.'

Paolo guffawed. 'I'll tend to Hugh. Chloe, here are some biscuits I made on the weekend. Plate them up and they can form part of a peace offering.'

Holly looked at the cheerful dahlias that a client had brought them, and that Chloe had put in a tall vase on the desk. Without the Greg drama, there was only Hugh drama. And while unpredictable, Hugh drama wasn't nearly as exciting. It was routine. Oh well, only a couple more months of heated tirades and she would be in Ascot. Judith had called to let her know the job at VetCo was definitely coming up at the end of the year, and that even though Holly would have to re-interview, it was a sure thing that the job would be hers. Apparently, the team in Ascot there had felt awful about her having to delay by a year.

Out of the corner of her eye, a shadow moved in front of the surgery door. She looked up from the dahlias and saw a box had appeared on the pavement.

They weren't expecting anything. Or if they were, most of their deliveries had to be signed for. As she approached it, she saw it was moving. She hoped to God it wasn't snakes. That had happened to her once before, and finding a clutch of abandoned corn snakes in a teeming heap hadn't exactly filled her with joy.

Cautiously, she opened the lid.

'Oh!' she gasped, and pulled out a tiny kitten, black with white socks.

Inside were two more. The mother wasn't there. Holly put the kitten back in the box with its siblings and carried it back to reception.

Chloe, back from her biscuit goodwill mission, was behind the desk. 'Placated him temporarily. What've you got there?'

Holly brought the box round. 'Look,' she said in a hushed voice.

'Wow! Where did they come from?'

'No idea. I didn't see who left it, and there's no note. I'll take them out the back and check them over and then we can work out where to send them.'

She took the box into the consulting room and beckoned Paolo.

He approached it with suspicion. 'Someone leaves a weird box and scarpers. Have you seen *Seven*?'

'I like to think I've won the townspeople over and that nobody would send me a head in a box.'

'Cute!' Paolo's eyes lit up as he fished one out of the box. 'We've got about twenty minutes before appointments start. Let's do as much as we can. Hugh'll be down in a second and can help.'

The door swung open. 'Christ! I've got two ferrets coming in a minute. What's all this about you having kittens?'

'Hello, Hugh!' Holly said. 'Someone left us a little present.'

'Och. Actual kittens. For heaven's sakes, the poor wee things,' Hugh grumbled. 'There's a cat charity in Inverness. I'll see if they can have them.'

Holly looked at the tiny kittens, shifting around in the box, and picked one up, causing it to emit a tiny mew. It was so helpless. They would need round-the-clock care for a good few weeks. An idea struck her.

'Hugh. You're going to see to the ferrets, right? I think I know someone who might take these. I'll be really quick . . . Just keep an eye on them for me.'

Ignoring Hugh's huffing, Holly slipped out the back door of the surgery and went through the alleyway to the front. At a jog, she made her way round to the harbourmaster's office. It was pretty early, but she was sure there'd be someone in. She took a breath and rapped loudly on the door. With a creaking clunk, one of the sash windows was hauled up.

'Good morning, Ms Anderson,' said Joe MacAllan, sticking his head out into the brisk late-autumn air.

Holly grinned, let herself in and ran up the flight of stairs. The door to the office was open, and behind a tatty desk sat Joe, sipping tea from an old mug. Holly composed herself.

'I know it's not long since we had to put poor Dora down,' said Holly. 'And I'm sure you miss her. She was a sweet thing. It's odd not seeing her out on her rounds of the harbour.'

'Aye.' A veil of sorrow fell across Joe's face. 'I miss that girl every day.'

'I wondered, if it isn't too soon, if you might want another cat. I know none will ever replace Dora, but someone dropped a box of three kittens on the surgery doorstop just now, and they'll need looking after. They're all healthy, and . . . I just think it would be nice for them to stay here, and maybe you would have the time. Just one of them. Not all. I'll ask around if anyone else wants to take the others.'

Joe leaned forward, his elbows on his desk. Holly really hoped he would say yes. And that she would be able to understand him. His accent still had the tendency to outfox her.

She continued. 'They'll go to Inverness otherwise. But I saw them and immediately thought of you.'

'Aye,' said Joe. 'I'll take them.'

'Really?' Holly clapped her hands together. 'What . . . all of them?'

'They've been separated from their mother, dumped by their owner. The least we can do is keep the siblings together.'

Holly put her hand on her heart. If she hadn't still been reasonably scared of Joe, she would have thrown her arms around him in gratitude.

'We'll keep them in for a couple of days, make sure they're definitely OK. If you have a moment this afternoon, come over and see them? They're lovely. Two girls and a boy.'

'Thank you,' said Joe. 'And thank you for thinking of me. It's very kind of you.'

'Not at all,' said Holly with a smile.

Later that afternoon, Holly found the confidence to ask Hugh a question that had been weighing on her mind.

'Can I have a word, please?' Holly asked.

Hugh looked up from the reception desk, where he was doing some paperwork, and huffed. 'Just the one?'

'A few,' said Holly, wanting to huff back.

'Go on, then. But be quick.'

Holly closed her eyes. This was it. A defining moment. The beginning of the end, in the best way possible.

'I was wondering if you'll be ready to write my letter of recommendation by the end of the year. I've seen so much, and feel like I've really grown, and been a credit to the surgery.'

At this, Hugh coughed and looked up. There was no reply, but she wasn't going to be intimidated by his silence. Refusing to be knocked off course, Holly continued.

'Ascot really depends on it. Twelve months was what you and Judith agreed, and I think I've spent my time well.' Or served her time, more accurately.

Hugh looked at her and smiled. 'I'll write you a letter.'

Holly grinned. Then she realized Hugh was most likely smiling because he was going to be rid of her. It was what he had probably wanted for the entire year. Or, as Hugh drew breath, maybe there was a catch.

'But only on the 31st of December, and only if you don't do anything daft between now and then. And on the proviso you judge the dog show.'

Holly stared at him. 'The *what*?'

* * *

On his lunchbreak, Paolo stepped out for some milk, only to spot Hamish, who waved and walked towards him.

'Paolo,' Hamish called. 'How are you?'

Paolo took a breath. Every time he'd try to say hello the last few months, Hamish had Daisy hanging off his arm, and Paolo had a feeling it would be awkward if he popped up next to them. Not that he was sure why. Nope — that was a lie. He knew full well why. He kept going back to that moment in the forest, asking himself what might have happened if . . .

He stopped his pointless exercise in alternate history. They'd been in the pub a couple of weeks ago, Daisy doing her usual hair-flicking routine while drinking vodka sodas, and Hamish had seemed happy, having decided to give things another go. Paolo had just stared at them, a mist of dissatisfaction seeping into his chest, until Holly had prodded him and given him a quizzical look.

'Good, ta. Just out for twenty minutes,' he replied. 'How are you? Things going well with Daisy?'

'You didn't hear?' Hamish looked surprised.

'Didn't hear what?'

'We broke up again. A fortnight ago. I suggested a weekend hiking in the Cairngorms, and then she countered with a boutique hotel in Glasgow, and it deteriorated from there. I'd had my doubts — you know that — but I was hoping that there was something there, anything.'

'I'm sorry. That's a real shame.'

Paolo hoped his tone came off as sympathetic, but secretly he was rather pleased. The news had instantly given him a warm, Ready Brek-style glow.

Hamish shrugged. 'I think I went back out with her to prove to myself that I'd not made a bad choice with her the first time round. That I had reasonably sound judgement.'

'And?'

'I confirmed my judgement is poor indeed.' Hamish ran a hand through his shaggy hair.

Paolo reached out and put a hand on his arm. 'Are you OK about it?'

'Aye. Fine, in fact. Thought I might take a break from the opposite sex, again. Do it better this time. Oh, look — Chloe's waving to you.'

Paolo turned to see Chloe shaking an empty bottle of milk at Paolo.

'She can be a right dictator if she's not had enough caffeine,' Paolo said. 'Look. Let me know when you're free soon. We can go for a drink.'

'Great. I'd really like that.'

Paolo headed towards the shop, wrapping and unwrapping his scarf, then wrapping it again, the fidgeting of someone to whom some options had opened up ever so slightly. Not that he was going to do anything about it, not yet. It was something to sit on. Whatever he was feeling could keep burning, slowly, for now.

CHAPTER 39

December finally arrived, and with it, the freezing temperatures that had shocked Holly when she first came to Eastercraig. The year was nearly out, and over the last week, she'd become painfully aware her time in Eastercraig was coming to an end. Living there felt like another world, and the more time she'd spent there, the more she realized she'd loved it. She would miss this meeting of heathery hillside, unexplored coves and unpredictable sea.

Holly walked along the front towards the fishing boats to collect some fresh fish — she had come to an arrangement where she paid shifty Sandy Alexander a fee each fortnight for fresh fish, which she picked up on Saturdays. Joe MacAllan leaned out of his window and gave her a cheery wave. On her way home, she greeted Lola, who was on her way to the shop, and then even got a smile from Doreen Douglas. Yes, she was *definitely* going to miss this place.

Later, after a run and a shower, Holly made her way to Eastercraig village hall. The day of the dog show had arrived. Over in a corner, Paolo and Chloe were moving staging around, under Hugh's direction. He'd taken his cue from Hollywood and was doing so in the most booming way possible, yelling "left" and "right a bit more" every two seconds.

His voice echoed around the hall, making it sound as if there were more than one of him, a thought that put her on edge.

'Hi, guys! What can I do?' she called, and the three of them raised their heads in her direction like startled meerkats.

'Run and hide, if I were you,' Paolo said. 'Hugh can't decide which way he wants the staging.'

Hugh huffed. 'It needs to be right. Honestly,' he muttered. 'If you want a job done properly, you have to do it yourself.'

He picked up one of the staging blocks and then teetered backwards. Holly, realizing he was about to topple, ran to his rescue. She might have her ups and downs with Hugh, but she didn't want to see him flattened in such an undignified fashion, like a geriatric pancake. Plus she had an unsettling vision of him dictating his wishes grumpily from a chair in the corner of the surgery, his mouth the only thing not bound in plaster casts.

'Tell me where to put it,' she said, taking a breath and summoning patience.

Eventually, after another ten minutes, Hugh seemed happy with the layout.

'So we're doing best in breed, best in show, some general agility. Any behavioural tests?' Holly asked.

'After last year we contemplated prizes for the dogs that didn't make a mess on the floor,' Chloe said with a grimace. 'Honestly. It was a disaster. We had to work hard to persuade the hall to let us use the space again.'

'And this year, we have . . .' Paolo ran out of the room and came back dragging a huge black tube. 'Ta-da! I can even produce an impromptu half-rhyme: Plastic sheeting / To protect against the sh—'

'Say no more,' Holly interrupted.

'And here are the forms,' said Chloe, pointing to the door. 'Lola Carlson from the shop is going to stand at the door and take the entry money.'

'And all I have to do is sit at a desk, examine all the dogs and choose a winner?' Holly said. It sounded too good to be true.

'Exactly,' smiled Hugh. 'Only, for the record, Mrs Wilkins's Labradors win the Family Dog of the Year category each year, and Rab Darling won Terriers last year so can't win again.'

Too good by half. 'Is there a crib sheet for this?'

This was meant to be fun. And now it sounded as fun as chasing invoices while simultaneously sticking pins in her eyes.

'I'll sit next to you,' smiled Chloe. 'I can stamp on your foot if you get it wrong.'

Holly stared, incredulous. 'This whole thing is rigged. I despair.'

'Don't be absurd,' Hugh retorted. 'It's nothing of the sort. About fifty per cent of it is formulaic, annually speaking.'

Holly rolled her eyes. 'OK. Half of this thing is rigged. This is ridiculous. You know what, considering I leave soon, it doesn't matter how I judge it. I won't be here to live with the repercussions.'

'But we will,' squeaked Chloe.

'Blame it on me,' said Holly. 'I'm going outside for a final breath of fresh air.'

She put her coat on and went to sit on the bench the other side of the road. The weather was getting colder — the peachy hues of the morning should have been warning enough. Under an iron sky, the sea rolled hypnotically back and forth, occasionally hurling up frothy spray as it hit the wall.

As she sat there, a shiny black lump emerged from the depths. For a second, she wondered if it was the top of a submarine. She'd read about them in the papers, that they occasionally patrolled the North Sea. But it was only Sporran.

'Hello, old friend,' she said, as he got close.

He barked loudly.

'Sorry. I don't have any chips. And even if I did, I wouldn't give you any. Don't want you getting seal diabetes. Why don't you swim off down the other end and get some fish? There's a catch just in.'

A boat was unloading, and a flock of seagulls screamed as they circled in desperate hope of a bite. Sporran, not keen, appeared to shake his head, and carried on bobbing in the water in front of her.

She was going to miss *all* of this. Beaches, inclement weather, seals, gorse, Paolo and Chloe, Dundee cake. Maybe not the weird workings of Hugh and the practice. Actually, she'd even miss him. And Greg, last but absolutely not least. Not that she had seen him since he'd gone to Edinburgh. But they had kept in touch with the odd call and text message. She hoped they would get to meet before she left. She still found herself thinking about him more than was healthy.

'Hi, Holly,' said a voice behind her.

She turned around and saw Hamish, reining Wolfie in. He'd seen Sporran and either wanted to play with him or sink him, and was threatening to drag Hamish over the edge.

'Are you entering that beast in the dog show?'

Hamish raised an eyebrow. 'That depends. Does winning rely on having had a wash and dry?'

'It might help,' said Holly, examining Wolfie, who looked as wild as they came. 'I mean, I'm very fond of him, but he does look like a hellhound.'

'Aye. But he's terribly good-natured,' he said, pressing his heels in as Wolfie strained against the lead. 'Can't you see how much he wants to kiss Sporran?'

'I think he wants to eat him.'

'Perhaps. Anyway, as for the show, I think I'll have to give it a pass,' said Hamish.

'You sure? I can give Wolfie his own category. Daftest dog in show?'

Hamish laughed. 'I'll think about it.'

'That's the spirit,' said Holly. 'Now, I ought to go and get changed.'

CHAPTER 40

Chloe welcomed and dreaded the dog show in equal measure. The animals were often on their best behaviour. The owners, on the other hand, didn't always manage to keep their emotions under control. Last year, as well as the dog muck all over the floor, Mrs Chambers had left in tears because Poppy, her chihuahua, had not won in any category. And Hugh had needed to do emergency surgery on a boxer that had found a bag of chocolate raisins in someone's handbag and scoffed the lot.

However, there had been a dog show in Eastercraig since 1957, and even though each year was accompanied by a heightened level of drama, there had never been any suggestion it be removed from the town's social calendar.

Holly had gone home and returned dressed in a pair of grey trousers and an olive jumper. Next to her, Chloe — who had worn shorts over pink tights, and a tweed blazer — felt like she was in fancy dress. She hadn't minded too much until Angus showed up at the door. She was still avoiding him, not feeling up to talking, hiding if she noticed him in the street. But now he was coming her way, and there were no doorways or alleys to duck into.

'Thought I might find you here,' he said, smiling. 'Looking good.'

'Not like Wee Jimmy Krankie?' Chloe joked, silently pleading he didn't agree.

'Not in the slightest.'

'Thanks,' she said, mildly encouraged by the response. 'Are you entering either of your dogs?'

'Nah. But I'll come along for the ride. This thing tends to throw up more excitement than you'd expect.'

'Don't remind me,' said Chloe, remembering the smell from last year, and the subsequent bill for disinfectant.

'I've got to grab some stuff from the shop. I'll be back later, though. And would you be keen for a drink after this finishes? I've not seen you for ages. There's a Chloe-shaped hole in my life.'

Chloe was stunned, almost speechless. 'I'd like that,' she managed.

Angus smiled. 'Great. Catch you later.'

She walked to the front door with him, and had barely given a wave when she was pulled sideways into the kitchen, narrowly avoiding falling over.

'So this is it!' said Paolo. 'You're back on!'

'No, we're not. He's being polite.'

'Why every time I mention it do you insist on coming up with reasons why you can't be with him. He just asked you out! He likes you.'

Chloe thought about it. Yes, Paolo had been pestering her, but ever since the Elle thing, she had given up. She didn't think she had any fight left in her.

How on earth Angus could like her was beyond her, and the thought of having to be in a room with him filled her with dread. She had done well in denying her feelings any voice, and it would take something massive for her to act on any residual ones she held for him. The drink, she told herself, was platonic — she needed to channel her inner Holly Anderson. Nothing was going to happen.

'I don't want to think about it,' she cried, suddenly feeling a rising panic. 'Oh gosh, I might faint. Or chunder. Help!'

'God, Chloe! If being asked out by him doesn't reignite your confidence, I don't know what will.'

'I don't know either.'

'Go along later, see how you get on.' Paolo gave her a stern look. 'Do I need to get my imaginary pompoms back out?'

Chloe closed her eyes and started breathing deeply through her nose, when Holly stuck her head round the door. 'Hey. I spy a queue. We should get going.'

'Cool,' said Paolo. 'Let's bounce.'

'*Let's bounce*?' Chloe removed her finger from the side of her nose and followed him out of the kitchen. 'What are you — twelve?' She steadied herself against the wall. 'Oh, I still feel weak.'

The three made their way to the main hall. Chloe took her position by the door, Holly went to sit at the judges' table with Hugh, and Paolo picked up the pile of entry forms. This would be a good distraction for now: she could dwell on her feelings for Angus and stress about going for a drink with him later.

Before long, the small, wood-panelled hall resounded with the barks of dogs of all shapes and sizes. Having calmed down, Chloe watched Holly judge categories including "Best Trick" and "Best Groomed". The miniature "dogstacle course" Chloe had set up for an agility competition was currently in use, and she leaned against the back wall, enjoying the spectacle.

A hairy shadow appeared beside her. 'Gah!' Chloe jumped, as it leaped up to kiss her. 'Wolfie!'

More obedient than normal, Wolfie put his chin to rest on her shoulder, and Chloe prayed he wasn't about to lick her ear.

'Sit, boy,' Hamish said, appearing next to him. 'Come on, ye cheeky sod. Sit. Siiiiit.' He smiled at her distractedly. 'Hey, Chloe.'

Eventually, with a firm hand, Hamish managed to get Wolfie to do as he was told. Chloe breathed a silent sigh of relief. All the same, she noticed Wolfie was positively drooling over some of the other entrants, a look of hungry longing in his eyes.

She checked her watch. A few hours and she'd be in the pub with Angus.

* * *

Holly gave a small gold medal to the owner of Dazzle, a terrier who had been the most obedient of the dogs in his category. Still a little dazed by the weirdness that was Eastercraig's answer to Crufts, she remembered to hand over a bag of dog biscuits too.

His owner shook her hand and thanked her enthusiastically. It might have been daft, Holly reflected, but everyone seemed to be enjoying themselves. She'd caught up with lots of her patients from the last year and met some new faces too. She was particularly taken with a glossy Scottie dog, who had been as well behaved as he was beautiful.

Picking up a cup of tea, she watched as Paolo rounded up the competitors for the next category.

Over by the door, she turned and smiled at Hamish. Wolfie, who was not competing, was lying on the floor, half asleep.

Then, before she turned back to announce the next category, Greg walked through the door with a beautiful Gordon Setter on a lead. Holly stared as he clapped a hand on Hamish's shoulder and engaged him in conversation. He'd not told her he was coming. Her heart began to pound, and she found herself feeling more breathless than after the run she'd done that morning.

Quickly, Holly looked forward, beginning to process her emotions. Greg was in there. In the flesh, mere yards away. She didn't know what she felt, but whether she was shocked, or overjoyed, she didn't want her expression to betray her. She looked away from him, needing to manipulate her face into its most neutral position before catching his eye.

'Are you all right? You look like you're about to eat your bottom lip.'

Holly startled and looked up. Greg was right in front of her. Her stomach twisted.

'Nope. I'm fine. I was trying to work out which of these dogs might win,' she lied.

'Come to the pub after this?' Greg said. 'We should catch up, now we're friends and everything. Before you head to Berkshire.'

The long road to Berkshire wound its way into her subconscious, extinguishing the spark of joy she'd felt at his suggestion of a drink. Holly had done her online interview the previous week with the lead vet at VetCo, who had said she had the job and that he would send over her contract soon.

'Sure thing,' she said, thinking she would like to see him one more time, after all, even if it was bittersweet.

'Great. I'll see you in the Anchor at seven-ish.'

He smiled and disappeared back through the door. Holly felt anticipation race through her body at the thought of the evening to come and tried to shove it away.

Focusing on the task ahead, she checked the competition list. Paolo appeared at her shoulder and gave her a nod. The next category was ready to go. At that moment, there was a rustling noise underneath the table. Spartacus, a chihuahua, was rooting around in her bumper bag of dog biscuits.

'Hey, you,' she said, reaching down. 'Cheeky blighter. Out of there.'

She went to pick him up and return him to his owner, when he growled at her, clutching the bag in his jaws. Holly rolled her eyes and summoned up her sternest voice.

'Come on. Stop that,' she said.

Spartacus's owner was nowhere to be seen and Holly went to retrieve the bag. Spartacus held tight, and as Holly pulled it, the bag split. Biscuits covered the floor.

'Rats,' she whispered, desperately trying to scrape the contents back in the packet. 'Honestly, Spartacus. You aren't half trouble.'

But the trouble had only just begun. Spartacus began to bark, a sound that was apparently contagious. Within seconds, the room was filled with yapping, barking and yowling. Hugh had gone to get some tea, and standing up, she looked around for Chloe or Paolo. It was all getting out of hand.

Paolo was the first person she spotted. He shrugged at her and clapped his hands. Very little could be heard over the din, so he moved to the centre of the room and bellowed for silence. But Spartacus wasn't done. This, he clearly realized, was a window of opportunity, and Holly watched in dumbstruck horror as he pelted out of the room with a biscuit in his mouth and towards the road.

Holly leaped up and sprinted out of the village hall. She squinted around, trying to spot him. There he was, running down towards the harbourmaster. She pursued him, catching up to him as he eventually stopped by the boats.

'You daft dog,' she said, scooping him up.

About to head back, she became aware of a huge furry shadow bounding towards her at great speed. Narrowly missing being knocked into the sea, she fell back and watched as Wolfie, caught up in the excitement, pelted past, disturbing a crowd of seagulls. Then, without warning, he ran alongside the harbour wall until there was a gap in the railings and launched himself off the edge and into the waves.

'Wolfie!' Holly cried, clambering up.

Wolfie, in his element, was paddling around, chasing the remaining bobbing gulls.

Holly rolled her eyes glancing over her shoulder to see Hamish, holding a stitch, jogged over, followed by Greg with Sadie.

'Has he gone in?' Hamish slowed down, panting.

'Afraid so,' said Holly.

'Then where is he?'

Holly spun round. 'Oh! He was right there.' She stared down at the spot where Wolfie had thrown himself in, but as she scanned the harbour, he didn't pop up. He'd gone.

'Wait! He's over there,' said Greg. 'Chasing Sporran.'

Holly gazed towards where Greg was pointing and, sure enough, Wolfie's black head was bobbing above the waves. A combination of the current, the dog's strength and his dedication to catching the seal had led him much further out than she had anticipated.

'I'll get him,' said Hamish. 'Ferdie's boat's down there.'

'No, Hamish—' Greg started, but Hamish was already heading towards the boat.

Holly watched as Hamish jumped on to the floating jetty then leaped into a small boat. The smell of petrol filled the air. The tide was going out, Holly noted, so it wouldn't take long for Hamish to get to Wolfie.

'Oh jeez,' Greg muttered.

'What's wrong?' asked Holly. 'If Wolfie can keep paddling Hamish will get there in seconds.'

'Hamish is *not* a good swimmer. He shouldn't go out alone. Take the dog, will you?'

His last words disappeared into the breeze as he ran towards the steps. Holly yelled after him: 'Is this a good idea?'

'Aye, I'll be fine. But, in case, go and get backup,' Greg called, leaping into the boat as Hamish guided it out into the sea.

For a brief second, Holly watched, tying Sadie's lead to the railings. Then she turned to run back to the hall, but already Paolo was sprinting towards her, Chloe and Angus not far behind. They'd know what to do. Along the front, a few people had gathered. They leaned on the railings, craning their necks to get a better view.

'What on earth's going on?' Paolo asked. 'We calmed all the dogs down, and realized you'd left. We said we'd reconvene the . . .'

His voice tailed off. Holly followed his eyes as he looked out to sea.

'Why are Greg and Hamish in a boat?' Chloe asked.

Behind Chloe, Angus was squinting as he looked across the waves. The wind had picked up even more, and black clouds were gathering.

'Wolfie went in after Sporran and he's been swept away by the tide,' Holly said.

'But Hamish can't swim,' Angus said, drawing appalled looks from Chloe and Paolo. 'Och — don't panic, you lot. Greg can. And they're not far out.'

They stood and watched. Holly's teeth started to chatter, and under her jumper her arms prickled. By now, the boat was nearing Wolfie, the noise of its engine fading as it bounced over the waves.

She pulled the hair out her eyes, only to realize they were watering, stung by the sharp wind. Wiping the tears away with the back of her hand, she blinked, her vision blurring. By the time she could see clearly again, one of the figures was leaning over the boat, trying to haul the dog back in. The other one was on the far side, stretching back to stop them capsizing.

'It's got pretty choppy,' Holly said, watching the waves as they grew bigger.

'Aye,' said Angus.

Holly turned to look at him. He was behind her, Chloe pressed up against him, his arm around her shoulder. For all the rotten luck that was running through Eastercraig, it looked at least as if something might be going their way. All it needed now was—

'Wolfie's on board!' Paolo cried and flung his arms around Holly. 'I can't believe it. I was completely on edge.'

Holly could feel the relief rolling off Paolo, her own shoulders dropping as she now made out the shapes of three beings in the tiny boat.

'Why are they waving?' Chloe asked.

'I don't know,' said Holly.

Her pocket began to vibrate, and she reached in for her mobile and picked up. 'Greg? What is it?'

Greg's voice was crackly. 'The engine's stopped. And there are no oars in this bloody thing. You need to get someone out to get us.'

'The coastguard?'

'Och, no. Anyone in a boat will do.'

Holly turned to look at her friends. 'They're stuck,' she said in disbelief.

'And someone's gone in,' Chloe shrieked.

Holly spun back. Among the choppy waves, a head bobbed up and down.

CHAPTER 41

For a split second it felt like a bad dream. Then Holly snapped out of it: she had never been one to stand by and watch. She was clear-headed and focused when the going got tough, and this wasn't going to be an exception.

'Can any of you drive a boat?' she said, quickly.

Angus put his hand up. 'Me. And I've been helping Hugh a bit with the *Dorothy-Jo*, and I know where the keys are.'

'OK, we're going after them,' Holly said. 'Chloe, Paolo you call the emergency services, then find Hugh and tell him we've taken his boat.'

She and Angus ran down on to the jetty and along to the *Dorothy-Jo*. Vaulting into the boat, she grabbed a lifejacket and threw another to Angus, who slipped it on before digging the key out from a corner and starting the engine.

'Untie us,' he called back to her.

She ran to the side, unwound the rope quickly, then pulled it into the boat. They were off.

The boat lurched over the growing swells, and Holly held on to the edge to stop herself falling. A drop of rain landed on her nose, then another, and she looked up to see any remaining blue sky had disappeared. She scanned the waters in front of her but couldn't see any sign of Hamish and Greg.

'I can't see them!' Holly cried over the sound of the gathering storm.

She moved to the front of the boat and stood next to Angus. The sea was black now, rain falling on it in heavy drops. The boat was shunted to the side by a large swell, and her hip hit the edge, causing her to gasp out in pain.

'They've been pulled round the headland,' Angus shouted.

Holly could hardly hear him above the whooshing of the wind. Ahead of them, the waves were gathering strength, ripples becoming giant curls, which broke in a fury over the rocks. Water crashed over the stern of the boat, leaving puddles on the deck. Her clothes were already drenched, sticking to her and chilling her bones.

'Are you sure this thing's seaworthy?' Holly asked, noticing Angus's jaw was clenched.

'Hugh said it was, though I'm not sure he planned to take it out on days like today.'

She wiped rain from her eyes, and as she did an enormous wave tipped the boat nearly on to its side. It paused, and then hit the water with a slap. Holly's heart was pounding now. Scanning the sea, she peeled back the wet hair that was plastered to her forehead. Still no sign.

'Hold on tight,' said Angus. 'I'm going to turn us around the headland, but it's going to be bumpy.'

Holly noticed his knuckles were white as he gripped the wheel. Out of the corner of her eye she spotted another giant wave. 'Is there a risk we'll capsize?'

'Aye. I'd say so.'

Holly felt a rush of fear. The wave broke before hitting the boat.

'There!' Holly yelled and pointed to a spot some thirty metres away.

'Where?'

'It was just—'

A wave smashed, and as the spray settled, the small motorboat came back into view. It bounced up and down in the tumultuous waters.

'Oh my God,' said Holly. 'There's Greg. And maybe Wolfie, lying low in the boat.'

'Right. I'll get as close as I can, and when we're side by side, I need you to haul them in. Can you see Hamish?'

Holly bit her cheek to stop the rising panic. 'No.'

* * *

On the shore, Chloe looked out to sea, watching the *Dorothy-Jo* as it disappeared around the headland. Turning to Paolo, she tried to hide the anxiety coursing through her veins, making her unable to focus.

'Do you think they'll be OK?' she managed.

'Aye. They'll be fandabidozi. Back on dry land before you know it and ready for a pint,' said Paolo, but she could see the lines on his brow.

'You know, if Angus comes back OK, I'm going to tell him how I feel. Go to the pub and ask him out properly.'

'Is that so? No bottling it?'

'Nope. I'm going to let him know I think about him all the time, and the minutes he was out on the boat were the longest ones of my life. That I want him to be mine.'

Paolo smiled. 'I'll hold you to that. Can I be there when you do it? I think it'll need a witness, because it sounds unmissable.'

Chloe was about to say "no", when she spotted Hugh making his way along the front. One of them had to tell him about the *Dorothy-Jo*. Her stomach dropped to a new low.

She looked back out to sea. There was still no sign of either boat. Taking a deep breath, she prepared to face her boss, and the inevitable onslaught that would follow.

CHAPTER 42

With titanium nerves, Angus guided them the last few metres until finally they were in line with the tiny motorboat. Holly didn't dare speak. She didn't want to distract him. Further out, there was a low rumble of thunder.

Greg, looking drenched and frozen, was hanging on to the side of the little boat. Holly felt another wave of fear — where was Hamish? She leaned over the side, and breathed in sharply. There, in the bottom of the boat, lay Hamish. He looked very pale, and his eyes were closed. Wolfie was curled up next to him, shivering.

'Greg. You need to help me get him out,' she shouted above the screams of the wind.

'Take this rope,' Greg shouted. 'I'll tie us together for a second.'

'No,' Angus's head spun round. 'If one of us capsizes it'll be a disaster.'

'Can you lift him?' said Holly. 'I'm strong enough to pull him from here.'

Greg looked at her. 'Sure?'

'Do it!'

She leaned towards the motorboat, and her eyes met Greg's. In that moment, her fear left her.

Greg pulled Hamish up. Hamish let out a groan, which filled Holly with relief. He was alive, at least. The motorboat banged up against the side of the *Dorothy-Jo*, and Holly grabbed a limp Hamish under his arms and dragged him across to their boat.

Trying not to slip on the deck, she laid him down as gently as possible, then went back to the side.

'Now the dog,' Greg said. 'I push, you pull.'

Holly gritted her teeth. Wolfie was as gangly as he was heavy, all tail and legs. And he was soaking wet.

'Hey, boy,' she said. 'Come up here. Come to me and Hamish.'

Wolfie reached out his paws weakly, and Holly pulled as Greg shunted the dog over the edge. Like a concertina, Wolfie scrunched up as he toppled on deck, and then lengthened back out, lying down next to Hamish, panting.

'Ready for me?' Greg called as Holly straightened herself back up.

'Hang on,' yelled Angus. 'After this one.'

The words had barely left his mouth than the wave approached. Holly said a small prayer as it hit the side and became airborne for a moment as the boats were hurled up by it. Her body felt weightless, as if going over a small bridge.

But while the *Dorothy-Jo* managed to ride it out, the motorboat didn't. As Greg gripped the side, the stern rose up into the air, before flipping over.

'Greg!' Angus yelled.

Holly couldn't see him. Surely, given a second, he'd emerge and they could throw the rope to him. The hull of the boat rocked. Perhaps he was trapped beneath it. But what if he'd hit his head? She pulled off her shoes, readying to dive, and turned to Angus. 'I can go in.'

There was a shout. Greg had surfaced ten metres from them. He was managing to remain afloat, but it looked like a tremendous effort. Holly went to climb up on the edge. She took the ring from the side, checked it was tied in, then hurled it out. With marked effort, Greg reached for it, missed then disappeared under the surface again. When he re-emerged, he was further away.

'He's exhausted,' she cried. 'I'll get him.'

'No! I'll go.' Angus yanked his boots from his feet.

'I'm the stronger swimmer.'

'He's my brother,' said Angus.

'But I can't steer the boat!' Holly cried.

But she couldn't stop Angus, who dived into the water. The sea was freezing. If he wasn't quick, he'd succumb to the cold. And so would Greg.

Angus swam a strong front crawl, but every current dragged him back. It was terrible to watch, and she could see that with the tide and the cold, each stroke drained him of energy. It took what felt like for ever to get there, but finally he managed. He wrapped his arm around his brother and began to pull him back.

In the meantime, her eyes barely leaving the scene in front of her, Holly had wound the rope of the ring up. Summoning every ounce of strength, she threw it towards them.

'Angus,' she yelled. 'The ring! It's behind you!'

She gripped the side, her hands bright pink from the cold. Her words were carried off on the wind. There was no way Angus had heard.

'Please, please get it,' Holly whispered through chattering teeth.

As if by some miracle, the message reached him and Angus craned his neck around and grabbed on to the ring, as the ocean threatened to submerge them. Water crashed over their heads, but when it settled again, Holly was overwhelmingly relieved to see them both still there.

Holly began to heave the rope in, feeling as if she was tugging an HGV from a standstill. Her nerves were beginning to make her hands shake. She had to do it.

Her feet locked on the edge of the deck, she heaved the rope. Angus was swimming, and she could feel some progress, but it was hard work. When they were at the edge of the boat, Angus boosted Greg up. Holly pulled him in and lay him next to Hamish, then reached for Angus. One last tug and he was in.

Through the cacophony of water that was trying to engulf them from all angles, Holly heard a juddering sound. Her whole body began to vibrate as a boat came into view around the headland. She waved furiously. Never had she been so glad to see anyone.

Weak with exhaustion and relief, she collapsed on her knees next to Greg. 'The coastguard's coming,' she said.

Next, she crawled on all fours to Wolfie, and placed her hand on his heart. Nothing. She moved her hands around. He was such a big dog. Maybe she'd got the wrong place. He had to be OK. Had to be.

There! She found it. It was faint. Too slow.

'Oh, Wolfie,' she whispered.

CHAPTER 43

Holly stayed remarkably calm in the hours after the rescue. She'd kept her emotions — and there were a bucketload of them — in check since they'd been in the hospital, where they had all been kept overnight. The sight of a pale Fiona Dunbar appearing on the ward should have moved her to tears. It didn't. Nor did Moira Glennis's weeping as she walked past Holly's room. Even Chloe's sobbing didn't break her. She put it down to shock. That would be it, she thought, as she ate her second Twix of the day.

But, of all things, what finally caused her to lose control was Hugh's visit.

He appeared at the end of visiting time, after everyone else had left. She recognized his silhouette through the blinds and gulped. Though the lives of four people could have been lost at sea, she found herself sweating over the boat. She'd all but forgotten it — but technically she *had* stolen it. And undoubtedly ruined it in the process. That nobody had told her anything about its fate led her to believe the *Dorothy-Jo* might have been swept into the North Sea and smashed to smithereens. And as for that reference for VetCo, she was never going to get it now. Oh God — she'd not even thought about that. She could kiss goodbye to that job.

She took a drink of water from the glass by her bed, but her mouth was growing drier by the second.

'Hi, Hugh,' she croaked as he came in. Before he could reply she said, in a rush: 'I'm so sorry about the boat. It was all I could think to do.'

'Good grief, woman!' Hugh sounded appalled. 'You lot could have died and you're worrying about the boat?'

'You're not furious?'

'Not in the slightest.'

Oh God! Relief and guilt ran through her veins — guilt for taking the *Dorothy-Jo*, and guilt for thinking Hugh could be so cruel as to hold it against her. As Hugh handed her a cup of vending machine tea, she burst into tears.

'You can take the money out of my wages,' she managed. 'I know how much the boat means to you.'

This was so embarrassing. Crying in front of Hugh. She'd spent damn near twelve months gritting her teeth and refusing to expose any weakness. She stared down into her cup, trying to hide her wet, blotchy cheeks.

'Why not fix it yourself?' Hugh's gruff tone had returned.

She looked up, frowning. 'Sorry?'

'Muck in with mending it,' he said, staring at her over his glasses.

'Of course. It's the least I can do.' Holly stifled another sob. 'But I'm leaving in a couple of weeks. I'm not sure we'd get it all done.'

'I think we could find time,' he said, a smile twitching at the corner of his mouth.

'What do you mean?'

'I'd like you to take over the practice.'

Holly blinked, repeating his words in her head. 'What?'

'You heard me.'

'But . . . Why?'

In all her time in Eastercraig, Holly would have never predicted this. Being offered a practice of her own. If she was down in Berkshire, it would take her years to make partner, let alone be in charge. She was so taken aback she couldn't speak.

Hugh sighed and took off his glasses, polishing them carefully. 'I need to take a step back. I'm not a young man anymore — far from it. And I've been waiting for the right vet to come along.'

'But . . . I thought you hated me?'

'Why on earth do you think that?'

Holly stared at him, finally able to find enough words to form a real sentence. 'You've spent the year shouting at me. Looking over my shoulder. And huffing. Occasionally you've offered some faint praise, but mostly you've been horribly grouchy.'

'I never hated you,' he said. 'I *resented* you.'

It dawned on her. 'Because you knew . . .'

'That I'd found a replacement.'

'But I heard you telling Judith in the summer that I was far from ready. That you wouldn't even write me a reference.'

'Och — she said someone was off on maternity leave and could you go earlier, and I had to find an excuse to keep you.'

Holly was excited enough by his offer to overlook the subterfuge. 'Are you sure you want to go? All that knowledge! I barely know half what you do.'

'It'll be a wrench,' he said. 'But I can't work five days a week anymore, and be on call. I'm nearing seventy. I want time to indulge my hobbies.'

'Wow,' said Holly.

There was silence. Her head spun from everything Hugh had said.

'So, what do you think?' Hugh asked. 'You can have a few days to think about it.'

Holly didn't need to think. 'I'd love to. But . . . would you consider staying on in some capacity?'

'Become the junior partner?' Hugh scowled.

'Senior,' Holly said. Then, knowing it was cheeky, added: 'Given your age and all that.'

'Insolence,' he said. Then he chuckled. 'I'd consider it. Maybe a day or two a week. And the occasional on-call. And

I'll still be in Eastercraig. You can ring me for advice if the circumstances arise.'

Holly felt herself welling up again. 'Hugh! You've been *so* unpredictable. And *so* shouty. And now you're forgiving me for wrecking your boat *and* offering me a job. I don't know what to say.'

'Say yes. Don't make me impatient.'

'I'll need to sort out somewhere to live.'

'Fabien's renewed his contract in Switzerland for two years, he tells me. He's offered a very reasonable rate, if you'd like to keep on at Sea Spray.'

Holly paused, feeling excitement swelling in her chest as she pictured herself in the role. She closed her eyes, visualizing her name on the gold plaque by the door, glistening in the late evening sun. She saw herself coming home to the cottage in the evenings, going for a run or enjoying the view with a glass of wine. Or sat outside the pub with Chloe and Paolo. A wide smile spread across her face. She opened her eyes.

'I'd love it,' she said. 'On the condition you stay on as partner. We can be MacDougal and Anderson.'

'Or even Anderson and MacDougal,' Hugh said, with a wink.

He held out his hand, and Holly took it, gripping it tightly.

'Thank you, Hugh. I promise you won't regret this,' she said.

'Of course not. You're a fantastic vet. You saved Wolfie, and by rights, that bloody dog should be dead.'

Holly began to cry at the thought, and Hugh pretended to look at something out of the window. Holly thought he might have been blinking away a tear too. After a moment, she took a shuddering breath and then let it all out, her shoulders dropping. This time, it was like when you turned the tap on, only to accidentally pull it off, water spraying everywhere with no means to stop it. She gulped back more tears, each breath shuddering in and out of her lungs as they tried to keep up with her emotions.

At the sound, Hugh turned back, then confronted with Holly's tears, he looked appalled he'd contributed to such floods.

'Ah! Here's a man who might be able to offer you some comfort,' Hugh nodded at the door, with a look of relief. 'I'll leave you to it.'

He got up and Holly glanced over at the door. There, with rings under his eyes and his hair sticking up, was Greg, his hands in his pockets.

'Hi,' he said, and tilted his head towards the chair. 'Is this seat taken?'

CHAPTER 44

'Greg!' Holly attempted to stop crying. 'How are you?'

'Not too bad!' he said. He sat down and leaned over to brush the last stray tears from Holly's cheeks. 'Could have been much worse.'

'Chloe and Paolo told me you were OK,' she said, and — without thinking — rested her head on his shoulder.

Her colleagues had appeared on the ward at the start of visiting time that morning, initially full of relief at seeing that Holly had been left physically unscathed. They'd told Holly how Greg and Hamish had been suffering from mild hypothermia and were being monitored. Angus too..

'Aye. And I've been sat next to my brother for a night, so we've had a lot of time to talk. When we're feeling a bit better, we're going to sit down and go over the finances. But, more importantly, we're friends again too.'

'I'm glad to hear it,' said Holly.

'How're you holding up?' he said, looking at her with concern.

'I was talking to Hugh about the accident, and it all hit me,' she said, pulling away from him.

Holly felt her eyes welling up again, and she wiped her face with her sleeve. There was a pause as she caught her breath again. Wanting to steady herself, she took a sip of water.

As she did so, Greg inhaled. 'Look. I wanted to tell you something. You know, after my near-death experience.'

A giggle escaped, and Holly flung her hand over her mouth. She hadn't meant to laugh. 'Sorry,' she said. 'It's just . . .'

'You're nervous about what I might say?'

'A bit. Yes. But I'd also like to reassure you I wasn't laughing at your near-death bit. Oh gosh — put me out of my misery.'

Greg fixed his eyes on hers. 'Holly. You were crazy to come after me. I know you're someone who always does the right thing, but you needn't have risked your life. It means a lot to me that you did.'

'All in a day's work.'

He smiled. 'I was going to tell you at the pub anyway. I like you, Holly. I think you're amazing. And I wish you weren't leaving.'

Emotions zinged through Holly's body. Instantly, she felt transported back to that fantasy of them together on Finnen Beach, realizing it might now happen after all.

Greg got up and wandered over to the window. He lifted up the blind and stared out, taking a quick glance over his shoulder at Holly.

Holly got up and went to stand next to him. Outside, the car park was an uninspiring sight. Hardly a picture from the romantic situations playbook. It was certainly no Finnen Beach. Nevertheless, there was no time like the present. 'What if I told you I might not go?'

Greg turned to her, narrowing his eyes. 'You might not go?'

'That I might change my mind and stay here?' Holly focused on a parking warden, who was doing his rounds. She was determined to stay a little nonchalant.

'Is it possible?' asked Greg, a note of hope in his voice.

'Perhaps I don't go to Berkshire. We could see how things go.'

'You'd talk to Hugh?'

'Underneath all that fury, he's all right.' Holly looked down, barely able to stop a grin breaking across her face.

'It would be a great place to start. My secondment is finishing early, so you can stay with me, if you need to for a bit, and commute. No, it's miles away.' He shook his head. 'Wow — I'm being way too forward. Maybe I can call Fabien and convince him what a great tenant you are.'

As he spoke, his face lit up. At once, Holly began to feel butterflies, hundreds of them. She was about to tell him about Hugh's offer when a knock at the door interrupted them, and Holly glanced over to see Chloe standing in the doorway, looking as if she'd won the lottery.

'You two look happy.' Chloe grinned, a twinkle in her eye. 'And I saw Hugh in the corridor. He told me you'll be taking . . .'

She trailed off, having spotted the "I haven't got to that part yet" look Holly was giving her. Holly looked to Greg, who tilted his head to one side.

'Taking what?' he asked.

A nurse appeared in the doorway, a clipboard in her hands. 'Mr Dunbar. I've been looking for you. If you'll come with me, I'll be able to discharge you. You'll not be long after, Ms Anderson.'

'Thank you,' said Greg. He turned to Holly. 'I ought to get back and see Mum, but can I call you in a bit and arrange something?'

Holly gave him a small smile. 'I'd like that.'

And then she could tell him her news.

CHAPTER 45

Chloe clutched her chest, holding her breath until Greg was out of earshot. When she was sure he had gone, she exhaled loudly. 'Did I interrupt a moment?'

'Perhaps,' laughed Holly. 'In a good way, though. I was about to tell him about the job, but it can wait a little bit longer. It'll be nice to surprise him with it. Hey — did you talk to Angus? Paolo was here earlier and he mentioned you'd promised to declare your undying love.'

Chloe couldn't help but grin wildly. She joined Holly at the window. 'I did. Well . . . Almost. I asked him out. Told him I liked him. Turns out life-or-death experiences, even when they aren't your own, give you a whole new kind of bravery. The "nothing to lose" type. When I thought for a moment I might lose Angus, I realized there was no point in putting things off.'

Holly gave an expectant look. 'And . . . What did he say?'

Chloe threw both hands in the air. 'That he'd never thought anyone would want to go out with him, let alone me. *Me*!'

She burst into unexpected tears. It was all too much. Holly wrapped her arms around her. 'Well done. I knew you could do it.'

'I think I did too. It just took me a while. Turns out you have to follow your heart. Talking of which, you're staying!'

'I know! I can't believe it.'

Chloe stepped back, wiping her eyes and laughing. 'Really? It's not the most ludicrous thing that's happened in the last twenty-four hours. When can we tell Paolo? He'll be stoked.'

'Shall we do it in person? I know it's a Sunday, but we ought to break with tradition and head to the Anchor.'

'Perfect. I'll go and call Paolo, then I'm off to the farm. I'm driving Angus home — Fiona's had enough to worry about and I think she's baking tons to herald the boys' return. I know it's usually the three of us, but can I bring him later?'

'Only if I can bring Greg.'

A thought struck Chloe. That Paolo would feel like a plum, sat between two loved-up couples.

'Do you think Paolo will feel left out?'

Holly paused. 'Maybe.'

'I'll ask,' Chloe said decisively. 'Better we all talk about our feelings, isn't it?'

* * *

Paolo was out for a walk on the cliffs when Chloe's call came through. The wild storm had dissipated, leaving barely any trace. The sky was icy blue, empty save for a few clouds and the odd gull soaring along on the light breeze. Maybe there was a little more driftwood than normal, and perhaps some of the grasses had been flattened, but aside from that, Eastercraig and Finnen Beach had come out of the storm remarkably unscathed. Aside from Wolfie.

Feeling his phone buzzing, he pulled it out of his pocket.

'Hey, Chlo. What's up?' he asked.

'I'm at the hospital. I offered to take Angus back to Auchintraid. And I've seen Greg, and he'll come with.'

'Sideline as a taxi service?'

'Kind of. Anyway, listen . . . Holly and I think we ought to go to the pub later. She has news. And Angus and Greg might come too — I'll invite them when I see them in a sec. But I wanted to let you know, in case you felt . . .'

'Like the odd one out?' Paolo finished the sentence.

Chloe sounded quieter. 'I wanted to warn you.'

Paolo considered it. 'I'm fine, but do you mind if I invite Hamish? Only, if I come, *he* might be the one feeling left out. You know, after the high-seas drama,' he said.

'Of course,' Chloe's voice sounded bright. 'See you there. Ah — here come the Dunbars.'

'Bye, Chlo,' Paolo said, and hung up.

CHAPTER 46

Holly commandeered the cosiest spot in the Anchor, a low table with armchairs and a settee. Actually, she was offered it — a couple of the fishermen vacated the threadbare sofa, telling her she deserved to put her feet up. Holly thanked them as Paolo and Chloe burst through the door.

'Oh. My. Goodness. It's *so* chilly outside,' Chloe shivered. 'I need to be by the radiator.'

'You need an industrial parka, that's what,' said Paolo.

'Yuck. I might as well wrap my duvet round myself and borrow one of my dad's belts,' Chloe said, sitting down next to Holly.

'Don't look at me,' said Holly. 'I think practicality trumps fashion every time.'

'We know,' said Paolo, laughing, slinging his jacket over the back of a wingback chair and collapsing into it. 'Say. Now you're staying, can we add a few tweaks to your wardrobe? A few date dresses, seeing as you might be going out a bit more.'

Holly was about to protest when Hamish arrived. He hung up his coat and sat down on the arm of Paolo's chair, giving his shoulder a squeeze. She resisted giving Chloe a look, who was also exercising some serious self-control trying not to do the same. Holly looked down, her mouth twitching.

A moment later, Greg and Angus appeared in the doorway of the pub. A hush fell over the crowd.

'What are you more surprised by?' Angus addressed the room. 'The fact we're all in the pub so soon after our wee ordeal? Or that I'm here with my brother?'

This caused a ripple of laughter to run through the tables, and then Mhairi began to clap. For a horrible moment, Holly thought she was about to lead a round of applause, then gave a sigh of relief as the fearsome publican yelled, 'Nothing to see! Back to yer drinks, the lot of you.' It was, Holly was glad to see, business as usual.

Angus plonked himself down next to Chloe, squeezing his frame into the gap between her and the end of the sofa. Chloe went bright pink but was clearly overjoyed. Holly looked at Paolo, who grinned back at her.

'I'll get a round in,' she said, and got up.

'Let me,' said Hamish. 'I insist. I've had a near-death experience and I want to thank you all for your efforts.'

Before Holly could protest, Hamish had made a beeline to the bar, Paolo hopping up and following him over. Holly looked to Greg, who was yet to sit down. They were stood right next to each other.

This was it. This was her moment.

'Seeing as your brother has taken my seat on the sofa . . .' Holly said to him, '. . . could we pop outside for a moment? I want to tell you something.'

'Sure,' he said, and followed her to the door.

They stepped into the freezing air. Holly looked out to the dark sea, then up to the heavens, wondering how she should start. Above them, the sky was a blanket of glittering stars. They all seemed to be winking, encouraging Holly to tell Greg how she really felt.

'Well,' said Greg. 'What did you want to say?'

Holly met his eyes. 'When we were at the hospital earlier, I was about to let you know something . . .' She paused, wanting exactly the right words.

'Let me know what?'

Taking a huge breath, she continued: 'Earlier, I told you I might not go. And . . . I *am* staying. Hugh has offered me the practice. To take over.'

Greg reached out and tugged her into a huge hug. Holly let herself be warmed by his arms, and held him tightly.

'I thought so,' Greg said. 'Congratulations! Chloe refused to cave on the drive home, but she'd basically already let the cat out the bag.'

She laughed, touched that Chloe had even attempted to keep the secret, to allow Holly to break the good news. She stepped back and shifted on her feet.

'I accepted, so I'm here for good. And if what you said earlier still stands, can we give it a try? Give *us* a try. I mean, you'd have to be sensitive of my inexperienced heart, and all that, but maybe we can see what happens. If you like . . . I don't want a fling though. You know how I feel about flings.'

She was gibbering, with no idea where she was going. Letting her heart lead the way was making her sound crazy. Greg put his arms around her again, and she prayed he hadn't changed his mind.

'I know how you feel about flings,' said Greg.

'Phew,' said Holly. 'I was beginning to get nervous.'

'I could tell.'

'Hey!' Holly gave him a playful nudge in the ribs. 'You're meant to say something romantic! Not confirm that my outpouring of emotion was a load of rubbish. But, wait, hang on . . . Can I double-check you want more than a fling too?'

Greg laughed. 'You can. And yes, I want more than that. Say . . . do we need to go back in? You're shivering.'

Holly hadn't noticed. Now she thought about it, though, she realized she was chilled to the bone. She had goosebumps but she'd assumed until that point it had been because of Greg, rather than the Baltic temperatures.

'Not yet,' she said, reaching her arms around his neck. 'There's one more thing I need to do.'

She stood on her tiptoes and kissed him. Greg pulled her closer, pressing his lips to hers, then moving them to her cheeks, her forehead and back to her lips. Holly let herself get lost in the embrace, not caring who saw them. She could stay here for ever.

When they pulled apart, Greg took her hand and rubbed his thumb over hers, and Holly felt a rush of emotion.

'Do you want me to talk to Fabien, by the way. See if you can stay in Sea Spray?' he asked.

'Already taken care of. Hugh's done the deal and it's mine for the next couple of years. Talking of which, how do you fancy staying over tonight?'

'I'd like that,' Greg leaned down and kissed her again.

'Great,' she whispered into his ear. 'There's a couch with your name on it.'

Greg laughed and, taking his hand, Holly led him back towards the pub. She couldn't stop smiling. This was going to be her local. These would be the people she saw every day. And this was the man she was going to be with.

Before opening the door, Holly looked up at him, grinning. 'Greg Dunbar. I think you're the best thing that ever happened to me.'

THE END

ACKNOWLEDGEMENTS

This is my first book to have made it out into the world, but it would never have got here had it not been for a number of brilliant people who helped it on its way.

Great big thanks to Emma Grundy Haigh at Joffe Books, for all your insight and kindness and all-round super editorial skills.

To Laura Macdougall at United Agents. Thank you for believing in *Let's Just Be Friends*, whipping it into shape and finding it a home. And for helping it find some darkness — but not too much darkness. Thanks also to Olivia Davies, audio wizard. Huge shout out to Amy Mitchell, who liked it in the first place and has found it homes abroad, and Lucy Joyce and the UA foreign rights team. Thank you so much.

I'm also eternally grateful to my friends who have read it and encouraged me along, especially: Polly Cowan, literary match-maker; Nina Bjurstrom, super doc; Emily Parker and Jo Archer. You all bravely agreed to tell me what you really thought . . .

To Mum and Dad, thank you for your unwavering confidence.

Gigantic thank you to Jake — you've been so supportive, patient and generally wonderful. And regularly taken the children out of my hair so I can write.

Thanks to Janet Gover and the readers on the Romantic Novelists' Association's New Writers' Scheme, which helped me get to the end of the book (more than once).

And, last of all, to my aunt Charlotte, the original supervet of the Highlands. Thank you for all your comments and suggestions, from the big picture right down to the tiniest details.

THE JOFFE BOOKS STORY

We began in 2014 when Jasper agreed to publish his mum's much-rejected romance novel and it became a bestseller.

Since then we've grown into the largest independent publisher in the UK. We're extremely proud to publish some of the very best writers in the world, including Joy Ellis, Faith Martin, Caro Ramsay, Helen Forrester, Simon Brett and Robert Goddard. Everyone at Joffe Books loves reading and we never forget that it all begins with the magic of an author telling a story.

We are proud to publish talented first-time authors, as well as established writers whose books we love introducing to a new generation of readers.

We have been shortlisted for Independent Publisher of the Year at the British Book Awards three times, in 2020, 2021 and 2022, and for the Diversity and Inclusivity Award at the Independent Publishing Awards in 2022.

We built this company with your help, and we love to hear from you, so please email us about absolutely anything bookish at feedback@joffebooks.com

If you want to receive free books every Friday and hear about all our new releases, join our mailing list: www.joffebooks.com/contact

And when you tell your friends about us, just remember: it's pronounced Joffe as in coffee or toffee!

Ingram Content Group UK Ltd.
Milton Keynes UK
UKHW040656120723
424996UK00004B/147